Praise for
Sleep No More

"You'll find yourself afraid to turn off the light after seven chapters, and after eleven, you may find yourself wondering if the person lying next to you is someone you really know or a dangerous stranger. This one gets under your skin, and then burrows deep. Imagine what *Rebecca* might have been if it had been written by a man. That will give you the idea of how successful this novel is. *Sleep No More* is that rarity, a thriller that really thrills." —Stephen King

"Completely engaging . . . irresistible pass-the-popcorn fun . . . a spirited chiller." —*People*

"A broody, moody writer whose books have the twitchy languidness of Tennessee Williams combined with the suspense of Alfred Hitchcock . . . a dazzling combination of guilt, obsession, and suspicion." —*St. Petersburg Times*

"Reads like a revved up go-kart, with surprises at every curve. Erotic, shocking, pulse racing, and a whole lot of white-knuckled fun." —*The Clarion-Ledger* (Jackson, MS)

"Iles presents whodunits that are a cut above. . . . His characters have some dimension. You usually can't see his plot twists coming."—*Fort Worth Star-Telegram*

continued . . .

BOOKS BY GREG ILES

SLEEP NO MORE

Greg Iles

NEW AMERICAN LIBRARY

New American Library
Published by New American Library, a division of
Penguin Group (USA) Inc., 375 Hudson Street,
New York, New York 10014, USA
Penguin Group (Canada), 10 Alcorn Avenue, Toronto,
Ontario M4V 3B2, Canada (a division of Pearson Penguin Canada Inc.)
Penguin Books Ltd., 80 Strand, London WC2R 0RL, England
Penguin Ireland, 25 St. Stephen's Green, Dublin 2,
Ireland (a division of Penguin Books Ltd.)
Penguin Group (Australia), 250 Camberwell Road, Camberwell, Victoria 3124,
Australia (a division of Pearson Australia Group Pty. Ltd.)
Penguin Books India Pvt. Ltd., 11 Community Centre, Panchsheel Park,
New Delhi - 110 017, India
Penguin Group (NZ), cnr Airborne and Rosedale Roads, Albany,
Auckland 1310, New Zealand (a division of Pearson New Zealand Ltd.)
Penguin Books (South Africa) (Pty.) Ltd., 24 Sturdee Avenue,
Rosebank, Johannesburg 2196, South Africa

Penguin Books Ltd., Registered Offices:
80 Strand, London WC2R 0RL, England

Published by New American Library, a division of Penguin Group (USA) Inc.
Previously published in G. P. Putnam's Sons and Signet editions.

First New American Library Printing, December 2004
10   9   8   7   6   5   4   3   2

This book is dedicated to my readers, who have allowed me to write something different each time out. We all like the familiar, but in the end I think we're all the richer for going new places with new characters. You may not like every book as much as your favorite, but at least you—and I—won't be bored. This novel is a wild one, so settle in and open your memory and imagination. (And for those who write in to ask, you may just see some familiar characters here and in the future, but probably where you least expect them.)

The normal man is a fiction.

—CARL JUNG

"Cathy! Cathy!"

—HEATHCLIFF, *Wuthering Heights*

chapter 1

Eve Sumner appeared on the first day of fall. Not the official first day—there was nothing official about Eve—but the first day the air turned cool, blowing through John Waters's shirt as though it weren't there. It was chilly enough for a jacket, but he didn't want one because it had been so hot for so damn long, because the air tasted like metal and his blood was up, quickened by the change in temperature and the drop in pressure on his skin, like a change in altitude. His steps were lighter, the wind carrying him forward, and deep within his chest something stirred the way the bucks were stirring in the deep woods and the high leaves were pulling at their branches. Soon those bucks would be stalked through the oaks and shot, and those leaves would be burning in piles, but on that day all remained unresolved, poised in a great ballet of expectation, an indrawn breath. And borne on the first prescient breeze of exhalation came Eve Sumner.

She stood on the far sideline of the soccer field, too far away for Waters to really see her. He first saw her the way the other fathers did, a silhouette that caught his eye: symmetry and curves and a mane of dark hair that made the mothers on both sides of the soccer field irrationally angry. But he hadn't time to notice more than that. He was coaching his daughter's team.

Seven-year-old Annelise raced along the sea of grass with her eye on the ball, throwing herself between eight-year-old boys nearly twice her size. Waters trotted along behind the pack, encouraging the stragglers and reminding the precocious ones which direction to kick the ball. He ran lightly for his age and size—a year past forty, an inch over six feet—and he pivoted quickly enough to ensure soreness in the morning. But it was a soreness that he liked, that reminded him he was still alive and kicking. He felt pride following Annelise down the field; last year his daughter was a shy little girl, afraid to get close to the ball; this year, with her father coaching, she had found new confidence. He sensed that even now, so young, she was learning lessons that would serve her well in the future.

"Out of bounds!" he called. "Blue's ball."

As the opposing team put the ball inbounds, Waters felt the pressure of eyes like fingers on his skin. He was being watched, and not only by the kids and their parents. Glancing toward the opposite sideline, he looked directly into the eyes of the dark-haired woman. They were deep and as dark as her hair, serene and supremely focused. He quickly averted his own, but an indelible afterimage floated in his mind: dusky, knowing eyes that knew the souls of men.

The opposing coach was keeping time for the tied

game, and Waters knew there was precious little left. Brandon Davis, his star eight-year-old, had the ball on his toe and was controlling it well, threading it through the mass of opponents. Waters sprinted to catch up. Annelise was close behind Brandon, trying to get into position to receive a pass as they neared the goal. Girls thought more about passing than boys; the boys just wanted to score. But Annelise did the right thing all the same, flanking out to the right as Brandon took a vicious shot at the net. The ball ricocheted off the goalie's shins, right back to Brandon. He was about to kick again when he sensed Annelise to his right and scooped the ball into her path, marking himself as that rarest of boys, one who understands deferred gratification. Annelise was almost too surprised by this unselfishness to react, but at the last moment she kicked the ball past the goalie into the net.

A whoop went up from the near sideline, and Waters heard his wife's voice leading the din. He knew he shouldn't show favoritism, but he couldn't help running forward and hugging Annelise to his chest.

"I got one, Daddy!" she cried, her eyes shining with pride and surprise. "I scored!"

"You sure did."

"Brandon passed it to me!"

"He sure did."

Sensing Brandon behind him, Waters reached back and grabbed the boy's hand and lifted it skyward along with Annelise's, showing everyone that it was a shared effort.

"Okay, *de*-fense!" he shouted.

His team raced back to get into position, but the opposing coach blew his whistle, ending the game with a flat, half-articulated note.

The parents of Waters's team streamed onto the field, congratulating the children and their coach, talking happily among themselves. Waters's wife, Lily, trundled forward with the ice chest containing the postgame treats: POWERade and Oreos. As she planted the Igloo on the ground and removed the lid, a small tornado whirled around her, snatching bottles and blue bags from her hands. Lily smiled up from the chaos, silently conveying her pride in Annelise as male hands slapped Waters's back. Lily's eyes were cornflower blue, her hair burnished gold and hanging to her shoulders. In moments like this, she looked as she had in high school, running cross-country and beating all comers. The warmth of real happiness welled in Waters at the center of this collage of flushed faces, grass stains, skinned knees, and little Jimmy O'Brien's broken tooth, which had been lost during the second quarter and was now being passed around like an artifact of a historic battle.

"Hell of a season, John!" said Brandon Davis's father. "Only one more game to go."

"Today was a good day."

"How about that last pass?"

"Brandon's got good instincts."

"You better believe it," insisted Davis. "Kid's got a hell of a future. Wait till AYA football starts."

Waters wasn't comfortable with this kind of talk. In truth, he didn't much care if the kids won or lost. The point at this age was fun and teamwork, but it was a point a lot of parents missed.

"I need to get the ball," he said by way of excusing himself.

He trotted toward the spot where the ball had fallen when the whistle blew. Parents from the opposing team nodded to him as they headed for their cars, and a warm sense of camaraderie filled him. This emerald island of chalked rectangles was where it was happening today in Natchez, a town of twenty thousand souls, steeped in history but a little at a loss about its future. In Waters's youth, the neighborhoods surrounding these fields had housed blue-collar mill workers; now they were almost exclusively black. Twenty years ago, that would have made this area off limits, but today there were black kids on his soccer team, a mark of change so profound that only people who had lived through those times really understood its significance. Before he knew why, Waters panned his eyes around the field, sensing an emptiness like that he felt when he sighted a cardinal landing outside his office window and, looking closer at the smear of scarlet, saw only the empty space left after the quick beat of wings. He was looking for the dark-haired woman, but she was gone.

He picked up the ball and jogged back to his group, which stood waiting for concluding remarks before splitting up and heading for their various neighborhoods.

"Everybody played a great game," he told them, his eyes on the kids as their parents cheered. "There's only one more to go. I think we're going to win it, but win or lose, I'm taking everybody to McDonald's after for a Happy Meal and ice cream."

"*Yaaaaaaay!*" screamed ten throats in unison.

"Now go home and get that homework done!"

"*Booooooooooo!*"

The parents laughed and shepherded their kids

toward the SUVs, pickups, and cars parked along the sideline.

Annelise walked forward. "You blew it at the end, Daddy."

"You don't have that much homework."

"No, but the third-graders have a *lot*."

Waters squeezed her shoulders and stood, then took the Igloo from his wife and softly said, "Did we have homework in second grade?"

Lily leaned in close. "We didn't have homework until *sixth* grade."

"Yeah? Well, we did all right."

He took Annelise's hand and led her toward his muddy Land Cruiser. A newly divorced mother named Janie somebody fell in beside Lily and started to talk. Waters nodded but said nothing as Janie began a familiar litany of complaints about her ex. Annelise ran ahead, toward another family whose car was parked beside the Land Cruiser. Alone with his thoughts for the first time in hours, Waters took a deep breath of cool air and savored the betweenness of the season. Someone was grilling meat across the road, and the scent made him salivate.

Turning toward the cooking smell, he saw the dark-haired woman walking toward him. She was twenty feet away and to his right, moving with fluid grace, her eyes fixed on his face. He felt oddly on the spot until he realized she was headed back to the now-empty soccer field. He was about to ask her if she'd lost her keys when she tilted her head back and gave him a smile that nearly stopped him in his tracks.

Waters felt a wave of heat rush from his face to his toes. The smile withheld nothing: her lips spread wide, revealing perfect white teeth; her nostrils flared with feline excitement; and her eyes flashed fire. He wanted to keep looking, to stop and speak to her, but he knew better. It's often said that looking is okay, but no wife really believes that. He nodded politely, then looked straight ahead and kept moving until he passed her. Yet his mind could not recover as quickly as his body. When Lily leaned toward Janie to say something, he glanced back over his shoulder.

The dark-haired woman was doing the same. Her smile was less broad now, but her eyes still teased him, and just before Waters looked away, her lips came together and formed a single word—unvocalized, but one he could not mistake for any other.

"*Soon*," she said without sound.

And John Waters's heart stopped.

He was a mile from the soccer field before he really started to regain his composure. Annelise was telling a story about a scuffle between two boys at recess, and mercifully, Lily seemed engrossed.

"Hey, we won," she said, touching her husband's elbow. "What's the matter?"

Waters's mind spun in neutral, searching for a reasonable explanation for his trancelike state. "It's the EPA investigation."

Lily's face tightened, and her curiosity died, as Waters had known it would. An independent petroleum geologist, Waters owned half of a company with more than thirty producing oil wells, but he now lived with a sword hanging over his head. Seventeen years of success had been thrown into jeopardy by a single well that might have leaked salt water into a Louisiana rice farmer's fields. For two months, the EPA had been trying to determine the source of the leak. This unpleasant situation had been made potentially devastating by Waters's business partner's failure to keep their liability insurance up to date, and since the company was jointly owned, Waters would suffer equally if the EPA deemed the leak their fault. He could be wiped out.

"Don't think about it," Lily pleaded.

For once, Waters wasn't. He wanted to speak of comforting trivialities, but none came to him. His composure had been shattered by a smile and a soundless word. At length, in the most casual voice he could muster, he said, "Who was that woman who looked at me when we were leaving?"

"I thought you were looking at *her*," Lily said, proving yet again that nothing got by her.

"Come on, babe . . . she just looked familiar."

"Eve Sumner." A definite chill in the voice. "She's a real estate agent."

Now he remembered. Cole Smith, his partner, had mentioned Eve Sumner before. In a sexual context, he thought, but most of what Cole mentioned had a sexual context, or a sexual subtext.

"I think Cole's mentioned her."

"I'll bet he has. Evie really gets around, from what I understand."

Waters looked over at his wife, wondering at the change in her. A few years ago, she never made this sort of comment. Or maybe she had—maybe it was her tone that had changed. It held a bitterness that went along with the now-perpetual severity in her face. Four years ago, the smiling girlish looks that had lasted to thirty-five vanished almost overnight, and the bright eyes dulled to an almost sullen opacity. He knew the date by heart, though he didn't like to think about the reason.

"How old is she?" he asked.

"How old did she look to you?"

Potential minefield. "Um . . . forty-two?"

Lily snorted. "More like thirty-two. She probably wants to sell our house out from under us. She does that all the time."

"Our house isn't for sale."

"People like Eve Sumner think everything has a price."

"She sounds like Cole."

"I'm sure they have a lot in common." Lily cut her eyes at him in a way that as much as said, *I'm sure Cole has slept with her.* Which was a problem for Waters, since his business partner was—nominally at least—a happily married father of three. But this was a problem he was accustomed to dealing with. Cole Smith had been cheating on his wife since the honeymoon ended, but he'd never let it interfere with his marriage. Cole's chronic philandering was more of a problem for Waters, who not infrequently found himself in the position of having to cover for a friend and partner whose actions he deplored. On another day he might have given a token grunt of skepticism in response to Lily's assumption, but his patience with his partner had worn thin of late.

He swung the Land Cruiser around a dawdling log truck on Highway 61 and tried to clear his mind. There was a low-grade buzz deep in his brain, a hum of preoccupation set off by Eve Sumner's smile but which had nothing to do with Eve Sumner. The smile on her face had risen straight from Waters's past; the word she'd silently spoken echoed in a dark chamber of his heart. *Soon. . . .*

"Damn," he said under his breath.

"What is it?" asked Lily.

He made a show of looking at his watch. "The Jackson Point well. Cole called and said it may come in about three in the morning. I'm probably going to have to log it tonight." Logging a well was the task of the geologist, who read complex measurements transmitted by an instrument lowered to the bottom of a newly drilled well in order to determine whether there was oil present. "There's some stuff I need to do at the office before I go out to the rig."

Lily sighed. "Why don't you swing by now and pick up your maps and briefcase? You can make your phone calls from home."

Waters knew she had made this suggestion without much hope. Whenever he logged wells, he had a ritual of spending time alone. Most geologists did, and he was thankful for that today.

"I won't be more than an hour," he said, a twinge of guilt going through him. "I'll drop you guys off and be home as quick as I can."

"Daddy!" objected Annelise. "You have to help with my homework."

Waters laughed. His daughter needed no help with homework; she just liked him sitting close by in the hour before bedtime. "I'll be back before you know it."

"I know what *that* means."

"I promise," he insisted.

Annelise brightened. Her father kept his promises.

*   *   *

Lily and Annelise waved as Waters pulled away from Linton Hill, the house that was not for sale, an antebellum home he'd bought five years ago with the proceeds from a well in Franklin County. Linton Hill wasn't a palace like Dunleith or Melrose, but it had four thousand square feet with detached slave quarters that Waters used as a home office, and many small touches of architectural significance. Since they moved in, Lily had been leading a one-woman campaign to have the house placed on the National Register of Historic Places, and victory seemed close. Having grown up in a clapboard house less than a mile from Linton Hill, Waters usually felt pride when he looked at his home. But today, watching his rearview mirror, he barely saw the place. As soon as Lily led Annelise up the steps, his mind began to run where it had wanted to for the past ten minutes.

"I imagined it," he murmured.

But the old pain was there. Dormant for two decades, it remained stubbornly alive, like a tumor that refused to metastasize or to be absorbed. Waters gave the Land Cruiser some gas and headed downtown, toward the north side, where live oaks towered overhead like the walls of a great tunnel. Most houses here were tall Victorian gingerbreads, but there were also plain clapboards and even shotgun shacks. Natchez was a lot like New Orleans on this side: half-million-dollar mansions stood yards away from crumbling row houses that wouldn't bring thirty thousand.

Waters turned right, onto Linton Avenue, a shaded street of middle-aged affluent whites that terminated near the Little Theater, where Maple Street rose sharply toward the bluff overlooking the Mississippi River. There he would break out of the warren of one-

way streets and into the last real light of the day. Like
biblical rain, the sunlight fell upon the just and unjust
alike, and in this deceptively somnolent river town,
the last rays always fell upon the tourists standing on
the bluff, the drunks sipping whiskey at the Under-
the-Hill Saloon, and upon the dead.

In 1822, the old town burial ground had been
moved from the shadow of St. Mary's Cathedral
Church to a hundred acres of hilly ground on the high
bluff north of town. Over the next century, this became one of the most beautiful and unique cemeteries
in the South, and it was through its gates that John
Waters finally pulled his Land Cruiser and slowed to
a near idle. Some of the stones he passed looked new,
others as though they'd been cut centuries before, and
probably were. Remains from the old cemetery had
been disinterred and transferred here, so tombstones
dating to the 1700s were not uncommon. Waters
parked the Land Cruiser on the crest of Jewish Hill,
climbed out, and stared down four breathtaking miles
of river.

In Natchez, the dead have long had a better view
than the living. The view from Jewish Hill always
stirred something deep within him. The river affected
everyone who lived near it; he had heard uneducated
roughnecks speak with halting eloquence of its
mythic pull. Yet he saw the muddy river differently
from most. The Mississippi was an ancient river, but it
had not spent its life cutting its way into the continent
like the Colorado. The Mississippi had built the very
land that now tried in vain to hem it in. Two hundred
fifty million years ago this part of America—from the
Gulf Coast to St. Louis—was an ocean called the Mississippi Embayment, but somewhere north of Mem-

phis the nameless proto–Mississippi River was already dumping millions of tons of sediment into that ocean, creating a massive delta system. That process went inexorably on until the ocean was filled, and 35,000 feet of soil covered the bedrock. It was from the upper layers of those deposits that Waters took his family's living, from the oil-bearing strata just a few thousand feet down. Tonight, thirty miles downriver, he would pull up core samples that would tell a tiny part of what had been happening here 60 million years ago. Compared with these notions of time, the vaunted "history" of his hometown—going back a respectable three hundred years in human terms—was as nothing.

Yet even in geological terms, Natchez was unique. The bluff that supported the antebellum city had not been built by the river but by the wind; aeolian deposition, it was called, or *loess*, according to the Germans. The city shared this rare phenomenon with parts of China and Austria, and drew scientists from around the world to study it. Sometimes, after saturating rains, whole sections of the bluff would slide like earthen avalanches to the river, and over the past few years the Army Corps of Engineers had fought a massive holding action to stabilize it. The citizens who lived along the kudzu-faced precipice clung tenaciously to their homes like bystanders to a war, human metaphors for the faith that had kept the town alive through good times and bad.

Waters turned away from the river and surveyed a gently rolling city of white obelisks, mausoleums, statuary, and gravestones you could spend a week exploring without beginning to fathom the stories beneath them. The surnames on the stones were still common in the town, some going back seven generations. Natchez was the oldest settlement on the Mississippi River, and while she had witnessed many changes, the names had remained constant. Standing in the midst of the monuments, each a touchstone of memory, Waters was suffused with hot awareness of the essentially incestuous nature of small towns, and of Natchez in particular.

As gooseflesh rose on his shoulders, he started down Jewish Hill toward the Protestant section of the cemetery, scanning the gravestones as he walked. He edged down a steep hill and through a line of gnarled oaks. Almost immediately his eyes settled on what he sought. Her stone was easy to spot. Black Alabama marble veined with grayish white, it rose three feet higher than the surrounding stones, its mirrorlike face deeply graven with large roman letters that could have been there a thousand years.

MALLORY GRAY CANDLER
Miss Mississippi 1982

As Waters neared the stone, smaller letters came into clear relief.

Born, Natchez, Mississippi
February 5, 1960
Died, New Orleans, Louisiana
August 8, 1992

"The flame that burns twice as bright
burns half as long."

He stopped and stood silent before the black slab. He visited the cemetery often enough, but he had never visited this grave. Nor had he attended the funeral. He was not wanted by the family, and he had no desire to go. He'd said his good-byes to Mallory Candler long before then, and the process had almost killed him. For this reason, the inscription surprised him. The quote was from *Blade Runner,* a film Mallory had seen with Waters. She had liked the line of dialogue so much that she'd written it down in her diary. The family must have discovered it there after her death and decided it captured her spirit—which it did. That Mallory Candler had sought out provocative films like *Blade Runner* while her peers numbed out to *Endless Love* or imitated *Flashdance* spoke volumes about her, and it was one of those traits few had known. Mallory played the Southern belle so well that only Waters, so far as he knew, had gotten to know the complex woman beneath. He was almost certain her husband had not.

The year Mallory reigned as Miss Mississippi, she told Waters she sometimes felt like the beautiful android woman in *Blade Runner*—so well trained, practiced, and seemingly flawless that her own sense of reality fled her, leaving an automaton going through the motions of life, feeling nothing, wondering if even her memories were invented. A few duties of her office had actually lightened her heart—the hospitals, the camps for retarded kids, the real things—but ceremonies for the opening of factories and car dealerships had left her cold and depressed.

Waters knelt at the border of the grave and laid his right hand flat on the St. Augustine grass. Six feet beneath his palm lay a body with which he had coupled

hundreds of times, sometimes gently, other times
thrashing in the dark with desperate passion that
would not be quenched. How could it lie cold and utterly still now? Waters was forty-one; Mallory would
have been forty-two. Her body *was* forty-two, he realized, but the passage of time meant only decay to her
now. Morbid thoughts, but how else could he think of
her, here, under the blank and pitiless stare of this
stone? Twenty years ago, they had made love in this
cemetery. They chased each other through tunnels in
the tall grass, trackless paths cut by an army of old
black men with push mowers, then fell into each
other's arms in the bright sun and the buzz of
grasshoppers, affirming life in the midst of death.

"Ten years gone," he murmured. "Jesus."

In the emotional trough left by this unexpected
wave of grief, myriad images bubbled up from his
subconscious. The first few made him shiver, for they
were the old vivid ones, shot through with violence
and blood. Waters usually steeled himself against
these and pressed down all other remembrance. But
today he did not resist. Because here, in the shadow of
this stone, reality was absolute: Mallory Candler was
gone. Here he could let the fearful memories go, the
ones he'd always kept close to remind him of the danger. That she had twice tried to kill him and might do
so again. Or worse, hurt his wife, as she had threatened to do.

In this silent place, less sanguinary memories rose
into his mind. Now he could see Mallory as he had
known her in the beginning. What he most recalled
was her beauty. That and her life force, for the two
were inextricably bound. The first thing you noticed
was her hair: a glorious mane of mahogany, full of

body, a little wild, and highlighted with a shining streak of copper from the crown of her head to the backs of her shoulders. Anyone who saw that streak thought it had been added by a stylist, but it had come in her genes, a God-given sign of the unpredictability in her nature. You couldn't miss Mallory in a crowd. She could be surrounded by a hundred sorority girls in the Grove at Ole Miss, and the sun would pick out that flaming streak of hair, the cream skin, rose lips, and Nile-green eyes, and mark her like a spotlight picking the prima ballerina from a chorus. Tall without being awkward, voluptuous without being plump, proud without conveying arrogance, Mallory drew people to her with effortless but inexorable power. Waters often wondered how he had grown up in the same town with her and not noticed her sooner. But they had gone to different schools, and a population of twenty-five thousand (the town was larger then) made it just possible not to know a few people worth knowing. Mallory also possessed an attribute shared by few women of her generation: regal bearing. She moved with utter self-possession and assurance, as though she had been reared in a royal court, and this caused men and women to treat her with deference.

Thinking of her this way, Waters could nearly see her standing before him. He'd always thought the truest thing William Faulkner ever said wasn't written in one of his novels, but spoken during an interview in Paris: *The past is never dead; it's not even past.* Trust a Mississippian to understand that. Maybe every man was haunted by his first great love to some degree. For Marcel Proust, it had been a scent that acted as a time machine, bringing the past hurtling into the present. For Waters it was a smile and a word. *Soon. . . .*

Staring at the gravestone, he thought its blackness looked somehow deeper, and then he realized the light was fading. He glanced over his shoulder, toward the kudzu strangling the trees across Cemetery Road. A gibbous moon was already visible high in the violet sky, and the sun would soon fall below the rim of the bluff. The cemetery gates were generally closed at 7:00 P.M., but the time wasn't absolute. If you were still inside the walls at dusk, you could see the dilapidated car of the black woman responsible for closing the gates, the woman herself sitting patiently in her front seat or standing by a brick gatepost, dipping snuff and watching the odd car or truck roll past on Cemetery Road. Waters knew she would be waiting for him at the "first" gate, where the old Charity Hospital had once stood. Now only a concrete slab marked the spot, but before it burned, the hulking hospital with its tubular fire escapes had towered over the cemetery, prompting tasteless jokes about doctors sliding the corpses of the indigent down into the cemetery like garbage down a chute.

He sighed and looked back at the gravestone: *Died, New Orleans, Louisiana.* He had often wondered about Mallory's death, whether the woman who had once claimed to despair of life, who had tried several times to kill herself, had fought death when it came for her. In his bones he knew she had. The New Orleans police had found skin under her fingernails. But the family had not been interested in giving him more details, and no one else in Natchez got them either. The Candlers were that kind of family: pathologically obsessed with appearances. Typical of them to think that having a daughter raped and murdered somehow reflected badly on *them*, or on Mallory herself, like medieval bourgeoisie believing physical deformity to be a mark of sin. Waters realized he was gritting his teeth. The thought of Mallory's parents could still do that to him.

For the first time, his eye settled on a smaller gravestone to the right of Mallory's. Not quite half as high, it appeared to be made of a cheap composite "stone material," so it stunned Waters to see the name *Benjamin Gray Candler* engraved on its face. Ben Candler was Mallory's father. More surprising still, the stone appeared to have been defaced with a heavy tool like a crowbar. He stepped that way to examine it but stopped before he reached it. The smell of stale urine seemed to permeate the air around that stone, as if a dog routinely marked its territory there each day. *There's justice after all,* he thought. Mallory's father occupied a special place of loathing in Waters's mind, but today all Waters pictured when he looked at the stone was a self-important man more than half in love with his daughter, trailing her with an ever-present camera, recording every social event, no matter how small, for what he called posterity.

The grinding whine of a pulpwood truck carried to Waters from the road. He glanced at his watch. 6:15. He'd already stayed too long. His wife and daughter were waiting for him at home. Across town, Cole Smith was priming two big investors with bourbon and scotch, preparing to drive them down to the well to await what they hoped was a huge payday. And thirty miles south, on a sandbar of the Mississippi River, a tool pusher and a crew of roughnecks were guiding a diamond-tipped drill bit the last few hun-

dred feet toward a buried formation Waters had
mapped five months ago, every man jack of them
earning his livelihood from Waters's dream. A lot was
in play tonight. Yet he could not bring himself to leave
the grave.

Soon....

He and Mallory had used that word as a sort of
code in college, after they'd become lovers, which was
almost as soon as they met. They spent every available moment together, but in the social whirl of Ole
Miss, "together" did not always mean together alone.
Whenever they found themselves separated by others
but still within eye contact—at parties, between
classes, or in the library—one of them would mouth
that word, *soon,* to reassure the other that it wouldn't
be long before they held each other again. *Soon* was a
sacred promise in the idolatrous religion they had
founded together, the rites of which were consum-
mated in the darkness of his dorm room, her sorority
house, or the Education Building parking lot, alongside the cars of others who had no more comfortable
or private place to go.

Soon.... To see their secret promise mouthed by a
stranger—a beautiful one, to be sure, but still a
stranger—had rattled Waters to the core. Kneeling in
the fading light, he tried to convince himself that he'd
misunderstood what Eve Sumner had said. After all,
she hadn't actually *said* anything; she'd only mouthed
a word. And had she even done that? She had certainly smiled the most openly flirtatious smile Waters
had received in years. But the word ... was it really
soon? Or something else? What else might Eve Sumner have said in that moment? Something mundane?
Perhaps it hadn't been a word at all. Now that he

thought about it, the movement of her lips was a lot like a pucker. Could she have blown him a kiss? Maybe he'd been too thick to recognize the gesture for what it was.

Evie really gets around, Lily had said. Maybe a blown kiss was part of Eve Sumner's come-on. Maybe a dozen guys in town had gotten the same smile, the same blown kiss. Waters suddenly felt sheepish, even stupid. That something so casual had sent him out to the cemetery in search of ghosts from his past . . . maybe the pressure of the EPA investigation *was* getting to him.

Yet he was not a man prone to misunderstandings. He trusted his eyes and his instincts. As he reflected on Eve's actions, a long mournful note echoed across the cemetery. He ignored it, but the sound came again, as though a bugler were warming up for "Taps" at day's end. All at once the sky went dark, and Waters realized the bugle call was a car horn. The woman at the gate was emptying the graveyard.

He got to his feet and wiped the seat of his pants, in his mind already walking back toward Jewish Hill. But he wasn't walking. He could not leave Mallory's grave without . . . doing something. With a hollow feeling in his chest, he turned toward the black stone.

"I've never come here before," he said, his voice awkward in the silent dark. "And you know I don't believe you can hear me. But . . . it shouldn't have ended like this for you." He raised a hand as if it could somehow help communicate the ineffable sorrow welling within him, but nothing could, and he let it fall. "You deserved better than this. That's all. You deserved better."

He felt he should continue, but his voice had failed

him, so he turned away from the stone and marched up through the oaks toward Jewish Hill and his Land Cruiser, the horn blowing from the cemetery gate like a clarion call back to the present.

chapter 2

Waters stopped at his office to pick up his maps and briefcase on his way home from the cemetery, and he said nothing to Lily about his side trip when he arrived. He sat at the kitchen table with Annelise, studying the maps that he hoped described the underlying structure around the well he would log tonight. While he rechecked every step of his geology, Annelise did second-grade math problems across the table. Now and then she would laugh at his "serious face," and he would laugh with her. The two shared an original turn of mind, and also a conspiratorial sense of humor that sometimes excluded Lily. Waters wondered if these similarities were attributable to genetics or socialization. Lily had been trained as an accountant, and her math skills were formidable, but Annelise's mind seemed to run along its own quirky track, as her father's did, and Lily herself often pointed this out.

While Waters and Annelise worked, Lily sat in the

alcove where she paid the household bills, typing a letter to the Department of the Interior, yet another skirmish in her campaign to add Linton Hill to the National Register. Waters admired her tenacity, but he didn't much care whether they got a brass plaque to mount beside the front door or not. He'd bought Linton Hill because he liked it, not as a badge of the quasi-feudal status that much of the moneyed class in Natchez seemed to cherish.

At 8:30 they went upstairs to put Annelise to bed. Waters walked back down first, but he waited for Lily at the foot of the steps, as was his custom. He had no illusions about what would happen next. She gave him a stiff hug—without eye contact—then headed back to the alcove to finish her letter.

He stood alone in the foyer as he had countless nights before, wondering what to do next. Most nights he would go out to the old slave quarters that was his home office and work at his computer, pressing down the frustration that had been building in him for more years than he wanted to think about. Frustration had been a profitable motivator for him. Using it, he had in his spare time developed geological mapping software that earned him seventy thousand dollars a year in royalties. This brought him a sense of accomplishment, but it did nothing to resolve his basic problem.

Tonight he did not feel like writing computer code. Nor did he want to telephone any investors, as he had promised his partner he would do. Seeing Eve Sumner that afternoon had deeply aroused him, even if he'd been mistaken about what she said. The energy humming in him now was almost impossible to contain, and he wanted to release it with his wife. Not the best motivation for marital sex, perhaps, but it was reality. Yet he knew there would be no release tonight. Not in any satisfactory way. There hadn't been for the past four years. And suddenly—without emotional fanfare of any kind—Waters knew that he could no longer endure that situation. The wall of forbearance he had so painstakingly constructed was finally giving way.

He left the foyer and walked through the back door to the patio, but he did not go to the slave quarters. He stood in the cool of the night, looking at the old cistern pump and reflecting how he and Lily had come to this impasse. Looking back, the sequence of events seemed to have the weight of inevitability. Annelise had been born in 1995, after a normal pregnancy and delivery. The next year, they tried again, and Lily immediately got pregnant. Then, in her fourth month, she miscarried. It happened at a party, and the night at the hospital was a long and difficult one. The fetus had been male, and this hit Lily hard, as she'd been set on naming the child after her father, who was gravely ill at the time. Three months after the miscarriage, her father died. Depression set in with a melancholy vengeance, and Lily went on Zoloft. They continued to have occasional sex, but the passion had gone out of her. Waters told himself this was a side effect of the drug, and Lily's doctor agreed. After two difficult years, she announced she was ready to try again. She got off the drug, began to exercise and eat well, and they started making love every night. Three weeks later, she was pregnant.

All seemed fine until a lab test revealed that Lily's blood had developed antibodies to the fetus's blood. Lily was Rh-negative, the baby Rh-positive, and because of the severity of their incompatibility, Lily's blood would soon begin destroying the baby's blood at a dangerously rapid rate. Carrying Annelise had sensitized Lily to Rh-positive blood, but it was in subsequent pregnancies that the disease blossomed to its destructive potential, growing worse each time. An injection of a drug called RhoGAM was supposed to prevent Rh disease in later pregnancies, but for some unknown reason, it had not.

Waters and Lily began commuting a hundred miles to University Hospital in Jackson to treat mother and fetus, with an exhausting round of amniocentesis and finally an intrauterine transfusion to get fresh blood into the struggling baby. This miraculous procedure worked, but it bought them only weeks. More transfusions would be required, possibly as many as five if the baby was to survive to term. The next time Lily climbed onto the table for an ultrasound exam, the doctor looked at the computer screen, listened to the baby's heartbeat, then put down the ultrasound wand and met Waters's eyes with somber significance. Waters's heart stuttered in his chest.

"What's wrong?" Lily asked. "What's the matter?"

The doctor took her upper arm and squeezed, then spoke in the most compassionate voice John Waters had ever heard from the mouth of a man. "Lily, you're going to lose the baby."

She went rigid on the examination table. The doctor looked stricken. He knew how much emotion she had invested in that child. Another pregnancy was medically out of the question.

"What are you talking about?" Lily asked. "How do you know?" Then her face drained of color. "You mean . . . he's dead now? *Now?*"

The doctor looked at Waters as though for help, but Waters had no idea what emergency procedures might exist. He did know they were in one of those situations for which physicians are not adequately trained in medical school.

"The fetal heartbeat is decelerating now," the doctor said. "The baby is already in hydrops."

"What's that?" Lily asked in a shaky voice.

"Heart failure."

She began to hyperventilate. Waters squeezed her hand, feeling a wild helplessness in his chest. He was more afraid for Lily than for the baby.

"Do something!" Lily shrieked at the stunned doctor. She turned to her husband. *"Do something!"*

"There's nothing anyone can do," the doctor said in a soft voice that told Waters the man was relearning a terrible lesson about the limits of his profession.

Lily stared at the fuzzy image on the monitor, her eyes showing more white than color. "Don't just sit there, damn you! Do something! *Deliver him right now!"*

"He can't survive outside of you, Lily. His lungs aren't developed. And he can't survive inside either. I'm sorry."

"Take—him—OUT!"

In the four years since that day, Waters had not allowed himself to think about what happened after that—not more than once or twice, anyway. Lily's mother had been reading a magazine in the hall outside, and she burst in when Lily began to scream. The doctor did his best to explain what was happening, and Lily's mother tried everything she knew to comfort her daughter. But in the ten minutes it took Waters's unborn child's heart to stop, his wife's soul cracked at the core. The sight unmanned him, and it still could now, if he allowed the memory its full resonance. This was how he had survived the past four years without sexual intimacy: by never quite blocking out the horror of that day. His wife had been wounded as severely as a soldier shot through the chest, even if the wound didn't show, and it was his duty to live with the consequences.

The ring of the telephone sounded faintly through the French doors. After about a minute, Waters heard Lily call his name. He went inside and picked up the den extension.

"Hello?"

"Goddamn, John Boy!"

Nobody but Cole Smith got away with calling Waters that, and Cole sounded like he already had a load of scotch in him.

"Where are you?" asked Waters.

"I've got Billy Guidraux and Mr. Hill Tauzin with me in my Lincoln Confidential. We're ten miles south of Jackson Point. You think this land yacht can make it all the way to the rig?"

"It hasn't rained for a few days. You shouldn't have any trouble. If you do get stuck, you'll be close enough for Dooley's boys to drag you in." Dooley's boys were the crew working the bulldozers at the well location.

"That's what I figured. When are you coming down?"

Waters didn't answer immediately. Normally, he would wait until the tool pusher called and said they had reached total depth and were bringing the drill bit out of the hole before he drove out to the rig location. That way he didn't have to spend much time doing things he didn't like. On logging nights—the last few anyway—Cole usually talked a lot of crap while the investors stood around giving Waters nervous glances, wishing the only geologist in the bunch would give them some additional hope that their dollars had not been wasted on this deal. But tonight Waters didn't want to sit in the silent house, waiting.

"I'm leaving now," he told Cole.

"Son of a bitch!" Cole exulted. "The Rock Man is breaking precedent, boys. It's a sign. You must have a special feeling about this one, son."

Rock Man. Rock. Waters hated the nicknames, but many geologists got saddled with them, and there was nothing he could do about it when his partner was drunk. He recalled a time when Cole had kept his cards close to his vest, but Cole had held his liquor a lot better back then. Or perhaps he was just drinking more these days. For all the pressure the EPA investigation had put on Waters, it had bled pounds out of his partner.

"I'll see you in forty-five minutes," he said in a clipped voice.

Before he could ring off, he heard coarse laughter fill the Continental, and then Cole's voice dropped to half-volume.

"What you think, John? Can you tell me anything?"

"At this point you know as much as I do. It's there or it's not. And it's—"

"It's been there or not for two million years," Cole finished wearily. "Shit, you're no fun." His voice suddenly returned to its normal pitch. "Loosen up, Rock. Get on down here and have a Glenmorangie with us."

Waters clicked off, then gathered his maps, logs, and briefcase. He kissed Lily on the top of the head as she worked, but her only response was a preoccupied shrug.

He went out to the Land Cruiser and cranked it to life.

Waters was four miles from the location when the rig appeared out of the night like an alien ship that had landed in the dark beside the greatest river on the continent. The steel tower stood ninety feet tall, its giant struts dotted with blue-white lights. Below the derrick was the metal substructure, where shirtless men in hard hats worked with chains that could rip them in half in one careless second. The ground below the deck was a sea of mud and planking, with hydraulic hoses snaking everywhere and the doghouse—the driller's portable office—standing nearby. Unearthly light bathed the whole location, and the bellow of pumps and generators rolled over the sandbar and the mile-wide river like Patton's tanks approaching the Rhine.

Something leaped in Waters's chest as he neared the tower. This was his forty-sixth well, but the old thrill had not faded with time. That drilling rig was a tangible symbol of his will. At one time there were seventy oil companies in Natchez. Now there were seven. That simple statistic described more heartache and broken dreams than you could tell in words; it summed up the decline of a town. Adversity was a way of life in the oil business, but the last eight years had been particularly harsh. Only the most tenacious operators had survived, and Waters was proud to be among them.

He turned onto a stretch of newly scraped earth, a road that had not existed ten days ago. If you had stood here then, all you would have heard was crickets and wind. All you'd have seen was moonlight reflecting off the river. Perhaps a long, low line of barges being pushed up- or downstream would send a white wake rolling softly against the shore, but in minutes it would pass, leaving the land as pristine as it had been before men walked the earth. Seven days ago, at Waters's command, the bulldozers had come. And the men. Every animal for miles knew something was happening. The diesel engines running the colossal machines around the rig had fired up and not stopped, as crews worked round-the-clock to drive the bit down, down, down to the depth where John Waters was willing it.

Drilling a well represented different things to different people. Even for Waters, who had pored over countless maps and miles of logs, who had mapped the hidden sands, it meant different things. First was the science. There was oil seven thousand feet below this land, but there was no easy way to find out exactly where. Not even with the priceless technology available to Exxon or Oxy Petroleum. In the end, someone still had to punch a hole through numberless layers of earth, sand, shale, limestone, and lignite, down to the soft sands that sometimes trapped the migrating oil that sixty million years ago was the surface life of the planet. And knowing where to punch that hole . . . well, that was a life's work.

In the 1940s and '50s, it hadn't been so hard. Oil was abundant in Adams County, and quite a few fellows with more balls than brains had simply put together some money, drilled in a spot they "had a feeling about," and hit the jackpot. But those days were gone. Adams County now had more holes in it than a grandmother's pincushion, and the big fields had all been found as surely as they were now playing out—or so went the conventional wisdom. Waters and a few others believed there were one or two significant fields left. Not big by Saudi standards, or even by offshore U.S. standards, but still containing enough reserves to make a Mississippi boy more money than he could ever spend in one lifetime. Enough to take care of one's heirs and assigns into perpetuity, as the lawyers said. But those fields, if they existed, would not be easy to find. No rank wildcatter was going to park his F-150 to take a leak in a soybean field, suddenly yell, *This here's the spot!* with near-religious zeal, and hit the big one. It would take a scientist like Waters, and that was one of the things that kept him going.

Another motivator was simpler but a little embarrassing to admit: the boyhood thrill of the treasure hunt. Because at some point the science ended and you went with your gut; you slapped an X on a paper map and you by God went out to dig up something that had been waiting for you since dinosaurs roamed the planet. Other guys were trying to find the same treasure, with the same tools, and some of those guys were all right and some were pirates as surely as the ones who roamed the Spanish Main.

Waters's Land Cruiser jounced over a couple of broken two-by-fours, and then he turned into the open area of the location. Parking some distance from the other vehicles, he got out with his briefcase and map tube and began walking toward the silver Lincoln parked beside the Schlumberger logging truck.

The car's interior light illuminated three figures: two in the front seat, one in back. Cole Smith sat behind the wheel. Once he spotted Waters, the Continental's doors would burst open with an exhalation of beer and whiskey, and the circus would begin. As Waters walked, he breathed in the conflicting odors of river water, mud, kudzu, pipe dope, and diesel fuel. It wasn't exactly a pleasant smell, but it fired the senses if you knew what it added up to.

Suddenly, the driver's door of the Lincoln flew open, and the vehicle rose on its shocks as Cole Smith climbed out wearing khaki pants, a Polo button-down, and a Houston Astros baseball cap. Cole had been an athlete in college, but in the years since, he had ballooned up to 250 pounds. He carried the weight well; some women still thought him hand-some. But when you studied his face, you saw his health fading fast. The alcohol had taken its toll, and there was a dark light in his eyes, a hunted look that had not been there five years ago. Once only infec-tious optimism had shone from those eyes, an irre-sistible force that persuaded levelheaded men to take risks they would never have dreamed of in the sober light of rational thought. But something—or a slow accretion of somethings—had changed that.

"Here's the Rock Man, boys!" Cole cried, clapping a beefy hand on Waters's shoulder. "Here's the witch doctor!"

These must be the mullets, Waters thought, as the two visiting big shots followed Cole out of the Lincoln. As a rule, he never used derogatory slang for investors, but these two looked like they might deserve it. There had been a time when he and Cole allowed only good friends to buy into their wells, but the business had

gotten too tough to be picky. These days, he relied on
Cole to find the money to finance their wells, and
Cole's sources were too numerous—and sometimes
too nebulous—to think about. The oil business attracted all kinds of investors, from dentists to mafiosi
to billionaires. All shared a dream of easy money, and
that was what separated them (and Cole Smith) from
Waters. Still, Waters shook hands with them—two
dark-haired men in their fifties with Cajun accents
and squinting eyes—and committed their first names
to memory, if only for the night.

"Everybody's feeling good," Cole said, his mouth
fixed in a grin. "How do you feel, John Boy?"

Waters forced himself not to wince. "It's a good
play. That's why we're here."

"What's the upside?" asked one of the Cajuns—
Billy.

"Well, as we outlined in the prospectus—"

"Oh, hell," Cole cut in. "You know we always go
conservative in those things. We're logging this baby
in a few hours, Rock. What's the biggest it could go?"

This was the wrong kind of talk to have in front of
investors, but Waters kept his poker face. In two hours
they could all be looking at the log of a dry hole, and
the anger and disappointment the investors felt
would be directly proportional to the degree their
hopes had been raised.

"If we come in high," he said cautiously, referring
to the geologic structure, "the reserves could be significant. This isn't a close-in deal. We're after something no one's found before."

"Damn right," said Cole. "Going for big game
tonight. We're gunning for the bull elephant."

He leaned into the Lincoln's door and pulled a Styrofoam cup off the dash, took a slug from it.

"What's the upside?" insisted Billy. "No shit. Cole says it could go five million barrels."

Waters felt his stomach clench. He wanted to smack Cole in the mouth. Five million barrels was the absolute outside of the envelope, if everything drilled out exactly right. The odds of that happening were one in a hundred. "That's probably a little generous," he said, meeting Billy's eye.

"Generous, my ass," Cole said quickly. "Our Steel Creek field was three million, and John was predicting one-point-five, tops." He poked Waters in the chest. "But Rock knew all along."

"So you said," growled Billy, his eyes on Waters.

"The statistics say one out of twenty-nine," said Cole. "That's the odds of hitting a well around here. John's drilled forty-six prospects, and he's hit seventeen wells. He's the goddamn Mark McGwire of the oil business."

"So you said." Billy was measuring Waters like a boxer preparing for a fight. "Five million barrels is a hundred and fifty million bucks at thirty-dollar oil. We like the sound of that."

"We'll know soon enough," Waters said, his eyes on Cole. "I need to talk to the engineer. I'll see you guys in a bit."

He walked up the steps of the Schlumberger truck, a massive blue vehicle packed to the walls with computers, CRTs, printers, and racked equipment. Schlumberger rotated engineers in and out of town pretty often—most of them Yankees—but the man at the console tonight had worked several of Waters's wells.

"How's it going, Pete?" Waters handed the engineer a surveyor's plat showing the well location and name.

A bookish young man with John Lennon glasses looked up, smiled, and answered in a northern accent. "The tool is calibrated. Just waiting to hit total depth."

"Cole been up here yet?"

The engineer rolled his eyes. "He's talking a pretty big game. You feel good about this one?"

"It's a solid play. But it's definitely a wildcat. It could shale out."

"God knows that's right. Happens to the best of them."

Waters grabbed a walkie-talkie off the desk and clipped it to his belt. "I'm going up to look at the rig. Holler if you need anything, or if Cole gets to be too much of a pain in the ass."

Pete grinned. "I'll do that."

Waters stood by the river on a patch of gray sand, watching a string of barges plow upstream in the darkness. The spotlight of the pushboat played across the surface of the river like the eye of a military patrol boat, and for good reason. There were sandbars out there that could turn that ordered line of barges into a lethal group of runaways floating downriver with nothing to slow them down but bridge pilings or other vessels.

The spotlight swung past him, then back, and he raised his hand in greeting. The light hung there a minute, then moved on. Waters smiled. The man behind that light was working through the night, just as he was, and that gave him a feeling of kinship. The same kinship he felt with the men working the rig behind him. He had made a point of speaking to the driller and crew when he went up to the rig's floor. Then he got a Coke from an ice chest on one of the workmen's trucks. The driller said Cole had brought crawfish and smoked salmon, but Waters didn't want to spend any more time with Billy and the other mullet than he had to. It was times like this—waiting out the last few hours when the chips could fall either way—that he sometimes questioned his choice of career. And that kind of thinking led to other questions, some better left unasked. But tonight the voice that asked those questions would not stay silent.

Waters had never planned to return to his hometown, much less enter the oil business. Nor had he planned to go to Ole Miss. He'd worked hard in high school, done well on his college boards, and received a full academic scholarship to the Colorado School of Mines, the most prestigious school of geology in the United States. But his father was dead, his mother had not remarried, and his brother was in the ninth grade. Henry Waters had not expected to die young, and so had not left enough insurance. Checks from his oil wells had been steady, but they wouldn't last forever, and the price of oil had already begun to drop. With all this in mind, Waters turned down Colorado and went to Ole Miss.

While his old friends drank, gambled, and chased sorority girls, Waters studied. Summers, he flew to Alaska and worked the pipeline. That was the best pay he could find, and his family soon needed it. His father's wells depleted rapidly, and the checks got steadily smaller. After the madness with Mallory peaked, he transferred to Colorado for his senior year.

There he met Sara Valdes, the woman with whom he would spend the next few years of his life. Sara was a vulcanologist who pursued her work with a single-minded passion that carried her to some of the most isolated and beautiful spots in the world. Waters began dabbling in her specialty just to be near her, and soon they were traveling the world together, doing graduate research. He spent nearly three years scuba diving beneath volcanoes to study marine ecosystems that lived off the heat of magma, and camping on pumice slopes to study active craters. In Argentina, they'd stumbled upon a meteorite of unusual composition and structure. In Ecuador, he found the frozen remains of a small mammoth dating back fifty thousand years. It was probably the nostalgic haze of selective memory, but he could not remember once being bored during those years.

Then his mother fell ill. His brother was in college, and Waters saw no alternative but to go home and take care of her. Sara Valdes loved him deeply, but she was not about to move to Mississippi, where the last volcanic activity occurred two hundred million years before she was born. That move was the start of the life Waters now lived. He'd been back in Natchez less than a month when Cole Smith—his old roommate and now a lawyer—asked if he thought he could find some oil. Since he had to do something for money, Waters set about mapping the region with a vengeance. Three months later, he was sure he had a cod-lock cinch. Cole sold the prospect in two weeks, and they prepared to make their first million dollars.

What they made was a dry hole.

Waters learned a hard lesson from that first failure, but the next morning he went back to his maps. He studied substructure for four months almost without sleep. And *this* time, he swore to Cole, he had it. It took Cole five months to sell that second prospect—split between sixty investors. Cole and Waters could barely afford to keep small shares for themselves. But at 4:00 A.M. in the middle of dense Franklin County woods, they hit twenty-nine feet of pay sand—a likely four million barrels of reserves—and one of the last big fields discovered in the area. After that, they couldn't put prospects together fast enough. Waters kept finding oil, and the money rolled in like a green tide. Even after the oil industry crashed in 1986, Cole somehow continued to sell deals, and Waters kept finding oil.

It was around this time that Lily Anderson graduated from SMU's Cox School of Business and returned to Natchez. A CPA, she planned to stay in town only long enough to help her father straighten out some tax troubles, but after she and Waters started seeing each other, she decided to stay a bit longer. Smart, quick-witted, and attractive, Lily kept Waters from slipping into the mild depressions he sometimes felt at a life that, despite the money, seemed significantly smaller than the one he'd left behind. But there were other compensations. His mother's health improved, and his brother graduated cum laude from LSU. When Lily expressed restlessness that their relationship seemed stalled, Waters took a hard look at his life—the old dreams and the new realities—and decided that he had not been born to roam the world in search of scientific adventure. He had built something in Natchez, a thriving company his father would have been proud of, and that—he told himself—was good enough. It was time to be fair to Lily.

"What the hell are you doing down here by yourself in the mud?"

Cole's voice was slurred from too much scotch. Waters heard him push through some weeds, then stop to keep his shoes out of the gumbo mud that bordered the river here. There'd been a time when Cole wore steel-toed Red Wings out to the locations, just like Waters. Now he wore the same Guccis or Cole Haans he sported at the office. Waters turned to face him.

"Have you lost your mind?"

Cole's eyes looked cloudy. "What do you mean?"

"You told them five million barrels?"

"You said yourself it could go that high."

Waters's frustration boiled over. "That's you and me! In the office! That's blue-sky dreaming. The outside of the goddamn envelope."

"We've hit it before." Cole's eyes narrowed with resentment. "Look, I handle the investors. You have to trust me about what makes them tick. It's the romance of it, John. They're just like women that way."

"You've obviously forgotten how women get when they're disappointed. You'd better start trimming their expectations a little."

Worry wrinkled Cole's fleshy face. "You don't think we're gonna hit?"

"You said it yourself: one out of twenty-nine."

"That's factoring in all the assholes who don't know what they're doing. You're one out of three, John."

Waters felt a hot rush of self-consciousness at this admission of the degree to which everyone's fortunes depended on him. "We can't ever rely on that."

"But I always have." Cole smiled crookedly. "And you've never let me down, partner."

"We've hit the last two we drilled. That ought to tell you adversity can't be far away."

Cole blinked like a fighter realizing that he has underestimated his opponent. A little clarity had burned through the scotch at last. Even in his inebriated state, Cole knew that fate was always out there waiting to hand you an ass-whipping.

"Who are those guys, anyway?" asked Waters. "The mullets."

"South Louisiana guys, I told you. I've hunted with them a few times. They got some land leased south of town this season. Paid thirty an acre."

"You don't hunt anymore."

"Not without a damn good reason." Cole grinned suddenly, his old bravado back in a flash. "You know deer season's my favorite time of year. While all the husbands are in the woods chasing the elusive whitetail, I'm back in town chasing the married hot tail."

Waters had heard this too many times to laugh. "Look, I know you want me up there. But I'd just as soon not spend much time with those guys. Okay?"

"Don't be an asshole. Investors like having the witch doctor around while they're waiting to log. Tones up the party. Unless it's a dry hole. Then nobody will want to see your ass." Cole grinned again. "Least of all me."

Waters started to walk up out of the mud, but more words came almost before he realized he was speaking.

"What do you know about Eve Sumner?"

Cole looked nonplussed. "The real estate chick?"

"Yeah."

"What about her? I thought you didn't want to know about any of my adventures."

"You've slept with her?"

"What do you think? She ain't no prude, and she looks like two million bucks. Besides, she likes married guys. Fewer complications."

"Is she—" Waters dropped the thought. "Never mind."

"What? Don't tell me you're thinking about hooking up with her. Not Ward Cleaver himself."

"No. She just came on to me a little, and I was curious."

"Yeah? Watch out, then. She's a hell of a lay, but too twisted for me. She's a sly one. Always looking for advantage. Reminds me a little of me. I like my women a little more . . . *pliable*."

"Yes, you do."

"Hey, though, Evie does this thing with her—"

Waters stopped him with an upraised hand. "Don't tell me, okay? I don't need to know."

Cole snickered. "You don't know if you need to know or not until I tell you what she does."

"I think I can live without that knowledge."

"Okay, fine. Now come on up here and hang out with the great unwashed, okay?"

"I will, if you lay off the scotch. I'm looking for two million barrels, but this baby could shale out in a heartbeat."

The levity that ruminating over sex with Eve Sumner had brought Cole vanished from his face. He stepped out of the grass and into the mud, his Guccis sinking ankle deep as he marched to within a foot of Waters.

"Listen to me, partner," he said. "I don't want to

hear any more negative waves, okay? Especially not around the mullets."

Negative waves? "Hey, I'm just telling it like it is."

Cole laid a heavy hand on Waters's shoulder and squeezed. "That kind of honesty's for the classroom and the confessional. This is sales, Rock. You're not so far up the ivory tower that you've forgotten that."

"Cole, what the hell is going on? Something feels wrong about this."

The big man smiled a beatific smile. "Nothing's wrong, John Boy. Nothing a few million barrels of crude won't fix." He leaned in as close as a lover and spoke with quiet earnestness, his breath a fog of scotch. "We need this one, partner. *I* need it."

Waters shook his shoulder free. "You know there's no way to—"

Cole waved him off and walked up out of the mud. "Don't be long. We're gonna be celebrating in a couple of hours."

Waters turned back to the dark river, his gut hollow with foreboding, his mind roiling with images of two women, neither of whom was his wife.

Claustrophobic. That's how it felt in the Schlumberger truck, where Waters sat in the glow of a CRT with Cole and the money men and the engineer crowded around him. The driller stood on the metal steps in the door, some roughnecks lined up behind him. Everyone wanted to know whether the work they had done was for a reason or not, and interest in the outcome— and the risk riding on it—increased with proximity to John Waters.

He watched the paper log scroll out of the printer like a cardiologist reading an EKG. The logging tool had been lowered down the bore hole to total depth and was now being slowly pulled up, electrically reading the properties of the fluids in the geologic formations around it as it rose. Waters's predictions were being proved or negated with every foot of rise, and soon he would know whether the potentially oil-bearing sand was where he'd predicted or not, and if so, whether or not it held oil.

Cole's face looked red and swollen, his eyes almost bulging, and Waters sensed that his partner's blood pressure was dangerously high. The tension slowly wound itself to an almost unbearable pitch, but Waters shut it out: the dripping sweat, the grunts and curses, white knuckles, taut faces. He was waiting for a moment none of the others had known and never would. There was a point when you didn't know what you needed to know and another when you did, the sliver of time between those two states not quantifiable, during which the human brain, trained by evolution to search for patterns and by rigorous education to interpret them, read the data as voraciously as any Neanderthal had searched the savannah for game. The slightest tick of the needle could trigger your instinct, and even before the actual data emerged from the machine the knowledge was there in your medulla, as sweet as the moment you plunged into a woman or as terrible as the ache of metastatic cancer in your belly. Fate's hand was revealed, and it was all over but the bullshittin' and spittin', as Waters's father had so often put it.

"I missed it," Waters said in a flat voice.

"What?" someone whispered.

"Shaled out." Waters clenched his jaw and took the

hit, accepting his failure as the price of courage. "It happens."

"What the fuck?" muttered Billy, the sullen-faced Cajun. "*What* happens? You sayin' there's no oil?"

Waters expected Cole to reply, but he heard nothing. He took his gaze away from the log tape long enough to see that the redness in his partner's face had vanished. Cole was as pale as a fish's belly now, his chin quivering.

"What the fuck, Smith?" bellowed Billy. Cole wasn't "Cole" anymore. The Cajun glared at Waters. "What about show? Gotta be some goddamn *show*, right?"

Waters shook his head. "Show" was the presence of oil in a sand stratum, but usually not enough to justify "running pipe," or completing the well to the point of production. After wells were logged, debates frequently arose over whether pipe should be set or not. Some people wanted to set pipe on marginal wells to be able to boast that they had made a well. Waters was thankful there would be none of that.

"This ain't right," said the other Cajun, silent up till now.

Waters focused on the log. *This ain't right?* What the hell was that supposed to mean? This was the way it worked. Every prospective well was an educated guess, nothing more. Had Cole not made that clear to them? Was this the first well they'd ever invested in?

Cole gave a little shudder that only Waters noticed. Then he straightened up with his old bravado and said, "Fate hammered our ass, boys. Let's give the man some room to do his paperwork."

"Hammered . . . my *ass*," said Billy. "I got money tied up in this well!"

Waters thought he heard the Schlumberger engineer snort.

"You got something to say, bookworm?" snarled the Cajun.

The engineer looked like he did, but he was working for Waters and Cole and would not speak without their leave.

Waters expected Cole to manhandle the whining mullets right out of the truck, but for some reason, Cole didn't look up to the task. Waters hesitated a moment, then dropped the log and stood up. At six foot one, he rose above both investors, and in the closeness of the truck, he stood well into their space.

"We gave it our best shot," he said quietly. "But we missed it. I'll lose more money today than either of you, and—"

"That's *shit*," said Billy. "You guys take a free ride on our money, and keep the override too."

"I don't get carried," Waters said, his palms tingling with potential violence. "I keep the major interest in every well. If it's a duster, I take it right in the wallet. So if you guys don't want to do anything but whine about what you lost, your partner needs to un-ass that chair and you go back to the car and drown your sorrows in scotch."

Billy looked like he wanted to knife Waters in the gut. Cole was staring at his partner as if he'd just watched a transformation of supernatural proportions. Rather than retaliate against Waters, Billy grabbed Cole's arm and growled, "This ain't over, Smith. Bet your ass on that. Now get out there and drive us back to town!"

Billy stomped down the steps of the truck, followed by his stone-faced companion, but Cole stayed behind.

"Been a long time since I seen you do something like that, Rock," he said. "I enjoyed it, but . . . Well, no use talking now."

Waters looked curiously at his old friend, but there was no time to delve into the morass of Cole's private life. He held out his hand, and Cole shook it with the iron grip he'd always had.

"We'll hit the next one," Waters said with confidence. "That's how it always goes, isn't it?"

Cole tried to smile, but the effect was more like a grimace. And though he hadn't spoken, Waters was almost sure he'd heard a thought passing through Cole's mind: *I hope there is a next one. . . .*

"I gotta drive those assholes back," Cole said softly. "What a ride that'll be."

"You've handled worse."

Cole seemed to weigh this idea in his mind. Then he laughed darkly, shook hands with the engineer, and climbed down the steps into the night. Waters picked up the log and reread the tale of his failure.

"Those guys really bugged me," said the engineer, speaking at last.

"Me too, Pete." Waters sensed that the Schlumberger man wanted to say more. He looked up and waited.

"I think Cole was scared when he left," Pete said, sounding genuinely concerned.

"Fear is an emotion Cole Smith never had to deal with," Waters said with a forced smile.

Pete looked relieved.

But as Waters looked back at the log, he thought, *I*

think he was scared too. After a few minutes, he got up and went to the door, then looked back and gave his final order.

"Rig down."

chapter 3

By the time Waters saw Eve Sumner again, he had nearly convinced himself that the strangeness of their initial encounter had been a distortion of his imagination. Their second meeting was as unexpected as the first, the occasion a party for a duke and duchess of the Mardi Gras krewe to which Waters and Lily belonged. Like New Orleans, Natchez had celebrated Fat Tuesday in the nineteenth century, and the tradition had been revived in the second half of the twentieth. Mardi Gras parties were not of a scale comparable to those of Natchez's greatest tradition, the Spring Pilgrimage, but they compensated for this by being less staid and generally more fun. Waters and Lily attended only two or three a year, and this accounted for Waters not knowing Eve Sumner was a member.

The party was held at Dunleith, the premier mansion of the city. If any single building personified the antebellum South as it existed in the minds of Yankees, Dunleith did. Standing majestically on forty landscaped acres and flanked by outbuildings styled after Gothic castles, this colossal Greek Revival mansion took away the breath of travelers who'd circled the globe to study architecture. At night its massive white columns were lit by fluorescent beams, and as Waters and Lily pulled up the private driveway in Lily's Acura, he saw a line of cars awaiting valets at the broad front steps.

"I hear Mike's done a fantastic job of restoration," Lily said, referring to Dunleith's new owner, a co-owner in Waters's largest oil field. "He's adding on to the B and B in back. I can't wait to see it."

Waters nodded but said nothing. The days following a dry hole were always long ones, filled with useless paperwork, regretful phone calls to investors, and consoling visits from colleagues. This time he felt more subdued than usual, but his partner had become almost manic in his desire to put together a new deal. That morning, Cole had pressed Waters to show him whatever prospects he was working on, claiming he was in the mood to sell some interest. "Can't let people think we're down," he said in his promoter's voice, but his eyes held something other than enthusiasm.

A valet knocked lightly on the Acura's window. Waters opened his door, got out, and went around for Lily. She wore a knee-length black dress that flattered her figure, but she carried a glittering gold handbag he had always thought gaudy. He had mentioned it once, but she kept carrying the bag, so he dropped the issue. He didn't know much about fashion, only what he liked.

"There's . . . what's his name?" said Lily. "That actor who bought Devereux."

Waters glanced up at a gray-haired man on the front gallery. The man looked familiar, but Waters couldn't place him. Natchez always collected a few celebrities. They arrived and departed in approximate five-year cycles, it seemed to Waters, and he never paid much attention.

"I don't remember," he said. As he turned away, he saw a formfitting red cocktail dress and a gleaming mane of dark hair float through the massive front door of the mansion. A spark of recognition went through him, but when he tried to focus, all he saw clearly was a well-turned ankle as it vanished through the door. Still, he was almost sure he had just seen Eve Sumner.

When Lily paused on the gallery to speak to the wife of a local physician, Waters was surprised by his impatience to enter the house. When she finally broke away, and they passed into the wide central hallway, he saw no sign of the woman in the red dress.

Tonight's party was larger than most Mardi Gras court affairs. About forty couples milled through the rooms on the ground floor, with more in the large courtyard in back. Two bars had been set up on the rear gallery, and a long wine table bookended by six-liter imperials of Silver Oak waited at the back of the courtyard. A black Dixieland band played exuberant jazz a few yards from the wine table, their brass instruments shining under the gaslights. Waters recognized every guest he saw. Many he had known since he was a boy, although quite a few new people had moved to town in the past few years, despite its flagging economy.

He left Lily engrossed in conversation with a tennis

friend and got himself a Bombay Sapphire and tonic. He and Lily had an understanding about parties: they mingled separately, but every ten or fifteen minutes they would contrive to bump into each other, in case one was ready to make a quick exit. Waters was usually the first to make this request.

Tonight he spoke to everyone who greeted him, and he stopped to discuss the Jackson Point well with a couple of local oilmen. But though he eventually moved through every room of the house, he saw no sign of the tight red dress. Seeing Lily trapped with a talkative garden club matron, he delivered her a Chardonnay to ease the pain. He was making his way back to the bar to refresh his gin and tonic when his eyes swept up to the rear gallery and froze.

Eve Sumner stood twenty feet away, looking down at him over a man's shoulder, her eyes burning with hypnotic intensity. She must be tall, he thought, or else wearing very high heels for her face to be visible over her companion's shoulder. The man was talking animatedly to her, and Waters wondered if the speaker thought those burning eyes were locked on him.

"John? Is this the line?"

Startled, Waters looked around and realized he was blocking access to the bar. "Sorry, Andrew." He shook hands with a local attorney. "Maybe I don't need another drink after all."

"Oh, yes you do. I heard about Jackson Point. Drown your sorrows, buddy. Go for it."

When Waters turned back to the gallery, Eve Sumner was gone. He looked to his left, toward the rear steps, but she was not among the guests there. He glanced to his right, at the northeast corner of the house, but saw only shadows on that part of the gallery. He was about to look away when Eve Sumner stepped around the shadowy corner, raised her drink in acknowledgment, then receded into the shadows like a fading mirage. Waters stood mute, a metallic humming inside him, as though someone had reached into his chest and plucked wires he had not even known were there.

"What can I get you?" asked a white-jacketed bartender. "Another Bombay Sapphire?"

"Yeah," Waters managed to get out. "Hit it hard."

"You got it."

Eve had *known* he was looking for her. Not only that. It was as if she had known the precise moment he would look up at the corner that concealed her. She could have been peeking around it, of course—spying on him—but that would have looked odd to anyone standing nearby. Yet one moment after he'd looked that way, she'd stepped from behind the wall and saluted the precise spot he occupied.

He took a bitter pull from his drink and glanced around for his wife. Lily wasn't the paranoid type, despite their troubles in the bedroom, but she did tend to notice the kind of eye contact Eve Sumner had just given him.

This time she hadn't. Before he could go looking for her, Lily appeared at the top of the courtyard steps, coming up from the rear grounds with the manager of Dunleith's bed and breakfast. She'd obviously been taking a tour of the new construction. A dozen women at the party would have liked to see it; trust Lily to simply walk up and ask the manager for a private tour. She caught her husband's eye and silently communicated that she was ready to leave. Though separated by only fifteen yards, Waters knew it would take her ten minutes to cross the space between, as she would be stopped by at least three people on her way. He sipped his gin and looked up at the crowded gallery.

The liquor had reached the collective bloodstream of the party. The Dixieland band launched into a rousing rendition of "When the Saints Go Marching In," and several couples began a chain dance. Most of the women wore sequined dresses and glittering masks that reflected the lamplight in varicolored flashes, and their voices rose and echoed across the courtyard in a babel of excitement. The men spoke less but laughed more, and tales of hunting deer in nearby forests mixed with quieter comments about various female guests. Waters felt out of place at these times. He hunted a rarer thing than animals, inanimate but maddeningly elusive. Sometimes he hunted in libraries rather than the field, but that didn't lessen the thrill of the chase. With three drinks in him, though, he felt the old wistful dream of getting back to Alaska or New Guinea, choppering over glaciers and rappelling into volcanoes. With this dream came a memory of Sara Valdes, but suddenly her guileless face morphed into the seductive gaze of Eve Sumner, and a wave of heat warmed his skin. Then Eve's face wavered and vanished, leaving the archetypal visage of Mallory Candler. Mallory had been gone ten years, but not one person at this party would ever forget her—

"*Stop*," he said aloud. "Jesus."

He set his drink on a table and rubbed his eyes. He felt foolish for letting Eve get to him this way. What was so strange about her behavior, anyway? Both Lily and Cole had told him she was sexually adventurous, and for some reason, she had picked him as her next conquest. Anything beyond that was his imagination. *She likes married guys*, Cole had said. *Fewer complications. . . .*

"John? Hey, it's been a while."

Waters turned to see a man of his own age and height standing beside him, a wineglass in hand. Penn Cage was an accomplished prosecutor who had turned to writing fiction and then given up the law when he hit best-seller status. Penn and Waters had gone to different high schools (Penn's father was a doctor, so he had attended preppy St. Stephens, like Cole and Lily and Mallory), but Penn had never shown any of the arrogance that other St. Stephens students had toward kids from the public school. Penn had been in the same Cub Scout pack as Waters and Cole, but only Penn and Waters had gone all the way to Eagle Scout before leaving for Ole Miss. They hadn't seen each other much since Penn moved back to Natchez from Houston, where he'd made his legal reputation, but they shared the bond of hometown boys who had succeeded beyond their parents' dreams, and they felt easy around each other.

"It has been a while," Waters said. "I've been working on a well."

"I'm working on a book," Penn told him. "Guess we both needed a break tonight."

Waters chuckled. "I already got my break. Dry hole. Two nights ago. Seems like everybody knows about it."

"Not me. I'm a hermit." Penn smiled, but his voice dropped. "I did hear about your EPA problem, though. Are you guys going to come out all right on that?"

"I don't know. When the EPA tells us whose well is leaking salt water, we'll know if we're still in business or not."

"The cleanup costs could put you under?"

"You don't know the half of it." Waters thought of the unpaid liability insurance. "But hey, I started with nothing. I can make it back again if I have to."

Penn laid a hand on his shoulder. "Sometimes I think we *wish* for some catastrophe, so we could fight that old battle again. Prove ourselves again."

"Who would we be proving ourselves to?"

"Ourselves, of course." Penn smiled again, and Waters laughed in spite of the anxiety that the author's mention of the EPA had conjured.

Penn inclined his head at someone on the gallery. Two men leaning on the wrought-iron rail parted, and Waters saw Penn's girlfriend, Caitlin Masters, looking down at them. She was lean and sleek, with jet-black hair and a look of perpetual amusement in her eyes. Ten years younger than Waters and Cage, she'd come down from Boston to knock the local newspaper into shape, and because her father owned the chain, a lot of Natchezians had groused about nepotism. But before long, nearly everyone admitted that the quality of reporting in the *Examiner* had doubled.

"Caitlin seems like a great girl," Waters observed.

"She is."

While Penn watched Caitlin tell a story to two rapt lawyers on the gallery, Waters studied his old scouting buddy. Penn had become famous for writing legal thrillers, but he'd also written one "real novel" called *The Quiet Game.* Set in Natchez, the book's cast of characters was drawn from the people Waters had grown up with, and the hidden relationships that surfaced in that book had left him in a haze of recollection for a week. Livy Marston—the femme fatale of *The Quiet Game*—had been inspired by Lynne Merrill, one of the two great beauties of her generation (the other was Mallory Candler), and Penn had clearly felt haunted by Lynne the way he himself was haunted by Mallory. Had Penn had an experience similar to his own at the soccer field? he wondered. Had *The Quiet Game* been an exorcism of sorts?

"Where's Lynne Merrill these days?" he asked.

The smile froze on Penn's face, but he recovered quickly and tried to play off his surprise. "In New Orleans for a while, I think."

After an awkward moment, Waters said, "I'm sorry I said that. I was . . . trying to figure something out."

The author looked intrigued. "Something besides whether Lynne was the basis for Livy Marston in my book?"

"I knew that from the moment I saw her on the page. No, I wanted to know if you ever get over something like that. An affair like that. A—"

"A woman like that?" Penn finished. He looked deep into Waters's eyes, his own glinting with the power of his perception. It was a bluntly penetrative act, and Waters felt oddly violated by it. "My answer is yes," Cage said slowly. "But somehow I don't think you'd answer that question the same way tonight."

When Waters said nothing, Penn added, "It's not a passive thing, you know? You have to work it out of you. Or something has to. Some*one*. If you're lucky, you meet a woman who finally obliterates all trace of the one who—who came before. Or knocks the memory down to a tolerable level, anyway."

"Penn!" Caitlin called from the gallery. "I need to get over to the paper. Get me a gimlet for the road."

At that moment, Lily touched Waters's shoulder and said, "Go take care of that girl, Penn Cage. I need my husband."

Penn smiled and walked over to the steps, but as he ascended them, he glanced back over his shoulder, and Waters saw deep interest in his eyes.

"Let's go," Lily said quietly. "I'd like to just slip around the side of the house, but we need to tell Mike we enjoyed ourselves."

Waters followed her up the steps and into the main hall. Conversation indoors had grown to a din, and most faces were flushed from alcohol. Lily walked quickly to discourage buttonholing, but she kept an eye out for their host as she picked a course through the crowd. As they neared the front door, she caught sight of him, but there were too many people between them to make progress. Mike helplessly turned up his hands, then blew Lily a kiss and waved good-bye. Waters nodded thankfully and started toward the door with Lily on his heels. He had his hand on the knob when an old woman cried, "Lily Waters, it's been a coon's age! You come here and talk to me this instant!"

Lily reluctantly broke away and walked to a lushly upholstered chair to pay her respects to a grande dame of the Pilgrimage Garden Club.

As Waters stood in the crowded hall, a cool hand closed around his wrist, and something feather-soft brushed the side of his face. Before he could react, a sultry voice said, *"You didn't imagine anything, Johnny.*

It's me. Me. *Call me tomorrow.*" Then something wet brushed the shell of his ear. Before he could jerk away, sharp teeth bit down on his earlobe, and then the air was cold against his skin. He tried not to whirl, but he turned quickly enough to see the red dress and black mane of hair vanish through the door.

He thought Eve was gone, but then she reappeared, the upper half of her face hidden by an eerily predatory mask of sequins and feathers. She did not smile, but her gaze burned through the eyeholes of the mask with such intensity that a shiver went through him. Then the door closed, and she was gone.

"I'm ready," Lily said from his left. "Let's go before someone else traps me."

Waters began to walk on feet he could barely feel. *You didn't imagine anything . . . It's me. . . .*

He hesitated at the door. If he walked outside now, he and Lily would have to go down the steps and stand with Eve while they waited for the valets to get their cars. He would have to make small talk. Watch the women measure each other. *Call me tomorrow. . . .*

"What's the matter?" asked Lily.

"Nothing."

Lily pulled open the great door and walked through. Waters hesitated, then stepped out into the flickering yellow light coming from the brass gasolier above their heads.

Eve stood at the foot of the wide steps, her back to them, waiting for her car. Her shoulders were bare, her skin still tanned despite the changing season. *You didn't imagine anything, Johnny. . . .*

As Lily started down the steps, Waters caught movement to his left and instinctively turned toward it. Standing on the porch smoking a cigar was Penn

Cage's father, Tom Cage. A general practitioner who had treated Waters's father until his death, Tom Cage took a token position in all of Waters's wells. He'd had a three sixty-fourths interest in the Jackson Point deal.

"Hey, Doc," Waters said, stepping over and extending his hand. "You recovered from that spanking we took?"

"I'm philosophical about losses," Dr. Cage replied. "I don't risk much. I never make a killing, but neither do I lose my buttocks."

"That's a good attitude."

Tom smiled through his silver beard. "You should recommend it to your partner."

"Cole?"

"Last time Smith was in my office, his pressure was way up. And that scotch isn't doing his liver any favors. Or his diabetes."

Cole had been diagnosed with adult-onset diabetes two years ago, but he ignored his condition so regularly that Waters sometimes forgot he had it. "I'll talk to him," he promised.

"Good. He doesn't give a damn what I tell him. And make him take that pressure medication. If it's giving him side effects, we'll find another drug."

"Thanks."

Waters looked down the steps and saw Lily standing alone as Eve Sumner swept toward the driver's door of a black Lexus. Eve didn't acknowledge Waters, but she winked at Lily before she disappeared into the car's interior. As Waters gaped, the Lexus shot forward with an aggressive rumble.

He descended the steps and stood beside Lily as the Acura pulled up the circular drive. "She must sell a lot of houses," he said, trying to sound casual. "That was an LS-four-thirty."

"I wonder who paid for it," Lily said archly. "But maybe she did. All the real estate agents drive more car than they can afford. They think image is everything in that business."

Waters got out his wallet and took out some ones for a tip.

"She told me she'd like to see the inside of our house sometime," Lily went on. "That means somone's interested in it."

"What did you tell her?"

"That Linton Hill won't be on the market for as long as I'm alive."

"That's pretty definite."

"It won't put Eve Sumner off for a week. Watch and see." Lily brushed something off the front of her dress. "I wonder if her breasts are real."

Even in his unsettled state of mind, Waters knew not to touch that one. Still, the question surprised him. Lily wasn't usually given to such comments. Eve Sumner seemed to bring out the cat in her. Maybe she had that effect on all women; hence, her reputation.

"Don't pretend you didn't notice them," said Lily. "She told some girls down at Mainstream Fitness they're real, but I think they're store-bought. She's a fake-baker too."

"A what?"

"Her *tan*, John. Here's the car."

Waters tipped the valet and got behind the wheel, his inner ear still cold from the saliva Eve Sumner had left on his skin.

chapter 4

"What do I *think*? I think you're losing your mind."

Cole Smith leaned back in his sumptuous office chair, kicked a pair of gleaming Guccis up on his desk, and lit a Macanudo. His eyes shone with incredulity.

"So how do you explain it?" asked Waters.

"Explain what? Evie wants to do the wild thing. Where's the mystery?"

"I'm talking about what she said."

"What she *said?*" Cole shrugged. "Okay, let's recap. At the soccer field she said zip. Right? She blew you a kiss."

"It looked like she said, 'Soon.' I told you that."

"It looked like she *might* have said that. But Eve Sumner has no way of knowing what secret things you and Mallory said to each other twenty years ago. And since she didn't actually say *anything*, I think we can assume she blew you a freaking kiss."

"And last night?"

" 'You're not imagining anything'? 'Call me tomorrow'?"

"Right."

Cole chuckled and blew a blue cloud of smoke across his desk. "She's just recognized what your partner already knows: that since your marriage, you're a little slow on the uptake where sex is concerned. You haven't hooked up in, what, twelve years? John Waters, Old Faithful. Last of a breed. Evie's telling you you're not wrong, that you're not imagining that she's coming on to you. You should call her."

"What about 'It's me'?"

"Maybe she's already tried to get your attention and you missed it. Sent you something, maybe. 'It's me.' Get it? 'I'm the one trying to get your attention.' "

"Nobody's sent me anything."

Cole sighed wearily but said nothing more.

Waters looked around the room. Cole's office felt more like a den than a working room. The walls were festooned with Ole Miss Rebels pennants and other memorabilia: a football helmet signed by coach Johnny Vaught, a framed Number 18 Rebels jersey autographed by Archie Manning, a Tennessee Vols jersey autographed by Archie's son Peyton, snapshots of Cole with pro athletes, a nine-pound bass he'd caught when he was seventeen, samurai swords he'd collected in his early thirties, and countless other souvenirs. Waters always felt a little embarrassed here, but the investors loved it. Even if they supported rival LSU, the Ole Miss relics made for lively conversation.

"What are you telling me, John?" Cole asked. "You think Eve Sumner is really Mallory Candler? Back from the grave?"

"No. I don't know what I'm saying. All I know is,

she knew that word, 'Soon,' and she knew the context."

"So what? I knew about it too."

"You did?"

"Sure. I saw you and Mallory do that a dozen times in Oxford."

Waters studied his partner's face, trying to remember how it had looked twenty years ago.

"You did it at frat parties, in the library, all kinds of places. And if I saw it, Mallory's friends saw it too."

"But Eve Sumner wasn't a friend of Mallory's. She's ten years younger than Mallory."

"Maybe Eve has an older sister who was at Ole Miss."

"Does she?"

"How the hell do I know? I doubt it, though. Evie's not even from Natchez. She's from across the river somewhere. I think she graduated from a junior college. Yeah, she told me that. Mallory was a whole different class than Evie, John. Though I hate to admit it."

"Why do you hate to admit it?"

"*Why?* Mallory couldn't stand having me around. Anyone or anything that took you away from her for five seconds, she hated with a passion. Do you remember how bad it got when she lost it? I don't even want to get into that. She almost fucked up your whole life. That bitch—excuse me, that *woman*—is dead. And any appearance of evidence to the contrary tells me my best buddy is losing his fucking grip."

Waters pressed down the disturbing images Cole's words had conjured. "I've never come close to losing my grip."

Cole nodded indulgently. "Not since Mallory. But

everybody has a breaking point. You're used to having all your ducks in a row. Your whole life is about that. Now everything you have is up in the air. We could both be dead broke in a month. That's bound to be affecting you down deep."

"I don't deny that. But it's not making me hallucinate."

"You don't know that. You've never gotten over Mallory, John. You almost did, but then she was murdered, and you actually started feeling sorry for her. Even though the chick might have killed you one day. Or Lily. Or even Annelise. You've told me that before."

"I know."

Cole leaned forward and laid his cigar in a Colonel Reb ashtray. "Drop this bullshit, Rock. Eve Sumner wants you in her pants—end of story. You got a decision to make: walk the strange road, or keep doing your martyr act."

"Goddamn it—"

Smith held up his hands in apology. "Sorry, sorry. Saint John of the great blue balls can't take too much honesty."

"You want me to be honest about *your* life?"

Cole sighed. "We'll save that onerous task for God."

They fell into silence and were quite comfortable with it. A partnership could be like a marriage that way; two people sitting in a room, neither talking nor feeling the need to, all communication made abundantly clear through a complex interplay of movement, sighs, and glances. Waters and Cole had a lot of practice at this. They'd grown up in the same neighborhood, and even attended the same school until the integration laws were enforced and Cole's parents moved him to St. Stephens Prep. Two years later, Cole's family moved to a more affluent neighborhood where all the houses had two stories and there were rules about what you could keep in your yard. Waters's parents had similar plans, but nine months after Cole moved, Henry Waters was standing beside a pipe truck in Wilkinson County when a chain broke and ten thousand pounds of steel pipe casing slid off the truck bed and crushed him.

He lived for three hours, but he never regained consciousness. The doctors never even got him stable enough for surgery. All Waters remembered was a horribly stitched and swollen face with a breathing tube going into the nose and his mother holding a shattered purple hand. John had taken hold of that hand for a few seconds. It was hot and stretched and did not feel natural. The calluses were still there, though, and they let him know it was still his father's hand. Henry Waters was a good geologist; he didn't have to do manual labor. But somehow he was always in there with the roughnecks and workover crews, cranking on three-foot wrenches, lifting pumps and motors, thrusting himself into the dirty middle of things. His biggest smiles had always flashed out of a face covered with grease or crude oil.

Cole was the only boy John's age to attend the funeral. Waters remembered sitting in the pews reserved for family, looking back into rows of old people, and seeing one thirteen-year-old face. After the service, Cole came up and shook his hand with awkward formality. Then he leaned in and quietly said, "This sucks, man. Your dad was a cool guy. I wish it hadn't happened." The adult that Cole Smith had grown into would have to commit a profound betrayal to erase the goodwill that this moment of sincerity—and others like it—had engendered. Cole had certainly tested Waters's patience through the years, but in sum, he was the one man John felt he could trust with his life.

"Speaking of meeting God," Waters said into the silence. "I saw Tom Cage at Dunleith. He told me you're not taking your blood pressure medicine."

Cole picked up his cigar and puffed irritably.

"I know you're not watching your diabetes. Your weight's still up, and I never see you check your sugar."

"It's under control," Cole said in a taut voice.

" 'Control' isn't the word that comes to mind when I think of you." Waters let a little emotion enter his voice. "You could stroke out, man. You could go *blind*. That happened to Pat Davis, and he was only thirty-seven. Diabetes is serious business."

"Christ, you sound like Jenny. If I want a lecture, I'll go home, okay?"

Waters was about to reply when Sybil Sonnier, their receptionist, walked in with something for Cole to sign. She did not smile at either of them; she walked primly to the desk and handed Cole the papers. This pricked up Waters's antennae. Sybil was twenty-eight years old, a divorcee from South Louisiana, and much too pretty to be working in an office with Cole Smith. Cole had "dabbled" with their receptionists before, as he called it, and one of his escapades had cost them over fifty thousand dollars in a legal settlement. At that point, Waters had vowed to do all the hiring himself. But when their last receptionist's husband lost his job and left town, Waters had been on vacation. When he got back, he found Sybil installed at the front desk: one hundred and twenty pounds of curves, dark hair, and smiles. Cole swore he had never touched her, but Waters no longer trusted him about women. When Sybil exited, Waters gave his partner a hard look.

"Sybil's been pretty cold for the past week. You got any idea why that might be?"

Cole shrugged. "PMS?"

"Cole, goddamn it. Did you sleep with her?"

"Hell no. I learned my lesson about employees when I had to pay reparations."

"When *we* had to pay them, you mean. Next time you pay solo, Romeo."

Cole chuckled. "No problem."

"Back to your health. You don't get off that easy."

Cole frowned and shook his head. "Why don't you use all this energy you're expending on paranoia and lectures to generate a new prospect, Rock?"

This was an old bone of contention between them. Their partnership was like a union of the grasshopper and the ant. Whenever they scored big, Waters put forty percent of his money into an account reserved for income taxes. The rest he invested conservatively in the stock market. Each time they drilled a new well, he maintained a large share of it by giving up "override," or cash profit up front. That way, if they struck oil, he was ensured a large profit over time. Cole preferred to take the lion's share of cash up front; thus his "completion costs" on the wells were smaller, but so were his eventual profits. Even when Cole kept a large piece of a well, he almost always sold his interest for cash—usually the equivalent of two years' worth of production—the day after the well hit. And Cole simply could not hang on to cash. He and his wife spent lavishly on houses, cars, antiques, clothing, jewelry, parties, and vacations. He invested in ventures outside the oil business, whatever sounded like big money fast. He had hit some big licks, but he always lost his profits by sinking them into ever-bigger schemes. And most damaging, Cole gambled heavily on sports. This addiction had begun at Ole Miss, where he and Waters had roomed together for three semesters. When Cole moved into the Kappa Alpha house and continued his partying and gambling, Waters stayed in the dorm. Only two things had allowed Cole to remain solvent through the years: a knack for buying existing oil wells and improving their efficiency by managing operations himself; and a partner who continued to find new oil, even in the worst of times. Thus, he was always after Waters to generate new prospective wells. As the attorney of the two, Cole handled the land work—leasing up the acreage where their wells would be drilled—but he saw his real job as sales. And a natural salesman without something to sell is a frustrated man.

In the absence of a prospective oil well, Cole set about selling what he had on hand—himself—usually to the prettier and more adventurous wives in town. He promoted himself to his chosen paramour with the same enthusiasm he gave to oil wells—though with slightly more discretion—ultimately convincing her that she had to have Cole Smith in her life, beginning in her bed. It was all about ego and acceptance. Cole had that manic yet magical combination of insecurity and bravado that drives sports agents, fashion models, and Hollywood stars. And in the oil business, Cole Smith was a star. That was why his name was first on the sign and on the letterhead. Years ago, Cole had suggested this order based on the alphabet, but Waters knew better. It made no difference to him. The proof of primacy in the partnership was in their private discourse and in the awareness of the close-knit oil community. The people who mattered knew who put the "X" on the map and said, "This is where the oil will be." The rest was showbiz.

"Oh, hey," Cole said casually. "I meant to tell you. I'm in a little bind over some margin calls on that WorldCom. I need some cash to tide me over the next thirty days."

Waters struggled to keep a straight face. Cole had said this as if he made such requests all the time, but in fact, it was the first time he had ever asked for a substantial loan. Cole had been in financial trouble from time to time, but he always found sources of emergency cash, and he'd never borrowed more than fifty bucks from Waters for a bar tab.

"How much do you need?" Waters asked.

"About fifty-five, I think."

"Fifty-five . . . thousand?"

Cole nodded, then pursed his lips. "Well, seventy-five might be better. It's just for thirty days, like I said. But seventy-five would smooth things out a little flatter."

"A little flatter," Waters echoed, still in shock. "Cole, what the hell's going on?"

"What do you mean?" A lopsided grin. "Business as usual in the Smith empire."

"Business as usual?"

The grin vanished. "Look, if you don't want to do it—"

"That's not it. It's just that I want to really help you, not—"

"You think I'm a bum on the street?" Cole's face went red. "You'll give me five bucks for food, but nothing for another drink?"

His bitter tone set Waters back in his chair. "Look, maybe we need to talk realistically about what could happen if the EPA investigation goes against us."

"Why? If it goes our way, seventy-five grand is nothing to you. And if it doesn't, that money won't help either of us."

He was right. But Waters couldn't help thinking that their exposure would be a lot less if Cole had paid the goddamn liability premium like he was supposed to. Cole had always said it was an oversight, but Waters was beginning to wonder if he had needed and used that cash for something else.

"Cole, why didn't you pay that insurance premium? Are you in real trouble?"

His partner toyed distractedly with his cigar. "John, you're like a wife who keeps dredging up some old affair. 'But *why* did you do it, Cole? *Why*.' I just forgot, okay? It's that simple."

"Okay."

Waters thought Cole would look relieved at his acceptance of this explanation, but he didn't. He glanced nervously through the cloud of smoke and said, "So, you can slide me the cash?"

Waters was searching for a noncommittal answer when the phone on the desk rang. Cole picked it up but did not switch on the speakerphone, as he once had with all calls. "What is it, Sybil? . . . Yeah? She give a name?"

Cole's face suddenly lost its color.

"What is it?" asked Waters. "What's happened?"

"You've got a phone call. A woman."

"Is it Lily? Is Annelise all right?"

"Sybil says she gave her name as Mallory Candler."

A cold finger of dread hooked itself around Waters's heart.

"Let me handle this," Cole said sharply. "I'll put a stop to this bullshit right now."

"No. Give me the phone."

Cole reluctantly passed the hard line across the desk. The cold plastic pressed Waters's ear flat.

"Who is this?"

"Eve," said a low female voice. "I thought you might hang up unless I said what I did."

"What the hell are you trying to do?"

"I just want to talk to you, Johnny. That's all."

Johnny . . . "I don't want to talk to you."

"I know you're suspicious. Maybe even afraid. You don't understand what's happening. I'm going to prove to you that I'm not trying to hurt you. Only to help you."

"How can you do that?"

"Your daughter's in trouble, Johnny."

Waters went into free fall. He covered the phone and hissed at Cole: "Call St. Stephens and make sure Annelise is in class."

"What? Why?"

"Just do it!"

Cole grabbed a different extension. "Sybil, get me St. Stephens Prep. The lower elementary office."

"What do you know about my little girl?" Waters said into the phone. "Have you hurt her?"

"God, no. She's fine right now. I'm just telling you that she's in danger at that school. That's all I want to say. Talk to her about it, then call me. I'm going now."

"Wait—"

"You'll understand soon, Johnny. I'll explain every-thing. But you have to trust me first."

"I'll understand what?"

"What happened to Mallory."

"What about Mallory? Did you—"

Cole whispered, "They just let the kids out of school. Your maid picked up Annelise five minutes ago."

Waters felt only slight relief. "Listen to me, Ms. Sumner. Did you have something to do with Mallory Candler's death? Did you know her?"

"I didn't know her," Eve said in a soft voice. "I am her."

Waters closed his eyes. His voice, when it finally came, emerged as a whisper. "Did you just say—"

"The world isn't how we think it is, Johnny. I know that now. And soon you will too. Soon you'll under-stand."

"What do you mean? What are you—"

The phone clicked dead.

Waters jumped to his feet and ran for the door.

"What the hell's going on?" Cole yelled.

"I'm going to get Annelise!" Waters veered into the hall, checking his pocket for his keys as he ran. "I'll call you when I find her."

"Let me drive you!" Cole shouted, but Waters was already halfway down the stairs.

Waters drove fifty miles an hour through the center of town, the Land Cruiser's emergency lights flashing. When he hit State Street, he accelerated to eighty. The beautiful boulevard tunneled through a large wooded area in the center of town that concealed two antebel-lum homes: sprawling Arlington plantation; and his own smaller estate, Linton Hill. He'd tried to reach Lily on her cell phone but failed, which meant she was probably swimming at the indoor pool downtown. That was why Rose, their maid, had picked up Annelise from school. He'd bought Rose a cell phone last year, but half the time she forgot to switch it on.

Annelise didn't have soccer practice this afternoon, and he prayed that she didn't have ballet or gymnastics or any of the other countless activities she pursued with the dedication of a seven-year-old career woman. He often wished the world were as simple as it had been when he was a kid; that there were long afternoons when Annelise would have nothing to do but use her imagination and *play.*

He slowed and swung the Land Cruiser into his driveway, then accelerated again. For the first thirty yards, trees shielded the house, but when he rounded the turn, he saw Rose's maroon Saturn parked in the semicircular drive, and his pulse slowed a little. He parked beside her and sprinted up the steps, then paused at the door and took a breath. He didn't want to panic Rose or Annelise if there was nothing to worry about.

When he opened the door, he smelled mustard greens and heard metal utensils clanking in the kitchen. He started to move toward the sounds, but then he heard Annelise's voice down the hall to his left.

He found her sitting on the floor in the den, playing with Pebbles, her cat. She was trying to coax Pebbles into a house she had built out of plastic blocks that reminded him of LEGOS but weren't.

"Daddy," she complained, "Pebbles won't check into the kitty hotel!"

Waters smiled, then struggled to keep the smile in place as tears of relief welled in his eyes. Seeing Ana playing there, it was hard to imagine what he'd been afraid of two minutes ago. Yet Eve Sumner had sounded deadly serious on the telephone. *Your daughter's in danger at that school. . . .*

"How was school today, punkin?" he asked, sitting beside Annelise on the floor.

"Good. Why won't she go inside, Dad?"

"Cats are pretty independent. They don't like being told what to do. Does that remind you of anybody?"

She grinned. "Me?"

"You said it, not me."

Ana pushed the cat's bottom, but Pebbles pressed back against her hand and glared like a woman groped in an elevator. Waters started to laugh, but stopped when he saw something that would normally have caused him to scold his daughter. The family's fifteen-hundred-dollar video camera was lying on the floor behind Annelise.

"Honey, what's the camcorder doing on the floor?"

Annelise hung her head. "I know. I wanted to make a movie of Pebbles in the hotel I built."

"What's the rule about that camera?"

"Only with adult supervision."

"We'll make a movie later, okay? I want to talk to you for a minute. We haven't spent enough time together lately."

She looked up at him. "It's always like that when you're drilling a well."

From the mouths of babes. "Has everything been going okay at school lately?"

"Uh-huh." Annelise's attention had returned to Pebbles.

"Are there any bullies bothering you?"

"Fletcher hit Hayes on the ear, but Mrs. Simpson put him in the sweet chair for an hour."

The sweet chair. "But no one's picking on you? Other girls, maybe?"

"No." Annelise grabbed a paw and earned a feline slap.

"Have you seen any strangers hanging around the school? Around the playground, maybe?"

"Um . . . no. Junie's dad hung around the fence for a while one day, but then a policeman came and made him leave. Her parents are divorced, and her dad's not supposed to see her except sometimes."

God, they have to grow up fast, Waters thought bleakly. Another idea came to him. He didn't want to consider it—Annelise was only in the second grade—but he knew that the dark side of human nature observed no rules. "Honey, has anyone . . . touched you somewhere they're not supposed to? Boys, I mean?"

Annelise looked up, her eyes interested. "No."

She said nothing else, but she continued to look at Waters, and he knew something was working behind her eyes.

"What is it, Ana?"

"Well . . . I think maybe Lucy and Pam have been doing something they're not supposed to."

Two girls, Waters thought. *This can't be too bad.* "Like what?"

Annelise clearly wanted to speak, but still she hesitated.

"You know you can tell me anything, baby. You're not going to get in trouble. No matter what it is."

"Well . . . they've been going to the closet during recess to see stuff."

"What kind of stuff?"

"Stuff Mr. Danny shows them."

A chill raced up Waters's back, and a vague image of a soft-faced thirty-year-old carrying a ladder came into his mind. "What does Mr. Danny show them?"

"I don't know. But I think it's stuff girls aren't supposed to look at."

Waters desperately wanted more information, but he didn't want to press his daughter on something sexual. "Have you been in that closet, Ana?"

"No *way*. I don't like Mr. Danny."

"Why not?"

"He reminds me of something. I don't know what. Something from a movie. When he looks at me, I feel creepy."

Waters realized his hands were shaking. "Rose!"

With a sudden clank of metal, Rose's footsteps sounded in the hall and she appeared in the door, a stout black woman in her sixties who looked as though she would make it through her nineties with ease.

"What is it, Mr. John?"

"I've got to run an errand. I want you to keep Annelise with you in the kitchen until Lily gets back. You understand?"

Rose often forgot things like switching on cell phones, but she was hypersensitive to the subtleties of human behavior.

"I'll keep her right by me. Is everything all right?"

"Everything's fine." He got to his feet. "I'll be back soon."

Rose smiled at Annelise. "You run in the kitchen, girl. I'll let you mix the cornbread today."

Annelise smiled, then stood and ran into the kitchen.

Rose's smile vanished. "Something bad done happened, Mr. Johnny? Is Lily all right?"

"She's fine. It's business, Rose."

Rose's look said she knew different. "You go on. I won't let that baby out of my sight."

"Thank you."

Waters hurried out to the Land Cruiser and roared down the driveway. Picking up his cell phone, he called directory assistance and got the number of Kevin Flynn, the president of the Board of Trustees of St. Stephens Prep. Waters had not known Flynn well growing up, but as a major contributor to the school's annual fund, he knew the man would bend over backward to accommodate him.

"Hello?" said Flynn.

"Kevin, this is John Waters."

"Hey, John. What's up?"

"I think we have a problem at the school."

"Oh, no. Air-conditioning gone again?"

"No. It's much more serious. I don't want to discuss it on a cell. I think we should meet at the school."

"Why don't you come by my office?"

An attorney with two partners, Flynn owned a nice building four blocks up Main Street from Waters's office. "The school would be better. Would that maintenance man still be there? Danny?"

"I think he stays till five, most days."

"Meet me there. Do you know Tom Jackson well?"

A hesitation. "The police detective?"

"Yes. He and I graduated from South Natchez together."

"Is this a police matter, John?"

"I'm not sure. But I'm going to have Tom meet us there if he can."

"Jesus. I'm on my way."

Waters tried to hold the Land Cruiser at the speed limit as he called the police department.

Kevin Flynn's Infiniti was parked near the front door of St. Stephens when Waters arrived, and the lawyer climbed out when he saw the Land Cruiser. An athletic man of medium height, Flynn had an open manner that made people like him immediately. Waters got out and shook hands, noticing as he did that some of the school's front windows were open to let in the autumn air.

"What's going on, John?" Flynn asked. "Why the secrecy? Why the cops?"

"Let's talk inside."

Flynn's smile slipped a little, but he led Waters through the front door and into the headmaster's empty office. He sat behind the desk, Waters on a sofa facing him.

"You look pretty upset," the attorney said.

"You're about to join me." Waters quickly recounted his conversation with Annelise, omitting any mention of Eve Sumner's initial warning. By the time he finished, Flynn had covered his mouth with one hand and was shaking his head.

"Jesus Christ, John. This is my worst nightmare. We do background checks on everyone we hire, for just this reason. We're required to by the insurance company. Danny Buckles came back clean."

A soft knock sounded at the office door. Waters turned and saw Tom Jackson leaning through the door, his outsized frame intimidating in the small space. The detective had light blue eyes and a cowboy-style mustache, and the brushed gray nine-millimeter automatic on his hip magnified the subtle aura of threat he projected.

"What's going on, fellas?" he asked, extending a big hand to Waters. "John? Long time."

Waters let Flynn take the lead.

"We're afraid we may have a molestation situation on our hands, Detective. Our maintenance man, Danny Buckles. John's daughter said Danny's been taking some second-grade girls into a closet to 'show them things.'"

Jackson sighed and pursed his lips. "We'd better talk to him, then."

"I have a civil practice. Nothing criminal. How should we handle this?"

"Is Buckles here now?"

"Yes. Or he should be, anyway."

"You're the head of the school board, right? Invite him in for a friendly chat. I'll stand where he can see me when he goes in to talk to you. You got a portable tape recorder?"

"Dr. Andrews has one, I think." Flynn searched the headmaster's desk and brought out a small Sony. "Here we go."

"Tell him you want to record the conversation as a formality. If he starts screaming for a lawyer, that'll tell us something."

"I'd scream for a lawyer," Flynn declared, "and I'm innocent."

"You never know what these guys will do," Jackson said thoughtfully. "Molesters are a slimy bunch. They frequently take jobs where they'll be close to children. At video arcades, camps, even churches."

"Jesus," breathed Flynn. "I wish you hadn't told me that. I've got six-year-old twins."

The attorney went into the front office and paged Danny Buckles over the intercom system. After about twenty seconds, a hillbilly voice answered, "I'm on my way." While they waited, Flynn got out Buckles's personnel file and scanned it.

"Here's Danny's background check. Clean as a whistle."

"That doesn't mean anything," said Detective Jackson. "You pay a hundred bucks, a hundred bucks worth of checking is what you get. All kinds of stuff slip through those."

A white man in his early thirties suddenly appeared at the window. Blades of grass covered his shirt, and his face was pink-cheeked from labor.

"That's Danny," said Flynn, giving the janitor an awkward wave.

Waters looked into the bland face, trying to read what secrets might lie behind it.

"We'll go out without saying anything to him," Jackson said to Flynn. "Then you bring him in."

Waters followed the detective out into the school's entrance area, a wide hallway lined with trophy cases. Jackson gave Buckles a long look as he passed, and Waters thought he saw the color go out of the maintenance man's face.

"Your little girl told you about this?" Jackson asked Waters as Buckles went through the door.

"That's right," Waters replied, watching through the window as Flynn led the younger man into the headmaster's private office.

"Just out of the blue?"

"Not exactly."

Jackson's face grew grave. "Did he touch your little girl, John?"

"I don't think so."

"You're not up here to do anything stupid, are you?"

Waters looked Jackson full in the face. He was six foot one, but he still had to tilt his head up to meet the detective's suspicious gaze. "Like what?"

The detective was watching him closely. "You're not armed."

"Hell no. If I was going to kill the guy, would I have called you first?"

"It happens. This kind of situation, especially. Fathers have killed molesters right in front of deputies and then turned themselves in on the spot."

"Don't worry about that, Tom."

A sound between a wail and a scream suddenly issued from the headmaster's office. Waters froze, but Jackson ran straight for the receptionist's door. As he opened it, Waters heard Kevin Flynn say, "Detective? This is a police matter now."

When Waters reached the office, he saw Danny Buckles sitting on the sofa he himself had occupied only moments before. Buckles's cheeks were bright red and streaked with tears, and his nose was running like a crying child's.

"I can't *help* it!" he sobbed. "I try and try, but it *don't . . . do . . . no . . . good.* It won't let me loose! I can't stop *thinking* about it."

A shudder of revulsion went through Waters, followed by an unreasoning anger.

"I don't hurt 'em none!" Danny whined in a tone of supplication. "You ask 'em."

"Danny Buckles isn't even his real name," said

Flynn. "God, what a mess. What am I going to tell the parents of those little girls?"

"The truth," Tom Jackson said. "As soon as you can. Call both parents of each child and get them up here right now. Twenty minutes after I get this boy down to the station, the story'll be all over town. I'm sorry, but you know how it works."

"Yes, I do," Flynn murmured.

For Waters, a different reality had suddenly sunk in. Eve Sumner had warned him of this danger, and her warning had proved accurate. Did the beautiful real estate agent know this blubbering pervert sitting on the couch? She must. How else could she know what he'd been up to? Waters started to tell Jackson about Eve, but even as he opened his mouth, something held him back.

"I'm going home, guys," he said. "I want to hug my little girl."

"I may need you to make a statement," said Jackson. "But I'll try to keep your daughter out of it."

"Thanks, Tom. You know where to find me."

Jackson told "Danny Buckles" he was going to place him under arrest. The janitor started crying again, then moaned something about how horribly he'd been abused in jail. Waters walked calmly out of the office and climbed into his Land Cruiser. He drove slowly away from the school, but as soon as he reached the highway, he accelerated to seventy and headed toward the Mississippi River Bridge. Eve Sumner's office was on the bypass that led to the twin spans, and if he pushed it, he could be there in less than five minutes.

chapter 5

Eve Sumner's office building stood a thousand yards from the Mississippi River Bridge. A false front of brick and wood molding had been grafted onto its front, but one glance would tell any passerby that it was an aluminum box. The familiar logo of a national brokerage company decorated the SUMNER SELECT PROPERTIES sign outside, and expensive cars crowded the asphalt parking lot. Waters remembered from newspaper ads that eight or ten agents worked for Sumner. He couldn't believe there were enough houses changing hands in Natchez to support those ten agents, much less the hundred or so whose pictures he saw in the newspaper every week. For the last six months, everything seemed to be for sale, but nobody was buying.

He parked in a reserved space by the front doors, then got out and pushed into a large open-plan office with two lines of desks and some partitioned cubicles against the right wall. Several women and two men sat at the desks, the women dressed to the nines and looking bored, the men reading newspapers. A receptionist with too much blue eye shadow sat near the door, half blocking the corridor created by the cubicles. Everyone looked up when the door banged open, and nobody went back to what they were doing.

"May we help you?" asked the receptionist.

"I'm here to see Eve Sumner."

"Umm . . . okay. She's with somebody right now."

"This can't wait."

"Can I have your name?"

"That's John Waters, Debbie," called one of the men in the cubicles. "Hi, John."

Waters didn't recognize the man, but he gave a half wave as Debbie picked up her phone and spoke softly.

"She said to go on back," Debbie said in a startled voice.

As though on cue, a door opened in the back wall and two female voices rode the air to Waters, one low and throaty, the other high and ebullient. Waters started toward the door, and two women emerged. One was Eve Sumner, wearing a blue skirt suit, a cream silk blouse, and heels; the other was a fiftyish woman in a bright blowsy dress. Eve tried to introduce Waters to her older guest, but he didn't slow down. He walked past them into the private office and closed the door behind him.

The room held a metal desk, glass shelves lined with real estate textbooks and photos of a junior high school–age boy, and a framed map of the city as it had appeared in 1835. Waters sat behind the desk and waited.

It didn't take long. Eve walked in, closed the door, and stood looking down at him, her eyes more curious than surprised. Before coming in, she had swept her dark hair up from her neck and loosely pinned it, which gave her a rakish air, and the generic skirt suit could not hide the sensual curves beneath it. Lily had guessed her age at thirty-two, but Eve's figure said twenty-five. She probably spent hours in the gym, but she clearly had genetics on her side. And she knew it.

"I thought you were going to call me," she said.

"The police just arrested Danny Buckles. You've got thirty seconds to explain how you knew about him before I get a detective over here to do the same to you."

Eve leaned back against the door. "Why didn't you bring one with you?"

Waters said nothing.

"It's because of Mallory, isn't it?"

Waters reached for the phone.

"What can you tell the police?" Eve asked.

"The truth. And Cole Smith can back me up."

"Cole needs a little backup himself these days." Her eyes gently mocked him. "I called you about a house I have for sale. I also have a buyer for Linton Hill. That's all we talked about."

"There a connection between you and Danny Buckles. There has to be. The police will find it."

Eve slowly shook her head. "No one could ever find it, Johnny. I advise you to trust me on that."

For some reason, he believed her.

"Besides, I saved Annelise a terrible experience. Why would you want to hurt me?"

"What are you really up to? This has to be about money. So let's go ahead and get to the bottom line."

She looked genuinely hurt. "I don't care about *money*. I want to talk to you. That's all."

"Talk."

She licked her lips as though about to confide in him, but then she shook her head. "Not here."

"Why not?"

"Because what I have to say can't be heard by anyone. Especially anyone here. We're going to be spending a lot of time together, and we don't want people suspicious from the start."

She was speaking to him like a fellow conspirator, and her low, confiding tone gave him a surreal feeling of complicity. "You're out of your mind, lady."

Eve glanced at the door and whispered, "Look, this one time, we could go to my house."

"Your house?"

"A house on the market, then. An empty house? That's perfect cover."

He couldn't believe her persistence. "Whatever you have to say, say it right here. Right now."

She took a step closer to the desk. Her proximity made his skin tingle. Here was a woman he had never really met, yet he felt as though they already shared the invisible connection of secret lovers.

"I'm not who you think I am, Johnny."

"Danny Buckles wasn't who anyone thought, either. Who are you? And don't tell me Mallory Candler."

Eve's dark eyes became liquid. "I'm the girl you first said 'I love you' to under the Faulkner quote on the front of the library at Ole Miss."

Waters's mouth fell open. *Who knows that?* he asked himself. *Who the hell knows that? Someone, obviously.*

She smiled at his reaction. "I'm the girl you first made love to at Sardis Reservoir."

His hand slipped off the desktop. "Who the hell are you, lady?"

"You know who I am. Johnny, I'm Mal—"

"Shut up!"

"*Please* keep your voice down. We have to figure out what to do."

He tried to think logically, but her knowledge of his intimate past had somehow short-circuited his reason. "I'm leaving," he said, and stood.

"Please don't. I'll meet you anywhere. You name the place. Somewhere we used to go."

"Where would that be?"

"The Trace?"

Waters couldn't believe it. He and Mallory had spent countless hours on the Natchez Trace, a wooded highway crossed by dozens of beautiful side roads and creeks. "Anybody could have guessed that. Lots of kids went there."

"Did they go to the creek under the wooden suspension bridge? Where we went skinny-dipping?"

Waters's skin went cold.

"Or we could go to the cemetery. Behind Catholic Hill, where the big cross is."

"*Stop.*" He realized that he had whispered, that he too was now trying to keep those outside from hearing their exchange.

Eve leaned across the desk. Perfume wafted to him as her silk blouse parted, revealing the deep cleft between her breasts. "Take it easy, Johnny. Everything's all right."

Waters shivered at the familiar way she said his name.

"It just takes some getting used to," she went on.

"It's really simple, once you understand. Like all profound things. Like gravity."

"Listen to me," Waters hissed. "I don't want to see you again. I don't want you to call me. If you come around my daughter, I'll have you arrested. And if you try to hurt her . . ."

Eve opened her mouth, feigning shock. "You'll what? You'll kill me?"

"You said that, not me."

"But you thought it."

He *had* thought it. That was the level of threat he felt in the presence of this woman. "Yes, I did. So . . . now you know the rules."

The mocking smile again. "I was never one for rules, was I, Johnny?"

He had to get out of the office. As he came around the desk, he half expected her to try to stop him, but she didn't. She stepped aside and watched him, letting her eyes do their work. He felt an almost physical tug as he broke her gaze, and then he was in the main office again, storming past the staring realtors and pushing into the sun of the parking lot.

He felt strangely grateful for the familiarity of the Land Cruiser, which he started and pointed up the bypass toward the bridge. As he turned right at Canal Street, toward his office, he punched Cole's number into the cell phone. Sybil answered and put him straight through.

"What's up, John?" Cole asked. "Is Annelise okay?"

"Yeah. But I want you to do me a favor. You still have a good relationship with your law school buddies in New Orleans?"

"More or less."

"They have investigators on their payroll, right?"

"Sure."

"I want a copy of Mallory's death certificate."

A pregnant silence.

"I also want to see the newspaper accounts of her murder. The *Times-Picayune*, *The Clarion-Ledger*, anyone who covered it. And if it's possible, I want to talk to the homicide detective who handled her case."

More silence. Then Cole said, "Okay, Rock. I think you've lost it, but if that's what you want, you got it."

"And I want everything there is on Eve Sumner. I mean everything. Pull out all the stops."

"What the hell did she tell you? Have you seen her?"

"I'll call you tonight and explain."

"You're not coming back to the office?"

Waters had intended to go back to work, but he was already passing the turn on Main Street, headed toward the north side of town. "Can you handle things for the rest of the day?"

"No problem, amigo."

"Thanks. And look, about that loan . . ."

"Forget it, man, I shouldn't have asked you."

"Bullshit. I'll cut you a check in the morning." Lily would kill him for doing this, but she didn't need to know about it.

"Thanks, buddy," Cole said softly. "You don't know how big a favor this is."

"I have a feeling I do. And when the mood strikes you, I want you to tell me what the hell is going on."

Cole gave a noncommittal grunt, and Waters clicked off.

Three minutes later, he found himself driving along Cemetery Road, looking off the bluff at the river.

When he came to the third gate of the cemetery, he turned in. Why he had come back, he wasn't sure. The open space and the silence had always drawn him when he had things on his mind, but something else had brought him here today. He parked atop Jewish Hill, but instead of walking to the edge of its flat summit, where the river view was spectacular, he walked toward the line of oaks that shaded Mallory's grave. Even from a distance it stood out, the imposing black marble amid a field of plebeian white and gray. Today he swung to the left of her grave and veered down one of the narrow asphalt lanes between cedar-shaded hills, into the depths of the cemetery.

Long beards of moss hung from the oaks, and a thin sprinkling of reddish-brown leaves dotted the grass. He passed ornate wrought-iron fences, markers for Confederate soldiers, countless metal plaques reading PERPETUAL CARE. Some days the cemetery was alive with the drone of push mowers and Weed Eaters, but today all was still but for an occasional breath of wind in the trees. The absence of sound heightened his senses. He felt the wind pulling at his shirt like invisible fingers, but what dominated his mind was his emotional state.

He'd been away from Eve Sumner for twenty minutes, yet the sense of being close to her had not left him. She had disturbed him on a level far deeper than that of reason. Against his will, she had reincarnated the feeling he'd had whenever he was close to Mallory Candler. He had no idea what subtle chemical signals were transmitted and detected by lovers—pheromones, or whatever the scientists called them these days—but whatever they were, he and Mallory had shared them, and Eve Sumner emitted exactly the same ones. And she *knew* it. She had known that her mere presence was working on him in a way that her secret knowledge of his past never could.

"It's some kind of scam," he murmured, as images of Mallory rose in his mind. "It has to be."

And yet, for a brief moment after leaving the real estate office, he had wondered if Eve Sumner might in fact *be* Mallory Candler. If Mallory might somehow have survived the attack that supposedly killed her. The two women had facial similarities; no one would deny that. And their bodies were not dissimilar, though Eve seemed bigger-boned than Mallory had been, and her features not quite as fine. But Eve Sumner was thirty-two at most, and looked ten years younger; Mallory would be forty-two now. What other explanation could there be? Could Mallory be alive and *helping* Eve to deceive him? For this to be true, there would have to have been a case of mistaken identity at Mallory's murder scene. He'd heard of cases like that before. Only it could not have happened in Mallory's case. He possessed few details of her murder, but he did know there had been little or no facial disfiguration, because Mallory—against her oft-stated wishes—had been given an open-casket funeral. Her parents' vanity had outweighed their loyalty to their daughter, and for once Mallory wasn't there to argue.

Waters started at a moving shadow, then ducked to avoid a quick beating sound above his head. When he straightened, he saw a large black crow light on a tree limb only a few feet above him. A female, he guessed. She must have a nest nearby. But fall was the wrong time of year for that. The crow stared back at him in profile, its solitary eye blinking slowly at the lone man standing in the narrow lane. Looking away from the bird, he realized he was practically in the shadow of the great cross on Catholic Hill. The ornate monument—easily fifteen feet tall—marked one of the secret meeting places he and Mallory had used before their affair became public in the town.

Catholic Hill wasn't actually much of a hill, just a few feet high at the front, but at the back it dropped off about eight feet at some places, where a cracked masonry wall held in the old graves. Between this wall and the kudzu-filled gully behind it was a narrow strip of grass, maybe fifteen feet wide, where a couple could lie in the shade on a hot day, shielded from the eyes of cemetery visitors, the only risk of discovery coming from the grass-cutters or another couple seeking privacy.

Waters walked up the steps and past the massive cross to a wooden gazebo built over an old cistern. Here the black men who eternally battled the cemetery grass and made good on the promise of "perpetual care" ate their baloney sandwiches from paper bags. The cistern was filled now with Fritos bags and RC Cola cans. Waters walked beneath the gazebo to the back of the hill and looked down at the grassy strip where he had lain so many hours with Mallory all those years ago. Nothing had changed. A few masonry cracks had deepened, a few more bricks had fallen. All else remained the same. What had he expected? The sun shone, the rain fell, the grass grew, the mowers came, the dead stayed dead.

He glanced to his left and felt a fillip of excitement. Across the lane, shaded by drooping tree limbs, lay two low-walled rectangles that bordered very old graves. Behind one of those walls Waters had once buried a mason jar beneath six inches of earth. If he or Mallory arrived late at a rendezvous—or early and had to leave—they would leave the other a message in the jar. *Sorry I missed you. I love you SO much.* Or *I'll come back at 3:30. PLEASE try to be here. I need you.* All the infantile gushing and obsessive logistics of clandestine lovers. He wondered if the jar was still there.

"What the hell," he said. He strode across the hill and down into the deep shade below the overhanging limbs.

He heard a scuttling in the undergrowth as he approached, probably a possum or armadillo startled by the drumbeat of his feet. A faint scent of flowers hung in the air, and as he stepped over the low wall, he had the sensation of entering a dimly lit room. Leaning over the far wall, he saw a thickly tangled web of weeds covering the ground. Though it had been almost twenty years, his hand went to the exact spot where he'd dug the hole, and in the act of reaching, he felt the same thrill he'd felt years before, the delicious anticipation of reading a declaration of love or a frank expression of lust. He also felt fear. He had nearly been bitten by a coral snake here, a beautiful harbinger of death sunning itself in the weeds beside the wall. You almost never saw coral snakes in Mississippi, but they were here, and far more lethal than the moccasins and rattlesnakes you bumped into during summer if you spent much time in the woods.

Beneath the weeds, Waters's fingers found a depression in the cool earth, like the shallow bowls that form over decomposing stumps. He drove his forefinger down through moist soil until it hit something flat and hard. Widening the hole with his finger, he scraped away some dirt, gripped the round lid, and pulled. The mason jar slipped easily from the ground, a translucent thing coated with a brown layer of soil, its once shiny brass lid now an orange-brown cap of rust. He was smiling with nostalgia when he saw a piece of paper lying in the bottom of the jar. Not a moldy yellow scrap, but a neatly folded piece of blue notepaper that could have been put there yesterday.

Powder blue paper . . .

His heart began to pound, and he whipped his head around, suddenly certain that he was being observed. More frightening, he had the sensation that he was following a trail of bread crumbs laid out by someone four steps ahead of him, someone who was pulling him along by the twin handles of his guilt and regret. If so, that person knew all his secrets, and Mallory's too. At least he knew she always used blue notepaper. He peered anxiously up at Catholic Hill, but he saw only gravestones, empty lanes, and gently swaying trees.

Looking down at the jar, he felt a sudden urge to shove it back down the hole and walk away. That would be the smart thing to do. But he couldn't. What man could?

He gripped the bottom of the jar with his left hand, the lid with his right, and twisted hard. The rusty lid squeaked but came off easily. Waters inverted the jar, and the notepaper fell to its mouth and stuck. He fished it out with his fingers and unfolded it. The flowing script sent his heart into his throat. Those words had been written either by Mallory Candler or by an expert forger with access to papers she'd left behind at her death.

Dear John,

I knew you'd come here sooner or later. I knew you'd look. You and I used to laugh at ideas like predestination, but I wonder if, even then, when we lay here kissing on the grass, what would happen to me in New Orleans had long been ordained, and even that you would one day be standing here with this note in your hand, wondering if you were going insane. You're not, Johnny. You're NOT. God, I love you. I LOVE YOU.

Mallory

"This isn't happening," Waters said softly, his hands shaking.

"Yes, it is," answered a low female voice.

He whirled.

Eve Sumner stood twenty feet behind him, as still as a stone angel. She still wore her work clothes, and her hair was still pinned up from her neck. As he gaped, her lips spread in a languorous smile, and fear unlike any he had known since Mallory lost her mind gripped him. The compulsion to run was almost over-powering, but some primal impulse held him in place. He would not let this woman see she had the power to drive him to flight.

"What are you doing here?" he whispered.

Eve shrugged and walked a few steps closer, down to the low wall that bordered the graves. "I knew you'd come."

"Do you know what this is?" Waters held out the note.

"It's the letter I left here the day after I saw you at the soccer game."

He closed his eyes and tried to keep his mind from spinning out of control. *Facts,* he thought. *Who knew about this jar? Did I ever tell Cole about it? Did Mallory ever tell anyone? She must have. How else could Eve know about it?*

"Why don't you just tell me what you want, Ms. Sumner? It would save a lot of time. Surely it can't be worth going to all this trouble."

"I want what I've always wanted. You."

Waters blinked. This was exactly what Mallory would have said, had she been standing before him.

"You want me *how?"*

The languid smile again. "Every way. In my life. In my bed. I want you inside me. I want to have your children."

The mention of children made Waters's stomach flip over. "You're not Mallory Candler. Your name is Eve Sumner."

"Legally, that's true."

"What do you mean? Were you born under another name?"

"I was born Mallory Gray Candler, on February fifth, nineteen sixty."

"You got that off her gravestone."

Eve looked skyward. "Sooner or later, you're going to have to listen to what I have to say."

"I'm listening now."

"You say that, but your mind is closed. To hear what I have to say, it's going to have to be open. To anything. Everything."

"I'm open."

Eve smiled sadly, then without a word turned away and walked toward the strip of grass behind Catholic Hill. Waters stood in the shadow of the woods, his eyes following her vanishing figure as though chained to it. He hesitated for nearly a minute. Then put the jar and the note back in the hole and went after her.

He found her lying on the grass, her eyes open to the sky, her arms outstretched like Christ on the cross. The navy skirt suit seemed totally incongruous with her relaxed posture.

Without looking at him, Eve said, "Ask me anything you like, Johnny. Things only you or I would know."

"I'm not playing that stupid fact game with you. God only knows how you found all that stuff out, and it doesn't matter anyway. No matter what secrets you know, you can't negate the single most important fact: Mallory Candler is dead, and has been for ten years."

Eve sighed and turned her head to face him, her eyes empty of artifice. "That's not true."

The boldness of her statement left him speechless for a moment. "Are you seriously trying to tell me you're Mallory Candler returned from the dead? Are you mentally ill?"

Eve bit her bottom lip, and Waters had the eerie feeling that he was talking to a small child concealing a secret.

"I'm not back from the dead," she said. "I never died."

Waters shivered at the conviction in her voice. "What?"

"I *never died*, Johnny. Not for more than a second or two, anyway."

"*You* may not have died, but Mallory Candler had an open casket funeral."

"And her *body* lay in it." Eve rolled up onto one

elbow and propped her head on her hand. "Do you think that's all a person is, Johnny? Has science jaded you so much? A woman is the sum of her flesh?"

"What else is there?"

"What about the soul? For lack of a better term. The spirit?"

"You're telling me you're the soul of Mallory Candler?"

Eve bit her lip again, as if seriously considering this question. "Maybe. I don't really know what a soul is."

"If you're the soul of Mallory Candler, where is Eve Sumner's soul?"

"Here. With me. Only . . ."

"What?"

"She's sleeping." Eve shrugged with childlike wonder. "Sort of."

"Eve Sumner's soul is sleeping?"

"That's what I call it. I'm awake now. Most of the time, really. It's something that's taken me a long time to learn. Years."

Three days ago, Waters could not have imagined having this conversation. "Is this craziness what you wanted to tell me?"

"Partly. But I knew it wouldn't convince you. I really wanted to tell you a story."

"About what?"

"My murder."

"Do you know something about Mallory's murder?"

Another sad smile. "Mallory's, mine, whatever. But she wasn't murdered. A man *tried* to murder her. Tried and failed."

"This is pointless, Ms. Sumner."

"Is it? You're still here."

He wanted to walk away, but he couldn't. And she knew it. He sat Indian-style on the grass a few feet away from her and said, "Talk."

Eve sat up and gracefully folded her legs beneath her, exactly the way Mallory had two decades before. Her smile disappeared, replaced by a look of deep concentration. Waters was reminded of Annelise when she tried to recall details of the house they had lived in when she was a small child.

"It was summer," Eve said. "We were living in downtown New Orleans. I'd driven across the river to the Dillard's Department Store in Slidell. On my way back, my Camry broke down. I couldn't believe it. That car was so reliable. This was nineteen ninety-two, and I didn't have a cell phone. I wasn't too worried, though. It was only nine-thirty, and I thought I could flag down a cop. I turned on my flashers, locked the doors, and started watching my rearview mirror. After forty-five minutes, I hadn't seen a single patrol car. I hoped my husband would come looking for me, but I'm not exactly the punctual type, and I knew he wouldn't really start worrying till at least eleven.

"I was a mile from City Park—the projects—and wearing a fairly skimpy outfit, so I didn't want to get out and start flagging people. But I did. After about five minutes, a truck with a blue flashing light pulled in front of me. It had a camper thing on the back, but it looked official. Like one of those canine units, or maybe a fire department thing. Anyway, I was blocked by a concrete rail on one side and zooming traffic on the other. A man got out and waved, then called out and asked if I needed help. I asked if he had a cell phone. He said he did, and I saw the little funny aerial sticking off his back windshield. He reached in and held out a phone on a cord, and I took a couple of steps forward. I knew it might not be the smartest thing to do, but I didn't want to have to jog down into the projects if I could help it.

"When I got close enough to reach the phone, he sprayed me with something that burned my eyes. Mace, I guess. I wanted to run, but traffic was flying past and I couldn't see where I was going. He hit me on the side of the head, and suddenly I was lifted and dropped onto metal. There was a roaring sound, and then . . . I don't remember anything else until I woke up in the dark. The truck was parked somewhere, with nothing but moonlight coming through the windows. I couldn't hear any traffic—just woods sounds—and I was more afraid than I'd ever been in my life. My hands were tied behind me, and I was lying on them, so my arms were numb to the shoulders.

"I thought at first that I was alone. Then I heard quiet breathing in the dark, and I knew he was in there with me. Close. I felt something touch my leg— fingers, I think—and I realized I was naked from the waist down. He started talking to me. In the dark like that. A voice in the dark. He told me he had a knife, and he pressed the blade against my thigh. It was cold. He said he was going to free my hands, because he wanted me to use them, but if I fought, he would cut my throat. He rolled me halfway over and cut whatever was tying me. Before the circulation came back to my arms, he climbed on top of me and started—" Eve's voice cracked and went silent, then returned. "Started to do what he wanted. It was terribly painful, and my arms were paralyzed, burning from the blood coming back into them. I could hardly see, and he was grunting and saying things I couldn't understand—something about how beautiful I was—and I remember thinking then how strangers had been leering at me and saying suggestive things since I was thirteen, and I was so goddamn angry that I'd been stupid, that one of them was finally doing what they'd all dreamed of doing.

"Anyway, I was trying to keep my head together, to decide how best to survive. Just lie there and wait for it to be over? Or fight? I mean, it was already happening. And he was holding the knife in one hand, right at my throat. As it went on, he got more violent. It was like he couldn't finish, and that was making him furious. He dropped the knife and put his arms around my throat and started choking me. I started to fight then, but he was so much stronger than I was. And suddenly . . . Johnny, suddenly I had this absolute flash of certainty that I was going to die there. Under him. In the dark. That this pathetic tragedy was going to be the last chapter of my life."

Waters wanted to argue, but there was no denying the pain in Eve's eyes and voice. Whatever else she might be, whatever ill intent she might ultimately have toward him, she was in this moment a woman in distress, remembering something that had actually happened to her.

Her voice dropped. "Then something very strange happened. My life didn't flash before my eyes, the way people say it does. Memories flooded into my head, but they weren't of my husband or my children. I saw *us*, Johnny." She looked urgently at him, her eyes wet with tears. "I saw *you*. I had this sense of a life unlived, of the road we'd never taken together, and that now we never would. And I knew that if I was thinking of you in that moment, then I had always been right about us."

Her words chilled him to the core, and still she went on.

"He was strangling me while he raped me, his eyes almost popping out of his head, and my vision started to go black. There was no white light or anything like that. No angels. Just awful blackness enveloping me from all sides. But suddenly in my heart, it was like this fire burst into life, this cold blue fire that screamed, 'NO! I'M NOT GOING TO DIE! I CAN'T DIE! I'M NOT DONE!' And then his hands loosened or slipped, because he was in the throes of finishing— I know that now—and suddenly . . ."

Eve's mouth was open but no sound emerged. Her eyes had the glaze of someone who had stared for an hour at the sun.

"What happened?"

"Suddenly I wasn't Mallory anymore. I was *looking* at Mallory. Looking at myself."

He blinked in confusion. "What?"

"I was looking at my dead body, Johnny. I was . . . in *him*."

Waters sat frozen, unable to break the spell her words had cast. If she was lying, she was either a first-rate actress or a delusional schizophrenic. As he stared, she rose onto her knees and hobbled to within two feet of him.

"You know I'm telling the truth," she said, her eyes pleading. "Don't you?"

He swallowed. "I think you believe what you're saying. But I don't understand. It's crazy. And it doesn't explain how you could be Mallory."

She nodded. "I don't want to think about that part

right now. I've waited so long for this moment." She reached out and touched his cheek, and a current of heat went through him. "Will you do me a favor, Johnny? One favor?"

"What?"

"Kiss me."

He pulled back slightly.

"Just one kiss," she said, sliding her finger down to his lips. "Where's the harm in that?"

"Why kiss you?"

"If you kiss me, you'll know."

"Know what?"

"That it's all true. That it's me."

He pulled her fingers away from his face. "I think you've suffered a terrible thing, Eve. But I'm not some fairy-tale prince. I can't magically solve your problems for you."

"Yes, you can. And I can solve yours."

"I don't have any."

Her eyes were serene in their knowledge. "Are you really so happy?"

He looked away.

"Kiss me, Johnny. Please. Just once."

She took his hands and pulled him up to his knees. Now his face was above hers as they knelt, inches apart. Her eyes seemed to expand and deepen, drawing him into her. Those eyes knew him in a way no others on earth did, and he felt that he knew them. He wasn't sure whether he leaned forward or she rose to him, but after a brief hesitation, their lips touched, and with the gentlest pressure they kissed. Her lips remained closed for a moment, and then he felt the soft touch of her tongue. He parted his lips, and she slipped her tongue inside, then took his lower lip between her teeth and tugged it toward her. A shock of recognition shot through him, and he almost pulled away, but with recognition came a wave of desire. He kissed her harder, slipping his tongue into her mouth to taste her. Eve did not taste like Mallory, but she *responded* like Mallory. Her mouth moved with perfect elasticity, yielding to the pressure of his lips, then reciprocating like a gifted dancer who senses her partner's every move. He had no idea how long they kissed, but when he felt her breasts swelling against him, he suddenly found himself unable to breathe. He broke the kiss and pushed her away.

Eve caught her balance and stared back at him, her cheeks flushed, her lips deep red as she panted for breath. "I told you," she said. "Oh God, I'm so happy."

He got to his feet and wiped his mouth, meaning to put more distance between them, but he wavered. Not the passion of her kiss but the *memory* of it had dislocated his sense of time. How could he remember kissing a woman he had never kissed before? He feared that if he walked back toward his Land Cruiser, he would find the old Triumph he'd driven in college waiting for him.

"I'm going," he said.

For a moment Eve looked as though she might panic, but she looked away and bit her bottom lip again. This too made him think of Mallory, of her infantile reactions to parting.

"Go on," she said, trying not to pout.

He took a few steps toward the edge of Catholic Hill, then looked back at her. "How did you know about Danny Buckles and the little girls at school?"

"If I told you that, you wouldn't believe me."

"If I stay, will you tell me that? And the rest of your story?"

"I'll tell you when you're ready. You're not there yet. You need time to think. And we need some more time together." She looked up at him and forced a smile. "You know where to find me, Johnny. I'll be waiting."

"I'm not going to call you," he said harshly.

She fell back on the grass as though he had not spoken, her arms outstretched again, her gaze lost in the clouds. Watching her, he was reminded of the young Natalie Wood playing Alva in Tennessee Williams's *This Property Is Condemned.* He waited, but Eve did not look his way again, so he turned and walked back to the lane.

When his feet hit the asphalt, a sudden sense of urgency rose in him, and he increased his pace to a jog, then a run. How had she simply appeared behind him? He'd seen no other cars, nor heard any before she appeared. It was as though she'd materialized on Catholic Hill at the moment he read the note, like a genie conjured from the buried jar. But as he neared his Land Cruiser, an engine rumbled to life somewhere among the stones far behind him. When he turned, he saw the black Lexus he'd seen at Dunleith slide between distant graves with reptilian stealth, headed for one of the far gates.

"Jesus," he panted, reaching for the Land Cruiser's door. "What the hell just happened?"

chapter 6

Waters lay awake in the dark beside his sleeping wife. His watch read 3:00 A.M., and he had not slept at all. The evening had not gone well. As he left the cemetery, Lily had called his cell phone, furious because she'd already heard one rumor of molestation at the school and another that her husband had brought it to light. She was angry primarily because she had not been the first to know of these events. Waters apologized for this, but what he really felt guilty about was what he had neglected to say once he got home.

When Lily asked how he had come to get the information about "the school closet" out of Annelise, he stood silent for a few moments, thinking of Eve Sumner's cryptic warning and all that had come after. And then he lied. He told Lily he'd simply asked Annelise about school and sensed something unusual in her answer, a feeling that she wanted to say more but was afraid to. By lying, he had entered into a tacit compact to protect Eve and her secret knowledge, whatever its source. This was a serious step, but hadn't she used her knowledge for good, as she said in her office? And yet . . . how had she known the abuse was happening in the first place?

If I told you that, you wouldn't believe me. . . .

Waters shut his eyes and tried not to think of Eve. It required concentrated thoughts of Annelise to banish the haunting face. He and Lily had spoken to Annelise about what kind of talk she was likely to hear at school tomorrow. Kids might call her a tattletale or talk about things she didn't yet understand. Conversing with a second-grader about child molestation was not easy, but he and Lily believed frankness was best, and Annelise didn't seem too upset by their explanation. They agreed to watch her closely and speak to her again tomorrow night.

When they finally got into bed, Lily read two pages of a Nora Roberts novel and fell asleep. Waters lifted the paperback from her chest and put it on the night table, then lay on his back as images from that afternoon spun through his mind, merging with memories from twenty years before. Eve's kiss remained on his lips as surely as Mallory's was engraved in the convolutions of his brain. That was easily enough explained: their kisses were identical. How this could be so was not so easily explained, and so he raveled threads in the dark.

Foremost in his mind were the intimate details Eve had thrown at him, things only Mallory could have known. He considered getting up and making a list, but the more he thought about it, the more trouble he had separating the memories Eve had mentioned from those rising from his own subconscious. Her irrational words and actions had shattered a dam he had built in his mind, freeing a river of memory that he was powerless to resist. Yet one bedrock reality refused to yield: Mallory Candler was dead. Eve Sumner might believe she was Mallory, but that did not make it so. At the very least she wanted *him* to believe she believed that, and to bolster her delusion, she'd told a heart-wrenching tale of rape culminating with an outlandish fantasy of soul transmigration. As a scientist, Waters found it difficult enough to accept the existence of an immortal soul; the idea that souls could move freely between human bodies he rejected out of hand. And despite a brief flirtation with Eastern philosophy in college, he had not one iota of belief in reincarnation.

What possibilities did that leave? Psychotic delusions seemed most likely. He suspected that the background information he'd requested from Cole's New Orleans connections would support this theory. The idea of demonic possession flashed into his mind and fled just as quickly. That was the stuff of medieval folktales, fodder for Hollywood filmmakers and religious fundamentalists. Besides, what Eve had described sounded more like possession of one person by another rather than some sordid satanic scenario. As best as he could recall, she had spoken of two personalities living inside a single mind: one "sleeping," the other "awake." Could she be some sort of schizophrenic? A victim of multiple-personality disorder? Waters knew little of such things, and since Natchez had no practicing psychiatrists, he knew no one to call about it.

As Lily began to snore, his wilder speculations gave way to scientific analysis. If a reasonable man studied what had happened since John Waters saw

Eve Sumner at the soccer field, what might he conclude? One: Sumner wanted to initiate a sexual affair. Two: Sumner was using knowledge of Waters's past to interest him. These conclusions alone were not remarkable. The fact that Eve was trying to persuade him that she was actually a dead lover from his past infinitely complicated matters. Assuming she was sane—and this question was still very much in doubt—what motive could she possibly have to do this?

First principles, he told himself. *What has been the result of Eve's words and actions? She's thrown a levelheaded man into a state of emotional disarray. How can she benefit from that? Who else might benefit?* Waters wasn't presently involved in business negotiations that would suffer due to a lack of concentration on his part. But perhaps Eve had only begun her campaign to disrupt his life. Maybe her ultimate goal was to draw him into an affair, then blackmail him. It seemed a great deal of trouble to go to, particularly since he stood to lose his fortune if the EPA investigation went against his company. But maybe she knew nothing about that.

And where had Eve gotten the intimate details of his old life? Given all she'd said, he half expected the background investigation to reveal some familial relation to Mallory. If none existed, Eve would almost have to have gotten her information from someone like Cole, or—

Waters blinked in the darkness.

Cole. Cole had known about *Soon.* He knew other things too. He knew Waters had first slept with Mallory on a camping trip at Sardis Reservoir. They had been roommates at the time. What else had Waters confided in the excitement of college love? And what had Cole confided to Eve? He'd already admitted they'd slept together. *She's a hell of a lay, but too twisted for me. . . . Watch out . . . She's always looking for advantage. Reminds me a little of me. . . .* Waters swallowed and tried to figure out what motive Cole could possibly have to give Eve private information about him. Maybe he was just drunk and answered anything she asked him. But that was unlikely, given the intimate nature of her knowledge. Try as he might, Waters could come up with nothing. Cole's fortunes depended on his partner remaining sane and healthy enough to keep finding oil—end of story.

Lily's snores stopped with a gasp, then resumed at a higher decibel level. Waters could stay in bed no longer. He got up and padded into the kitchen in his boxers, more awake than he'd felt in years. His mind and body thrummed as though rushing on the pure cocaine he'd snorted with Sara on the slope of a volcano in Ecuador. His blood was *singing*. And he knew why. The strange encounters with Eve had stirred his long-suppressed desire, and like a bear waking from hibernation, that desire would not return to sleep. It stretched and breathed, feeling its power, and beneath that power a hunger that had grown steadily through the long night of winter.

Almost before he knew what he was doing, he lifted a phone book from Lily's alcove and looked up Eve's number. He found two listed: work and home. The kitchen clock read 3:40 A.M. He looked at the phone but did not touch it. Yet some part of him knew that Eve was waiting at the other end for the connection to be made. Sleeping perhaps, but waiting still. The soft ring would come, and before it faded, the phone would be in her hand, her voice already weaving its spell.

Waters left the alcove and walked to the marble-topped island where Annelise's schoolbooks awaited her. *School*, he thought. *Where we learn to read and write and add and subtract while learning subtler but more important lessons: how to speak and listen, how to lie and tell the truth, how to honor and betray, how to strive, to whisper, to hold hands, to kiss, to insist and evade, to make love, to marry, to honor and again betray—*

"Jesus," he muttered, feeling his mind slipping off its tracks. He went to the laundry room and pulled a pair of jeans and a T-shirt from the wicker basket. He slipped the jeans over his boxers, put on the T-shirt, then laced on the running shoes he kept by the back door. This time of night, Lily slept too soundly to hear him start the Land Cruiser, but just in case, he scribbled a note saying he was going to Wal-Mart for some ice cream. Then he grabbed his keys, wallet, and cell phone and went out the front door.

The streets of Natchez were deserted at this hour. He drove slowly down Main Street, past the Eola Hotel and his office, then turned onto Broadway and coasted down the long precipitous drop of Silver Street to the river. The Under-the-Hill Saloon was shut tight, but the Steamboat Casino threw a garish Las Vegas light over the water, and a few rumpled patrons stumbled along the gangplank toward the shore. Waters accelerated up the sweeping lane that led back up the bluff, then turned right onto Canal and headed toward the bypass.

To honor and betray . . . Eve Sumner no longer filled his mind; memories of Mallory had driven her out. Waters's relationship with Mallory had been born from a double betrayal: one of a friend, the other of a lover. During his sophomore year of college, he'd been home for a weekend in mid-October, when the sun still burned down like summer. He was dating a sophomore from Tulane, a Natchez girl who had graduated St. Stephens a year ahead of Cole. They'd been invited to the home—estate, really—of a young local internist, Dr. David Denton, for a Sunday picnic. Through several unusual connections, Waters knew Denton well. Waters's mother worked as a reception-ist for Denton's older partner, but their real bond had grown through baseball. During Waters's senior year of high school, when his team made a run for the state championship, Denton went along as an unofficial coach. Fifteen years earlier, David Denton had been the star third baseman for the St. Stephens state cham-pionship team, and since Waters played third base, they spent many hours together. Waters missed his fa-ther badly, and his association with the young doctor had helped him with a lot more than baseball. Some people thought Denton arrogant, but Waters re-spected him, and always looked forward to seeing him.

When Waters and his date arrived at Denton's house that Sunday, they did not find the large party they expected. They found two blankets laid out with food worthy of a five-star restaurant, and no people in sight. As they tried to figure out what was going on, two figures walked out of Denton's stables. One was the doctor himself, tall and handsome at thirty-six; the other was Mallory Candler, twenty years old and as beautiful as any woman Waters had ever seen. Wa-ters's date squealed, ran over to Mallory, and gave her an exaggerated hug. Though Mallory attended Ole

Miss and she Tulane, they belonged to the same sorority. Waters would later learn that Mallory had no close
female friends, but other women were always drawn
to her, as though to learn the secrets of her remarkable
self-possession.

Hiding his shock at the age difference, Waters
shook hands with Denton and sat down to eat. Because of Mallory's beauty, he expected her to reveal
herself as the vapid creature many Ole Miss sorority
girls turned out to be, but he was surprised. She did
not gossip or squeal; she conversed with erudition on
politics, religion, literature, and sex. Denton was
clearly enamored with her, and he seemed amused by
Mallory's attempts to draw Waters out during the afternoon. When they went riding, Mallory cantered
alongside Waters while Denton lectured on the line-
age of his horses, and all the while Waters felt her ap-
praising him: the way he talked, moved, handled his
horse.

When they retired to the house for late-afternoon
drinks, Waters's date asked him to play the grand
piano in Denton's living room. With half a bottle of
pinot noir in him, Waters agreed. He had never taken
formal lessons, but his mother was a fine pianist and
he had been blessed to inherit her ear. He ran through
a few songs from the period—mostly Elton John and
Billy Joel—singing in a voice made confident by wine,
and Denton professed amazement that a third baseman could do anything requiring that much talent.
Only Mallory did not compliment his playing, but
when Waters glanced up from the keyboard, he saw
that she had been profoundly affected by his performance.

During one song, the phone rang, and Denton took

the call. Holding the phone against his chest, he told them that Mallory's ride back to Ole Miss was leaving, and would be by to pick her up in fifteen minutes. Clearly unhappy, Denton asked Waters how he was getting back to school. Waters explained he was driving back in his drafty thirdhand Triumph convertible. Would he mind, Denton asked, driving Mallory back so that they could continue their evening? In that moment, Waters had a sense of massive stones sliding into place somewhere, and he saw a glint in Mallory Candler's eye that he would see many times over the next two years.

No, he replied. *I wouldn't mind at all.* . . .

Denton treated them all to dinner at a restaurant on the bluff, and then it was time to begin the five-hour journey back to Oxford. In the parking lot of the restaurant, Waters's date climbed into the doctor's BMW, and Mallory crammed her suitcase into the trunk of Waters's TR-6, a symbolic switching of partners that gave Waters a chill.

They began the ride in silence, and the silence lasted forty miles. Occasionally he or Mallory would glance over the console, but their eyes did not meet. Then—at the turn for the northbound interstate—they shared a gaze during which a full conversation took place without words. With Ole Miss still four hours away, Mallory entwined her hand in his and began to talk.

She spoke first of Dr. Denton, how she had accepted his request for a date to prove that "age was no big thing" to her, and also because he was a close friend of her parents. She'd continued dating him because it was fun to shock people and because she liked watching how far Denton would go to win her approval. But he was more a businessman than a physician, she said, and she knew she could never be with "someone like that." She asked Waters about his relationship with her Tulane sorority sister, and he was cautiously frank. He was sleeping with her, and they had agreed not to see other people. Mallory asked about his family but confided little about her own. She wondered aloud how they had lived in the same town for so long without more than a cursory acquaintance. Waters pointed out that she had attended preppy St. Stephens, while he'd graduated from public school "with the blacks." Mallory made light of this difference, but that was easy to do when you were from the rich side of the tracks.

Soon she was asking Waters about his dreams, his thoughts on God, his sexual history. As for her own past, she professed one "serious" relationship in high school with an older boy who had known nothing beyond "basic high school football player stuff," and another in college during which she'd done a lot of experimenting. Her relations with Dr. Denton had not progressed to intercourse; the age difference made him especially solicitous of her, and she'd taken advantage of that. By the time they hit Oxford—at 3:00 A.M.— Mallory said there was really no point in going to sleep. Better to push through till morning and do Monday classes on adrenaline.

Instead of driving to campus, Waters drove out to Sardis Reservoir, a massive, man-made lake held in check by a three-mile-long dam. At one end of the dam was a single-outlet spillway, where a juggernaut of water thirty feet thick blasted through the concrete with earth-shaking force and spent itself in a rocky channel. A narrow catwalk crossed above this spillway, where you could stand above the thundering jet and feel the spray swirl around you like gravity-defying rain as the primal roar filled first your ears and then your mind.

On this catwalk Mallory took Waters's face in her hands and kissed him with infinitely more passion than he had known in his nineteen years. When she pulled back, he looked into her bottomless green eyes and knew that he was lost. He had a sense of being chosen—by her and also by something greater, something unknowable, the same amorphous force he had felt when Denton asked if he would drive Mallory back to Ole Miss. A sense that his destiny, whatever that might be, was gathering itself around him at last.

After the kiss, they walked hand in hand back to the car. Waters drove back to the campus, but when they reached the sorority house, Mallory simply shook her head. He needed no prompting. He drove to an empty athletic field on a hill above his dorm and parked the convertible in the predawn darkness. Mallory lay across him, and he leaned down to her up-lifted face. In the timeless hour that followed, his hands never went below her waist, but the two of them left the physical domain of that car as surely as if they had lifted into the dark with wings. He sensed in Mallory a sexuality of limitless scope, like a man looking through an open door at a closed one, yet sensing that behind that door lay still another, an end-less succession of doors, each concealing its own mystery, each mystery folding into another, the inmost circle unreachable, impenetrable, an essentially feminine core that he had no choice but to try to reach and understand.

Waters went through the next day in a trance, wondering if Mallory had felt what he had, whether she had seen that night as a beginning or merely an interesting Sunday diversion for a beautiful woman with nothing better to do. At four that afternoon, his telephone rang. Mallory had slept through all her classes, but she wanted to see him again. His exhaustion left him in a moment. They spent most of that night together, watching a movie, eating dinner, driving for miles, talking, and then not talking.

In the span of two weeks, they became inseparable. A wild euphoria permeated their days, yet it was shadowed by an unspoken reality. Mallory was still technically dating Dr. Denton, and Waters, the girl from Tulane. For this reason, and others, they kept to themselves much of the time, and stopped their impassioned couplings short of intercourse. But by the end of the first month, it was becoming difficult to restrain themselves. One rainy night in Waters's dorm room, Mallory straddled him, took him in her hand, and guided him to her opening. She started to sit, moaned softly, then sobbed once and got off the bed. While he stared in confusion, she pulled on her jeans and ran from the room. Waters put on his pants and gave chase. By the time he reached the door of the dormitory, Mallory was running up the hill toward the library, her hair flying behind her in the rain. Barefoot, he sprinted after her, dodging cars to cross the road, finally coming within earshot on the library lawn. Under foot-high letters trumpeting Faulkner's assertion that man would not merely endure but prevail, he screamed for her to stop. When she turned, he saw that her eyes were not red from tears, but filled with wild joy.

"Do you love me?" she cried.

"What?"

"Do you *love* me?"

He stood there in the rain, knowing only that he could not stand to be physically apart from this woman. "Yes," he replied.

"What?"

"I love you!"

She came back to him and kissed him, and then the tears did come. After a time she dragged him toward the library door.

"Where are we going?"

"You'll see."

Just inside the doors were two pay phones. Mallory lifted a receiver and handed it to him.

"Who am I calling?"

"You know."

And then he did. She wanted him to call his girl-friend at Tulane and break off the relationship. He hesitated only a moment. He told the girl he was finding a long-distance relationship too hard to sustain. She asked tearfully if he had met someone, and he said yes. When she asked who, he looked at Mallory, and for the first time she looked uncertain. Waters lied and said he'd met someone from another state. As they spoke, he felt strangely detached, as though discussing the death of a distant relative, but as he hung up, he felt angry. He handed Mallory the phone.

"Do you want me to call David?" she asked.

"You're damn right."

She bit her bottom lip, then took the receiver and started to dial his number.

"Wait," he said.

"Why?" She kept dialing. "You're not sure?"

"I'm sure about you. About how I feel. But . . . telling David is different from what I just did."

She looked intrigued. "How?"

"He's a friend of mine . . . of my mother's. Of your parents. My brother's supposed to work for him next summer, for God's sake. Taking care of his horses."

Mallory nodded. "I know all that."

"Is he in love with you?"

"He says he is."

"Shit."

She laid a hand over his and looked deep into his eyes. "I'm ready, if you think I should."

"You should do it face-to-face."

She hung up the phone. "This weekend. There's a big party at his house."

His anger took him by surprise. "You didn't tell me that. You were going home this weekend? To see him?"

"No. I wasn't going to go."

He wasn't sure he believed her.

"You should come too, John."

"No, I shouldn't. Besides, I wasn't invited."

"You weren't?" Her eyes narrowed. "That's weird. A lot of college people are going."

A shiver of apprehension went through him. "Jesus. You think David's heard something?"

Mallory shrugged. "We haven't been as careful as we should have been. And there are only, what, like five hundred students here from Natchez?"

He nodded, wondering if David Denton already saw him as a son of a bitch.

"You should come anyway," Mallory told him. "It's a masquerade party. For Halloween. No one will know."

"You're crazy."

"Sometimes I think so. You really should come though." She laughed and hugged him tight. "In fact, I'm not going unless you do."

So he went. Mallory rented him a Sir Lancelot costume in Memphis, and three nights later he walked into David Denton's house wearing a visored metal helmet. If anyone asked who he was, he planned to say he was Cole Smith. Cole had been invited to the party but had chosen to go deer hunting instead (which struck Waters as hilarious now). There were between eighty and a hundred masked guests, so remaining incognito turned out to be no problem. People drank in grand Natchez style, and dancers spilled from Denton's great room onto the huge stone patio behind his house.

Mallory had come as a ballerina, with a white tulle skirt blossoming over her leotard and a glittering mask adorned with pearls. Her regal bearing and fluid dance style drew the eyes of everyone, and Denton—dressed as Louis XIV—almost never left her side. Waters watched them dance from a distance, mingling with people who didn't know him well. Mallory seemed to be having the time of her life, and after an hour—and three stiff drinks—he began to feel resentful. Mallory had asked him to the party, even rented his costume, yet she acted as if he weren't there. He was at the point of doing something monumentally stupid—like asking her to dance—when he realized he'd lost sight of her. Suddenly, a hand squeezed his behind.

"Feeling neglected?"

He was almost sure the person whispering in his ear was Mallory. Reaching back, he felt the tulle skirt and pinched her thigh hard enough to hurt. He heard a laugh and another whisper: *"Meet me behind the stables."*

He slipped outside as quickly as he could and made his way across the lawn to Denton's capacious stables. He waited in the dark with the smell of hay and horses, wondering if Mallory would be able to get away without Denton noticing. Suddenly, a white apparition materialized out of the night, floating toward him as though borne on the wind.

"I thought you weren't coming," he hissed as she neared him.

Mallory pulled up her mask and smiled mischievously. "Do you want to talk or do you want to kiss me?"

He pushed her against the stable wall and kissed her, and in seconds they were panting in the dark.

"Have you told David anything?"

She shook her head. "I'm going to do it after. When everyone's gone."

He kissed her again. Her fingers dug into his back, then raked around his ribs to his chest. He wanted her badly, but he could almost see Denton searching the house for her now.

"You'd better get back."

She nodded and put a finger to his lips. "Are you all right?"

"No."

"I didn't think so."

She smiled knowingly, then put her mask back on, slid to her knees, and lifted the tunic of his knight's costume. He sucked in his breath when she took him into her mouth, then closed his eyes and tried to stay silent as she went to work with feverish intensity.

Once, he thought he heard voices nearby, but when he touched Mallory's head to warn her, she slapped his hand away and continued with more fervor. Seconds later he cried out and started to push her away, but she grabbed his wrists and finished while music and laughter echoed across the lawn and horses stamped in their stables and he shuddered in the dark.

She rose to her feet, her eyes twinkling. "Better now?"

Without waiting for an answer, she kissed him, then took off across the lawn, the tulle skirt trailing after her like a fallen angel's wings.

When Waters returned to the party, Mallory was dancing with Denton on the patio. Through the mesh of her skirt he saw two oblong grass stains on her knees, but no one else seemed to notice. He went inside for another drink.

All masks were to be removed at midnight. At five 'til, someone turned off the stereo, and Waters prepared to slip out a side door. Before he could, he heard someone ask Denton to play his piano. The doctor looked thoughtfully at the Kawai concert grand and said, "I wish Johnny Waters was here. I thought that kid couldn't play anything but third base, but he's a genius on piano."

"Why didn't you invite him?" Mallory asked casually.

"I meant to. It just slipped my mind. I'll remember next time."

A wave of guilt surged through Waters, and instead of leaving, he signaled Mallory to follow him down the hall to the bathroom. When she did, he pulled her inside and said, "Don't tell him tonight."

She shook her head. "I knew you were going to say that."

"You still want to?"

"No. But we're just putting off the inevitable."

"I know, but . . . Look, just do whatever feels right to you."

Mallory nodded and went back to the main room, where guests were beginning to remove their masks and pop the corks on champagne bottles. Waters stole a last glance at Mallory and Denton at the center of the crowd, then faded through the garage door, more confused than he'd been in a long time.

At 2:00 A.M., Mallory knocked at his window, and he learned that she hadn't told Denton anything. Thus began a two-month period of secrecy that nearly caused both of them to fail the semester. When they returned to Ole Miss, they camped for a weekend at Sardis and made love for the first time. But they did not go out together in public. They frequently drove the hour to Memphis to avoid prying eyes, and even there they spent most of their time in hotel rooms. When they returned to Natchez for the Thanksgiving holiday, Mallory accepted only one date with Denton, and that night she made excuses and went home early, so that later—as she had every other night—she could slip out to meet Waters and make love in his car. It was a ridiculous situation, but Waters couldn't bear the idea of hurting the man who had helped him so unselfishly during high school. Beyond this, he knew that Mallory's parents would be enraged when they learned she had cheated on their ideal suitor to "go in the street" with a boy from the wrong side of town. But as the Christmas holidays approached, Natchez students started to gossip at Ole Miss, and it was only a matter of time before Denton heard what was going on.

It took an almost unbearable irony to bring things to a head. Three days before Christmas, Denton called Waters and asked him to accompany him to an ante-bellum home to look at a piano. The doctor was think-ing of buying an antique Bösendorfer brought from Berlin to Natchez during the 1850s. Driven by a desire to maintain the illusion of normalcy—and not least by morbid curiosity—Waters agreed. As he and Denton examined the piano and discovered dry rot inside, Denton asked him what he thought of Mallory Can-dler. Waters swallowed and said he thought she was a "great girl," which was the ultimate Ole Miss stamp of approval. Did Waters see Mallory much in Oxford? With his nerves stretched to maximum tension, Waters replied that it was a small school, and everyone saw everyone pretty regularly. Denton said he was only asking because Mallory had been acting a bit distant, but he thought he knew the reason. Mallory Candler was the kind of girl who didn't get too involved with a man unless she knew the relationship was more than a passing affair. Then he smiled and confided that he planned to ask her to marry him on Christmas Eve. She was a little young, Denton conceded, but Mallory's father was all for it, and he was sure Mal-lory would be too. As Waters sat frozen, his heart thundering in his chest, Denton said he'd just wanted to make sure he wasn't reading Mallory wrong, that there wasn't another man in her life. Waters almost confessed everything then, but he stopped himself. That was Mallory's duty, not his. Besides, if Denton was considering a marriage proposal, maybe Mallory had been encouraging him more than she let on to Waters.

When Waters recounted this conversation to Mallory, she turned white. That night, she went to Denton's house and told him she was in love with another man. Yes, it was someone he knew. She elided some details, such as the rendezvous behind the stables, but for the most part she told him everything. At two that morning, Waters, his mother, and his brother awoke to a pounding on their front door. Waters answered in his underwear, and found a drunken David Denton on the front porch, his BMW idling in the street behind him. Denton greeted Mrs. Waters with a rant against her "worthless" son, and Waters asked her to go back to bed. He listened to Denton's railing for as long as he could. Then he looked at the doctor and said, "David, I'm sorry it happened the way it did. We should have told you from the start. But the woman chooses in these things. Okay? The woman chooses, and there's nothing any of us can do about it."

"You could have done the decent thing!" Denton yelled. "You could have been a friend! And if not that, you could at least be a goddamn gentleman!"

This wounded Waters deeply, but he'd only begun to wallow in his guilt when Denton added, "I should have known better though. You're no gentleman. You're trash. That's why you live over here with the rest of the goddamn trash. I ought to kick your ass."

All his guilt forgotten, Waters clenched his quivering hands into fists. In his mind he saw his father, and he felt as though Denton had just called his father trash. In a barely audible voice he said, "Go ahead, if you think you can. But you'd better be ready to kill me."

Denton took a wild swing, and Waters easily ducked it.

"You're drunk, David," he said, trying to restrain himself.

Denton punched him in the stomach. As Waters drew back his fist to throw a punishing right, he saw his mother silhouetted in the window behind him.

"Go home!" he shouted. "And don't come back!"

Denton blinked in confusion, mumbled something unintelligible, then turned around and stumbled back to his BMW, cursing and sobbing as he went. When Waters walked back inside, his mother shook her head.

"Is this over that Candler girl?" she asked, her face tight and vulnerable without makeup.

Waters nodded.

"She's no good, John. I know you won't listen to me, but that girl's not right, not for you or anybody else."

He asked what his mother knew about Mallory, but she just turned away and went back to bed. That night was the beginning of his public relationship with Mallory, a brief window of bliss during which all seemed golden, when the horrors to come still lay out of sight.

Now—driving down the deserted road by the paper mill—he thought again of Mallory at Denton's party, but this time, when she pulled down her mask by the stables, he saw not her face but Eve Sumner's. He tried to push the image from his mind, but the harder he tried, the clearer Eve became. He could *not see Mallory's face*. It made him crazy, like trying to remember the name of a familiar actor whose face was right in front of him on television. Frustration built in him with manic intensity, like the feedback loops he'd read about in obsessive-compulsive people. He *had* to see Mallory's face.

He swung onto Lower Woodville Road and sped up to sixty. He kept a rented storeroom less than a mile away, a climate-controlled cubicle filled with furniture and boxes from his mother's house and his own. His mother saved everything, and somewhere in that cubicle was a footlocker containing whatever junk was left from his Ole Miss days.

He turned into the storage company lot, punched a code into the security gate, and parked by a long aluminum building. The room was near the end of the inside corridor, the PIN code for its lock his social security number. When he opened the door, the musty smell surprised him, but he felt for the light switch, flicked it, and went inside.

Furniture and boxes were stacked nearly to the ceiling. Plastic bags held old clothes—some his father's—and broken lamps sat on all available flat surfaces. Even his father's old power tools were here, saved like the instruments of a renowned surgeon. Another time, Waters might have stopped to go through some of the stuff, but tonight there was only one thing on his mind.

He found the old footlocker behind some boxes of books. It wasn't locked, and he tore open the lid like a heart-attack victim searching for nitroglycerin. Here lay several chapters of his past, deposited in no particular order and with no particular intent. He found football programs, grade reports, the tassel from his graduation cap, love letters with a rubber band around them, geological specimens, a guitar pick from a Jimmy Buffett concert, a box of snapshots from Ole Miss and another from his summers working the pipeline in Alaska. He was about to go through the photos when he saw a banded portfolio near the bottom. Something clicked in his mind. Inside the portfolio he found everything dating from the time he spent with Mallory—everything that had survived, anyway. At some point he must have grouped it all together, but he didn't remember doing it.

The first thing he saw was a copy of the campus newspaper, the *Daily Mississippian,* with Mallory Candler filling most of the front page. MISS UNIVERSITY 1982! proclaimed the headline. ON TO MISS MISSISSIPPI PAGEANT? asked a smaller font. Below the type, Mallory stood facing the camera with a dozen roses, flashing her megawatt smile and wearing a sequined gown that could have been made for Grace Kelly. The instant Waters saw her face, Eve vanished from his mind. Eve Sumner had the sensual but not uncommon gifts of good bones, good tits, and sultry eyes. Mallory's beauty was the once-in-a-decade sort, her features drawn from and sharing in some portion of eternity. As he lifted the newspaper to look for other photos, the cell phone in his pocket rang, startling him. When he answered, he heard Lily's worried voice.

"I woke up and found you gone," she said sleepily. "Are you still at Wal-Mart?"

"I didn't go to Wal-Mart."

Silence. "Where are you?"

"I went for a ride. I couldn't sleep."

"What's wrong?"

Mallory stared out of the newspaper photograph with eerie vitality. "I don't know. The dry hole . . . the EPA thing."

"Come home, and I'll make some coffee. It's five a.m., John."

"All right."

He hung up but did not stand. Even when reduced to a millimeter-thick sheet of paper, Mallory seemed more alive than the people he saw in town every day. He shook his head. If anyone in that audience on that night had known what was going on behind those hypnotic green eyes, they would have left the auditorium in shock. But of course they hadn't. No one had, except John Waters. He started to fold the newspaper and bring it with him, but then he slid it back into the portfolio and carried the portfolio out to the Land Cruiser. Lily never drove the SUV. He could leave the portfolio under its seat with no worries. And if he got the desperate feeling that he could not recall Mallory's face, all he'd have to do was pull it out and look at her picture.

Waters had driven most of the way home when a blue dashboard light flashed and swirled wildly in his rearview mirror. Though reminded of Eve's rape story, he pulled over, rolled down his window, and waited. He heard heavy footsteps, and then a man said, "John? You're out kind of early, pardner. Or is it late?"

The speaker was Detective Tom Jackson, the man who'd arrested Danny Buckles the day before.

"Hey, Tom. Was I speeding?"

Jackson stopped at Waters's window and gave him a friendly nod. "No, I just recognized your vehicle. I wanted to make sure you were okay. All that molestation stuff yesterday . . . I know it's tough to deal with."

"Yeah. I couldn't sleep. I'm just doing some thinking."

Jackson gave him a sympathetic smile. "Your little girl okay?"

"Oh, yeah. She took it better than I thought she would."

"Good. You know, it looks like the guy didn't touch the girls at all. He just did some looking, exposed himself, that kind of thing."

"Thank God."

"Yeah." The detective sniffed and looked up the road. In the darkness, his size and his cowboy mustache gave him the look of a Frederic Remington bronze. "Well," he said, looking back at Waters. "You have a good day, John. Try to get some sleep. You look like you need some."

"I will. Thanks."

"Anytime."

Waters drove away slowly, wondering how long Jackson had been following him.

chapter 7

"I got a preliminary report on Eve Sumner," Cole said, setting down his morning cup of coffee. "You want to hear it?"

Waters put down his briefcase, sat in a leather chair, and looked around Cole's one-room shrine to the Ole Miss Rebels.

"You look like shit," Cole said.

"I didn't sleep much. Let's hear what you've got."

"Eve was born Evie Ray Sumner in St. Joseph, Louisiana, in 1970." Cole read from a faxed page. "Sounds right for St. Joe, doesn't it? Evie Ray?"

Waters nodded. St. Joe was a center of cotton and soybean farming, an hour north of Natchez.

"She got knocked up when she was fifteen and had an abortion in Baton Rouge."

"How did they find that out?"

Cole shrugged. "Made some calls, I guess. Old friends talk. For money, anyway."

Waters felt more than a little sleazy to be funding that sort of muckraking. But he had to know about her.

"Evie graduated St. Joe High at seventeen. Salutatorian, if you can believe it. She lit out for Los Angeles, married a cop, got pregnant, and split town six months later. May have been some spousal abuse involved. She came back to Louisiana to have the kid, and her mother mostly raised it. Evie enrolled in Hinds Junior College and spent her time dating jocks. She didn't graduate. She did try about eight different lines of work. Beauty school, paralegal school, massage therapist, you name it. Nothing worked out for long. Then she came to Natchez and got a job as a dealer on the casino boat. She studied nights for her real estate license, then went to work for Hubert Hartley's company. After a year, she was leading salesman, or salesperson, whatever. Then she went out on her own."

"Any evidence of mental illness? Depression? Suicide attempts?"

"Nothing they could find. And I myself would class Evie as irritatingly sane. You want them to keep looking?"

"Keep looking. What about Mallory's murder?"

"We've got copies of all the newspaper stories coming FedEx. The law firm is trying to set up a call between you and the lead homicide detective on the case."

"Good."

Cole put down the papers and sipped his coffee. "John, what are you going to ask this detective if he does call?"

"I'm not sure."

"Okay. So . . . are you going to tell me what happened after you stormed out of here yesterday?"

Cole had called twice last night to ask that question, but Waters and Lily had been in tense discussion, and he hadn't answered the phone. Now, recalling the crazy conversation at the cemetery and the kiss, he didn't want to answer at all. If he told that story with a straight face, Cole would think he'd lost his mind.

"It's no big thing. Eve warned me about Danny Buckles. I checked it out. I don't know how she knew about it, but she did a good thing. There's some connection between her and Buckles, and I'm trying to find out what it is."

"I haven't heard Evie's name in any of the rumors," Cole said. "Did you tell the cops she was the one who warned you?"

"No."

"I see. And that's no big thing."

Waters sighed and looked out the picture window at the sweeping vista of the rust-colored river below.

Cole's chair groaned in protest as he heaved his bulk forward and dropped his heavy hand on the desktop to get Waters's attention. "John? It's never a good idea to keep things from your partner."

Waters gave him a hard look. "I agree. Let's start with you. You have anything you want to tell me?"

Cole rolled his eyes. "Look, I just don't want you to get in trouble. Sailing the strange river is always murky waters. And you don't have any experience at that kind of navigation."

"I'm fine."

"Great. Well . . . Evie's been around. If you're going to do it, double up."

"Double up?"

"Wear two pairs of gloves."

"Ahh." Cole's practicality surprised him.

"How's Annelise doing? The Danny Buckles thing mess her up?"

"No. She didn't go into that closet or anything."

"Good. You know, there's already a couple of lawsuits coming out of that."

"Does that surprise you?"

"No, but if we don't hurry up and sell another deal, I'm going to wish I was representing one of the plaintiffs."

This was as good an opening as Waters was likely to get to question Cole about his financial problems, but for once he wasn't in the mood. "I've got a couple of prospects in West Feliciana Parish that look good. One's a close-in deal. If you really want to sell something, I could probably have that ready in a week."

Cole's face lit up. "Are you serious?"

"Yeah."

"You been holding back on me, Rock!"

Waters stood. "I'm going to my office to do some mapping on it right now."

Cole grinned. "Don't let me stop you. Get Evie Ray's ass off your mind and start thinking crude oil. I'll have lunch sent to your office."

Waters took an envelope from his pocket and laid it on Cole's desk. Inside was a check for fifty thousand dollars.

"That's what we talked about yesterday."

Cole started to reach for the envelope, then seemed to think better of it. "John . . ."

"Don't worry about it. I'll see you in a while." He picked up his briefcase and went down the hall to his door.

Entering his own space was a relief after Cole's chaotic office. When they remodeled the two-story warehouse, Waters had taken the office with the most frontage on the bluff. Now he had two massive windows that gave an unsurpassed view of the Mississippi River, and unlike Cole, he had planned his *sanctum sanctorum* around it. He'd even added an outdoor balcony, fighting the Historical Preservation Commission all the way.

People were always surprised by the modernity of the room, but living in an antebellum home was all the nostalgia Waters could stand. During his years of postgraduate work—often living in tents on volcanic slopes—he had learned an economy of materials that stayed with him to this day. He liked his lines clean and sharp, his artificial lighting indirect, his corners empty. Four large skylights allowed natural light to fall onto the original heart pine floors, and tasteful displays of rare rocks in unexpected places gave a zenlike quality to the space. Each geological specimen represented a chapter in his life, and each had two provenances: one that chronicled its origin and life, and covered millions of years; the other much briefer, the story of Waters's discovery and analysis of the specimen. On the walls hung framed satellite photos of global regions he had worked, river deltas and volcanoes and oceans, their unusual colors blending into abstract art to the untrained eye.

He set his briefcase on his desk and went to his drafting table, where a map showing 252 square miles of West Feliciana Parish awaited his attention. On a normal day, he would sharpen his colored pencils and go straight to work. But today was not normal. When he looked at the map, he felt no inclination to study it.

He walked back to his desk, opened his briefcase, and took out the portfolio he'd found in the storage room. Inside was the newspaper reporting Mallory's Miss University win. There was also a copy of *The Clarion-Ledger*, trumpeting her victory in the Miss Mississippi pageant. Mallory had never entered a pageant before the Miss University contest, and she had only entered that because her sorority sisters begged her to do it. This was during one of the darkest times in her life: Waters was in Alaska, and she had just left there one step ahead of the state police. When her sorority and family pleaded with her to advance to the Miss Mississippi pageant, she entered it only to prove to Waters that she was sane enough to handle something "normal." She acted stunned when she won the crown, but he wasn't surprised in the slightest. By that time, he knew she could play her chosen role with the world falling in flames around her.

He set aside the newspapers and looked at a bundle of her letters. The handwriting on the envelopes evoked only dread. He was not yet ready to delve into the circular logic of Mallory Candler's unhinged mind. He might never be ready for that. But he could not resist the boxes of photographs. One was filled with Ole Miss scenes: Waters and Cole drinking Coors at the annual shrimp boil; tailgating in the Grove during homecoming; mugging for the camera at a football game, their hands wrapped around bourbon and Cokes. There were also some night shots from a gonzo road trip to Vanderbilt, when Cole had driven Waters's Triumph right through the campus on its brick sidewalks (and later told the police he'd thought they were narrow streets). The snapshots showed Waters just how much kinder the years had been to him than to his partner. Cole had lost hair and gained weight, while Waters's lean build had hardly changed. And mercifully, Waters had received his mother's genes where hair was concerned. But the most profound changes in Cole were subtler. Waters couldn't put his finger on it; perhaps it was merely the air of dissipation that had hung around Cole for the past few years. But strangers tended to guess Cole was closer to fifty than forty, while many thought Waters was in his mid-thirties.

He slid aside a photo from a fraternity party and looked into Mallory's incomparable face. The copper streak in her dark hair shone in the light of the flash-bulb, and the stark intensity in her eyes pierced him to the core. The next thirty pictures were all of Mallory, some taken in and around Oxford, others shot on the shoestring vacations they'd taken together. Crested Butte, Chaco Canyon, the Yucatán, Zihuatenejo, points in between. Seeing her in such varied settings—laughing in the snow, dancing in the surf, crouching outside a kiva in New Mexico—buttressed rather than diminished his memories of her beauty. The adjectives that New York models struggled to bring to life in their faces, Mallory conjured with effortless grace. With each flip of a photo she was by turns haughty, warm, insouciant, sentimental, naive, knowing, a little cold, a little mad. Every image brought back a vignette from their early lives together, but none more so than one taken in the mountains of Tennessee: Mallory standing nude beneath a sparkling waterfall. It had not been posed; Waters had simply turned the camera on her as she washed her hair in the falls, and her radiant smile had filled the lens with its power. Nothing in the image linked it to the modern world; it could have been shot ten thousand years before, had someone possessed a camera. *Here is a twenty-one-year-old woman coming into the full flower of her sexuality, fully conscious of the process. She stands naked in the wilderness with no more embarrassment than a doe would feel drinking at the pool beneath the falls.* Looking at her standing in the glittering mist, Waters felt a bittersweet awe, a faint echo of what it had felt like to hold that remarkable body in his arms. To be *inside* her. To look into eyes so alive with . . . *life.* He was staring entranced at the picture when Sybil pushed open his door and walked toward his desk.

"I've got some papers from the Oil and Gas Board," she said. "You need to sign the last page."

He slid a newspaper over the nude photo just as Sybil set the papers on his desk; he couldn't be sure if she'd seen it or not. Sybil was no prude, but the woman in the snapshot was clearly not Waters's wife, and he didn't want his receptionist getting the wrong idea. He signed the papers, then picked up a remote control and switched on the small Sony television he kept behind his desk to monitor market reports and news crises. As Sybil walked slowly to the door, he flipped through the channels. At sixty, the numbers began to recycle. When he hit channel four, he lifted his thumb, his chest tightening. Eve Sumner was staring at him from the television screen. Her sudden appearance disoriented him, but he soon realized he was watching Natchez's local cable access channel. A real estate program. Eve was leading viewers on a tour of an antebellum home that was on the market. Waters watched her with fascination.

She was wearing the navy suit skirt again, with

nude hose and high heels. Her alto voice and precise diction intrigued Waters; Evie Ray may have come from rural Louisiana, but somewhere along the way she had sweated blood to free herself from redneck syntax. Using her hands gracefully, she pointed out various attributes of a "thoroughly modern" kitchen, then began walking backward toward a door. As she led the cameraman into the dining room, Waters went rigid in his chair.

Pausing in the doorway, Eve had twisted a strand of hair around her right forefinger, tightened it, and begun pulling. As he stared, she popped her finger out, leaving the strand momentarily curled. It was an automatic gesture, probably developed in childhood, but it betrayed a touch of self-consciousness that let you know Eve was not quite so confident as she seemed. In that moment, she became Mallory Candler. For all Mallory's beauty and self-possession, when she was under close scrutiny, she had twisted her hair in exactly that way. A lot of women probably did the same thing, but some gestures are uniquely one's own; in this way we recognize family members or loved ones from behind. That unconscious twisting of hair was Mallory to the life, and in her it symbolized a more private and dangerous habit, one whose memory deeply unsettled Waters.

Rotating his chair back to the desk, he looked down at the photos spread across his desk. Then he turned to his computer keyboard and looked up Eve Sumner's real estate company on the Web. Without pausing to second-guess himself, he called and asked to speak to her, giving the receptionist the name of a local surgeon.

Eve came on the line brimming with enthusiasm.

"Dr. Davis? This is Eve Sumner. How may I help you?"

"You mean *Evie Ray* Sumner, don't you?"

Silence. "Who is this?"

Waters did not reply.

"Johnny?" A whisper. "Is that you?"

"I'm watching you on TV right now."

She exhaled with obvious relief. "God, I knew you'd call. I look awful on that show. It's the lighting or something."

"I want to ask you some questions."

"Ask away."

"Where did I take a nude picture of you?"

"What?"

"You heard me."

"Well . . . the bedroom, of course."

He started to pounce on her response, then stopped. They *had* taken some photos in his bedroom, but he had destroyed those long ago. "Outside, I mean."

"Outside? Let me think. Oh. Fall Creek Falls State Park? In Tennessee?"

He couldn't speak. No one else knew about that. No one.

"My God," Eve said softly. "You don't still have that picture, do you?"

He pushed on, his face uncomfortably warm. "How many men did you sleep with before me?"

"Two."

"Why did you have to leave Alaska the year you won the pageants?"

"Because I threatened your Alaskan girlfriend."

"I didn't have an Alaskan girlfriend."

"French girlfriend, then. Or French Canadian or whatever the slut was."

Real anger in her voice, enough to send a chill down his back. "What else did you do to her?"

"I put sugar in her gas tank and stranded her on the tundra. She nearly froze to death."

He shook his head. Eve's cadence and pronunciation were nothing like those of the woman on television. But for the timbre of her voice, she could *be* Mallory. "How did you get back to the lower forty-eight without the police getting you?"

"I chartered a private plane."

"What kind?"

"Um . . . a Piper Saratoga."

Confusion settled over Waters like a fog. Some of these details he may have confided in Cole, but not all. Close to desperation, he searched his mind for something that no one but Mallory could possibly know.

"What did we do behind the stables at David Denton's party?"

"*You* didn't do anything." Eve's voice sultry now. "I went down on you."

He could go no further.

"Johnny, I want to see you."

"No."

"I know you want to see me. You wouldn't have called if you didn't."

"No."

"Ask me more questions, then. Anything. Eventually you're going to believe me, because there's nothing I don't know."

He sat silent for half a minute, listening to her breathing. "How did you try to kill me?"

He thought the phone had gone dead.

"Johnny . . . I'm so sorry for that."

For the first time, he sensed evasion. "How did you try to kill me?" he asked in a harsher voice. "What did you use? You don't know, do you?"

"The first time? A gun. The other time, your car."

He was gripping the phone so hard his hand hurt. Cole knew about the time with the car, but not about the gun. No one knew about the gun. The phone squawked on the desktop, and he realized he had dropped it.

"Johnny? Are you there?"

"Here."

"I want you to meet me somewhere. You know where Bienville is, right? The antebellum home? The Historic Foundation owns it, and it's for sale. I can get the key. I'm going to be there in twenty minutes, waiting for you."

"I'm not coming."

"I'm leaving now. I'll see you in twenty minutes."

"Eve—"

She had rung off.

He sat numb at his desk. She had answered so damn *quickly.* Any hesitation could be attributed to surprise. Mallory herself might have paused in the face of some of those questions. Waters looked back at the television, where Eve was concluding her presentation. He could not put that face and body with the voice he had spoken to on the telephone.

He didn't know what to do. He did know that the last thing he should do was drive across town to Bienville. With anxiety turning to panic in his chest, he picked up the phone and called Linton Hill. Rose answered. In a barely controlled voice, he asked to speak to Lily. He didn't know what he was going to say to his wife, only that he needed to hear her voice.

"Lily gone with her walking group," Rose replied. "And she left her cell phone right here on the counter."

Waters hung up and went to his drafting table. The wavy substructure lines and numbers on the map looked as foreign to him as they would to a layman. He turned away and began pacing out the perimeter of his office. The room was more than a thousand square feet, but today it felt like a cage.

Opening a subtly concealed door, he stepped out onto his balcony and inhaled the cool air blowing up off the river. He looked south toward the bend that led to Baton Rouge and New Orleans, then north up the stretch that led to Memphis and St. Louis. He could see Weymouth Hall from here, an antebellum mansion with a widow's walk sitting on a promontory a mile upriver. Across the street from Weymouth Hall stood Jewish Hill, and under the oaks below that hill lay Mallory's grave. Mallory's corpse.

So who in God's name was waiting for him at Bienville?

He put the photos and newspapers back into the portfolio and locked it in the bottom drawer of his desk. Then he took his keys from his pocket and walked to the back stairwell of the office. Sybil gave him a questioning look, but he said nothing.

He couldn't even manage a lie.

chapter 8

Sited on half a city block on the north side of town, Bienville was a world unto itself. The foundation of the Greek Revival mansion had been laid into a hill twenty feet above the street, and high stucco walls rising from the sidewalk presented a blank face to passersby. Only a narrow gravel drive that tunneled off Wall Street through thick foliage led up to the terraced gardens behind the mansion, a sun-dappled world of spreading oaks, shrubs, azaleas, jasmine, and banana trees.

Eve's black Lexus was parked near an opening in the garden wall. Waters pulled his Land Cruiser in behind her, blocking her exit, and walked through the gate. To his right rose the rear elevation of the mansion. Its scored concrete walls were relieved by jib windows, and its steeply sloped roof had several chimneys. To his left lay intricate gardens laced with brick walkways and shadowy paths, the centerpiece a fountain surrounded by statuary inspired by German fairy tales. The frozen figures of boys and girls had nothing in common with the stone angels from the cemetery; they captured an elusive quality of childhood, wonder mixed with boredom, a feeling that time had no meaning beyond the present moment.

As Waters approached the house, something made him look up. Through one of the jib windows, he saw the silhouette of a standing woman. She leaned forward and spread her palm against the pane like a starfish. His heart stuttered. Through the distorting blur of the century-old glass, she could be Mallory Candler. Her palm left the pane, and a forefinger pointed downward. A door stood immediately below the window, one of three in the back wall of the house. When he looked back up at the window, the figure had vanished.

He walked to the door, then hesitated with his hand on the knob. He felt like a man walking into a brothel, or a hospital, or a monastery. Once he walked through this door, he would never be the same. Some part of him even feared that he might not come out again.

The knob turned in his hand, and he jerked back his arm. He half-expected the door to open, but it remained closed. After several moments, he turned the knob and pushed open the door.

It led to a narrow, carpeted staircase. Looking up, he saw Eve Sumner standing at the top of the steps. Gone were the navy skirt suit and heels. She wore a bright yellow sundress that looked like something a St. Croix islander might wear. Her feet were bare, and her hair was tied back with a ruby scarf, exposing her fine neck and jaw. Waters was sure he remembered Mallory wearing a dress exactly like it on their Yucatán trip. Eve did not speak but watched him intently. She was waiting for him to enter on his own.

He stepped over the threshold.

"I'm glad you came," she said, her eyes suddenly bright with tears. "I've been waiting for this for a long time."

He closed the door behind him.

She lifted a hand and beckoned him up the stairs.

As he ascended, he took in details of the room that served as a backdrop to her stunning figure: fourteen-foot ceilings, massive crown moldings, a carved medallion above the chandelier.

"I'm not sure why I came," he said, reaching the top step.

She took his hand in hers, and he realized she was shaking. "You don't have to be sure. Just be here."

Waters looked around in wonder. The mansion was furnished with period antiques, giving him the feeling it was 1850 and that the owners had simply gone out for a carriage ride. To his left stood a massive, coffin-shaped piano, a Broadway from England, he guessed. Six doors led off of this central room, some to bedroom suites, the others to a kitchen, a marble-floored foyer, a dining room.

"We're alone," Eve said. "I have the only key."

He looked at her.

"Come with me, Johnny." She pulled him toward a half-open door. Through it he saw a short corridor, and beyond that a bedroom furnished with two tester beds. He pulled back against her hand, stopping them by a grandfather clock that stood beside the door. The heavy chimes in the clock gonged softly from the impact of their feet on the hardwood.

"Do you want to talk some more?" Eve asked, looking nervous.

"I don't know."

She blinked, her dark eyes still moist. "Do you want to kiss me again?"

He flashed back to the cemetery, to the kiss that had thrown him twenty years into the past. "I've thought about it. The way you kiss. It's . . ."

"Just like her. Is that what you were going to say?"

"Yes."

"Think of it that way, if it makes it easier. Right now I don't care. Just kiss me again."

Even as he shook his head, he moved forward. She dropped his hand and touched his face, her fingers tracing the line of his jaw, his lips. Her fingertip opened his mouth, and then she parted her lips and softly pressed her mouth to his. A shock like a static discharge went through him, leaving him tingling as the pressure of her lips increased. Her tongue slipped into his mouth, cautiously exploring. She bit his lower lip, tugging insistently, just as she had at the cemetery, letting him know the kiss was only a beginning, the opening movement of a symphony they both remembered. Or so she wanted him to believe. And God help him . . . he almost did. The desire she'd awakened yesterday had wound itself to an unbearable tension. He wanted Eve Sumner as he had not wanted a woman in more years than he could remember. He slid his hands up to her face and held her cheeks, searching her eyes for . . . what?

"Who *are* you?"

She didn't blink. "You know."

He shook her with sudden violence. *"What do you want?"*

"You, Johnny. That's all. I want you. Right now."

Her hand slid below his belt and gripped him with painful force. Had she done anything else, had she followed a subtler line of seduction, he would have repulsed her. But her animal directness—so unfamiliar to him now—shattered the cerebral restraint of loyalty to legal vows that had not been honored in this way for too long. All thought, all doubt flew out of his head. He bunched the yellow sundress in his hands and yanked it up over her hips. She wore nothing underneath. As he stared, she held her arms straight up, and he slid the fabric right off her.

She stood before him without a hint of self-consciousness, the way Mallory had at the falls, letting him absorb all of her. Then she pulled him to her and kissed him again, her hands working frantically at his clothes until he stood naked before her.

"In there?" he asked, nodding to the bedroom.

She shook her head and pulled his hand down, and he knew then that she'd been ready for some time. When her arms slipped around his neck, he slid his hands beneath her hips and simply lifted her onto him. There was momentary resistance, then none. They gasped and clutched each other like climbers caught in an ice storm, clinging together for warmth. He did not move within her; holding her suspended as she shivered around him was almost more sensory input than he could stand. After a time, a strange purring sound began in her chest. As it built slowly, another, deeper sound blended with a ululation in her throat, creating a strangely haunting music; it was the chimes of the grandfather clock vibrating in sympathy with their moving bodies, the waves transmitted through the seasoned floorboards. The quivering in

Eve's body suddenly focused in the pit of her belly, then radiated out through her limbs like the seizure of some hill woman about to speak in tongues. When the trapped cry finally burst from her throat, Waters's legs trembled violently, and his vision went black as all the frustration and regret of the past four years poured into her. She was still screaming when his legs gave way, and he flung out his arms to break the impact of the floor.

They lay two feet apart, panting like winded sprinters stunned to find themselves naked together. The clock chimes still clanged on their chains, sending resonant waves through the room. Waters looked down at his hand as though at the hand of a stranger. But it was his hand, unchanged. After twelve years of fidelity, he had finally yielded to this ancient impulse, and the sky had not fallen. The earth had not opened at his feet.

Eve sat up and took his hand. She did not speak, but simply pulled him to his feet and led him down the corridor to the bedroom, where she drew back the covers on one of the three-quarter beds, gently pushed him under the sheet, and slid in beside him.

He lay on his back, looking up at the gathered fabric of the canopy, which radiated from a central circle like the rays of the sun. The light in the bedroom had a fluid consistency, as if a golden liquid were being filtered through the heavy lace curtains. Eve lay close and warm along his left side, for the bed was too small for them both.

"What are you thinking?" she asked. "Are you thinking about your wife?"

"No."

She kissed his shoulder. "What, then?"

"This. It's insane. The whole thing."

"You're wrong. This had to happen. It was always going to happen."

"I have no idea what that means."

"I know. Johnny . . . look at me. Did you feel me?"

He refused to look at her. "I don't want to talk about Mallory."

She kissed his shoulder again. "All right. As long as you're here. That's all that matters. There's time for all the rest later."

All the rest. He turned onto his side and looked into her eyes. "I don't know why I came here. And I don't know what you're doing. What you want out of this. You could be crazy for all I know. The things you say are crazy."

She nodded, her eyes filled with patience. "But I'm not crazy. You know I'm not."

He knew no such thing, but he saw no point in telling her that.

She took his hand and placed it over her breast. Her heart beat strongly beneath the swollen bosom.

"I know they don't feel the same," she said. "Not exactly the same. But this is a very nice body." She averted her eyes for a moment. "Better than some I've known."

He pulled his hand away. "What the hell does that mean?"

"I told you, Johnny. You're not ready for the truth."

"We just had sex. We didn't use any precautions. How much crazier can it get?"

"Don't worry about me getting pregnant. Eve had her tubes tied."

Her use of the third person confused him; he shook

his head, trying to keep his mind clear in the face of her delusion.

"And as far as other worries, I've been tested. Eve wasn't very selective in the past, but I changed her. Slowly."

"I feel like I'm on acid," Waters murmured.

Eve giggled, an odd sound after all that had come before. "Johnny? You've done acid?"

"When I worked in Alaska, I did a couple of tabs. Nobody in this town would believe that, thank God." He brushed a strand of hair from her eyes. She had very fine hair; it made him think of an animal pelt.

"Mmm," she purred.

He let his hand fall to the concave curve of her abdomen, then slid it down to the silkier hair there. She rose against his fingers, pressing into his touch. He moved his hand back up to her face and caressed her cheek.

"We're through the looking glass," he said. "I want to hear the rest of it. Finish the story you started in the cemetery."

Fear flickered in her eyes. "Only if you promise not to leave. You have to let me finish."

"Why would I leave? I'm the one asking you to tell it."

"You've never heard anything like this before. It might be hard to listen to."

"For God's sake. Just start talking."

She nodded hesitantly, and he lay back, letting his gaze wander along the underside of the canopy as her low voice trembled.

"I told you how it was. The rape. How at the moment I felt I was going to die, when he was strangling me and finishing, I suddenly wasn't looking at him—

I was looking at me. Mallory. I was *in him,* right? Looking at a woman who lay under him, not breathing. And that woman was *me.*"

The anxiety Waters had felt in the cemetery returned like a shadow falling over him. She spoke lunacy with absolute conviction. Yet what was the harm in listening? An absurd parallel came to him: it was 1955, she was a communist agent, and he had already slept with her. The damage was done. What difference could it possibly make if he listened to her crackpot manifesto now?

"Everything went blank after that," Eve whispered, oblivious to his thoughts. "It was like being in a coma, I guess. Or a drugged sleep. Now and then I would wake up and see things—rooms, furniture, the interior of a car—but they were alien to me. It was like a nightmare where you're trapped in someone else's body. The things I saw . . . I eventually began to make sense of them. The man who raped me led a double life. He had a wife, a house in Marrero, a mindless job as a technician in a plant. To the people he worked with he seemed like a normal person. But inside his head, it was like . . . Hell. There was so much anger and pain, so much hatred. I knew all his thoughts, his memories. They would ambush me in the dark, things that were done to him as a child. It was sickening. The way he treated his wife . . . the way she cowered and took it. Sometimes I shut down my consciousness—went back to sleep—just so I wouldn't have to see or feel any of it. But as time passed, that became harder to do. When I was awake, I tried to think. I didn't understand how it had happened, but I was *alive* in this man. And I was growing stronger. Sometimes I'd be awake for an hour or two. And he wouldn't know it.

He didn't remember any of it. I could tell by people's reactions. It was like he blacked out during those times. He became terrified of the blackouts. I had no idea what I was going to do." Eve swallowed, as though trying to keep her vocal cords working. "Then he raped another woman."

A ball of ice formed in Waters's stomach.

"He raped and killed her . . . exactly the way he had done it to me. I had to experience that, Johnny. *As if I were doing it.* She wasn't as strong as I was. She just lay there, praying it would be over quickly, hoping she would be all right in the end. But she wasn't. He strangled her. I knew he was going to do it. I knew all along, Johnny. And there was *nothing I could do to stop him.*"

Waters pulled the covers over his chest.

"I nearly went mad. Maybe I did, a little. I don't know. I wanted so badly to get out of him. I imagined killing him during one of the times that I was in control. I knew I could stop him from hurting women if I did that. But I didn't want to die. I'd *seen* my dead body. I'd seen that other woman, lying there like a candle someone had blown out. God forgive me . . . I didn't want that to happen to me, Johnny."

Eve wiped her eyes. Waters reached down and took her hand, and this seemed to steady her enough to go on.

"His wife was a pathetic creature, totally dependent. He abused her, but on some level she seemed to need that. He didn't have sex with her very often. Sex to him was what he did to his victims. But when he was with his wife, it was very rough and seemed to satisfy something in her, some yearning for punishment. It was so twisted. Once, while I was thinking of suicide, he had sex with her. During the act, I started to feel like I had when he had raped me. Not the same feeling, but the same *intensity* of feeling. I wanted out of him so badly. And I was so near to this other person, this person who was not a monster. I was physically inside her, you know? As they thrashed against each other, she started to climax, and I felt . . ."

"What?"

"Like a door was opening. As she started to peak, the person she was—the individual part—began to fade away. All thought and memory was vanishing into this . . . nothingness. The ecstasy of her climax wiped out her individuality. Do you know what I mean? In those seconds she became like a shell—a body without a soul—and in the instant that I understood what was happening, it was over. One moment I was looking at her, the next I was looking at him. I was inside her, Johnny. In her *mind*. And it was like being released from prison." Eve looked at him, her eyes begging for understanding. "Do you understand what I'm telling you?"

"You're saying that your soul—"

"I don't know if it's my soul! That's beyond me. But whatever we are—whatever human consciousness is—that part of me moved from him into her, just as it had gone into him when I so desperately wanted to survive." She squeezed his hand. "Please tell me what you're thinking."

"Don't stop. Tell me the rest."

She looked up at the canopy. "That was ten years ago. The time between then and now . . . I don't want to think about."

"Tell me."

Eve closed her eyes and spoke in a detached voice.

"The woman's mind was much less crowded than her husband's. She'd endured terrible things as a child too, but she hadn't reacted the way he had. She'd turned the anger inward, against herself. That's why she responded to his abuse. She thought she deserved it. Once I was inside her, I understood that. I could control her much better than I could him. I could stay awake for much longer periods. I could *think*. And the more I thought, the more I realized that I had been given a unique chance. I had no idea how, and I still don't. But I *had* to do something with that chance. It was as though I'd been lost in a shipwreck. Everyone I knew thought I was dead, so the old obligations didn't apply. My husband, my children . . . I was dead to them. And all I could think about was what had happened when I thought I was going to die. What I had thought of. I decided then that I would do whatever I had to do to find you."

For the first time, Waters truly felt he was lying beside Mallory Candler. The single-minded possessiveness that had led Mallory to insanity was there in Eve's voice. She opened her eyes and rose up on one elbow.

"I mean, I knew *where* you were. But I had to come to you in a way—in a form—that you would listen to. Someone you could be attracted to. Someone like I was when you knew me before."

Waters felt her gaze upon him like heat from a candle. "Are you saying you went through many different people to get to where you are now?"

"Yes."

He felt a manic compulsion to jump out of the bed, but he didn't trust her to stay rational if he did.

"What are you thinking?" she asked, her voice edged with anxiety.

"I'm trying not to think. I'm just listening."

But he *was* thinking. He was thinking he had read that paranoid schizophrenics were capable of constructing incredibly complex delusions, filled with detail and interwoven with reality. If it weren't for all the secrets Eve knew about Mallory, he would be positive this was just such a delusion.

"How many people did you go through to get to Eve?"

"Nine."

As the implications of her words hit him, his face felt cold. "And one of them was Danny Buckles? That's how you knew about the molestation at the school?"

"Yes."

Jesus God. . . .

"I know things about those nine people that no one in the world would ever believe. Things they'd kill themselves over if people discovered. Human beings are corrupt creatures, Johnny. I remember you talking about Thomas Hobbes when you were taking political philosophy. Well, Hobbes had human nature right."

Her easy reference to a class he had taken twenty years ago pierced him like a blade. In this empty mansion, logic held no sway. On one hand she was telling him a story that could have been written by Poe while on opium; on the other she was casually bringing up things only Mallory could have remembered, thus lending credence to her hallucinations.

"And you can move through people at will?" he asked, not believing his own voice.

"No. Only the way I described."

"Only during sex?"

"Not just any sex. The other person—the person I move into—has to climax. Their individuality has to be wiped out by that. So, as you'd imagine, it's very easy for me to move into a man, but harder to pass into a woman."

"But how could it take nine years?"

"I made some mistakes." Bitterness had entered her voice. "I was trapped in a prison for a while. Literally in jail. In a man. There was sex there, but"—she shivered—"not with anyone who could get me out."

Who could make up this insanity? he asked himself.

"The farther along the chain I got, the easier it became to move closer to you. But still, it was hard. It took me a long time to learn to control my . . ."

"What? Your what?"

"My host, I was going to say."

Icy fingers closed around his heart. The "soul transfer" she had been describing had a direct analogue in the real world: viral infection. In Eve's world, souls moved through people in the same way a sexually transmitted disease did. Could her whole fantastic delusion be some paranoid response to contracting the AIDS virus?

"Is that what you're doing now?" he asked, trying to keep his voice steady. "Controlling Eve?"

"Yes."

"Is Eve ever really Eve anymore?"

She bit her lip and turned her face away. "Sometimes."

"What does she feel like when she is?"

"She's afraid. She went to a doctor about it. He referred her to a psychiatrist, who put her on medication. That didn't work, of course. Eve's confused, and sometimes she breaks through when I least expect it. She's a strong personality. Some people are easy to dominate. Others . . . it's exhausting. I'm never quite myself—not completely—because part of my energy is always devoted to maintaining control of the person."

Waters nodded as though it all made perfect sense, but there was a scream behind his lips.

Suddenly Eve turned back to him and squeezed his shoulder. "Johnny, what are you feeling?" She clung to him as though sensing he wanted to leave. "Tell me."

As he searched for some innocuous lie, he suddenly realized that deception was ridiculous. He looked her in the eyes and took her hand. "Eve, are you ill? I want you to be completely honest with me. You said you were tested before. You didn't tell me the result. Has someone made you sick?"

She pulled away, her eyes filled with hurt. "Do you really think I would do that to you? Put you at risk like that?"

"I don't know. Think about everything you've just told me."

"I know it sounds crazy. But think for a minute, Johnny. Millions of people go to church every Sunday and profess faith in their immortal souls. Christianity is built around that. Do those people believe what they say or not? Because if they do, they're admitting that something exists apart from the body, some *force*. And if that's true, then why is what I've described so crazy? Are you only your body, Johnny? If during the good times between us, I'd been paralyzed in a car wreck, would you have left me?"

She had clearly thought about this much more deeply than he had.

"You know you wouldn't have. I know it. Well, this is like that. My old body is useless now, it's gone. But *I'm still here.* And I need you."

He sat up in the bed.

Eve got onto her knees and grasped his arm. "Are you leaving?"

He looked at his watch. "I need to."

"Don't go yet. Please. I don't know how you feel. Where you are."

"I don't either."

"Will you see me again?"

He looked toward the corridor. His clothes lay strewn on the antique rug outside the door. "I don't know."

Eve closed her eyes tight, as though suppressing panic. "Please don't say that, Johnny. Please."

Her reaction threw him back twenty years, to the worst times with Mallory. This yo-yo journey between present and past had been happening ever since the soccer field, and it left him dizzy, like a man trapped on a carnival ride. As soon as Eve opened her eyes, he would calm her down, then make his exit.

While he waited, she raised her right hand to her neck and twisted a lock of hair around her forefinger. Instead of releasing it, she pulled tighter and tighter, clearly hard enough to cause pain. With deep shock spreading through his chest, Waters reached across her body and took hold of her left wrist, exposing the inner forearm. Eve's eyes popped open, but she did not release her hair. He scanned the length of the forearm but saw only smooth skin. Eve gave him an eerie smile.

The watch, he thought. She wore a large watch for a woman, a platinum Rolex. Before she could stop him, he grabbed the watch and yanked it two inches up her arm, keeping his fingers beneath the band to hold the arm still. Where the face of the watch had been, he saw four parallel scars in the skin. A cold wave of dread rolled through him. The scars were not fresh, but deep cuts had made them. Not just four, but cuts over cuts. Repetitive lacerations and scratches in the same place, a spot no one would see.

As Eve watched him with a mixture of shame and triumph, he jerked the covers off her nude body and looked at her legs. She didn't try to hide. On her inner thighs, a few inches below her vulva, he found a crosshatched pattern of scars. Some were old, others made perhaps a week ago. He pulled the covers back up and sat motionless on the bed.

The scars were not evidence of suicide attempts, but part of a complex coping phenomenon of self-mutilation practiced by many adolescent girls. Mallory had cut herself in secret for much of her life, but Waters had been her lover for six months before he discovered this. At the time, he could find no information on the subject. Now he knew that self-mutilators inflicted pain on themselves to drown out a deeper pain, something inexpressible in any other way. Cutting was usually a later phase of the phenomenon. It often began as scratching, banging one's head against the floor, or even hair-pulling. Mallory's had begun that way, but even after she stumbled on cutting, she continued her hair-twisting as a public substitute for the bloody ritual that gave her relief in private.

"I didn't want to show you that," Eve said quietly.

Waters could not speak. The implications of the
scars had shut down part of his nervous system. He
simply could not process what he had seen. A man
with any sense would run, but how could you escape
from something in your head? Knowledge was in-
escapable, irrevocable. The sight of the scars had
scrambled his sense of time, of history, of identity.

"Johnny?"

He turned and slid his legs off the bed. Before he
could get up, Eve draped her arms around him and
laid her head on his shoulder. Her breasts compressed
against his shoulder blades, and her voice sounded in
his ear.

"Do you really have to go?"

"Yes."

She licked the back of his neck, then slid her tongue
up behind his ear. "Do you *want* to go?"

Her tongue entered his ear, then disappeared. Despite the insanity of the situation—or perhaps because
of it—he felt himself stir again. She let go of him then,
and backed away on the bed. Turning, he saw her
kneeling three feet behind him, her eyes glowing with
heat.

"Come here," she said.

"I have to go."

"No. You need me."

Her body seemed to generate some sort of mag-
netic field. And though he tried not to see them, the
small scars on her thighs seemed to blaze like fresh
wounds. "I can't do this."

She reached out and took his hand, pulling until he
lifted his legs back onto the bed. "Get like me," she
said, tugging his wrist.

He got up onto his knees.

She leaned forward and kissed him, lightly running her fingers across his chest, down his stomach. He felt himself swelling again.

"Eve—"

"Don't say that," she whispered, enfolding him in her hands.

"Don't say what?"

She closed her eyes and squeezed him. "That name. I listen to it all day. Not from you . . . please."

Suddenly she turned away, leaving him staring at her finely muscled back and the cleft of her behind. The sudden disappearance of her hands left him quivering with desire to be inside her.

"Remember?" she said to the wall.

His face felt hot. He could not move.

Eve slid backward, reaching for his hand as she neared him. "You know what I like." She caught his hand and pulled his arm over her shoulder, then leaned into him. "And I know what you need."

"Eve—"

"*Shhh.*" She threw herself forward, pulling him across her back as she went down on all fours. "You remember," she said, her voice hoarse now. "Come on, Johnny."

Sweat filmed his face, cold at the temples as she pressed back against him, leaving no doubt about where she wanted him.

"Are you sure?"

She turned and looked back at him, her eyes filled with dark knowledge, her lips curved in a serene smile. "I'm totally relaxed. Do it."

He shut his eyes and obeyed.

*   *   *

It was dusk when he swung the Land Cruiser out of the narrow drive and onto Wall Street. As he crossed to the next block, he glanced in his rearview mirror and saw her black Lexus nose out of the drive, then pull into the street. He looked at his cell phone and thought of calling home, but decided against it. Rose would be gone by now. Lily and Annelise would be in the kitchen, talking about homework, wondering where Daddy was. Daddy was wondering the same thing.

His arms and legs felt shaky, as though he couldn't trust them. Memories of his last hour with Eve flashed through his mind like flares in the darkness, blanking out his thoughts. She came back to him in pieces, like quick cuts in a film. The nape of her neck, beaded with pearls of sweat. Her hip, already bruised in the pattern of his fingertips. And the sounds . . . her mouth at his ear, whispering, urging, taunting, begging. Nonsense words. Profanity. Prayers. But always she returned to the same three words: a pleading command, a mantra, the soundtrack to her remarkable movement, her controlled abandon. *"Say my name, Johnny. . . ."*

"Eve," he'd grunted.

She shook her head and splayed her fingers against the wall to brace herself against him. *"No.* Say it."

"Eve . . ."

"No! Say my name!

"I did."

"Say it!" Anger now, as she thrust violently backward, using her well-muscled arms to anchor herself on the wall. "You know me now! You remember!"

He shook his head, unable to vocalize anything, though the word she wanted so desperately was swelling in his mouth like a balloon, bursting to be freed with all its transformative power.

"Say my name, damn it!" she screamed. A river of sweat ran down the valley created by the muscles on either side of her spine. His eyes tracked up her arm to the four scars her watch had concealed. "I can't feel my head," she panted. "Johnny? I can't . . . say it . . . *say my name!"*

He never did.

chapter 9

He saw Eve every day for the next two weeks. In the beginning he tried to resist, but it was pointless. The awareness that she was within a few miles of him yet not with him made it impossible to concentrate on the smallest things. His work did not suffer, because he did not work. When forced to be in his office, he stared out the window at the river or riffled through the portfolio he kept in the locked desk drawer.

Then his cell phone would chirp. He developed a Pavlovian reaction to the sound. Out of silence it came, and before the first chirp ended, his heartbeat had accelerated, his respiration had gone shallow, his self-awareness had tripled in intensity. Then Eve would speak, her voice a clipped command.

"Ten minutes."

"I'm gone," he'd reply, already standing with his keys in his hand. Eve always called from pay phones, and she always managed to be waiting for him when he arrived at their assignation.

In the beginning they used Bienville. Waters had suggested that they meet in various empty houses, as though Eve were showing him properties for sale, but she rightly argued that this would create more problems than it would solve. If she toured him around town in a sham of house-shopping, word would quickly get back to Lily that her husband was looking at antebellum homes, and she would wonder why, since they already owned one that she had no intention of selling. Moreover, few other properties had the advantages of Bienville. Though situated in the middle of town, the mansion was totally isolated by its elevation and its verdant gardens. The only risk of being seen came when either of them turned into the narrow gravel drive that led off of Wall Street. From that moment until they drove out again—usually hours later—they were safe from the prying eyes of passersby.

Waters came to know the mansion in a way he did not know his own, the way the child of a house knows its secret spaces and idiosyncrasies. They made love in every room, not by design but by serendipity. Exploring the house between sessions, they would find a cozy nook they hadn't noticed before, or a bathroom countertop set at just the right height, and a different sort of exploration would begin. Sometimes they would look down at the street from the half-moon window on the third floor, watching the people passing below, oblivious to the naked lovers above. Their hands would intertwine, they would kiss, and the rest followed as naturally as flowers opening to the sun.

These were moments of searing purity to Waters, existential epiphanies that made irrelevant all that had come before and all that might come after. But this purity had nothing to do with morality, or even with light. There was more darkness in the house than light. Darkness within Eve, and also within himself. That darkness was the shadow of Mallory Candler, who haunted the empty mansion with them during these lost hours. When they made love, Mallory was always there, watching from beside the bed or from over Eve's shoulder. The whole experience was a kind of shared madness, but Waters had lived without passion for so long that he would deny almost any insanity to drink of it. Before long, he found a way to think about it that he could live with. It was like dating an insatiable schizophrenic; the conversations could be eerie, but the sex was explosive.

It was in her sexuality that Eve most resembled Mallory. For just as Eve and Waters avoided dwelling on the underlying truth of their situation—riding the wave of passion without looking beneath the dark water that carried them forward—Mallory too had used sex as an escape. Even before the "black wings" that she later named broke loose in her head, Mallory fled into the sanctuary of physical ecstasy, struggling to drive back an amorphous threat that Waters felt but could not see. With Mallory, directness was the thing. Foreplay was exactly that, and she was not much interested in play. Sex was penetration; all else was secondary. Even now, he could see her near-mindless stare as she bucked and strained toward her peak, her renowned beauty shed like a husk as some primal thing took her over, the way a woman in childbirth is hijacked by larger forces, primordial compulsions that drive her through pain that a conscious body could not otherwise endure.

After Mallory's deepest drives had been sated to

some degree, she could spend hours exploring, ca-
ressing, and kissing—but all that was lagniappe.
What had stuck in his mind was her aggressiveness.
She was usually ready for him before they were alone,
and she could not get her clothes off fast enough.
Sometimes she didn't bother to remove them; she
wore skirts so that she could simply climb astride him
in the car, or lift her leg in a fortuitous hallway or
bathroom and take him into her standing up. She
dared him to take her in crowded places, where discovery would have instantly shattered the perfect
image grafted onto her by the town and then the state.
She brought inanimate objects into their coupling,
things Waters would never have thought of as sexual,
and which frightened him for her when he did. The
perversity of her needs—and her ruthless directness
in seeking to satisfy them—kept him in a state of con-
tinuous arousal. He went through his days with a
woman whom young and old alike admired and
adored, whom many Mississippians thought of in the
way they thought of the models for Ivory Snow, all
the while knowing that her true nature was such that
no one in their insular world could have imagined or
believed it.

All this Eve Sumner resurrected in the empty mansion on Wall Street. Rather than analyze her behavior,
Waters shut his mind and embraced it, reveling in her
unrestrained eroticism. Eve gave orders; he obeyed
them. He abased himself before her. He worshiped at
the pagan altar of her sex. Only one heresy did he
cling to in the shadows of this hidden world. When
she demanded that he call her "Mallory," that he give
voice and thus legitimacy to the shadow that lived
with them in the house, he refused. To do so, he

sensed, would be to leap from the thin ledge of sanity where he now perched into the depths of madness.

The manifold dangers of their repeated trysts he saw but ignored. Blackmail was the most obvious risk, yet he no longer believed Eve intended anything of the sort. The fear of disease lingered until the day she casually left a copy of her blood tests on the piano, dated a week before their meeting at the soccer field. Being caught was always possible, and sometimes images of Lily's face passed through his mind, how she would look if what was happening in the house on Wall Street were somehow revealed to her. Yet it was Eve who insisted they adhere to strict rules of security: no calls between their homes; no actual conversations when she called his cell phone; no following each other; no "surprises" in the mall or the grocery store. Her preoccupation with these matters gave him a feeling that some dark purpose underlay all her actions, but to think too much about this might have broken the spell she had cast upon him, and he had no desire to do that.

Eve questioned him often about guilt. His feelings surprised her, and she seemed not to trust his honesty on this point. Ever since Lily lost the baby on the ultrasound table—and with it her passion—Waters had worked hard not to feel resentment about his wife's inability to let go of that pain. But he was human, and eventually the thousand small humiliations he endured accreted into resentment. Lily's emotionally detached efforts to relieve his frustration only made the problem worse, and as months—and then years—passed, he struggled to keep his resentment from twisting into something worse. He thought he had succeeded. But now, experiencing all that Lily had denied him, and that he had denied himself, he could not feel guilt. He knew he *should* feel it, yet he did not. What he was experiencing with Eve, he desperately needed. He had wanted that ecstasy with Lily, but it was simply beyond her power. Lily's inmost self had been wrapped in chains to which Waters did not have the key.

When he was home, he walked through the house like a secret stranger, a double agent who believed his own cover. *I am a husband,* he would tell himself. *A father. I love this woman. I love this child.* And he did. Sitting with Annelise in the evenings, he would listen in wonder as she told him about her day, each experience a suspenseful drama seen through the stark lens of seven-year-old perception. When he kissed Ana good night, her smile warmed him in a way nothing else could. Yet even before he passed through the door leaving her room, images of Eve would rise into his mind, as impossible to ignore as a fever in the blood. The urge to telephone her was almost irresistible, but he remembered her proscriptions and forced himself to wait until the next day, when she would call his cell phone. One night, though, the fever overcame him. He went to a pay phone and called her home. Eve was furious until he explained where he was. She met him on a deserted county road and made love with him on the ground, her dark eyes reflecting the moonlight, her voice weaving its ceaseless spell in his ear as he grunted like an animal into the surrounding forest.

The next day, when he took the portfolio from his desk drawer to look at Mallory's picture, his eyes settled on the unopened bundle of her letters. That he had not yet opened this forced him to realize how badly he wanted to experience a reincarnation of Mallory without exhuming the darker remains of her personality. But that was as impossible now as it had been twenty years ago. Ominous flashes of her instability had already broken through the bright facade Eve worked so carefully to maintain.

More and more during their time together, she brought up Lily's name. She questioned him endlessly about her. What had initially drawn him to her? Why had he married her? Was Annelise more like her father or mother? Eve asked these questions as though the answers were of only passing interest, but whenever he said anything even mildly complimentary about Lily, Eve's face tightened in a way that sent a chill through him. More disturbing, as the days passed, she wanted him to stay later and later at the house. Twice he drove out of the narrow driveway after dark, distressed by the knowledge that Lily and Annelise were waiting for him at home. At first, Eve kept him late by increasing the intensity of the sex as evening approached. But when Waters tore himself away in spite of this, she reversed strategy and drew out the foreplay, so that he stayed late in order to find the release that days before had come in the first hour after his arrival. Beneath Eve's subtle games he sensed a battle beginning with Lily, and in this Eve truly bore out Mallory's shadow side. For the Grendel that lived in the dark cave of Mallory's mind was jealousy, an unthinking possessiveness that could swallow a man whole and not be sated. The fact that Lily did not even know she was in a war began to work on Waters's conscience in a way that simple sexual betrayal had not. Yet still he returned to Eve, diving ever deeper into the well of her passion, and leaving farther behind all that he deemed precious.

One night, as dusk fell outside the half-moon window on the third floor, he was trying to find a graceful way to make his exit. Sensing his mood, Eve shook her head and began to caress him. He had thought himself spent, but with patient ministrations, Eve brought him back to a state of arousal greater than that in which he'd begun the afternoon. They started with him above, but as he tired, she rolled him over and sat astride, taking control of their movements. Waters hovered in a purgatory between ecstasy and exhaustion, striving for release but unable to achieve it. With tireless rhythm Eve brought him to a point of exquisite torture, a tightrope in the dark, with pain on one side and pleasure on the other. As he strained against her, feeling as though he might faint, her mantra began again.

"Say my name, Johnny . . ."

He shut his eyes and tried to lose himself within her. Her teeth bit into his neck.

"Say it, Johnny . . . say it and you'll be there. It's so easy. It's your magic word . . ."

Blood pounded like drums in his ears, and his muscles burned, but still he could not find release. Panting for oxygen, he opened his eyes and found himself staring at the place of their joining. The crosshatched pattern of scars on Eve's inner thighs had grown red and prominent with her arousal, scars he hadn't seen for twenty years.

"Say it, Johnny," she begged, not even slowing her motion. *"Say my name. . . ."*

As she repeated her eternal demand, he heard another voice answer hers. Three whispered syllables filled the room as completely as the screamed confession of a heretic.

"Mallory."

Eve froze above him, her eyes locked onto his. Then she gave a moan riven from the depths of her being.

"Mallory," he said again.

She gripped his head between her hands. "Say it again! Say it! Save me!"

"Mallory? Mallory, Mallory, Mallory . . ."

Tears poured from her eyes like rivers of grief and joy. She sat down with all her weight, the tears dropping onto his face, into his mouth, not warm but cold against his superheated flesh. And though she was not moving, something suddenly broke loose in him, and the point he had struggled so hard to reach came without effort, leaving him shivering beneath her like a malaria patient. Eve lay prone atop him, breathing shallowly.

"Do you love me, Johnny?"

Before that day she had often said, "I love you," but she'd never insisted that he do the same. At those times he'd sensed a careful vigilance over her emotions, as though she knew that moving too fast could ruin everything. Now she had thrown caution to the wind.

"I don't know," he replied. "I honestly don't know."

"I do," she said. "I know you do."

As Waters drove up to his house that night, he felt like a man on the verge of madness. Eve had not demanded that he call her Mallory again before leaving, but neither had he called her Eve. And having surrendered this ground to her, he sensed that only one moral redoubt remained: the renunciation of his love for Lily.

*   *   *

The next morning, Cole walked into Waters's office, sat down in the chair opposite his desk, and asked if he had the new maps ready.

Waters looked blank.

"You said you had a prospect in West Feliciana Parish," Cole reminded him. "A close-in deal. You said you'd have it ready in a week."

"Oh. Right."

"Can I see it?"

"The mapping's going to take a little longer than I thought."

Cole gave him a hard look. "What the fuck are you up to, John?"

Waters shrugged. "Nothing."

"Nothing but banging the bejesus out of Eve Sumner. Which would be fine by me, except you ain't doing any *work*."

A flash of temper covered Waters's shock. "I do more than my share of work around here, and you know it."

Cole's face reddened. "And you make more money."

Waters dismissed this with a flick of his hand. He should have known Cole would be on to him. It wasn't hard to figure out. For no apparent reason the partners had suddenly swapped lifestyles. Cole, usually absent from the office during the odd hours he catted around town, was coming in early every day, making phone calls, evaluating producing wells for possible purchase and workover. Waters, the obsessive workaholic, arrived at nine but usually left by ten, and sometimes didn't return until four. When he was in the office, he locked his door and took no calls.

"Come to think of it," Cole said, leaning back and crossing his legs, "your banging Evie isn't fine by me for another reason. 'Cause you're breaking rule number one."

"What would that be?"

"Don't lose your perspective. That gets you in big trouble. And you have a lot on the line, John Boy."

"I should take advice from you?"

"In this case, yes. That chick ain't worth it."

Waters stiffened. "What do you know about Eve?"

Cole looked incredulous. "What do I *know* about her? I fucked her, remember? I know plenty. Evie's hot to trot, and you're just the latest in a very long line."

The words stung Waters like the lash of a whip. The knowledge that Cole had been inside Eve nauseated him. He knew how ridiculous he must look. He was like a young soldier in love with a whore, defending her honor to a laughing village. But he couldn't control his feelings.

"She's not the same woman you slept with," he said quietly.

"No?" Cole's eyes narrowed. "What do you mean?"

"Nothing."

Cole shook his head, his eyes filled with amazement. "Holy shit. At first I thought you meant she'd reformed or something. Changed her ways. Got born again. But that's not what you mean, is it?"

Waters looked away, not sure just what he had meant.

"You're still on your Mallory kick, aren't you?" Cole leaned forward, his forehead knotted in thought. "Don't tell me you were right about 'Soon,' and all that? Eve's not actually trying to run that line on you? That she's Mallory?"

Waters said nothing. A saying of his father's had always stuck with him: *Two people can keep a secret, if one of them's dead.* Yet the temptation to confide in Cole was strong. As far as he knew, his partner had never spilled any of his secrets.

"Eve knows things," Waters said softly. "Things no one but Mallory ever knew."

"We talked about that, John. You don't know what Mallory told people about you. She lived for, what? Nine years after you two split as a couple?"

"I know. But that's not all. Eve . . ."

"What?"

"She kisses the way Mallory did. *Exactly* like her."

Cole barked a laugh. "Do you really remember how Mallory kissed? Does a guy remember that? There aren't really any unique ways to do it. This is *in your head*, mon."

"I remember how she kissed. It was unforgettable. It's like muscle memory. Like riding a bike. You can't forget it. It's deeper than conscious thought."

"You're losing your mind, Rock. You need a week in Cabo."

Waters shook his head. "I've seen her handwriting. It's identical to Mallory's. She left me a note at the cemetery, just like Mallory used to, and the handwriting was exactly the same."

For the first time, Cole looked intrigued. "Do you have this note?"

"No. I think I left it at the cemetery. I may have put it back in the jar."

"Back in the jar." Cole nodded like a cop humoring

an escaped mental patient. "I see. And this note was signed 'Mallory'?"

"Yes."

"John, Eve Sumner is either batshit crazy or running a scam on you."

Waters thought of the scars on Eve's arm and thighs, but he did not want to mention them. Since he had never told Cole about Mallory's self-mutilation, Cole might think he had made it up on the spot.

"Personally, I think it's a scam," Cole asserted. "She's looking for money, baby."

Waters shook his head. "She doesn't want money."

"What, then? You think that forty-one-year-old dick of yours is different from the last ten she had? She wants your money, boy, nothing else."

"Eve doesn't want money!" Waters snapped. "*You're* the only person who's asked me for money recently."

It was a reflexive blow, but Cole snapped back as though he'd been dealt a mortal wound. After a stunned moment, he stood and walked to the door, but before he went through, he turned and spoke in a quavering voice.

"I'm going to forget you said that, partner. And you're right about one thing. Where you dip your wick is your own business. I just don't want to see you lose Lily and Annelise. You're not me, and Lily isn't Jenny. Lily won't take this well if she finds out. She won't look the other way. And if you keep this shit up, she *will* find out. That's the only sure bet I know. Because they always do."

Waters stared out the window until Cole closed the door. He knew his partner's advice was the fruit of bitter experience, but he didn't much care. All he cared about right now was the cell phone on his desk. He wanted it to ring.

It didn't. It lay there like an insult for an hour, then two, its silence a goad to his pride and to his faith in Eve. Like a junkie going cold turkey, he fought the urge to call her office. He tried a dozen distractions, but none worked.

Ten minutes before noon, it finally rang. With two chirps of the ringer, he was back on the crest of the wave, Cole's warnings forgotten. But when he answered, Eve did not say, "Ten minutes." She said, "We've got a problem. Don't say anything."

It was a measure of how much perspective Waters had lost that her words did not cause him panic.

"Some film producers are flying in from Los Angeles," she explained. "The ones who bought Penn Cage's novel. They're considering shooting the film on location here."

"Uh-huh." Waters had no idea what this could have to do with him.

"The Historic Foundation is coordinating the visit, and they're putting the producers up in Bienville for the week."

"Ahh." The strung-out addict's feeling returned with a vengeance as he wondered if they would miss today's rendezvous.

"Today's no good," Eve went on, confirming his fear. "But check the jar."

He started to say something, but she'd already clicked off. Locking the portfolio in his bottom drawer, he got his keys and walked quickly to the back stairs, his mind already at the cemetery.

When he arrived at Catholic Hill, he parked and ran behind the wall to dig up the mason jar. Inside lay a piece of blue notepaper and a hotel key card. When he unfolded the paper, he saw Mallory's flowing script.

Johnny,

This is a key to Suite 324 at the Eola Hotel. I've rented it for the week. I know the Eola is right in the middle of town, but it's the safest place for us. It has a bar inside the Main Street entrance, so if anyone sees you go in, you can always say you were going to the bar. The Pearl Street entrance is best for you, though. It's possible to get all the way to our suite without being seen. The security guard sits deep in the lobby, and he probably won't see you. Even if he does, he won't look at you more than a second if you're dressed nice. Go in and immediately turn left. You'll see a staircase leading to the mezzanine. Walk up, then take the elevator to the third floor. There's an exposed walkway just before the suite's door, where you can be seen from the courtyard or from rooms above, so walk fast there. I'll be there by 10:30 p.m.

M

He put the jar back in its hole, but this time he kept the note. As soon as he got back to the office, he got the portfolio back out and did something he had not yet found the courage to do: he opened the bundle of Mallory's old letters.

The handwriting matched perfectly.

chapter 10

When he arrived at the Eola suite that night, he saw that she'd been right to choose it. The brick and stone hotel was a local landmark; it occupied most of a city block, and at seven stories had held the title of tallest building in the city for decades. Two popular night-clubs operated nearby, and their patrons frequently spilled out into Main Street, go cups in hand as they laughed and danced to the beat of live bands thumping through the walls. On any given night, those bars were filled with people who would recognize Waters on sight, but he felt reasonably safe approaching on foot from Pearl Street, as Mallory had told him to do.

Entering the doors of the grand hotel hurled him back in time, not twenty years but thirty. When he was a boy, his father had often brought the family to the Eola for Sunday dinner. He still remembered his passage through the lobby as they walked to the restaurant. Old men sat in club chairs, smoking cigars and playing checkers; a black shoe-shine man quietly solicited business; an attendant with a gold-braided uniform manned the elevator, which had a brass cage door that Waters always dreamed of opening and closing. He could still hear his father ordering shrimp rémoulade from the red-haired waitress, still see the sliced yellow pound cake, strawberries, and whipped cream that awaited them for dessert.

On the first night he met Eve, the lobby was empty but for a lone security guard who sat far away with his back to the door. A bell rang somewhere, but as Eve had predicted, the guard did not challenge him. A dark business suit provided all the bona fides he needed for access.

When he opened the door to suite 324, he found Eve lying naked across the bed like Marilyn Monroe, a huge red bow tied around her waist, a champagne flute in her hand. The Rat Pack campiness of it broke the tension that had built inside him on his way up, and they celebrated their new digs with wild excess.

It was a good beginning for a week that would end badly. For after that first night, things began to change. Lily was behaving differently toward Waters at home. Her tone of voice became more affected, and sometimes he caught her watching him from the corner of her eye. He began to worry that he'd made some mistake, that she could smell Eve on him despite the fact that he always showered before returning home. And not all the clues to his betrayal were as subtle as scent. Eve was so physical that she sometimes left marks on him, even though she tried not to. If he and Lily had had a normal sexual relationship, his infidelity would have been discovered in the first week. But though she did not discover the marks of passion, Lily did notice changes in his behavior.

The move to the Eola had necessitated that the trysts become nocturnal, and Waters's nightly ritual never varied. He would put Annelise to bed, wait for Lily to retire, then go out to the slave quarters to "do some mapping." After he was sure Lily was asleep, he would slip on a sport coat, drive down to Pearl Street, park under some trees, and walk two blocks to the Eola.

One night, though, Lily varied *her* ritual. She came into the kitchen after they'd put Annelise to bed, and remarked that he'd been cold to her for the past few days. Waters could not believe she'd used the word "cold." When he asked for clarification, she said he seemed unusually distant, and she didn't think it was just the EPA investigation. He hadn't hugged or kissed her for ten days, she said. Waters almost pointed out that Lily hadn't made love with him for seven weeks, and that effort was only a painful charade she suffered through to keep him from going out of his mind with frustration. But he didn't. As he stood awkwardly by the refrigerator, Lily walked up and laid her head on his shoulder, then said she was going to take a hot shower. Waters stiffened. Lily normally took baths. "Taking a hot shower" was one of her rare preambles to sex.

Afraid she would sense his anxiety, he hugged her, then said that he had a full night's work ahead, mapping a new prospect. Lily gave him a hurt look, but he did not relent. He went out to the slave quarters and sat looking blankly at his drafting table while he waited for Lily to fall asleep. As his mind drifted, an underlying irony of his marital sex life hit him. As long as Lily knew that he wanted to go to bed with her, she was quite content not to have sex. But the moment she sensed real indifference on his part, she felt compelled to take him to bed.

He went to the Eola that night in the hope of forgetting the tension at home, but he found only more tension. That night, when Eve said, "I love you," she held eye contact, waiting for her declaration to be returned. When Waters didn't comply, he saw anger in her eyes. Later, after sleep deprivation had caused him to doze off, he awakened to find her sitting Indian-style at the foot of the bed, staring at him in the half dark.

His bladder almost emptied at the sight. Coming out of sleep, he was not sure whether the woman watching him with shining cat's eyes was Eve or Mallory. He had found Mallory like that countless times, and he'd hoped never to see the sight again. Mallory *never slept*. If she did, it was while he was sleeping, and she always woke before he did. He couldn't count the times he had surfaced out of slumber to find her propped on one elbow, watching him with luminous unblinking eyes. It unnerved him. And after her mind slipped its moorings, the cutting became part of her nocturnal vigil. He would awaken to find her sitting at the foot of the bed, her eyes glazed as she slowly raked the point of a safety pin along her inner forearms, leaving little trails of blood behind. Sometimes she used only her fingernails, but other times a key or a pocketknife. To wake and find Eve in the same position made him shudder beneath the covers. He was trying to think of some banal words to mask his fear when her lips parted and her low voice floated to him.

"Do you ever think about our babies, Johnny?"

"What?" he asked, hoping he'd misheard.

"Our babies."

Memories too traumatic to face flooded his mind, and his fear morphed into panic. He could no longer convince himself that the woman sitting three feet from him was Eve Sumner. Her face was lost in shadow, her eyes seemed to burn with cold light, and her question reflected the central preoccupation of Mallory Candler's broken mind. During her time with Waters, Mallory had terminated two pregnancies, both babies fathered by him. The first abortion had triggered her descent into madness, and Waters knew—if no one else did—that even after marriage and the birth of three healthy children, Mallory had never fully recovered from those abortions.

"Tell me, Johnny," Eve insisted, her eyes never leaving his face.

He could hardly bring himself to address her as Mallory in a nonsexual situation, but what choice did he have? "I've thought about what happened," he said cautiously. "I've thought about it a lot. And I still think it was the right thing to do at the time. I know you don't agree, but—"

"I don't mean that," she said. "Do you think about what they would have been *like*? Blends of you and me. They would be twenty-one and twenty-two now. Do you realize that?"

The skin on Waters's neck rippled as though he'd touched a snake.

Eve hugged herself and rocked slowly. "I don't think of them that way," she went on. "I think of them as children. Three and four. A boy and a girl, Johnny. That's what they were. I asked the doctors."

He had heard this a thousand times, but that did not lessen his anxiety. When Mallory let herself think this way, she entered a psychological danger zone, in which thoughts of her lost children drove out all else, and her guilt and anger searched desperately for an object upon which to discharge themselves. Eve might only *believe* she was Mallory, but that wouldn't lessen the violence of her actions if she carried her delusion that far. She sat three feet away from him, her nude body as still as that of a meditating yogi. Yet danger radiated from her as from a coiled cobra.

"Are you afraid, Johnny?"

He fought to keep his voice under control. "No."

"There's nothing to be afraid of."

"I know that."

"Good. Then go back to sleep. I'm fine."

"I probably should go," he said, looking at his watch.

She slowly shook her head. "No. Go back to sleep. I'll wake you up in plenty of time."

He rolled back over and closed his eyes for an hour, but he did not sleep. He lay like a man spending his first night in prison, waiting for a fist, a knife, or worse. It took all his willpower not to leap out of bed and run from the room.

After he finally escaped the suite, he vowed never to see Eve again. When she called his cell phone the next day, he lied and told her Lily was leaving town for the night, and that he had to stay home with Annelise. Eve offered to come to his house and wait for him in the slave quarters, but he told her he couldn't possibly see her with Annelise in the house. She tried to act casual, but thirty minutes later she called back. Couldn't he find a sitter for a few hours and come to the hotel during that time? No, he told her. Annelise would tell Lily what he'd done, and that wasn't their agreement. Eve called back twice more and tried various approaches, but Waters held firm. That night, after he and Lily put Annelise to bed, he sat on the porch at Linton Hill until dawn, like a lone settler guarding his family on the Great Plains. He wasn't sure what he feared, but he knew he could not sleep.

Several times, headlights slowed as they passed the house, and one car actually nosed into the driveway and parked, its engine idling. This was not uncommon in a tourist town; people got lost all the time. Yet as the vehicle sat at the end of the drive, obscured by the trees and darkness, Waters felt in his blood that behind those bright lights was a black Lexus, and behind its wheel Eve Sumner, her eyes as watchful as the previous night when she had watched him in sleep. He thought of switching on his cell phone, but he did not want to give Eve a chance to interrogate him or persuade him of anything.

Just before dawn, he went out to the slave quarters and crashed on the twin bed he kept there. When he awakened that afternoon, Lily was gone. His cell phone showed fourteen missed calls, all from pay phones. He knew that if he didn't answer soon, Eve would show up in person at his home or office. Just as Mallory would have done.

As he drove to his office, his phone chirped. The caller ID showed a pay phone. Despite Eve's recent behavior, the Pavlovian response still kicked in: desire stirred in him, utterly detached from the misgivings in his mind. He picked up the phone.

"Here."

"Tonight," Eve snapped, her voice so clipped it was hard to read. She might have been crying.

"Um—"

"You don't want me anymore?"

"Of course I do."

"I know I scared you, Johnny. I know I'm going too fast. It's just that I've waited so long—"

"I know," he cut in, not at all sure what he knew. "Look, are you going to keep on with the Mallory stuff? All the painful things from the past?"

"No. I swear to God. No talking. Let's go back to what we know. I need you inside me."

Even if it was a lie, her words dulled his anxieties like Valium.

"We could go right now," she whispered. "I'm ready now. You know how I get."

Images bloomed like night flowers in his mind: Eve's dark hair lying across her shoulder blades; the river of sweat running down her spine; her mouth as she growled in a way that was not quite animal and not quite human—

"Not now," he whispered. "Tonight."

"Tonight," she said. "Don't stand me up, Johnny."

"I won't."

Rain lashed the walls and windows of the Eola in silver sheets turned pink by the streetlamps as Waters drove his Land Cruiser down Main Street toward the old hotel. At the corner of Main and Pearl, he turned right, and his breath stuck in his throat. Police and ambulance lights arced like antiaircraft tracers from the intersection of Pearl and Franklin streets, a block to the north. This was close to where Waters normally parked. Braking, he saw that an old Grand Am had smashed into a Mississippi Power & Light truck with its cherry picker extended. He considered cruising slowly past the scene and parking farther away than usual, but something made him stop. Perhaps it was the memory of Detective Tom Jackson recognizing his vehicle and stopping him that night. In any case, the police and rescue vehicles were blocking most of the intersection, and no one working the scene seemed to notice when he reversed the Land Cruiser back onto Main Street and continued toward the river.

Passing the bars near the Eola, he saw the silhouettes of several patrons through neon-lit rain. He turned left on South Wall, then made another left and parked in a law firm's lot on South Pearl. He'd brought an umbrella with him, but it was almost useless. The rain blew at a forty-five-degree angle, soaking his coat and slacks. As he ran across Main Street, he used the umbrella to hide his face from any curious drinkers in the bars.

He walked through the hotel doors like a businessman late for an appointment, despite the hour. The bell chimed through the spacious lobby, and he heard the scrape of the security guard's chair, but as usual no one challenged him. He ascended to the mezzanine and pressed the elevator button. Waiting, he fought the urge to look back over the mezzanine rail. If he did, he would be visible to the desk clerk working below and to his right. The ancient elevator always seemed to take forever. At the sound of groaning cables, he willed the car to be empty, as it had been on most nights he'd come.

It was.

He reached the door of the suite without seeing a soul or—he hoped—a soul seeing him. But as he turned the doorknob, he felt a disquieting premonition, like the one he'd had when he first touched the door at Bienville. *Nerves*, he thought. *Suck it up.* He shook his head and pushed open the door.

Tonight Eve wasn't sprawled across the bed or hiding naked in the dark, as she had been on some nights, and for a moment he thought he had arrived first. Then he felt wind blowing through the suite. He looked across the bed at the door-sized windows and saw Eve silhouetted on the balcony, her unmistakable curves framed in the pink glow of the streetlights below. She was leaning on the rail with her back to him, naked, apparently oblivious to the rain that had stung his face only moments ago.

As he stared, she looked back over her shoulder, and her eyes glinted in the dark. The rain and the halos of the streetlights created the impression that the balcony was superfluous, that Eve was floating in space. He started to go to her, but she stopped him with an upraised hand.

"You lied to me," she said in a voice devoid of emotion.

"What?"

"Lily didn't leave town. She was home with you. I saw her leave the house this morning."

Waters swallowed and tried to marshal his thoughts. This was Mallory to the life: paranoia, surveillance, confrontation. She would begin with cold fury, then escalate to the inevitable explosion. He felt himself tensing for violence.

"I know why you lied," she said. "You don't have to be afraid."

Lightning strobed, freezing her body in time, burning eerie images onto his retinas: her soaked hair hanging limp, rainwater spattering her breasts and abdomen, her skin almost blue from cold. Then a colossal peal of thunder shook the building, and she seemed to shudder in place. He saw confusion in her eyes, as though for a moment she had forgotten who and where she was.

"I'm not afraid," he told her.

Eve blinked several times, then folded her arms across her breasts. "I'm cold," she said, her teeth chattering.

Waters grabbed the comforter off the bed and went to her. He gathered the fabric around her shoulders and pulled her inside. His shoes made sucking sounds in the soaked carpet as he shut the windows.

Standing by the bed, he switched on a lamp. Dark circles shadowed Eve's eyes, and her cheeks looked drawn. She might not have slept or eaten for days, yet thirty-six hours ago she had looked the picture of health.

"How do you feel?" he asked.

She did not reply.

"I'm worried about you."

Now she looked up at him. "Are you? What are we going to do, Johnny?"

"What do you mean?"

"Are we just going to keep fucking like animals in the dark?"

He drew back, stunned by the bitterness in her voice.

"Every day you go back to sweet little Lily, but at night you come to me. Everything's just fine for you, isn't it?"

"No."

"Don't *lie*. You'd keep going like this forever, if I would. Do you think this is all I want? *Do* you?"

"What do you want me to do? You want me to leave my wife and daughter?"

She looked away from him and stared straight ahead. "Yes."

He closed his eyes and tried to keep himself together. Cole was right: he had lost his perspective. He had lost his perspective and now Eve had expectations. Reasonable expectations, by any fair standard.

"You can't do it, can you?" she said.

He wanted to tell her the truth, but he feared her reaction. He wanted to hug her, but she clearly did not want that. She was still shivering despite the comforter, and her teeth still chattered. There was a glass of red wine under the lamp on the end table. He picked it up and held it up to her mouth, but she ignored it. He drained it himself, thankful for the heat in his throat.

"Listen," he said softly. "We should—"

"I want you to cut me."

Now she was looking at him, her face almost empty of humanity.

"I can't do that."

"You've done it before."

It was true. Once, at Mallory's request, he had cut her arm during sex. He had done it in the hope that they could somehow uncover the source of the pain that she mutilated herself to alleviate. He used a knife, and the act had brought them closer than he thought human beings could get. But it did not have the desired result.

"I'm not going to cut you."

She let the comforter fall and held out her arms. The surfaces of both inner forearms had been deeply scratched, by her fingernails, probably. She had bled, but the comforter had wiped most of it away.

"What's a few more?" she asked. "You don't know how badly I need it."

"Why? Why do you need it?"

She grabbed his wrist and pulled him onto the bed. He tried to resist, but she covered his mouth with hers in an almost vicious kiss. She didn't even try to remove his clothes. She pulled him on top of her, reached down, and freed him from his trousers, her fist closing around him like the hand of a demon. He cried out in pain.

Rolling him over with frantic movements, Eve placed him against her opening and tried to sit down. She wasn't ready, but she did not intend to wait. She shut her eyes and settled hard upon him.

He cried out again, but Eve made no sound. She began to move with slow insistence that escalated to a blank-faced urgency and left Waters feeling he was not even part of the act. One concentrated minute was all it took, and she finished with facial contortions that looked as though she had lost control of her nerves. When she collapsed upon him, he thought surely she would surrender to sleep at last. But only a few seconds later, she wrapped her arms around his back and, using all her strength, rolled him over in the bed, so that he lay on top of her.

As he looked into her eyes, they went wide, as though a bolt of electricity had shot through her, and he saw something in them he had not seen before: fear.

"What is it?" he asked. "What's wrong?"

"*Shut up,*" she hissed, sliding her hands down his back and pushing him deeper. "You're not done."

"Eve—"

"Don't call me that!"

She made claws of her hands and dug them into his pectoral muscles, then locked her heels behind his thighs. The conditioning of the past two weeks took over, and he began to move, his body charged with the energy stored during the twenty-four hours he'd gone without her. With every thrust she urged him on, her hands raking his back. The reciprocal rhythm of her hips drove him toward his peak, but he held himself in abeyance, unsure of what she needed from him.

"Scratch me, Johnny . . . please."

"No."

"I need you to cut me!"

He had never seen Eve this way. Beneath her carnality he had always sensed arrogance, a confidence that she could rule and possess him. Tonight uncertainty clouded her eyes. She was like Mallory fleeing her demons, using sex as an escape. But from what? And why did she want to be cut? Until tonight she had wanted only to be called Mallory. Now there was no mention of that.

"Please," she begged. *"Make me hurt."*

Waters slid his hands beneath her back, set his knees against the mattress, and heaved her up off the bed. Now he had all the leverage, and he yanked her to him or held her back as he chose, driving her mad with hesitations and sudden reversals. She fought only to hold herself against him.

"Please," she rasped, her breath ragged. *"Make me . . . make her go away."*

Her words registered only as encouragement, their specific meanings lost in the violence of their union. He drove harder, yet still she demanded more, her cries no longer a language but guttural syllables any mammal could understand. He let go his conscious mind and thrashed wildly, as a man pursued senses that his only hope of survival is to battle his way through an unyielding wall before him.

"*Make it stop!*" she screamed. "*Make her stop!*"

His heart thundered as it fought to feed his starving tissues, and for an instant his vision faded. Fearing he might faint, he let himself fall forward, pinning her to the mattress. Her fingernails dug into the flesh of his upper arms, and the sudden pain made him open his eyes.

Eve was staring at him as though she had no idea who he was, her mouth frozen in an O that he read as a symbol of a shattering climax. When she began to flail her arms, he used his last reserve of energy to magnify her sensation to the limit, thrashing inside her like a man possessed. Had he not been so lost within the act—or had his partner been someone else—he might have realized he was in one of those situations in which the woman later claims she tried to stop and the man refused. But the idea of Eve stopping sex *in medias res* was incomprehensible. Her screams of ecstasy were indistinguishable from those of agony. Yet this time, tears were streaming from her eyes.

Her movements became disjointed, as though she were having a seizure rather than an orgasm. In the moment that doubt truly entered Waters's mind, her spastic movements drove him past the point of no return. All that remained of his conscious mind shot out across light-years of space and time, while the animal in him ejaculated with withering force. Eve faded, flashed, and then his mind went black.

*   *   *

He awoke facedown on the bed, shivering like a wet dog. At some point while he slept, the wind had driven the rain across the balcony and into the suite. The bed was drenched, and him with it. He lay half across Eve, his hips between her legs, his torso to the right of hers. He tried to pull off the wet covers, but the twisted sheet was pinned beneath her.

"Hey," he said. "Wake up."

Even before the silence stretched into eternity, he sensed something wrong with her skin. It felt only slightly warmer than the sopping bedclothes. He recoiled and threw himself onto the floor.

At first he could not bear to look at her, to confirm with his cerebral cortex what his medulla already knew. Kneeling beside the tall tester bed, he reached out and placed the tip of his forefinger beneath her jawbone. There was no pulse beneath the bluish skin, only a waxy resilience that had nothing in common with the rich pink tissue he had kissed a short while ago, soft skin animated by thrumming nerves and oxygenated blood.

In death, Eve finally looked her age. The breasts that had piqued Lily's curiosity now lay flat on her chest like Baggies half-filled with water. Her face was stiller than a statue's, for statues are sculpted to look alive, and Eve had lost all semblance of life. Her mouth hung open as though gasping for air, and around her eyes were small pinpricks of dark blood. Something ticked in Waters's brain at this sight, something from a film or novel, and he remembered that such small hemorrhages were petechiae, telltale side effects of strangulation.

He looked at Eve's neck.

The skin there was bluish red, bruised from pressure and abrasion. She had definitely been strangled. This realization led to another—*I was alone with her*—and nausea hit him in a sickening wave. He staggered into the bathroom and emptied the contents of his stomach into the commode, the spasms racking his body down to his cramping groin muscles.

"Jesus God," he croaked, hugging the toilet.

He got to his feet, washed his face, and went back into the bedroom. A thousand irrational thoughts assailed him, but the cold center of his mind knew there was only one thing to do. Taking a wet rag from the bathroom, he methodically wiped down every surface in the suite that he might have touched. He didn't look at the corpse on the bed. If he stopped to think about what he was doing, he might pick up the phone and call the police. With Lily and Annelise to think about, he could not risk that.

After wiping down the room, he searched for anything he might have left behind on previous visits. Socks, underwear, a scrap of paper. Finding nothing, he went back to the bathroom. There was something here, he knew. Something dangerous. His vomitus? No. The drain trap. He had showered here every night before returning home. There would be hair in the drain, hair that could be matched to that on his head with a hundred percent certainty. He crouched in the shower stall and examined the drain. It was held down tight with tiny Phillips screws. He had no screwdriver with him. Not even a pocketknife.

Cut me, Eve had begged.

What had she wanted him to use? He walked back into the bedroom and searched her purse. Sure enough, he found a small pocketknife inside. A Gerber. He took it into the bathroom, but its thin point made no headway with the Phillips screws. Digging into the purse again, he found a scrap of blue notepaper with his home phone number written on it. As he put the paper in his pocket, he saw a small flat case made of faux leather. Inside he found a mini tool kit, and one of the tools was a screwdriver. Not a Phillips head, but a standard one that would probably do the job. He went back into the shower stall and removed the drain trap, dug the hair and funk out of it, then flung the mess off the balcony onto the rain-slicked parking lot. As he screwed the drain back down, he felt his composure fragmenting. It was time to leave.

Holding the doorknob with a washcloth, he looked back at the suite one last time, not out of sentiment, but because he had left evidence here that he could not destroy. Inside the body on the bed. Inside Eve. It might be possible to destroy that evidence, he supposed, or at least corrupt it (an image of a maid's cleaning cart came into his mind), but he was not up to that task. The best he could manage was hanging a DO NOT DISTURB sign on the outer doorknob.

Standing frozen in the hallway with his umbrella, he saw his journey to the first floor as fraught with peril. The hallway. The elevator. The mezzanine. The staircase. The lobby. The security guard. For a moment he considered going back into the suite and trying to climb down the outer balconies to the parking lot, but that was ridiculous. They were slick with rain, and even if he didn't kill himself, anyone passing on the street below could easily see him climbing down.

Move! shouted a voice in his head. *Do you want to lose your wife and daughter? Do you want the remainder of your sex life to happen in Parchman Prison?*

He put out his right foot, halted, then began to walk briskly toward the elevators, his eyes watching the carpet. His mind was already two blocks away, at his car. *See it*, said the voice. *All you have to do is get your body to the place where your mind is already.* He opened his umbrella as soon as he reached the lobby, and used it to conceal his face from the security guard. When he hit the street, rain whipped him like a vengeful spirit, and thunder reverberated off the walls of the hotel, buffeting the air in his lungs. He clutched the umbrella close over his head and began to run.

chapter 11

A hotel maid discovered Eve Sumner's body just after noon. The news didn't travel quite as fast as the news of Danny Buckles's molestations at St. Stephens, but by 2:00 P.M., buzzing telephones and flying e-mail had informed most of the Natchez business community of her death. Shortly thereafter, Sybil came into Waters's office with a stunned expression on her face and told him that "that real estate lady, Eve something" had just been found dead in the Eola Hotel. Raped and murdered, her throat cut, said the rumor. This distortion helped Waters put on a show of shock, but when he asked Sybil for details he found she had none.

When she closed the door, Waters got up, walked out onto his balcony, and stared across the river at the Louisiana lowlands. His vision seemed unusually acute. Last night's rain had knocked the dust out of the air, and behind it came the cold telegram of approaching winter. In the bracing wind, his body felt numb, disconnected, as though his mind were trying to leave it behind as part of a survival strategy. A sense of inevitability permeated his consciousness, a dark conviction that during his presence in the hotel room last night, distant stars had shifted position, forever altering his fate, and that the millstones of the gods were aligning themselves to grind another mortal to powder.

His sense of time had fled him. During the two weeks of his affair with Eve, he'd had difficulty keeping track of the days, largely due to sleep deprivation. But when he returned home after fleeing the Eola, he'd had to stop the Land Cruiser at the head of the driveway and pick up the newspaper to learn what day it was. His last coherent memory was of Tuesday, but the top line of the paper said it was Thursday. He felt like a coma patient waking up to find himself in a different year than the one in which he'd had the accident that put him in the hospital. He had lost himself in a dream, and he had awakened to fear. Cold, nauseating, sphincter-twitching fear. All that he'd risked like so many plastic poker chips now filled his mind with heart-wrenching clarity.

Exactly what had happened last night, he was still unsure. He felt like the hapless senator in *The Godfather Part II* who went to bed with a laughing girl and woke up with a dead whore. Only in the real world there was no Tom Hagen standing by to make everything go back to the way it was before. In the real world, you were left alone with your horror and guilt, desperately needing to talk to another human being but afraid that any confession—even to a priest— could set you on a road that ended in the barred hell of Parchman Farm, strapped to a padded table while white-coated technicians helped you ride the needle down into the smothering dark.

Despite these anxieties, some part of Waters's brain continued to operate in survival mode, the way a soldier with a blown-off arm remains cogent enough to search for his bloody limb, then carry it back to the aid station with blank doll's eyes, instinct driving him forward long after his higher brain functions have shut down. Waters was pretty sure no one had seen him leave the hotel. The security guard was sleeping, and the raging thunderstorm had cleared the streets. As he ran across Main Street toward his car, he did see a distant figure down near the bluff, a man with an umbrella standing over a urinating dog, but he didn't think the man saw him. Even if he had, he would not have recognized Waters from so far.

As he drove home, he considered breaking into Eve's house to see whether she kept anything there that would incriminate him. There was a good chance that she did, but he had never been to her house before. If he was seen trying to get in, tonight of all nights, that would be the end for him, even if there was no evidence inside.

When he pulled into his driveway, he noticed the kitchen light on. It had not been on when he left the night before. Disquieted, he parked the Land Cruiser on the side of the house and walked around to the slave quarters. From there he could look across the patio at the rear windows of the main house. He did not see Lily moving around, and the master bedroom was still dark. He watched the windows for an hour. While he did, the events of the past two weeks played through his head like a surrealistic film, intercut with horrifying stills of Eve's lifeless body.

When the bedroom light clicked on, he went into the house and put on a pot of coffee, then walked back to the bedroom to check on Lily. She was using the bathroom. Standing by the partly open door, he asked how she'd slept.

"Not too well," she said in a tired voice. "What about you?"

He paused, waiting for some clue to what she had seen last night, if anything. None came. "I couldn't sleep again," he told her.

She said nothing.

"I'll get Ana up," he offered.

"Thanks."

He walked to the foot of the stairs and yelled for Annelise to roll out of bed, then went into the kitchen and began to make biscuits, bacon, and eggs. By the time Lily came out of the back of the house, Annelise was munching on a biscuit and watching the Disney Channel on the satellite.

Sitting in this Norman Rockwell illusion of normalcy, he was nearly overcome with regret. How could he have put this blessed, well-ordered universe at risk? Was he that perverse? Was the memory of Mallory Candler so powerful? Apparently so. But he was not so far gone that he did not see his duty as a father. To protect Lily and Annelise, he would have to construct an unbreakable alibi for last night. He needed to know exactly what Lily had seen last night, but he would have to wait until tonight for that information. Even if she had noticed him AWOL, she wouldn't bring it up in front of Annelise.

As domestic life unfolded around him, he contemplated grim realities. The stakes riding on his remaining free were incalculable. The EPA could rule against his company at any time, and all his assets could be seized. Lily might retain the house, but she would have no income. If Waters was sitting in prison for murder, he would be unable to generate any, and Lily wouldn't be able to earn more than thirty thousand dollars in the first year if she went back to accounting, *if* she could get a job in Natchez's declining economy. Waters had two million in life insurance, but unless he received the death penalty—and unless it was carried out with unprecedented speed—Lily wouldn't see that insurance money for decades. His wife and daughter could fall from the affluent middle class to poverty in a matter of weeks. As he passed Annelise jelly for her biscuit, he made a mental note to check the suicide clause in his life insurance policy, and also to see whether it would pay its death benefit if he should be executed by the state. That he had brought himself to a point where this kind of thinking was a necessity left him feeling hollowed out, like a man dying from a wasting disease.

Soon the whirlwind of getting Ana off to school with the proper books, her Coke money, and her ballet things was in full swing. Waters kissed Lily and his daughter, then went back to the master bedroom to "take a shower." When he heard the Acura roll down the drive toward State Street, he sat down on the bed and began to shake.

His next clear memory was of sitting at his office desk, looking down at a photograph of Mallory. Somehow he had cleaned himself up and driven downtown, but he could not remember doing it. He had to get himself together. If anything should bring him under suspicion—phone records, something inside Eve's house, a witness he knew nothing about—

he would not be able to fool the police for five minutes in this mental state. Of course, if he really came
under suspicion, he was lost anyway. The police
would sample the semen taken from Eve's corpse and
test that DNA against the DNA of any suspects. With
that evidence, nothing else would be required. In the
harsh light of hindsight, he cursed his squeamishness.
He should have steeled himself and found a maid's
cart with some powerful bottled cleaner, carried it
back to the room, and used it to contaminate or destroy that conclusive evidence. But of course he had
not. Such was the work of monsters, not men. And
yet . . . the thought was in him.

"Rock Man, are you okay?"

Waters looked up to see Cole's bulk bearing down
on him. He swept Mallory's photo into the portfolio
and dropped the portfolio into an open drawer.

"Why would I not be?"

"Sybil said she told you about Eve."

"She did. Sounds horrible."

His eyes alert to the slightest tic in Waters's face,
Cole walked back to the door and closed it, then came
and sat down opposite the desk.

"What's going on?" Waters asked.

Cole took a deep breath and sighed. "This is your
partner talking, John. We go way back, right? *Way*
back."

"Right."

"Were you with Eve last night?"

"Eve Sumner?" Waters didn't blink. "Hell no."

Cole nodded slowly. "You were home with Lily?"

"Of course."

"All night?"

Waters said nothing.

"Because, if you weren't," Cole went on, "if you were . . . alone, say. You were alone, and you thought that wouldn't look good to certain people? Well, Jenny went to sleep early last night. She took a pill. So I watched HBO and drank Wild Turkey for most of the night."

Waters's mouth had gone dry. "And?"

"I'm just letting you know, before it becomes any kind of *thing*, that if you needed to be with me last night for some reason . . . then you *were*. *Capisce?*"

Despite the pressure he was under, a preternatural calm settled over Waters. He had always had the gift, in dire circumstances, of seeing to the heart of things. It had saved his life more than once during the years that he studied volcanoes, and also with Mallory. As Cole sat watching him, his face a perfect expression of loyalty, Waters realized two things. First, Cole had offered him the alibi he needed, should he fall under suspicion for Eve's murder. If Cole swore that Waters had spent the night at his house, then the presence of Waters's semen in Eve's corpse could be explained. Yes, he'd had sex with her that day, but he had not been anywhere near the Eola Hotel that night. There would be a scandal. It might even end his marriage. But it would probably keep him out of prison, and he would then have a chance at salvaging his family. However—and this was the mother of all caveats—if he accepted Cole's offer and went with that alibi, he would be placing his life in his partner's hands. Cole would own him, now and forever.

"You've got that look," Cole said.

"What look?"

"That deep-shit look. Your cold face."

Waters had known Cole since he was four years

old. They'd experienced the frictions common to any friendship over time, magnified by the tensions of a business partnership, but Cole had never truly screwed him. Waters wasn't worried about outright betrayal. What worried him was weakness. Cole had vices. All men did, but Cole was exceptionally bad at resisting temptation. He drank, gambled, and chased women, and he was loose with money. In his youth he had been good about keeping his own counsel, but lately even that virtue had begun to erode.

"Let me help you, Rock," Cole said in a quiet voice. "Everybody needs a little help sometimes."

"I don't," Waters said, suddenly sure. "But I appreciate it."

He saw disappointment in his partner's eyes. It was human nature. When we feel weak, it comforts us to know that others share our vulnerabilities. But Waters could not afford to reveal his. Not to Cole. If he needed a confessor, he would have to choose very carefully.

"I need to get to work on that map," he said. "The one you were after me about last week."

Cole nodded but did not get up. "Be sure, Rock. Because once you take a fork in the trail, you can't always get back to the same spot. You know?"

"I'm good," Waters assured him. "No worries."

Cole looked far from convinced, but he heaved himself out of the chair and walked to the door. Before he went out, he turned and gave Waters a mock salute that seemed to say, "I did my best. You're on your own. Good luck." Then he went out.

The rest of the day passed in a disjointed sequence of detached, fuguelike states interrupted by mundane phone calls. At one point he buzzed Sybil to bring him the newspaper, then remembered that Eve's body had been discovered six hours after the paper hit the streets. There would be plenty of coverage tomorrow, though. Penn Cage's girlfriend had probably been working the story like a pit bull from the moment Eve's body was found. But he needed a faster source of information than tomorrow's paper. He needed to know what the police knew. Had any hotel guests heard screaming from room 324? Had anyone come forward with knowledge about Eve's recent activities? What kind of trace evidence had they taken from the scene?

His phone buzzed, and he snapped out of his reverie.

"Your wife on line one," Sybil informed him.

"I've got it." He hit the button. "Hey, Lil."

"Have you heard about Eve Sumner?"

"I heard."

"Isn't it just unbelievable?"

No. . . . "It is."

The open line hissed in his right ear.

"John, I've been thinking."

He waited.

"The rumor is, Eve was meeting someone at the hotel, and whoever it was killed her."

"I haven't heard that."

"Oh, you know she was. Having an affair, I mean. That was what Eve did. She couldn't find the love she needed, so she just kept looking. And ever since I heard about it, all I can think about is us."

"Us? Why?"

"Because . . . I know you were gone last night."

His chest tightened so suddenly that he found it hard to breathe.

"I know you were probably just taking a ride like you do sometimes. But think if you had been doing something. I couldn't blame you if you were. Not with the way things have been between us. And what happened to Eve . . . that kind of thing could happen to anybody. When you're desperate, and you go looking in the wrong places for something you should have at home—"

"Lily, don't," he said, surprised by the hysteria in her voice.

She sobbed, then choked it back. "I'm so *stupid*. It makes me so angry to know something is wrong with me and not be able to change it. I know I've said that before, but now . . . I just have to, John. I have to change. Life's too short."

Why hadn't Lily said these things two weeks ago? Maybe he could have resisted Eve's siren song. "It's all right, babe. Everything's okay."

"No, it's not. And I want to stop pretending that it is. I don't want to lose you, John."

And I don't want to lose you and Annelise. "We'll talk about it when I get home. Why don't you go for a swim? That always helps you feel better."

"I might. Are you coming straight home after work?"

"I think so."

"Good." She paused, but he sensed that she wanted to say more. "I want to put Annelise to bed early tonight," she added. "And I . . . I want to make love with you. The way I used to."

"Lily—"

"I love you, John."

"I love you too."

After a few moments, she hung up, and he set the phone in its cradle.

Her call almost pushed him into a manic state. How could things unfold this way? How could the death of a near-stranger change his wife's attitude about sex when all his most patient efforts could not? And how could that stranger be the woman he had turned to for succor in his need? He felt trapped in some crazy Greek tragedy where only the Fates and Furies knew their roles well enough to carry them off.

He wanted to leave the office, but for appearance's sake, he felt he should stick it out until five. He soon found himself pondering morbid ironies, like the fact that Eve's body almost certainly now lay on the same embalming table that Mallory's had lain upon ten years ago. Natchez had come a long way in race relations, but it was still segregated in death. If you died white in this town, or were to be buried here, there was only one funeral home to go to. Of course, her body might not be there yet. There would have to be an autopsy. He had no idea where that would be carried out. Would a Natchez pathologist do it? Or would the body be shipped to the state capital, Jackson?

What would the autopsy reveal? Was he right about strangulation? Or was there some other possibility? He had seen marks on her throat and petechiae around her eyes. But what if those marks had been made during the last minutes of their lovemaking, when he held her down on the mattress? What if something else had killed her? A heart attack? Or a stroke? Natchez was a small town, and Waters knew two women in their forties who had died of strokes in the past few years. Lily thought it had something to do with birth control pills. Eve wasn't on the pill. She'd had her tubes tied. She was also in her early thirties. On the other hand, she'd led a wild life. Who knew what was possible? Eve might have been taking drugs the whole time he'd known her, which was only two weeks, after all. Cocaine caused heart attacks all the time. Strange as it seemed, these thoughts lifted his spirits. The alternative was to face the fact that he had strangled a woman for whom he had cared a great deal.

He went to a small refrigerator under his wet bar and took out a bottle of water, then returned to his desk. That brief activity exhausted him. He was puzzled until he remembered that he hadn't slept last night. Laying his head on the desk, he tried to resist the worries that had been eating at him all day.

"John? Hey, John!"

Waters started and looked up into Sybil's concerned face.

"What is it? What's the matter?"

"It's five-thirty. Do you want me to stay?"

He looked at his watch. He'd slept for two hours. "No, no. You go home. I'm sorry. Is Cole still here?"

"No, he left around four. He didn't say where he was going."

Sybil sounded put out by this, but it could have been Waters's imagination. "Let's shut it down and go home," he said. "I want to see my daughter."

Sybil smiled, but her eyes were sad. "Ana's a lucky little girl. One day she'll know that."

I hope she stays lucky, he thought.

*   *   *

Turning into his drive, Waters stopped at the mailbox from habit. Junk mail and a couple of party invitations were stuffed between copies of the *U.S. Geological Review* and *USA Today*. As he laid the mail on the passenger seat, a four-door diesel pickup pulled in behind him. Its sudden appearance startled him, but when a leather-faced man of sixty got out, Waters calmed down and got out to shake hands.

Will Hinson was a well-checker. He monitored the daily operations of oil wells all over the county for a monthly fee. Though he checked about a dozen Smith-Waters wells, most communication was handled by telephone.

"How do, John?" Hinson said.

"Fine, Will. How're you doing?"

"Not bad. Don't want to bother you, but I saw you pull in."

"I'm glad you stopped. Everything going okay?"

"Oh, fair. Always something to fix, but you know. You get the bills for it. Reason I stopped, I saw 'em hauling off the pumping unit at your Madam X well."

Waters blinked in confusion. "You what?"

"I thought you might be replacing it, but then I remembered it was a three-twenty. Didn't figure you wanted to push any more fluid than that."

Waters wondered if Hinson was getting what Rose called "old-timer's disease." "Are you sure this was on our lease?"

"Yessir. I don't check that well, but I stopped and asked the crew what they thought they was doing. They said you boys had sold the unit to a Texas outfit. That's where that rig's bound right now. Oil City, Texas."

This news was shocking enough to bring Waters

out of his haze. "I'd better make some calls. Somebody made a mistake somewhere."

The older man nodded, but it was clear he had more to say.

"What is it, Will?"

"It was me? I'd call my partner first."

Waters went still. "Tell me what you know."

"I'm not one to talk behind anybody's back. But you're a pretty trusting fella, John. Just like your dad."

"Come on. Out with it."

"Word is, your boy Cole's in a bind. A bad one. I heard all kinds of things he's trying, but I don't know what's true, so I ain't repeatin' nothing. But you better look to your business. People get in money trouble, they do things they might not normally do. Like selling a pumping unit out from under a partner when they need cash."

Waters nodded slowly, not believing his ears. "I appreciate you stopping, Will."

"I hope I did the right thing."

"You did. You take it easy, now."

"Nope. I never do. I'll die in the saddle. Only way to go."

They shook hands again, and the older man got into his truck and backed out of the driveway. Waters climbed into his Land Cruiser and drove slowly up to the house. The unreality of his situation was growing by the minute. The Madam X well was currently down, and due for a workover in two weeks. Cole was in charge of that. If someone like Will Hinson had not stopped out of the blue, Waters might not have known the pumping unit was gone for three weeks or more. Maybe longer, if Cole planned to lie about production runs. A used 320 pumping unit would bring about thirty thousand dollars on the open market. Would Cole betray his trust for thirty thousand dollars? He didn't want to think so. But . . . how much trouble was Cole really in?

When he opened the front door of the house, his exhausted mind and body told him to go straight to bed. That wasn't an option tonight. He walked into the kitchen and hugged Lily, who looked like she would have broken into tears, were not Annelise sitting at the table doing her homework.

"Sit down," she said. "Supper's ready."

He sat, and she brought him a plate of shrimp and pasta that Rose had cooked during the afternoon. He had no appetite, but he made a show of picking at his food. His mind was on Cole and the pumping unit. After serving Annelise, Lily laid her hands on his shoulders and massaged them as Ana told a story about a new music program at school. When Ana finished, Lily got a plate for herself and sat opposite Waters. As she ate, she watched her husband and daughter as though she had never really seen them before. Under the circumstances, it made him uncomfortable.

Waters had a feeling that something about her had changed. It wasn't her hair, which was the same dark blond it had always been and still fell to her shoulders. She might have on a touch more makeup, but not enough to give him an odd feeling.

"You look different," he said.

"I ran today. Maybe that's it."

"You ran?"

"Mom, that's cool," Ana said. "I want to go next time."

Lily had been a long-distance runner in high

school. As a tenth-grader she'd won the state championship in the two-mile run. She had kept up her running well into their marriage, staying almost obsessively in shape. But after the first miscarriage, she couldn't seem to find the energy to get outside. She gained weight, and that intensified her depression. Today was probably the first time in four years that she had "hit the road," as she used to call it.

"I'm tired of being fat," Lily said.

"You're not fat, Mom."

"Definitely not," Waters agreed, though he knew that by Lily's once rigid standards, she was overweight. She probably weighed a hundred and thirty-five or forty now; in the old days that would have driven her crazy.

"Just three miles," Lily said. "Seven-minute miles, at that. Embarrassing, but it's a start. In a week I want to be down to six minutes."

"Don't overdo it, babe. You haven't run in a long time."

She nodded thoughtfully. "I haven't done a lot of things for a long time."

Waters smiled, but he was worried. Changes this sudden could signal deep discord. "Anything else happen at home today?"

Lily shook her head. "Oh, Tom Jackson called a little while ago. The detective. He wants you to call him."

Waters's throat constricted. "Did he say what it was about?"

"Rose talked to him. Just the same old thing, I'm sure." She cut her eyes at Annelise, who was looking at her plate. *Probably the Danny Buckles business*, she was telling him.

Jackson had called a couple of times over the past two weeks to keep Waters abreast of the Buckles prosecution, but that was pretty much on track. This might be something else. Like Eve Sumner's murder. Tom Jackson worked all homicides for the Natchez Police Department.

"I'd better call Tom before it gets late."

Lily gave him a soft look. "Why don't you wait until tomorrow? I don't want to think about that stuff right now, and I don't want you to either."

"What stuff?" asked Annelise, looking up.

"Taxes," Lily replied, which was their catchall euphemism for anything Ana didn't need to hear about.

"Oh. Do you know what Fletcher did today? You won't *believe* it."

Waters tried to clear his mind to listen to the story of a playground standoff, but a hundred thoughts nibbled like fish at the edges of his consciousness. As he tried to hide his anxiety from his daughter, he felt Lily's foot touch his ankle beneath the table. She had removed her shoe, and was now rubbing his calf with her toe. She never did this kind of thing. He didn't know how to respond. When Ana finished her story, he got up and rinsed his plate.

"You want to watch some TV together?" he asked Annelise. "I got a new DVD from Amazon yesterday."

"What is it?"

"The Princess Diaries."

Annelise jumped up, grabbed his arm, and dragged him toward the den. While Waters started the movie, he heard Lily cleaning up the kitchen. Normally, she would now retire to her alcove or go to work on a project around the house: stripping paint, making curtains, whatever. But tonight she came into the den, sat beside him on the sofa, and halfway through the film intertwined her hand in his. Her obvious intention to make good on her promise of the afternoon surprised and worried him. His experience in the Eola was still fresh in his mind, and he didn't want any flashbacks while he made love to his wife.

As the movie wore on, he felt himself zoning out, his mind on Tom Jackson's phone call. Lily went upstairs and got Annelise's pajamas, and Ana changed while they watched the conclusion. When the credits rolled, Waters snapped out of his trance and carried Annelise upstairs, Lily close behind him. They tucked her in beside her stuffed rabbit, Albert, then walked back down, Lily in front. Reversing their usual ritual, she waited at the foot of the stairs, and when he reached the bottom step, she reached out and pulled him to her. He tried not to stiffen, but given the stress he was under, it was all he could do to remain still.

"Hug me like you mean it, John."

He tightened his arms around her.

"That's better."

She pulled him off the step and climbed up onto it herself, putting them eye to eye. Then she kissed him on the mouth. Her lips were closed, but just as he expected her to pull away, she brushed her tongue against his teeth. He froze in surprise. Her tongue pressed insistently until he opened his mouth. She slipped it inside, then took his hand and placed it over her breast.

Moments like these were painfully awkward for him. He still remembered the first time she had come to him after losing the baby. She was sleeping fifteen hours a day, eating nothing. He sensed a fearsome anger buried under her depression, but she held it in, the way a bed-wetting child threatened with a beating holds his urine. Clenching, repressing, paralyzed by fear. Waters had gently broached the subject of adoption and earned himself a white-knuckled dinner without a word. Four months had passed without any sex at all. Yet Lily was not blind to his suffering. One day, without telling him, she dropped Annelise off at her parents' house for the night. Then she followed the old psychological map she had laid out years ago, the one that relaxed her enough to respond fully. She locked the doors, washed the dishes, paid the household bills, fed the cat, turned off the phones. He almost wept when he saw her standing by the bed removing her gown. The first few minutes went well enough, but at the moment of penetration, Lily snapped back to that ultrasound room, and her body went as rigid as that of a catatonic, her eyes draining tears. Waters got off her as fast as he could and gave her the sedative her doctor had prescribed.

Months passed before she tried again. But gradually, when she sensed Waters grinding his teeth from animal frustration, she would roll over in the dark and use her hands on him, or pull him onto her for a quick mechanical release, during which her face remained painfully tight, her eyes glassy. Sex performed out of duty was almost worse than no sex at all, but how could he tell her that? Occasionally the quality of those experiences improved slightly, but never did they last more than a few minutes, and afterward Lily always looked like a lost and embittered child.

Tonight's kiss at the foot of the stairs, her placing his hand over her breast: these were not part of her repertoire of marital duty. If it had been any night other than this one, he would have been filled with joy.

"Lily—"

She put a finger to his lips. "Shhh."

"I don't really need to right now."

"It's not for you," she said. "For me." She pressed his hand hard against her breast, and he was shocked to feel her nipple stiffen.

"Are you serious?"

She nodded. "Let's don't talk about it, okay? Let's just do it." She took his wrist and pulled him toward the master bedroom.

By the time they reached the door, she had undone her blouse and pants enough to slip out of them in seconds. She turned and knelt before him, undid his belt, and roughly pulled down his khakis. Then she slid down the comforter and pulled him into bed.

"Lily?" He took hold of her shoulders. "What's going on? What's changed?"

"I don't know." Urgency filled her eyes. "I just want you. I know I can feel good right now. Let's don't talk anymore."

She kissed him again, deeply this time. He felt trapped in a dream, his movements clumsy and unreal. Instinct told him to get the act over with quickly, lest he do something to trigger one of Lily's depressive episodes. He slid gently over on top of her, but when he moved to kiss her mouth, she pushed down on his shoulders, something she had not done for years.

"Down there," she whispered. "Hurry."

He closed his eyes, then slid down her belly, kissing as he went. She responded forcefully, startling him with her moans. He had not heard such sounds from her in so long that he felt he was with a stranger. On the verge of climax, Lily dug her nails into his shoulders and pulled him up to her mouth. He kissed her and went inside, stunned by the intensity of his own arousal. The woman beneath him now he had thought gone forever. It was as though four years of self-imposed deprivation were being exorcised in minutes. Her face was flushed, her skin blotchy and covered with perspiration, her breaths quick and labored. As he shut his eyes and went with her movements, her cries became so loud that he put his hand over her mouth. The last time sounds like that had come from this room, Annelise was four years old. She would panic if she heard them now.

Suddenly Lily locked her legs around him and screamed, her cry breaking through his fingers, her arms locking around his neck, cutting off his air. Still he pressed down with his back muscles, trying to intensify her climax if he could. Dimly, he realized that he could not breathe, but that was a small price to pay for the emotional transformation he was witnessing. Mallory used to let her head hang off the bed to deprive her brain of oxygen during orgasm. Something similar was happening to him now. He was torn between jerking his head free of Lily's grasp or remaining still while she finished. In seconds, his will no longer mattered. He began to peak with her, and her arm came loose from his neck, flooding his brain with oxygen.

"Jesus," he gasped, rolling off of her. "Lily . . ."

"I know," she panted. "It's been so long. I honestly forgot what that felt like."

She started to speak again, but her words disappeared into a sob. Turning, he saw her cover her face with her hands. Tears ran from beneath them.

"I'm so sorry . . . I don't know why I've been like I have."

"It doesn't matter, Lily. Don't think about it. You just broke through a wall. Let your feelings out and try to sleep. Thinking doesn't help with things like this."

She reached out and took his hand. "I'm so glad I haven't lost you."

"Don't worry," he said softly. "You don't have to worry about that."

From nowhere, the specter of Tom Jackson rose in his mind. What could the detective want with him? Waters felt a sudden compulsion to go out to the slave quarters and get a zero-gauge Rapidograph in his hand. Make a list. Do an analysis of his situation. Vulnerabilities. Options. Possible solutions. He'd have to burn it after he made it, of course.

And what about Cole? The pumping unit? Should he drive over to his partner's house and confront him? Or make a few discreet calls and try to discover if the rumors Will Hinson had mentioned were true? When Lily's breathing deepened, he started to slide out of the bed, but she caught him by the arm.

"Don't go," she said sleepily. "Stay with me."

"I need to brush my teeth. And call Tom Jack—"

"No. No worrying about anything tonight. Stay close to me. I feel so good right now."

He sighed and lay back down, so hyperalert that he felt like running three miles himself. Lily's breathing continued to deepen, but her hand did not release his arm. As he lay there, anxiety building to a crescendo in his chest, he heard the den phone ring. If the volume was up on the machine, he could sometimes hear

the outgoing and incoming messages from the bedroom.

"You've reached the Waters house," said Lily's
perky recorded voice. "Leave a message at the beep,
and we'll call you back as soon as we can."

The machine beeped.

"John? Tom Jackson here. I hate to bother you at
home, but I'm trying to run down some leads in this
Eve Sumner mess. Just routine stuff, really, but I need
to talk to you when you get a minute. Thanks, bud.
See you."

This Eve Sumner mess? Waters felt sweat beading on
his brow. If it were really routine, why would Jackson
be calling after ten at night? And why the hell would
he be calling John Waters, unless the police had found
something incriminating? Evidence Waters knew
nothing about. Something from Eve's house, for example. A scrap of paper. A photograph. God only
knew what she had kept there. Or maybe someone had
told them something. A witness Waters hadn't seen.
Someone drinking in one of the bars near the Eola. Or
the man holding the umbrella over the pissing dog. It
could be anyone. Anything. A million variables came
into play when you started leading a secret life. The
things you feared most were often no threat at all,
while those you never thought about could tip the
balance and bring your life crashing around your
ears.

"*Shit,*" he whispered, listening to Lily's steady
breathing. "I need help."

chapter 12

"And when I woke up," Waters said, "Eve was dead."

Penn Cage did not speak or even blink. He looked exactly like what he was, a former lawyer who had heard almost everything in his time.

"And now Detective Tom Jackson is trying to reach me," Waters added. "He says it's about Eve, but that it's routine. That's all I know."

"Do you think you killed her?" Penn asked.

"I don't know. I honestly don't think I did, but as far as I know there was no one else in the room."

Penn sighed and focused somewhere in the middle distance. Waters had made his choice of confessor in the depths of the night, after long reflection. He had no desire to talk to a psychiatrist. For one thing he didn't know any. For another, a shrink couldn't give him legal advice. He had known Penn Cage since he was a child, and though Penn no longer practiced law, he had served for years as a prosecutor in Houston,

Texas, where he'd sent more than a dozen killers to death row. Penn Cage knew about murder.

He also knew about human frailty. After writing several successful legal thrillers, he had given up the law. Then his wife died of cancer, and his writing stalled. When he returned to Natchez with his young daughter to try to make sense of his life, a widow's emotional appeal had caught him up in an old civil rights murder. Penn had ultimately turned those experiences into a novel called *The Quiet Game*, the book that the Hollywood producers staying in Bienville this week had come to Natchez to explore filming.

Some people might see Penn as a straight arrow, but those same people probably saw Waters as one too. Waters had read *The Quiet Game* very closely, and it was clear to him that its author was haunted by the past in a way not unlike the way he was haunted. This, combined with their childhood friendship, had finally convinced him that Penn Cage was the best possible confidant under the circumstances.

When he arrived at Penn's home that morning, a stately town house on Washington Street, a maid had shown him to a spacious office at the back of the ground floor. Penn seemed pleased by the surprise visit, but he resisted any talk of legal representation.

"John, you know I don't practice law anymore."

"You took the Del Payton case," Waters pointed out. On the bookshelves behind Cage, he saw studies of criminology and law, but also an extensive collection of psychology and philosophy.

"That was different. I was essentially defending myself."

"Penn, I need help."

"Is it the EPA thing?"

"Compared to why I'm here, the EPA investigation is nothing."

"Something that could wipe you out financially is nothing?"

"Yes. You don't have to represent me. I just need the benefit of your experience. And I need . . ."

"What?"

"Your confidentiality. And to absolutely ensure that, I need to hire you."

"I could take that as an insult."

"Please don't. If you're put on the stand one day and asked questions about me, I don't want you to be held in contempt for trying to protect me. You can plead client privilege."

"Jesus, John. What the hell have you got into?"

"Real trouble."

A deep stillness settled over Cage. "Give me a dollar."

Waters took out his wallet and slid a bill across the desk. Penn took it and slipped it into a drawer.

"Talk to me."

Waters began at the soccer field and went on from there. The Dunleith party, Eve's warning about danger at the school, the kiss at the cemetery, the matching handwriting, all of it, omitting nothing. Penn listened with absolute concentration, rarely interrupting except to ask for clarification. *And you told Cole about this? She actually stated that she was Mallory Candler?* Waters concluded with his blackout and waking up to find Eve dead, but the expression of shock he expected did not come.

"And you don't remember strangling her," Penn said.

"No."

"Not even as erotic play?"

"No."

"You say you passed out during your orgasm?"

"As best I remember."

"Had you ever done that before?"

"Never."

"Were you taking drugs of any kind? Cocaine? Amyl nitrate? X?"

"X?"

"Ecstasy. MDMA."

"God, no."

"This isn't the time to hold anything back, John."

"No drugs."

"Not even a prescription drug?"

"No."

"Was Eve using cocaine? Any other drugs?"

"I have no idea. I never saw any."

"But you drank some wine."

"One long swallow. Half a glass, maybe."

"There could have been something in the wine."

"I suppose so. But I never felt drugged with her before. What do you think?"

Penn moved back in his chair and picked up a blue Nerf basketball from the floor. "I don't know yet. I'm processing what you've told me. Obviously, you could be in very serious trouble soon."

"I wouldn't be here otherwise."

"This is why you asked me about Lynne Merrill. Whether you ever get over a relationship like that. You were talking about Mallory."

"Yes."

"She was only a year ahead of me at St. Stephens. I thought I knew a fair bit about her. I see now that I didn't. I didn't see much of her at Ole Miss. Obviously, you did."

Waters nodded.

"John, you've referred to Mallory's psychosis, to terrible things that happened, evil things she did. But you haven't said what those things were. You did say that Eve had started to display the kind of behavior Mallory did when she started to lose her mind."

"She did."

"Then you had better tell me about Mallory. What started her slide into madness, as you called it?"

Waters looked to his left, where a large window gave a view of the backyard. There was a nice play set made of treated lumber; he'd built one like it for Annelise. "I don't know if that's possible, Penn. I mean we're two guys sitting here in the light of day, twenty years after the fact. I'm not sure I can communicate the reality of what went on then. Not with the impact that it had."

Penn smiled. "I'm a writer. I wrestle with that every day. If words could convey human emotion with sufficient force, we wouldn't need to shed tears, hug, or kill someone. Because I know that, I listen in a different way than most people."

Waters felt encouraged, but still he hesitated. "When I graduated from South Natchez, I weighed one hundred eighty-five pounds. During my freshman year at Ole Miss, I gained another fifteen. After one year with Mallory, I weighed one hundred sixty-five. I looked like a skeleton."

"I'm going to ask some questions," Penn said, "but don't feel bound to answer them in a narrow way. Say whatever comes to mind."

"Okay."

"If you had to give me one word that summed up the root of Mallory's mental problems, what would it be?"

"Jealousy."

"Elaborate."

"Mallory was pathologically jealous. You wouldn't think she would be, as beautiful as she was, but that didn't seem to matter where I was concerned."

"Was she jealous in her previous relationships?"

"I don't know. She only slept with two guys before me. One was a football player from St. Stephens, older than she was."

"Wade Anders, probably. I remember them dating for a while. He was an asshole."

"Then she was with a guy at Ole Miss, before I really knew her. Her freshman year. When I asked who it was, she told me he was older and already gone. I assumed she meant he was a senior who had graduated. I was curious, because she told me they'd done a lot of sexual experimentation. And I believed her, because there was nothing she didn't know or do."

"And?"

"I found out later that the older guy had been an English professor, thirty-eight years old. He lost his job over it. Resigned or was fired, I'm not sure which. He basically flipped out when Mallory dumped him. He stalked her, the whole nine yards. I also later learned she was lying about the sex. They hadn't done all that experimentation. She'd got him to tell her all the exotic things he wanted to do to her, and what he wanted her to do for him, but she didn't *do* those things with him. She basically tortured the guy, I think."

"But she did those things with you."

"Yes. And that's where the problem began. I was the first person she ever really took off her mask for. She gave herself to me totally. Showed me the darkest corners of her personality . . . and there were some dark ones. And once you do that with somebody, and they reject you . . ."

"What happens?" asked Penn.

An image of Mallory's face, desolate and cold, filled Waters's mind. "I once saw an Oprah show where these distraught parents were talking about their college kids, kids who couldn't get over a romantic relationship. Some had committed suicide, others simply couldn't move forward with their lives. Their parents couldn't help or even reach them. And they couldn't understand why parental love couldn't alleviate some of the suffering of these kids. These are healthy families I'm talking about."

"That made you think of Mallory?"

"Some of those parents were describing Mallory perfectly. But I already knew the answer they couldn't seem to see. Not even the shrink on the show. When a young woman gives herself completely to a man—sexually and every other way—she shows him parts of her personality that her parents have never seen and never will. The guy knows everything about her, things she may have seen as shameful for her whole life, but he loves her in spite of these things. Or maybe because of them. But if he then *leaves* her, if he stops loving her, the rejection is absolute. You know? There's no way parental love can console the girl, because *her parents don't really know her.* 'If they really knew me like he does,' she thinks, 'they wouldn't love me either.' That's what takes her to the brink of suicide."

Penn seemed intrigued by this theory. "And you rejected Mallory?"

"Yes."

"Tell me what happened."

"She got pregnant."

"When?"

"My sophomore year. She was a junior."

"How long had you been together?"

"Six months."

"She terminated the pregnancy?"

Waters nodded.

"Jackson? Memphis?"

"Memphis."

"Did she want the abortion?"

"I don't think any woman really wants an abortion."

"Point taken. But she agreed to its necessity?"

"She went through with it."

Penn mulled this over. "You talked her into it."

"I don't like thinking about it, and maybe I didn't admit it to myself for a long time. But yes, I basically made her do it."

Penn nodded with understanding, if not sympathy. "You went with her for the procedure? Stayed through it, before and after, all that?"

"Yes."

"Tell me about it. What do you remember most?"

Waters didn't have to think. "You couldn't just go get it and be done. You had to go for counseling first. This huge impersonal building on Union Avenue, like an office building. The waiting room was full of girls. We could hear them talking. Some were there for second or third abortions. We couldn't believe it. We felt so stupid for letting ourselves get into that situation even *once*. These women were talking like it was an alternative form of birth control. Mallory felt sleazy just being there. She hated it."

"Go on."

"They show us into this room with an older woman in a wheelchair. She starts questioning us. Why were we having sex? Did we understand the implications of having sex? It was surreal. Then she starts asking why we want to abort the baby. Why can't we get married and have it?"

"Is that what Mallory wanted?"

"Penn, do you remember what Ole Miss was like when we were there?"

"Sure. Reagan in the White House. Young Republicans on campus. Conformity was the school religion. The de rigueur uniform was Izod shirt, Levi's rolled at the ankles, and white canvas Nikes with the baby-blue stripe. I think of the early eighties at Ole Miss as a sort of superrich version of the nineteen-fifties."

"Exactly. We grew up in the seventies, with dope and sex and rock and roll, but all the old double standards were still very much in force in Oxford. Especially for the girls. The good-girl/slut dichotomy still applied."

"Sorority girls didn't have babies and stay in school."

"No," Waters agreed. "Not Chi Os anyway."

"Did Mallory want the baby, but know deep down that she couldn't keep it?"

"That's pretty close, I think. I don't think she could have handled disappointing her parents to that de-

gree, even though she hated her father at some level.
But she wanted *me* to want the baby. You know?"

"Yes."

"So the counselor starts in on adoption. Mallory
didn't want to do that, and neither did I. We couldn't
deal with the idea that part of us would exist in the
world, and we wouldn't know where. I'm sure that's
a callous, selfish way to think, but that was the only
thing we agreed on."

"And after the counseling?"

"They made you wait seven days to have the procedure. Agonizing reappraisal time. Those seven days
were hell. Mallory stopped going to class. Her face
showed nothing, but she was barely keeping it together. One day she wanted the abortion, the next she
wanted us to run off to Canada, have the baby, and
live like Bohemians."

"Why did she finally agree to the procedure?"

Waters looked back at the window, wishing he did
not have to speak this truth. "I made a devil's bargain.
She made me promise her—in the dark of the night,
parked on Sorority Row—she made me promise that
if she got rid of that baby, I would never leave her.
Ever. And she meant it."

"And you promised that?"

"Yes."

Penn sighed heavily. "Go on."

"A week later, we were back in Memphis. Mallory
was so tense, I didn't think she could handle it. This
was all supposed to be secret, right? But when she
checked in, they asked for her parents' phone numbers, everything. They said if anything went wrong, if
she started to hemorrhage or something, they had to
notify next of kin." Waters could still smell the hotel-

like scent of the place. "Mallory gave the numbers. They checked her in and told me it would be a minimum of two hours before I saw her again."

"What did you do?"

"I tried to sit in that waiting room, this sterile room full of women—only two guys there besides me—and I started to lose it. I couldn't believe I was there, or what was about to happen to Mallory. I got into the elevator, rode down ten floors to the ground, and walked out into the daylight. That's when I first realized that terrible things happened in the light of day. That things like the Holocaust happened while the sun was shining and people were having picnics. Anyway, there was a Burger King outside this building. I walked over there and ordered a cheeseburger, then sat there without eating it. I knew what Mallory was going through up there—the counselor had made sure of that—and I felt sick. I was growing up, I guess, learning that actions have real consequences."

Penn listened like a patient priest, his eyes alert for the smallest clues to motivation. "Go on."

"I was positive something terrible was going to happen. She was going to start hemorrhaging, maybe even die. There was this awful certainty in my gut that things were going to go very wrong."

"Did they?"

"Not that day. When she came out, she was like a zombie. Literally in shock. The next day, she did start to hemorrhage. I took her to the ER in Oxford. They gave her six birth control pills, and it stopped the bleeding, but the whole experience was more than she could take. Everything went downhill from there."

"How?"

"She was just never the same after that. But she

didn't react the way you would expect. I mean, when my wife lost a baby, she lost her sexual desire. But Mallory was the reverse. She became sexually ravenous. She constantly pushed the envelope, as though she were trying to use sex to banish whatever demons were in her head. She'd always been a little like that, but now it was scary. Do this to me. Do that. Hurt me. Rape me. Things I thought were demeaning, and I'm no prude when it comes to sex."

Penn was nodding slowly. "And Eve resurrected some of this. What other changes did you notice?"

"Paranoia. She didn't want me apart from her. If I left her for a few hours—even to go to class—she interrogated me endlessly. When I registered for the next semester, she asked who was in all my classes. She told me I couldn't take two that I wanted, because of girls she knew who were going to be in them."

"Did she ever get violent?"

"Yes. I'm talking clock you with a closed fist, and she was a strong girl. She'd try to claw my eyes out. The subtext of it all was, 'You don't really love me. You're going to leave me the first chance you get.' And this was the most beautiful woman in the state."

"Her fear became a self-fulfilling prophecy, of course. When did the violence start?"

"Toward me? After the abortion. I don't think I understood how deeply the maternal desire is embedded in the female psyche. Even in women you might think wouldn't feel it so much—gung ho career women—it's there. And in Mallory . . . I think terminating that pregnancy so violated her fundamental nature that it snapped something in her mind. She *loathed* herself for doing it. And she projected that hatred onto me."

"I think you're right. And obviously, you couldn't stand that kind of pressure for long."

"No. That's when I lost all the weight. My grades went to hell. I felt like I was holding Mallory's mind together by sheer force of will. I started talking to a girl in one of my classes, just from a desire for simple contact. It was such a relief, talking to a normal person. It was like coming out of a cave. And I knew then that I had to end it with Mallory."

"Is this when she became suicidal?"

"How did you know she attempted suicide?"

"When I asked about the violence, you said, 'Toward me?' That told me she'd probably done violence to herself."

"She tried with pills first," Waters told him. "In my apartment, so I was almost certain to find her when I got back from class. I carried her to the ER again, and they pumped her stomach. That scared the shit out of me."

"Which was exactly what she wanted."

"Yes, but it didn't stop me. She was smothering me. I had to get free. I don't clearly remember the sequence of events after that, but the fights became unendurable. One night, she tried to run me over with my car. I jumped off a fifteen-foot embankment to avoid being hit."

"Do you really think she would have hit you?"

"Absolutely. Looking back, I don't think she would ever have killed her*self*. Deep down, she was too selfish for that. But me? No doubt about it. The same goes for any woman I was with. Mallory could have killed any of them under the right circumstances."

"You sound like you have evidence of that."

"I do." Waters looked at his watch. "Jesus, I've

talked for over an hour and I haven't told you anything yet. She tried to kill me twice, herself four or
five times. She attacked a girl I was riding in the car
with in Jackson. She almost killed a girlfriend of mine
in Alaska, and that was the year she won Miss Mississippi. She even got pregnant again, on purpose." Waters heard hysteria in his voice, but he couldn't seem
to control it. "All this is so mixed up in my mind . . .
her insanity, the secrets I've kept, the things Eve
said—"

"John?" Penn dropped the foam basketball and
came around the desk and squatted by Waters's chair.
"Hey. Take it easy." Penn waited a moment. "I have a
theory. But you haven't told me enough yet to be sure
about it. I need to know everything you know, and
now's the time for you to tell me. After today, we
could be talking to each other at the jail."

His casual mention of this reality shook Waters to
the core of his being.

"I don't think that will happen," Penn went on,
"but we have to be realistic. The odds of carrying on
an affair like you and Eve did without anyone knowing about it are very small. Even if it only lasted two
weeks. Someone always knows. Lovers confide in
friends. Neighbors are nosy. It's almost inevitable."

"So what do I do?"

Penn got up and went back to his seat. "I need you
to give me the basics of the other stuff you mentioned.
You said Mallory tried to kill you again after the time
with the car?"

"Yes."

"Tell me about that."

"I had a hunting rifle in my apartment, a Winches-
ter thirty-thirty. During one of her 'You're going to

leave me' fits, she got hold of it and threatened to kill herself. I figured the best thing to do was walk out of the room. Remove her audience, you know? She ran after me, held the barrel below her chin, and got her finger inside the trigger guard. I was more worried about her killing herself by accident than by design, so I grabbed the barrel and we fought for the gun. She screamed that she'd kill me if I didn't let her kill herself. I let go and yelled, 'Go on and do it, then!' She stuck the barrel under her chin and went for the trigger. I grabbed the rifle again, and this time it wound up jammed into my side. I saw something happen in her eyes, a kind of crazy triumph, and then she yanked the trigger. I felt that pull all the way into my bones."

"It wasn't loaded?"

"It *was* loaded. The lever had gotten half cocked in the struggle, so when she pulled the trigger, the action wouldn't operate. That's the only time I ever hit her. When I realized she'd meant to kill me, I backhanded her across the face. She laughed. She *wanted* me to hit her." Waters's mouth was dry. "God, it was so twisted by then."

"What about the thing in Alaska?" Penn asked. "She almost killed a girl?"

"You remember I worked the pipeline in the summers. I had a French-Canadian girlfriend named Marie. Mallory flew up and followed us for a few days before I even knew she was there. She put sugar in Marie's gas tank and stranded her in a blizzard. It was a miracle she was saved. Mallory barely got out of the state without being arrested. Alaska tried to extradite her, but her father pulled some juice in Jackson and got that quashed."

"Jesus. And you said Mallory got pregnant a second time. Was that by you?"

"Yes."

"Before or after she was Miss Mississippi?"

"Just after she gave up the crown."

Penn shook his head in amazement. "God, the things that stay hidden in small towns. The women in Natchez would snap their garters if they heard this. How did the next pregnancy happen? I thought you were trying to leave her."

"I was. I spent most of the year she was Miss Mississippi trying to stay away from her. Her duties made it a little easier, but she spent a lot of terrible nights alone in hotel rooms. I talked her through a lot of them on the phone. But eventually the bad episodes got farther apart, and she came to realize I wasn't going back to her.

"After she gave up her crown, she took a job in Dallas at one of the TV stations. Some political big shot had arranged it for her. Well, she didn't have a car. Since she had completely alienated her parents by this time, I agreed to drive her the three hours down to the New Orleans airport. She told me she was scheduled to fly out at seven p.m., so I got her there at five-thirty. That's when I found out her plane had left at five. She said she'd made a mistake, but that was bullshit. I should have made her show me the tickets. There was no flight to Dallas until the next morning."

"You spent the night together?"

"We got a hotel in the Quarter. We went to dinner at Galatoire's, and the waiter just had to tell us what a perfect couple we were. Mallory asked where in the Quarter we could go dancing. He said we were too nice for the Quarter. Go to the old Roosevelt Hotel, the

Blue Room. So we did. What else were we going to do? Go back to the hotel and stare at each other? We danced to a piano and bass. It was poignant, because I really thought that was the end of it all, and I was proud of her for leaving. Soon we were the only two people left in the place. The pianist played 'As Time Goes By,' and Mallory reminded me how we saw *Casablanca* together at the Hoka in Oxford, and how the first person you see *Casablanca* with is supposed to be the person you're going to marry, and . . . shit, you can guess the rest."

"When did she tell you she was pregnant?"

"She called from Dallas six weeks later. I can't even describe how I felt, the talks we had, but the bottom line was, I told her I couldn't marry her. It would have been insane after all we'd been through. And she'd told me she was on the pill, for God's sake, though I admit I was stupid to believe her."

"Take it easy, John."

"She agreed to have the abortion, but only if I would go out to Dallas and be with her. This will show you the real Mallory, Penn. She had no car out there, right? No way to get around, make arrangements. So what does she do? She sleeps with some poor college kid, then tells him he got her pregnant."

"You're kidding."

"God's truth. She told me this herself. So this kid hauls her around the city, doing whatever she needs done. Then she tells him he's finished, that her brother is coming into town to be with her during the procedure."

Penn took a Mont Blanc from a drawer and made a note on his desk pad. "I'm starting to understand your fear of her. Was that experience like the time in Memphis?"

"No. It wasn't corporate sterile with five doctors and fifty girls waiting. It was a little house with two nurses and one old doctor. They brought me into the examining room as soon as the procedure was over, and they left me there. Mallory's lying on a table, crying and shivering. I held her hand, but she wouldn't look at me. So I look to my right, and there's this damn stainless-steel machine. And inside that machine is what's left of our baby. I know it without anybody telling me. *That's where the vacuum hose hooks up. There's the vent for the motor.* It was the most unnatural feeling I'd ever had in my life. That metal machine was absolutely against nature, *created* in opposition to nature. I'm not religious or anything, but I felt like the hose that had sucked up that fetus could suck up the entire world, that the whole universe could be sucked into the black maw of that vacuum pump. And when I realized that thing had been inside Mallory two times . . . I started to understand her insanity. And I started to cry. The whole situation was beyond belief. I feel like an asshole telling it to you now."

Penn nodded. "Try to keep yourself in the present. Sum up the rest, if you can. From then until Mallory's death."

"She never got over it. Any of it. Ever. And I never got free of her. She dated other people, but it was all an act. Even after she got married and had kids, she never stopped trying to contact me. I eventually had to get a restraining order. She still found ways to threaten me. I would walk out of a store when I thought she was two hundred miles away, and there she'd be, waiting for me, looking at me with this haunted face."

"What did she want from you?"

"I think she never really gave up on us having a child together. But the way she put it, she just wanted to be together, any way that I would. She tried to use sex that way. 'Let's go somewhere. I know you want me. We can do it in the car.' I was in San Francisco once for a meeting, and she turned up there. How the hell did she know I'd be there? She must have been paying detectives to tell her everything about my life. All the time."

"She may well have been. How much of this did you tell Lily?"

"As little as possible."

"She knew Mallory was dangerous, though?"

"Yes. I told her it was a *Fatal Attraction* kind of thing. Everybody thinks they've had a similar experience, so it made Lily take it seriously, but not *too* seriously. You know? I told her that if Mallory ever suddenly appeared at the house, or came around her anywhere, she should call the police and get the hell away from her."

Penn stretched his arms, then reached into a cooler and brought out two bottles of water. He handed one across the desk to Waters.

"I know it took a lot out of you to tell me all this."

"It's a relief to tell some of it, honestly."

Penn took a long sip of water, then set his bottle aside. "John, do you think it was the abortion that caused all Mallory's problems? Or was it something from much farther back?"

"Why do you ask that?"

"Just a feeling."

"Remember when I told you she'd shown me the darkest corners of her personality? That's not completely true. I don't think I ever saw the darkest corner. There was something buried so deep in there I could never get to it. And I don't think she could either. What it was . . . I don't know."

"Sexual abuse, maybe?"

Waters thought about it. "Maybe. Once, during a really bad spell, she told me her father had sexually abused her."

"Did you believe her?"

"Do you know what a 'cutter' is, Penn?"

"You're not talking about a surgeon?"

"No. I'm talking about people who cut themselves in secret. Girls, mostly."

Penn's eyes went wide. "You mean self-mutilators?"

Waters nodded.

"Caitlin told me about them. It's somehow related to bulimia and anorexia, isn't it?"

"It can be. I know a lot about it now, but twenty years ago I knew nothing."

"Mallory cut herself?"

"Yes. I didn't know for a long time. Cutters cut places where they can see the blood but others can't. But eventually I caught her. After that, she did it in front of me."

"Is self-mutilation caused by sexual abuse?"

"It can be. The immediate pain of the cutting is used to distract the victim from chronic inner pain that she can't escape. That could be sexual abuse. Mallory sometimes scratched and cut herself during sex. Sometimes she wanted me to do it."

Penn shook his head. "So, did you believe her when she told you she was sexually abused?"

"No. I'm not sure why. I just . . . didn't feel in my gut that it was true. That could be male stupidity, of course."

"If her real problem wasn't sexual abuse, then what?"

"I think Mallory had undiagnosed clinical depression. And no one really knows what causes that. I had a class under Willie Morris at Ole Miss. He had William Styron speak to our class. I read *Lie Down in Darkness* for that, and I remember thinking Mallory was a bit like Peyton Loftis, when she went mad in New York. Peyton wound up killing herself, I think."

Penn nodded. "She did."

"Styron himself was later a victim of suicidal depression, though he managed not to kill himself. I think Mallory may have been bipolar. Manic depressive. Not like Styron or my wife, who both had major depressive disorder. Nowadays this stuff is no big deal. I mean, half the people we know are on Zoloft or Paxil. There are ninth-grade girls taking it out at St. Stephens, for Christ's sake. But back in 1980, there was still a heavy stigma. And you knew the Candler family. You think they'd send their little princess to a shrink?"

"Not in a million years," Penn agreed.

"I feel like I've told you nothing but bad things about Mallory."

"I remember the good things," Penn assured him. "What she did for the Children's Hospital when she was Miss Mississippi. And the Protestant Home, and the Women's Shelter. I remember when her father tried to use her crown to get himself reelected to the legislature. Mallory wouldn't have any of it. Ben Candler damn near disowned her over that. I also know that her mother's a first-class bitch hiding behind a smiley face she paints on for the world. It's a miracle Mallory turned out as well as she did.

"Let's get the hell out of here," Penn said, getting to his feet. "I'm tired of being under a roof."

Waters stood too. His muscles felt tight, his joints creaky, and he was glad to follow Penn through the door to the backyard. Washington Street was one of Natchez's most beautiful thoroughfares, and Penn's yard was a showplace. There were dogwood and crape myrtle trees, azaleas, rafts of ivy, and perfect circles of monkey grass around the trees. Oddly, there was no division of any kind between Penn's backyard and the one next door. Together they formed a huge garden with several play areas, and it seemed as though Penn and his neighbor had collaborated to make a fantasyland for children.

"Who lives over there?" Waters asked, pointing at the three-story town house next door.

"That's Caitlin's house. I had to live somewhere, so I picked the most convenient place."

Waters started to smile but didn't. Caitlin Masters was not only Penn's girlfriend, but also the publisher of the local newspaper.

"I know what you're thinking," Penn said. "Don't worry. Caitlin and I won't be exchanging information. Not from me to her, at any rate. We had to deal with this situation on the Del Payton case. It wasn't a problem."

"You didn't have to say that. But thanks."

Penn walked over to a flower bed, knelt, and started pulling up weeds.

"So," Waters said, "are you going to tell me about this theory you mentioned?"

Penn continued to pull weeds. "Do you know why I asked for all the details about you and Mallory?"

"No."

"I wanted to know why you were so susceptible to the things Eve told you."

"And now you know?"

"Yes. I have a lot of thoughts about you and Mallory, actually, but we'll save those for another time. The bottom line is that Eve didn't have to try very hard to resurrect Mallory Candler for you, because for you, Mallory never died."

Waters didn't know what to say.

"Oscar Wilde was firmly convinced that men are the more sentimental sex, and I think he was right. Don't feel bad. It would probably be easy to do something like this to me, if Lynne Merrill had been murdered ten years ago."

"Something like what?"

Penn looked up from his work like a doctor about to give a terminal diagnosis. "John, someone is trying to drive you crazy. Probably someone very close to you."

"*What?*"

"They may even be trying to frame you for murder. I saw something like this in Houston once. A man married a woman for her money. Not surprisingly, he grew to hate her. He didn't think he could murder her and get away with her money, so he tried to convince her family that she was insane. And it almost worked."

"Who would want to drive me crazy?"

Penn shrugged. "That shouldn't be hard to figure

out. Who would benefit by your being declared incompetent?"

An image of Cole Smith came into Waters's mind.

"I know that's an unpleasant line of thought, but
you're in real danger. We have to go to the wall on
this. We have to ask everything of everyone. Who's in
a position to blackmail you? Besides Eve Sumner, I
mean, since she's dead. Would anyone benefit if you
were to go to prison for murder? And finally, does
anyone hate you enough to destroy you simply for revenge?"

"Jesus."

Penn went back to pulling his weeds. "I think we
both know who we're talking about. But let's follow
the logic before we name names. Who could possibly
know all the facts that Eve used to convince you she
was Mallory?"

"No one. I've been thinking about that for three
weeks."

"Could two people have pooled what they knew
and put together the information Eve had?"

"I don't think so."

"What about a diary?"

"What?"

"Did Mallory keep a diary? A journal? Something
like that?"

"My God," Waters thought aloud. "She did keep a
diary. She had several, going way back. After the
craziness started, I don't remember seeing them as
much. But she could have been writing a lot of that
stuff down."

"That may be our answer. You need to find out who
has those diaries. I'd start with Mallory's mother."

"She won't talk to me. Certainly not about that."

"I might be able to help with that." Penn yanked out a stubborn weed and tossed it on the ground. "Now, let's get to the ugly stuff. I hear your partner's in financial trouble."

Waters nodded. "That's what I hear too."

"But not from Cole?"

"He hasn't exactly been forthcoming." Waters told Penn about the pumping unit Cole had apparently sold without permission.

"You've got real problems, John." Penn looked up and smiled. "But they're *worldly* problems, okay? Not supernatural ones. That ought to make you feel a little better."

Waters felt light-headed. "It does, actually."

"Let's go back to Eve for a second. The way you told it to me, you were unconscious when she died."

"As best I can remember."

"It's hard to imagine Cole slipping in and killing her to frame his best friend."

"It is."

"But he might not be above *paying* someone to kill Eve, and then framing you. We don't know what problems he has. How much danger he's in. I've seen things done between lifelong friends that you wouldn't believe. There is literally no depth to which human beings cannot sink."

Waters crouched beside Penn and spoke softly. "Cole offered to give me an alibi for the time of the murder."

Penn's head snapped toward him. "Did you ask him to do that?"

"Hell no."

"Okay. You told me you didn't use a condom with Eve that night, right?"

"No."

Penn expelled a lungful of air, then stood and wiped his hands on his pants. "You screwed two people when you did that, John. Eve and yourself. Only you're going to stay screwed. If they put you in that hotel room using DNA, it'll take the archangel Gabriel to keep the D.A. from nailing you. They could say anything. Eve seduced you, then tried to blackmail you, and you killed her. Or you promised to leave your wife and then reneged. Eve threatened to tell, and you killed her. The scenarios are endless."

Waters got to his feet. "You're a real optimist, aren't you?"

"I'm a lawyer. You have two choices. One: Turn yourself in to the authorities, which I don't recommend at this juncture."

Waters closed his eyes and sighed with relief.

"Two: Find out who's trying to turn your life inside out, and nail them before they—or the police—nail you."

Penn's theory, combined with the prospect of action, gave Waters his first real hope since waking up next to Eve's corpse. "How would you start?"

"Confront Cole about the pumping unit. Be aggressive. See how he reacts. I'll do what I can to find out about Mallory's diaries. We'll talk again tonight."

"What about Tom Jackson? Should I just avoid him? I have no idea what he's going to ask me."

"You went to school with Tom. What do you think about him?"

"The old cliché. Tough but fair. He'd hate to bust me for murder, but he'd do it."

"Do you have your cell phone with you?"

Waters nodded.

"Call him right now. If he asks something you're not sure how to answer, tell him you're out in the county checking a well, and you're getting a dropped signal. You'll call him back when you get in."

Penn's deviousness brought a smile to Waters's face. He took his phone from his pocket, called the police department, identified himself, and asked for Detective Jackson. After about a minute, Jackson came on the line, his voice deep and seemingly casual.

"Thanks for calling, John."

"Glad to, Tom. What's up?"

"I'm running down some leads on this Eve Sumner thing. She was a pretty complicated lady, I'm finding out. Anyway, I was down at her office, and they told me you stormed in there a couple of weeks ago and read her the riot act. What was that about?"

Waters was about to evade the question when Eve's own lie came back to him. "She was trying to sell my house out from under me. I don't want to speak ill of the dead, but she was kind of a pushy lady. She called me at the office and said she'd told some couple they could look through our house, when she knew it wasn't for sale. That pissed me off."

"I can see how it would," Jackson said. "She pissed off a lot of people doing that kind of thing. Anything else you can tell me about her?"

"No. You guys got any suspects?"

A long silence. "We're working it hard. That's about all I can tell you."

Waters felt himself sweating. "Well, good luck, Tom. Call me if I can do anything else for you."

"I will. Thanks."

As Waters hung up, Penn said, "You handled that smoothly. Maybe a little too smoothly."

"Shit, what was I supposed to say?"

"I'm just kidding. Hey, remember you told me you felt like the senator in *The Godfather Part II*? He went to bed with a laughing girl and woke up with a dead whore?"

"Yeah."

"The senator didn't kill that girl. He was framed by the Corleones, who later gave him his alibi."

Waters felt a chill as he thought again of Cole. "You're right. I didn't think it through that far."

"It's hard to think when you believe you just committed murder."

Waters nodded.

Penn brushed off his hands. "It's time to start thinking again, *paisan*."

chapter 13

Driving south on Highway 61, Waters was nearly to the Saragossa Country Club when his cell phone rang. What would be a normal occurrence for most people sent a spasm of shock along his body. Eve might be dead, but the sound of his cell phone instantly resurrected her. He checked the LCD, half expecting it to read PAY PHONE, but instead he saw his wife's cell phone number.

"Hey."

"Where are you?" Lily asked.

"On my way to Saragossa for lunch. I'm going to meet Cole out there." Actually Cole had no idea he was coming. "How's your day?"

"Fine. Ana's staying over at Lindsey's tonight."

Lindsey was a classmate who lived in one of the white-flight neighborhoods that had sprung up around the country club. "On a school night?"

"Tomorrow's Lindsey's birthday, so I said it was all right."

"Okay."

"Besides, that gives us some more time together."

Waters had thought last night's lovemaking an anomaly, despite Lily's professed commitment to change. "That's true," he said neutrally.

"Have you checked your voice mail?"

"No."

"You should. I haven't left a message like that in a while. I'll see you later on. Or call me, if you like the mail."

"I'll do that."

"I love you."

"You too," he said, nonplussed by her forwardness.

He clicked off and punched in the code for his voice mail.

"It's just me," said Lily. "I'm not calling to ask you to pick up something at the store or bug you about some household junk. I'm calling to tell you I wish you were inside me right now."

Waters swallowed. Lily had not done anything like this for *years*.

"I know you don't believe me, but it's true. That's what I'm thinking about right now. What we did last night. And I'm touching myself. I wish you could do this for me. *Mmm.* If you were, you'd know I'm telling the truth. Well . . . I hope you get home soon."

He hung up and made the turn into Saragossa. As the clubhouse came into sight, he decided not to call Lily back. He was glad she was making an effort to close the distance that had separated them for so long, but he simply didn't know how to respond.

He parked the Land Cruiser and walked through the front doors, then headed to the card room. Cole didn't play golf anymore; he played gin or Bourée.

Waters found him sitting at a table with three men ranging in age from thirty to sixty. All four had stiff drinks in front of them. On any given day you could find the same crew here, talking, drinking, and gambling. If there was a game on TV, there would be money riding on that as well. Waters couldn't imagine wasting his life this way, but he knew that men like Cole didn't really have a choice. They followed their appetites, their appetites led them this way, and that was that.

"Rock!" Cole called. "You come out to play a few hands with us?"

"No. I need to talk to you for a minute. We've got some problems with a flow line in Jefferson County."

"Flow line? What are you talking about?"

Waters jerked his head to the side, leaving no doubt that he wanted privacy. Cole stared at him for a few moments, then said, "Deal me out for a hand, guys. Duty calls."

The other players grunted, and Cole got up and followed Waters through a side door that opened near the putting green. A retired surgeon was practicing there, so Waters walked out of earshot, Cole wheezing along behind him. They had taken walks like this many times, but always as brothers in arms, discussing strategy on deals they were putting together. Now events had divided them. Waters could feel it in his bones. Cole might not be his enemy, but a chasm had opened between them. When he stopped and turned by an iron bench, Cole squinted against the sunlight, then raised his right hand to protect his eyes.

"You wouldn't drive out here over any damn flow line," he said. "What's going on?"

"Didn't you tell me it's not a good idea to keep things from your partner?"

Cole's neck tensed with the effort of remaining expressionless. "That's right."

"I hear we sold our three-twenty pumping unit off the Madam X well."

Cole's mouth opened slightly; then he drew back his head as if expressing shock at a gross misunderstanding. "Rock, we've talked a half dozen times about replacing that old three-twenty."

"In a couple of years, maybe."

Cole tilted his head to the side and pooched out his bottom lip. "Well, that's a difference of opinion."

"One I wasn't aware of."

"Look, am I in charge of that workover or not?"

"You were until today. But if you don't give me some straight answers, you're not going to be in charge of jack shit."

His face reddening, Cole stepped forward like he meant to deck Waters. Instead, he looked at the ground and shook his head.

"Look, goddamn it. I just needed a few thousand to tide me over. I was going to replace the unit in a couple of weeks."

This was a ludicrous statement, but it served as an admission of guilt. "Jesus, Cole, what about the fifty I lent you the other day?"

"I told you I needed seventy-five!"

"What the hell are you into? Is this gambling debt or what?"

Cole stared off over the eighteenth fairway. "Yeah."

"Football? What?"

"Mostly football. Some high-stakes poker from the last trip Jenny and I took to Vegas. The vig on that is pretty tough. You know how it is. I tried to make back what I owed by going for broke." Momentary excitement flashed in Cole's eyes. "I had a sure thing, Rock. The Tulane–Ole Miss game. I had the inside poop from the team doctor. A guy in New Orleans clues me in—"

"But he was wrong, right?"

Cole shrugged. "I just didn't catch the right spread."

"Would you listen to yourself? You'll never get out of the hole like that."

"Shit, I know. I'm like a drunk with the gambling."

"You're like a drunk with the scotch too."

Cole whipped up his arm. "Get off me, okay! You were screwing the local slut because she told you she was your dead girlfriend. That's *necrophilia*, man."

Waters felt his hands go cold. He wanted to scream back that he knew it was all a scam, that Cole and Eve were behind the whole thing, but he would not let his partner sidetrack him. He needed to get all the information he could. After today, the only communication he had with his partner might be through attorneys.

"What else have you done? Is this why you didn't pay the liability premium? You used that money to pay debts?"

"No."

"Am I going to have to audit every goddamn line of our books? Tell me the truth."

Cole distended his cheeks like Dizzy Gillespie and expelled air in a repentant rush. "Okay . . . I was in a bind then too. Not as bad as now, but bad enough. I slid the premium money into a different account and cashed it out."

Waters felt like the earth had opened beneath his

feet. "Do you realize that I could lose everything because of that? My retirement? Ana's college money?"

"Uh-huh," Cole said in a dead voice. "I've agonized over it ever since they found the leak. But goddamn it, John, you put all that at risk yourself when you started screwing Eve. What's going to happen to them if you go down for murder?"

"Why would I go down for her murder?"

Cole's eyes glinted. "You can't fool your partner, Rock. I know you were with her that night."

"You're full of shit. What do you think you know?"

Something like satisfaction crossed Cole's face. "I know what I know."

"You don't know shit."

"No? Maybe I got curious about why you'd given up your true-blue work ethic after seventeen years. Maybe I followed you for a couple of days. Maybe I saw you go into the Eola to meet Evie. You should have taken me up on that alibi offer."

"You couldn't have seen me go into the Eola that night, because I wasn't there."

"Whatever you say, Rock. Just don't push me, okay? Don't even dream about going to the cops over this pumping unit thing."

Waters shook his head in disbelief. "Is that what you think I'd do? Turn you in to the police? I'm trying to *help* you, man."

Cole looked uncertain.

"You know what this tells me? You wouldn't hesitate to turn *me* in for something. Is that what you're doing? Threatening to turn me in if I don't pay off your debts?"

"Have I done that?" Cole snapped. "Have you heard me say that?"

"It sure sounded like you were leading up to it."

"Goddamn it, Rock, everything's just gotten fucked up. And I can't see how to unfuck it."

"This is a sad day, partner. We've known each other almost forty years. And this is how it ends up?"

Cole suddenly looked close to tears. "You don't understand, John. This isn't just about money. I don't pay these guys? They take it out of my hide. And maybe they don't stop there, you know? There's no way Jenny can make it if something happens to me. I gotta find a way to pay this off."

"Such as?"

"I don't know. I been doing stuff like selling that pumping unit just to keep up the interest on the debt. I mean, what the hell? If the EPA thing goes against us, we're going to lose it all anyway."

This was true enough. And given his present difficulties, Waters could care less about the dollar value of a pumping unit. "Listen to me," he said. "Think about when we were kids together. Those summers by St. Catherine's Creek. The forts we built . . . the stuff we did together. You at my father's funeral."

Cole nodded. "That was a long time ago."

"Not for me. For me it was yesterday. Now I want you to tell me something. Were you in with Eve on this thing from the start?"

"What thing?"

"Don't *lie*, Cole. This is me. Did you feed Eve a bunch of stuff about Mallory and me so she could make me think I was going crazy?"

Cole did a first-rate impression of being shocked. "Why the hell would I do that?"

"You could sell a lot more pumping units with me out of the picture. Maybe even some production, if you forged my signature. And if you did it before the EPA lands on us with both feet, it might just buy your ass out of the hole."

Cole's mouth was hanging open. "Are you drunk?"

"I'm stone sober. I'm as sane as I've ever been, and I'm not going anywhere. You got it? I'll be running this company till the EPA chains the door shut. And as of now, you're making no solo decisions regarding cash flow, production, or anything else."

"If you're not drunk, you *have* gone crazy. You think I'd fuck my best friend like that?"

The hurt in his voice almost made Waters turn away, but this was no time to be soft. "I don't know what to think anymore, partner. We've come to a pretty bad place."

Cole shook his head, stepped forward, and put his beefy hands on Waters's shoulders. "Rock," he said in a cracked voice. "I'm under some real pressure, no lie. All told, I'm over six hundred grand in the hole. But I'd go down with my legs broken and a bullet in my head before I'd do something to hurt you or your family. That's God's truth."

Despite his shock and fury, Waters felt tears sting his eyes. There was no doubt that Cole at least believed what he said. He started to press on with his accusations, as Penn would have wanted him to do, but he simply didn't have it in him. He squeezed Cole's arm and said, "I know you would, partner. I know." Then he gave Cole a hug. He felt the big man shaking, and he knew then that Cole really was in the kind of trouble that some people never walked away from.

"Don't sweat the little shit," he said.

"And it's all little shit," Cole replied automatically.

They forced a laugh, and then Waters took out his keys.

"What are you going to do?" Cole asked.

"I don't know. You just stay safe, okay? And don't worry about that three-twenty."

Cole took a step toward him. "Listen, John. I don't know what you did exactly. But my offer for an alibi still stands. If you can't figure a way out, come see me. We've dug ourselves out of holes before. Maybe we can do it again, if we stick together."

Waters tried to smile but couldn't manage it. Cole sounded so sincere, yet every word of it could be a lie.

The office was busy that afternoon. Monthly billing was going out to the coowners in all the wells, and Sybil couldn't handle it alone. Since Cole was busy drinking and playing cards, that left Waters to fill in for him.

The printer jammed halfway through the job, and as he helped Sybil clear it, he felt tempted to ask her some questions. If she was sleeping with Cole, as he suspected, she might know a lot about his financial problems. She might also know if he'd had any recent contact with Eve. But Sybil seemed to be in a down mood, and he didn't want her to think the company was in more trouble than she knew about already.

At a quarter to five, Sybil headed out to the post office to mail the bills. Cole still hadn't returned, so Waters locked the office and headed home. He was nearly there when his cell phone rang, and he saw a mobile number he didn't recognize.

"Hello?"

"This is your fellow Eagle Scout," said a male voice.

Waters almost laughed at Penn Cage's choice of code. "What's going on?"

"We're both on mobile phones. Where are you?"

"State Street, on my way home."

"We need to talk. Your house?"

"Ah . . . I'd rather meet elsewhere."

"Okay. How about the parking lot of Heard's Music Company?"

The lot was only a few hundred yards from Waters's driveway. "I'll see you there."

Waters hung up and sped past his driveway, then crossed one boulevard and turned into the music store parking lot. Waters had bought his last piano here, a nine-foot concert grand. As a boy, he and his mother could only dream of an instrument like that; now he owned a house that seemed incomplete without one. *But for how long?* he thought.

As he parked the Land Cruiser, Penn leaned out of a green Audi TT and motioned for him to get in. When Waters climbed into the convertible, Penn shook his hand and smiled.

"What's up?" Waters asked. "Do you know something?"

"The police have a new lead. They're keeping quiet about it, but Caitlin has a source inside the department."

"And?"

Penn grimaced. "The guy thought he heard your name mentioned."

"*Shit.*" A wild, unreasoning fear hit Waters in the bowels. "Was he sure?"

"Nothing's sure yet. I don't know what they have. Do you have any idea what it could be?"

Waters thought of the week at Bienville, then the

nights at the Eola. "I don't know. Maybe someone saw us, but we didn't see them?"

"That may be it."

"I've always been worried about Eve's house. She's bound to have had stuff about me in there."

"Well, until we know something for sure, you should sit tight and stay calm. Go back over everything and try to anticipate the situation."

Waters's face suddenly felt cold.

"What is it, John?"

"I just talked to Cole, like you said to. Confronted him."

"And?"

"He told me he knew I was with Eve at the Eola."

Penn's eyes narrowed to slits. "How could he know that?"

"He was coy about it. Said he followed me for a few days. But I think that was bullshit. I can't see him doing that."

"No. If he knows, it's because Eve told him you would be there." Penn tapped the steering wheel. "What if she called him to come up after you passed out, thinking he was going to do something to *you*? When in reality he was going to kill her all along, and frame you."

Waters shook his head. "Cole couldn't do that."

"Are you so sure? What did he say about selling the pumping unit?"

"He admitted it. He's up to his eyeballs in debt. To bookies, Vegas casinos, everybody."

Penn turned up his palms, as if this proved his case.

"Did you find out anything about Mallory's diaries?" Waters asked, wanting to change the subject.

"As a matter of fact, I did. I talked to Mrs. Candler for quite a while. I told her I was thinking of doing a nonfiction book about Natchez, and naturally I'd want to include a chapter on our second Miss Mississippi. I got a good bit of information out of her before she got suspicious."

"Such as?"

"About a year ago—sometime around her husband's death—some of Mallory's things disappeared from their house."

Waters felt a strange premonition, but of what, he wasn't sure. "Like what?"

"Mallory's diaries, for one thing."

"You're joking."

"No. Also some jewelry, all Mallory's. And some personal things of Mallory's that wouldn't mean anything to anyone but her."

"What do you think?"

"That tells us that someone has been planning this scam on you for over a year. They broke into the Candler house and took personal things that would help authenticate Eve's story."

"How could they take things that no one would know were important but Mallory?"

"John, they were taken from her room. Obviously she had saved them for some sentimental reason. My guess is that if you hadn't swallowed Eve's story so quickly, those little items would have started making appearances in your life. On Eve's arm, or in her purse, maybe."

Waters felt a strange lightness in his limbs. He leaned back in the seat, unable to believe what he was hearing.

"I've been thinking about what you told me about

Mallory cutting herself," Penn said. "You said you didn't believe her when she told you that her father had sexually abused her."

Waters nodded.

"Well, I've been asking questions about her family. Nobody could be very specific, but I got the feeling that Ben Candler was a little strange where sex was concerned."

"How so?"

"A little pervy about young girls. He made inappropriate comments sometimes. He and his wife apparently had a nonsexual relationship. That's the gist, anyway. The mother had an affair at some point, but when it threatened Ben's political career, she ended it."

"Political career? Shit, he was only a state representative."

"Ben Candler took that very seriously, as you know."

"Oh, do I. He liked to give you the impression that if the country went to DEF CON Three, he would be making the critical decisions about launching nuclear missiles."

"You got it. And he held that job for six terms."

"Old Ben knew how to kiss ass."

"Yes, he did."

"I'll tell you this," Waters said. "When I visited Mallory's grave after the soccer game, I noticed two things I didn't tell you. They didn't seem important then. Her father is buried next to her. He has a small, cheap gravestone. And it was defaced, like someone had taken a crowbar to it."

"Ben Candler only died about a year ago," Penn said. "So Mallory couldn't have defaced the stone. It could be his wife, I suppose. Or someone else he sexually harassed."

Waters nodded, but that wasn't what he was thinking. "I'll tell you something else. It stunk by his grave."

"What do you mean, stunk? Like what?"

"Urine. Like an animal came there every day and pissed on his grave."

Penn looked incredulous. "I can't see prim old Margaret Candler driving to the cemetery to piss on her husband's grave every day." He shook his head and laughed. "Maybe once a week, though."

"Mallory would," Waters said quietly.

"Mallory would what?"

"Go there every day and piss on his grave. She'd do it rain or shine for ten years. That's the way she was."

"*Was*," Penn echoed. "That's the operative word there, John. Focus on the present, all right?"

"Something's been bothering me, Penn."

"Jesus. Are you starting with the supernatural stuff again?"

"You tell me. One of the things that convinced me Eve was really Mallory was her scars. I didn't tell you that before for fear you'd think I was crazy. Eve Sumner had cutting scars beneath her watch, and also on her inner thighs, just the way Mallory used to. And they weren't all new. She'd been doing it for a long time."

Penn was staring at him with worry in his eyes.

"And the night she died," Waters went on, "she asked me to cut her during sex. She was really upset, and she wanted to be cut, just like Mallory did sometimes."

Penn took hold of his wrist. "John, listen to me.

They got those details from Mallory's diaries. They had to."

"You're telling me Eve Sumner mutilated herself to convince me she was Mallory? And for a long period of time? Do you really think that's possible?"

"People are quite capable of maiming themselves in pursuit of a goal, John. In the nineteen-fifties, inmates at Angola Prison slashed their Achilles tendons to draw attention to their plight. They permanently crippled themselves. What's a few cuts on the surface of the skin compared to the money involved in this case? And we know from the break-in at the Candler house that they were planning this scam for at least a year."

Waters pondered this in silence. He wanted to believe Penn, but his memory of Eve's desolate face as she begged him to cut her was too vivid to call a lie.

"Stick to realities," Penn urged him. "Things still look good for you. If the police had something concrete, they would already have brought you in for questioning. If they do call about questioning you, refer them to me. I'll try to arrange for it to take place in a law office downtown. I don't have one, but I can borrow a friend's." He squeezed Waters's knee. "You just keep cool."

Waters nodded.

"Get some sleep if you can. Play with your kid. Bring her over to play with Annie."

"I will."

He shook hands with Penn and got out. The owner of the music store was standing in the display window, looking right at him. As Penn's Audi pulled away, Waters waved, then got into the Land Cruiser and drove out of the lot. Home was only a few hun-

dred yards away, but as he neared it, he felt suddenly
sure that he would find the police waiting when he arrived. He closed his eyes and thanked God that Annelise was spending the night away from home, and
would not have to see him led away in handcuffs.

The driveway was empty.

The house felt empty too. Without Ana clattering
around and Rose clanking utensils in the kitchen, Linton Hill seemed like a museum.

"Lily?" he called.

No answer.

He went into the den and sat on the sofa. For once,
the remote control was actually on the table beside
him. He switched on the TV and clicked up to CNN.
The local news out of Jackson always had murders to
report, and he didn't want to see anything about murder. The images on CNN weren't much better, though,
war casualties overseas. Wherever you went, death
was news.

"I thought I heard you come in."

Waters looked over his shoulder, and his mouth fell
open. The woman standing in the doorway was his
wife, but she looked as though she had stepped out of
a time machine. Her shoulder-length blond hair had
vanished. Now cut boyishly short, with only a few
locks curling around the neck, it looked the way it had
when Lily first moved back to Natchez, and was still
in her athletic phase. Tight slacks, drop earrings, and
a deep V-neck blouse made the transformation complete.

"*Wow,*" he said. "You cut your hair."

She smiled. "I had them lighten it a bit too."

"You look ten years younger."

"Was I that bad? You look like you're in shock."

"Did you run again?"

Lily walked into the room and spun before him like a runway model. "Actually I slept most of the day. I was really tired. But after going to the salon, I felt better. What about you? You look exhausted."

"Just worried," he said, searching for some excuse. "The EPA won't tell us a damn thing."

"Screw the EPA." Lily smiled again. "As soon as I start rubbing your shoulders, you're going to forget all about those tree-hugging fascists."

Waters couldn't believe his ears. Lily hadn't sounded this carefree in ages. She was wearing a little eyeliner and shadow too, he noticed. She hadn't overdone it, but there was enough to give her an air of mystery.

She walked behind the sofa and said, "Turn off the news and put on some satellite music. Atmospheres or something."

Waters fiddled with the remote, and soon the soothing sounds of a well-played acoustic guitar filled the room.

Lily laid her hands on his shoulders and began a soothing massage. She started with gentle pressure, but before long her fingers were digging into the muscle fibers of his neck, working out the tension that had been building there ever since he left Eve lying dead in the Eola Hotel.

"God, that feels good."

"Don't think," she said. "Clear your mind."

Her command was impossible to obey, but he tried. Lily thoroughly massaged his neck and scalp, then moved to his face. She worked the tension out of muscles he never knew he had: below his eyes, over the joint of his jawbone, below his nose, around his mouth. He jumped when her fingers slid into his mouth and began to rub his gums and upper palate, but it felt so good that he laid his head back and gave himself to it. When Lily flattened the pad of her thumb against his back teeth and pushed down, the sensation was amazing.

"Let go, baby," she murmured. "Don't fight it."

The sensuality of her fingers inside his mouth aroused him. After a couple of minutes, she removed her wet fingers and slid them down into his shirt. His nipples constricted at her touch. She played there for a few moments, then leaned over him and slid both hands down to his lap.

"God, Lily. . . ."

"*Shhh.*"

She unbuttoned his trousers and slid her hands inside, working on him with shocking directness. Then she climbed over the back of the couch and knelt before him.

"Close your eyes."

He didn't want to, but he obeyed. What followed was a selfless application of attention so focused that it pointed up everything Lily had neglected to do for the past four years. Longer, really. Even before losing the baby, this act for Lily had always been a brief stage of foreplay. She would touch and kiss him there, but it was never an end in and of itself, simply a prelude to intercourse. She didn't seem to understand that what made the act so arousing was the complete focus of effort where it was most needed, with every movement assuring him that contact would never be broken or even lessened in intensity unless it was to heighten his reaction and magnify his final release. But by her

actions now, Lily made it clear that she had understood this all along. Had it not felt so wonderful, Waters would have brooded over the fact that his wife
had possessed this knowledge and ability all along,
yet had not used it.

"*Jesus,*" he gasped.

She took his right hand in one of hers and
squeezed, but she did not break contact.

"Lily, I can't hold back. . . ."

Suddenly he felt nothing but air on his wet skin.

"Yes, you can."

She pulled him to his feet and ran back toward the
master bedroom, pulling him behind her. "I'm going
in the bathroom for a sec," she said. "Get in bed and
wait for me."

She disappeared behind the bathroom door, leaving him alone in the room where he had known only
frustration in the past. He removed his shirt and pants
and dropped them to the floor. Lily would normally
make a point of picking them up and hanging them in
the closet when she came out of the bathroom, but he
had a feeling she wouldn't even notice today, or at
least would let it go if she did.

He pulled back the bedcovers and started to get beneath them, but something held him back. He wanted
to know what she was doing in the bathroom. Walking up to the half-open door, he leaned slowly to his
left.

Lily was standing naked before her mirror, one
breast in each hand, as though testing their weight.
She smiled to herself, then ran her hands down to her
hips, where a pink blemish marred the white skin
over her right hipbone. Taking some makeup from a
blue container by the sink, she rubbed a bit on her fin-

ger and covered the blemish. Then she surveyed herself again, turning her back to the mirror and looking
over her shoulder.

Fascinated by this glimpse of his wife alone with
her vanity—something he hadn't seen for far too
long—Waters took a half-step backward so that she
wouldn't catch sight of him. As he watched, she
turned to face the mirror again, looking quite satisfied
with what she saw. He was about to tiptoe back to the
bed when Lily raised her right hand to her neck and
entwined one of the newly chopped locks around her
forefinger and began to twist it into a tight curl.

His skin rippled from his toes to his scalp, and his
scrotum withdrew as fear flushed adrenaline into his
system. There was hardly enough hair to twist, but
Lily twisted it anyway, a childlike look of rapture on
her face. *She has no idea she's doing that*, he realized. He
wanted to run from the room, but that was crazy. How
would he explain it? He hurried back to the bed and
slid under the covers, a film of sweat already covering
his skin. He wanted to wipe the image of Lily twisting
that curl from his mind, but he knew he would remember it on his deathbed. Worse, a horrifying movie
began to screen itself in fast motion behind his eyes.
He saw Eve flailing under him that last night, screaming at the top of her lungs, then himself waking to
find her dead, fleeing the hotel like a craven killer.
Then he was sitting in his office the following day, trying to puzzle out his strange disorientation, his losses
of hours, the long naps. When Sybil came in with
coffee, her face bled into Lily's, red and blotchy from
her shattering orgasm, the first in so long. . . .

"Are you ready?" Lily asked, stepping naked from
the bathroom.

Waters was so far from ready that he doubted he could perform.

"Last night made me remember what I've been missing," she said, pulling back the covers and sliding in beside him. "I hope you've got a lot of stamina tonight."

Struggling to control his wild thoughts, he tried to keep Penn's reassurances in his mind. But all Penn's logic weighed as nothing against the power of his own instinct.

"What's wrong?" Lily asked, touching him beneath the covers. "A minute ago you were ready to burst."

"I don't know," he said, trying not to recoil from her touch.

Lily looked at him with concern, then kissed his cheek. "Don't you worry, baby. Mama knows how to make it all better." She smiled and vanished beneath the covers.

When her lips touched him, his stomach heaved, and despite her efforts he remained soft. *Stop!* he told himself. *This is what you've wanted for four years.* Yet it wasn't. Why it wasn't was another question altogether. The answer his autonomic nervous system was giving him was the kind of thing they sent you to the state hospital at Whitfield for.

Desperate not to reveal his feelings, he shut down his emotions and posed a thought experiment. *If I were to accept everything Eve told me as the truth, what conclusion could I draw from the way she died and all that's happened since?* The logic came as easily as stacking blocks did to a toddler. *One: Mallory's soul survived the death of her body. Two: Mallory's goal is to be with me forever, to live the life we left unlived twenty years ago. One way to accomplish that would be to tempt me to leave my wife for "Eve Sumner." But what if Mallory decided I would never leave Lily and Annelise for Eve? Then the most logical strategy would be for Mallory to enter Lily and remain inside her forever. And to do that, she would have to move through me first. . . .*

As Lily stroked and kissed him beneath the covers, he flashed onto Eve standing nude on the balcony of the Eola. The lightning strobed, briefly illuminating her face, and in that moment he saw total confusion in her eyes, the confusion of an amnesiac or a schizophrenic. Later, in the throes of sexual ecstasy, Eve had begun to scream and flail her arms as if in terror. He saw it much more clearly now than he had at the time, and the possible implications of what he had witnessed in those penultimate moments hit him with a wave of nausea. Had the real Eve Sumner—the "sleeping" Eve—suddenly awakened to the reality of being raped by a man she did not know? Had she literally come to her senses with a total stranger thrashing inside her? Waters shuddered with horror.

He heard a soft plop, then Lily's voice. "Stop thinking," she said. "You have to help a little."

"I'm trying."

"Try harder."

As she went back to her work, he thought, *I saw Eve freak out, then I lost consciousness. When I woke up, she was dead. I was the only one in the room. My hands strangled her. But . . .*

"That's it," Lily said, squeezing him forcefully.

Waters felt as though a steel band had been removed from his chest. Penn would say he was crazy for thinking this way, but for the first time, he saw a real possibility that he had not killed Eve—

"Now we're in business," Lily said, sliding quickly

up his chest and climbing astride him. "You just stay like that, and I'll do all the work."

Looking up into her eyes, Waters saw a combination of emotions he had never before seen in his wife's face: pride, triumph, lust, greed. The woman above him now knew exactly what she wanted, and she would do anything to get it. Right now she wanted sexual pleasure. As she began to move, flexing her abdominal muscles with perfect control, he thought, *What will she want tomorrow?*

Waters lay in the dark with his back to Lily. He was mentally alert but physically spent. Lily had been sleeping for the past hour; he knew by her snoring. For a while he'd feared she didn't intend to sleep at all. Once aroused to orgasm, she had remained in a heightened state in which any additional stimulation brought yet another climax. Waters survived the first hour without reaching release himself, but when he finally did and thought himself done, Lily went feverishly back to work on him. She used her lips and fingers with ruthless assurance, invading his most intimate spaces with techniques she had not picked up by reading some *Cosmo* article in a grocery checkout line. Time blurred, and he found himself in a disturbing dimension where pleasure and pain merged into something beyond both. These sensations were not new to him. He had felt them only days ago, with Eve. And before that . . . twenty years ago. The effort of concealing his fear while performing sexually left him a quivering wreck, and he felt blessed relief when Lily finally collapsed onto her pillow.

Now, lying in darkness, he began to doubt his sanity. Paranoia might be the subject of endless jokes, but it was a dangerous condition. Once tuned to threatening scenarios, the paranoid mind made ominous connections between patently unrelated events. He'd seen it a thousand times in Mallory. Was the same force now at work in him? Were the fears that had gripped his mind for the past two hours merely fallout from the shock of killing Eve? Were—

Waters went rigid in the bed.

Lily had stopped snoring. He listened for breathing but heard nothing. How could there be no sound? She had to breathe. He listened harder, and the hairs on his back and neck rose to prickly stiffness. *She's watching me*, he thought. He felt the pressure of her gaze upon his back like the beam of a laser. He tried to prepare himself for her touch, for the sound of her voice. *What are you thinking, Johnny?* Or would she go further? *I know what you're thinking . . .*

But she couldn't know. People couldn't read other people's minds. And souls could not move between bodies. Waters didn't even believe in souls, when it came right down to it. He believed in experience. Of course, part of his experience was waking in the dark to find Mallory staring at him with the lidless gaze of a reptile. The same thing had happened with Eve. If he turned over now and found Lily staring at him like that, he might start screaming—

Turn over, he told himself. *You're not some scared kid.*

He steeled himself against the sight of a nightmare made real, then rolled over and looked into Lily's face.

Her eyes were closed.

Her mouth was open, her head cocked in the mindless gape of sleep. As the fear drained out of him, she began to snore again. Lily was no hyperaware Fury awaiting her moment to strike, but an exhausted wife resting from exertions and ecstasies she had too long denied herself.

"Jesus," he whispered. "This is out of hand."

chapter 14

"John? Is this John Waters?"

Waters blinked himself awake and found the phone in his hand. Lily was gone, the bed was a wreck, and daylight shone around the edges of the drapes.

"This is Waters," he mumbled. "Who's this?"

"It's Tom Jackson, John."

He instantly came to full alertness. "What can I do for you, Tom?"

"Sounds like I woke you up."

Lily's clock radio read 9:15 A.M. Waters was usually in his office by 8:30. "I had a headache last night. Guess I overslept."

"Sorry. Look, I have another question for you."

"Shoot," said Waters, remembering Penn's warning: *The police have another lead. Caitlin's source thought he heard your name come up . . .*

"We got a lady says she saw you and Eve Sumner

going into the driveway of Bienville two days in a row the week before the murder."

Waters waited for more details, but Jackson offered none. He swallowed hard.

"That's right," he said, as the skin of his face seemed to tighten around his skull. "Is that a problem?"

"Well," said Jackson, "last time I talked to you, you didn't seem like a big fan of Ms. Sumner. You went down to her office to give her an earful after she tried to sell your house out from under you. That's what you said."

"That's right."

"Well, I'm sort of confused, John. What were you doing with her at Bienville a few days after that? And not once but twice?"

"She was showing me the house. Simple as that."

Silence. "You in the market for a new house? You already got a pretty nice one."

"Bienville has a lot of architectural significance."

"I don't know too much about that kind of thing. Is Lily interested in it too?"

A flash of the knife. Tom Jackson was quicker than he liked people to think. "Here's the thing, Tom. I've been thinking about buying it as a surprise for Lily. She thinks it's too expensive. And it *is* expensive. But I've had a good couple of years, even though the oil business as a whole is in the toilet. And I knew if I just went ahead and did it, she'd love it. You know what I mean?"

"I can't really say I do, John. That's thirty years of my salary."

Jackson had already checked the price of the house. "Well, that's why I kept quiet about it, anyway. I didn't want anyone knowing I was looking at the place. You know how this town is. People hear I'm looking for an antebellum home, every realtor in town is calling me, and my wife knows about it by dinnertime."

"Now *that* I understand," Jackson said. "But why'd you pick Eve Sumner to show you the place? She's not the realtor for the Historic Society."

Waters thought fast. "To be honest, I felt bad about raising hell at her office. She was nice that day, and I felt guilty later. I figured a commission like that would more than make up for it."

"I see." The detective covered his phone and said something unintelligible to someone else. "What did you think about Eve as a person?"

"Very professional."

"People say she could get a little unprofessional with certain male clients."

"Cole told me something like that. But she was totally professional with me. I did notice she had the equipment for what you're talking about, though."

"That's the damn truth," Jackson said in an unguarded moment. "In the right outfit, she was something to see."

Any outfit, Waters thought, recalling how Eve had looked dancing gloriously naked in the parlor of Bienville.

"John," Tom said in a quieter voice, "this is you and me, right?"

"Right."

"Did you tap that stuff out on one of those afternoons? I wouldn't blame you a bit, if you did. I just need to know."

"Hell no. I'm married, man."

"So were a lot of guys who spent time with Eve. That doesn't seem to stop too many people these days, men or women."

"You're right. But it does me."

More silence. "John, I'm going to ask what I asked you the other day. And I want you to think before you answer, okay?"

"Okay."

"Did you have any other contact with Eve Sumner that I should know about?"

Waters let some time pass, as if he were thinking. "No," he said at length. "Nothing I can think of."

"Okay, then. I appreciate your time."

"Sure. Still no prime suspect?"

"With this gal, it's more a process of elimination than a search. You know what I mean?"

"I hear you. Good luck, Tom."

"Yeah."

Waters hit the disconnect button with a shaking finger. Then he pulled Penn Cage's phone number from his memory and punched it into the keypad.

Penn gave Waters a cup of coffee and led him out to the backyard. Today he did not pull weeds from his flower beds. He sat on a wrought-iron bench, crossed his legs, and sipped his coffee.

"If the police were going to call you in for questioning over this," he said, "Tom wouldn't have questioned you on the phone."

Waters paced the grass in front of the bench. "I'm not sure he bought my explanation."

"He may not have. He may think you were screwing her, in which case he won't let this drop. But unless they find something else to support this, you've probably got at least a few days' grace. I'll tell you something else encouraging. They must not have found anything in Eve's house that incriminates you. If they had, they would already have searched your house and office."

Waters stopped pacing, relief washing over him like a cool balm.

"So," Penn said. "You told me you needed to talk about something else. Something disturbing."

"Yes." Waters sat on an iron chair opposite Penn and set his coffee mug on the ground. "Lily wasn't herself last night."

Penn drew back his head as if he sensed where Waters was going. "What do you mean?"

"I mean in bed. She was totally out of character. She was very aggressive, and she did things she'd never done before."

Penn shrugged. "Sometimes women do that. Didn't you tell me that Eve's death had made Lily more aware of your marital problems?"

"Yes. She said she was going to make an effort."

"There you go. Don't look a gift horse in the mouth."

"You know women don't go from sexual dysfunction to supreme confidence overnight. But that wasn't all. When Lily was in the bathroom before we made love, I walked over to look at her. She couldn't see me. She was looking into the mirror like she hardly recognized herself. And then she twisted a lock of hair tight around one finger and pulled it out into a curl."

Penn shook his head. "This is nuts. You think because Mallory twisted her hair, and because you saw Eve do it a few times, that Mallory's soul is now in your wife?"

"I know you're not open to—"

"I've seen Caitlin twist her hair a hundred times."

Waters waited a moment before continuing, in the hope that Penn would really listen. "I'm sure you have. It's a basic human gesture, okay? But in Mallory, it was a precursor to her cutting behavior. It's called trichotillomania. She pulled it very hard. So did Eve. And now Lily."

"Even in this fantasy universe of yours where the laws of physics are suspended, how could Mallory's soul be inside Lily?"

"I told you how Eve said it worked. Through sex. Eve *died* while we were having sex, Penn. Or soon after. And the next day I was totally disoriented. I had blackouts I remember absolutely nothing about."

"And that's exactly what I'd expect from a man who believed he'd just committed murder."

"That same day, I made love with Lily. She climaxed, and after that I was fine. But then *she* spent half the next day sleeping, and then started acting like a totally different person."

Penn got up from the bench and motioned for Waters to follow him along one of the paths through the large garden area formed by his and Caitlin Masters's yards.

"There's one other option, John. I hesitated to mention it when we first spoke, but now . . ."

"This isn't the time to pull any punches."

Penn met his eye. "Remember you said that."

"Tell me."

"Lily could be involved in this thing. She could have been in it with Cole from the start."

"*What?* That's insane."

Penn nodded and kept walking. "I'm sure you're right. I thought I should mention it."

"Why?"

The lawyer looked almost apologetic. "If you were to be declared incompetent by a court, or sentenced to prison for murder, Cole's corporate power would be enhanced, but his ability to turn that power into ready cash would be limited."

"He could sell a lot of equipment on his own."

"Yes, but the real money in your company is in oil production. Correct? The monthly runs, and the reserves you hold. I assume those are worth millions of dollars?"

"Yes."

"And I'm sure you've held on to a lot more production than Cole has."

"Yes."

"You see what I'm getting at?"

Waters did. "It would take Lily's help for Cole to sell off my existing production."

"I know this is a painful line of thought, but we have to look at the facts. Last night, Lily acted in a manner that furthered your belief that Mallory Candler has somehow returned to haunt you. What logical explanation could there be for that? Does Lily have any romantic history with Cole?"

"No."

"She was three years behind Cole and me at St. Stephens?"

"She was a freshman when you guys were seniors."

"Did she and Cole ever date?"

"Not at St. Stephens."

"What about Ole Miss?"

Waters felt strangely uncomfortable. "They did have a few dates there. Two or three. We always laugh about it when it comes up. Lily despises Cole."

"Let's talk about Ole Miss for a minute."

"There wasn't anything to that, Penn. Nothing sexual, anyway."

The lawyer didn't look convinced. "Cole doesn't strike me as the kind of guy who'd spend much time with a girl who didn't put out in college."

Waters felt his face coloring.

"I'm not trying to piss you off, John. I'm trying to make you look at things objectively."

"I hear you. But I really think Lily would have told me if she'd slept with Cole."

"Women are funny about their sexual pasts. So are men, for that matter. They say that when a man gives you his number of conquests, you should divide by three, and when a woman does, you should multiply by two."

Waters tried to think about it without emotion. "Okay, what if they did sleep together in college? What you're suggesting now is that they've revived that relationship, and they're using their knowledge of my past to drive me insane or send me to prison. That's crazy."

"It may sound crazy. But you find yourself in extraordinary circumstances. So extraordinary that you've attributed them to a supernatural cause rather than face potentially painful facts."

"We don't have any facts. Only circumstances."

"Highly suggestive ones." Penn stopped beside a complicated wooden play set, reached over his head, and closed his hands around a horizontal ladder.

"You have to be strong, John. Your freedom is at stake. Maybe even your life."

"I know it is. I don't want to lose my wife and daughter."

Penn dropped his hands from the ladder, sat in a swing, and looked up at Waters with sadness in his eyes. "You're still not grasping what I'm telling you. You may already have lost your wife. I want you to drop all your preconceptions and try to answer a truly terrible question."

"I'll try."

"Is it possible that Lily hates you? Secretly, I mean."

"What?"

"You heard me."

Waters was stunned by the anger he felt at his old friend. Penn seemed to be trying to make him suffer as much as he could, and for no good reason. "You've got to tell me why you asked that."

Penn swung slowly back and forth. "I've been trying to look at this situation without making any assumptions whatever. Just analyzing what's happened so far. And I've tried to think like a woman. Perhaps a mentally disturbed woman."

"You mean Lily?"

"Yes. Does Lily know about Mallory's abortions?"

Waters thought about it. "I told her about the first one. To explain Mallory's fixation, you know? Why she was a threat."

"Could she know about the second one as well?"

"I don't think so."

"Did Cole know about both abortions?"

"Yes. What the hell are you getting at?"

"Your wife lost two children to miscarriages. One was very traumatic. I think it's possible that Lily blamed you for those miscarriages. Not in some vague subconscious way, but very specifically. That she believed you caused them, and that she hates you for it."

"Why would she blame me for that?"

"In a state of grief and clinical depression, she might be quite capable of deciding that her miscarriages were some sort of karmic payback for Mallory's abortions. You basically forced Mallory to kill the children you conceived with her, and Lily might think you were owed some sort of divine punishment for that."

Waters was outraged by the suggestion. "That's the most twisted thing I've ever heard!"

"But not outside the realm of what a grief-stricken mother might seize on as a reason for her suffering." Penn stopped swinging, his eyes somber. "Tell me the truth. After Lily lost those babies, did you never feel— even for a moment—that what you had forced Mallory to do was somehow the cause of it?"

Waters stood with his mouth open. Though he wanted to deny it, he could not.

"Guilt is a powerful thing, John. Especially in a man like you, with a highly developed conscience. I know, because I'm the same way."

Waters walked over and sat in the swing beside Penn. He had to cling to the chains to hold himself steady. "If your goal was to blow my mind, you succeeded. I'm willing to consider your theory. You say Lily and Cole are in this together. Sleeping together. But Lily doesn't even *like* sex. After she lost those babies, we basically went without it for four years."

"Maybe that should tell you something."

"Like what? That she's sleeping with my best friend? A guy whose sexual habits she despises?"

"After Lily lost the baby, were you patient with her about resuming sex? Very careful and considerate?"

"Of course!"

"Maybe that wasn't what she needed. Maybe that made her think about it too much. Maybe she needed someone to just take her and be done with it."

"No way." Waters struggled to control his temper. "That's not Lily. I know my wife."

Penn reached out and touched his shoulder. "None of us really knows anyone. Not even our own parents or siblings. And last night, Lily showed you that she has a lot more sexual knowledge and skill than you ever suspected."

"This is *bullshit*." Waters got out of the swing and kicked it against a wooden post. "I can't even remember what it felt like to be normal!"

"The normal man is a fiction," Penn said. "There is no 'normal.' Not for women either. Your life is on the line now, John. You have to face reality, no matter how terrible it might be."

Waters had heard all he wanted to. He got out his keys and started walking back toward the house.

"Where are you going now?" Penn called.

"The office. I want to talk to Sybil."

"About Cole and Lily?"

"Maybe. I don't know."

"Be careful. Call me if you find out anything important. And let's talk later today in any case."

"I'll call you."

"Don't forget."

Waters gave him a dispirited wave and walked around the side of the house to the street.

*   *   *

Sybil Sonnier walked into Waters's office wearing a Black Watch skirt and a forest-green blouse. He had buzzed her the way he normally would, and she stood waiting as though expecting a request for photocopies. He wasn't sure how to begin. He'd never gotten to know Sybil very well, and her mood had not been the best for some time. As the silence dragged on, her dark Cajun eyes widened, and she gave him a look like *Am I in trouble?*

"Is this about my work?" she asked finally, making Waters realize he'd been sitting there like a department store mannequin.

"Not exactly."

He motioned her to the oxblood chair across from his desk. She folded her skirt over her knees and sat primly on the edge of the seat. Looking at her shapely calves, Waters knew his partner would not have been able to resist at least trying with her. But Sybil was no schoolgirl. She was twenty-eight and divorced, and Waters had seen her angry enough times to know she could handle herself.

"It's actually a personal matter," he said. "Do you mind if I ask you a few personal questions?"

Her cheeks pinked, but she shook her head.

"I'm worried about Cole," he said, and waited for a reaction.

"I am too," she said.

"May I ask why?"

"I think he's in trouble. Bad trouble."

"Do you have any idea what kind?"

"Money trouble." Sybil looked suddenly self-conscious, or perhaps she was just being cautious. She might think her job was at stake. She was paid much better than most assistants in town, mostly for her discretion in business matters.

"What makes you say that?"

"I spend half my time telling his creditors he's working lawsuits in Memphis or New Orleans."

This shocked Waters. "I'm sorry, Sybil. I didn't know you were having to cover for him to that extent."

She shrugged. "I figured it went with the job."

"It doesn't. Though I'm sure Cole appreciates it."

She closed up then, with a hard tightening of the skin around her lips and eyes.

"I didn't mean to suggest—"

"I know," she cut in. "But that's what this is about, isn't it? You want to know if I'm sleeping with him."

Waters started to deny it, then gave up. "Sybil, if you're having a relationship with Cole, it's unprofessional and dangerous for the company. But you're both adults, and that kind of danger is the least of our problems right now."

"I know."

"You do?"

She nodded, and something seemed to come loose inside her. "I'm really scared, John. I think he owes some Vegas loan sharks. I'm from South Louisiana, and I know what they do to you when you don't pay your debts."

"I can tell you really care about him. I care about him too. May I just ask you what I need to?"

"Go ahead."

"Are you having sex with him?"

She averted her eyes for a moment. "Not now," she said finally. "But I was. Until about a month ago."

Until just before I saw Eve at the soccer field, Waters thought. "What ended it?"

"I'm not really sure. I think it may be the trouble he's in. I don't think he's sleeping with anyone else."

Penn's theory came back to him like a knife in the belly. "Let's change the subject for a second. Has my wife called up here for Cole lately? Or in the past few months? Or has he called her?"

Sybil looked as if something had suddenly occurred to her. "Do you think he's having an affair with Mrs. Waters?"

"No, no. This has to do with money."

"Oh." She sniffed, then looked at the ceiling as she thought back. "No, I don't think so. Wait—your wife did call for him once or twice in the past month. I just didn't think anything of it at the time."

"How many times did they talk, do you think?"

"Three, maybe? Four at the most."

"Do you know what they talked about? Did you ever listen in?"

"No!"

"Did they have any other contact that you know of?"

"No."

Waters made a mental note to request Lily's cell phone records. "Sybil, what do you think about Cole?"

"I'm not sure what you mean."

"Your bottom-line opinion, as a woman. Is he a good guy? A bad guy? What?"

She sighed and looked at the floor. Clearly she had spent a good deal of time pondering this question. "I'm really mad at him right now. Sometimes I think I hate him. But deep down, I think he's a good man. I wouldn't have slept with him if I didn't think that. Will he ever leave his wife for me? I doubt it. But he has a good heart."

Until this week, Waters would have agreed with her assessment. "Do you think he'd ever betray me, Sybil?"

"How? Like, do I think he'd sleep with your wife?"

"No. I mean over money. To save himself."

"Never. He might sleep with your wife. Sex is an exception to every rule. But hurt you to save himself? No way. You have no idea how much your good opinion means to him. You're sort of like a father to Cole, even though you're the same age. He says you always do the right thing, and he never does. And he's pretty close to right."

"I don't always do the right thing."

"Well, nobody does, do they? But I've known a lot of men, and I've never known one like you. Your wife is really lucky. I hope she knows that."

Waters could see how Cole could fall for this woman. The sincerity in her eyes made you want to please her, to make her feel all the happiness she could.

"Cole hasn't come back in, has he?" he asked.

She shook her head. "I don't think he will today."

"Okay. Look, I appreciate your being so forthcoming. Why don't you go home? There's nothing going on. Take a long nap, and then get yourself a good dinner tonight. Go to the Castle, and bring me the receipt."

Sybil gave him an ironic smile. "Wendy's tonight. I'm too bummed out for anything else."

He laughed with her, then motioned for her to go.

"Don't worry, Sybil. I'm not going to let anything bad happen to Cole."

She paused by the door and nodded gravely. "I just hope it's not too late."

"I do too," he said softly, after she'd gone out.

At 1:50 P.M., Waters stood on top of Jewish Hill, looking out over the Mississippi River. After Sybil left, he'd called St. Stephens to verify that Annelise was in class. Then he'd shut down the office and driven straight to the cemetery. He needed time to think before he faced Lily again, and this was the place that drew him. He hadn't much time. Ana would be dismissed from school at 2:30, and he wanted to be there to pick her up. He didn't want her alone with Lily until he knew exactly what was going on.

As he watched a large sailing vessel make its way beneath the twin bridges over the river, a funeral cortege pulled up to the first gate of the cemetery and turned into its new section. The new section looked like any cemetery in any town in America. The gravestones were low and the ground flat, and there were few trees to break up the view. Waters was glad he'd managed to purchase a family plot in one of the older sections, shaded by oak trees and bordered by walls and wrought iron. It probably didn't matter to the dead where they came to rest, but for those left behind, atmosphere made a difference. He'd spent enough time at his father's grave to know that.

About five hundred yards from Jewish Hill, a green burial tent faded by the sun awaited the funeral procession. He hadn't noticed it when he drove up. The tent kept the sun or rain from the open grave, the coffin, and the immediate family and close relations. The

cars in the procession parked bumper-to-bumper in a
long line, thirty or forty of them blocking the narrow
lane. The headlights were extinguished, and then
dark-suited mourners emerged from the vehicles and
gathered in a somber circle around the tent. Waters
had been to a hundred burials exactly like this one:
the same tent, the same hearse, virtually the same
crowd. That was how it was in small towns.

As he watched, a late arrival turned in through the
wrong gate and began looking for a lane that would
lead to the burial service. A sign on the car's door
read, SUMNER SELECT PROPERTIES. It took a moment for
the significance of this to register, but as the latecomer
turned and drove toward the green tent, Waters's face
felt cold.

Eve Sumner was lying under that burial tent. Cold
and still with an ugly Y-incision stitched into her torso
from the autopsy. She was about to be buried right before his eyes.

His first instinct was to flee. Tom Jackson might be
in the crowd of mourners, watching to see who
showed up at the murder victim's funeral. Waters
looked back at his Land Cruiser. Satisfied that it was
parked out of sight of the burial tent, he walked over
to a wrought-iron fence bordering old Jewish graves
from Alsace and Bohemia and sat down against it.
Anyone at the burial would need binoculars to make
out his face at this distance, and sitting in front of the
fence, he was unlikely to be noticed at all.

Eve's mother and teenage son would be under that
tent, grief-stricken and confused, roses and Kleenex
clenched in their hands. Morbidly, Waters wondered
how many men in that crowd had coupled with Eve
while she was alive. It would probably please her to

know they had come to her final farewell. Then again, he reflected, he might have no idea what Eve would have wanted. Because he might never have known the real Eve.

No matter how imaginatively Penn Cage twisted events to fit his logical explanations, Waters remained unconvinced. And not because of denial. No man wanted to think his wife and best friend might be trying to drive him mad. But he had not accepted Eve's story of soul transmigration simply to avoid an unpleasant truth. He'd believed the things Eve told him because they *felt* true. Her intimate knowledge, the way she kissed him, her pushing of every limit in search of ecstasy, her desire to possess him totally— all these were the essence of Mallory Candler. Penn might believe Waters was enmeshed in a complex conspiracy designed to deprive him of his sanity, his freedom, and finally his money. But Penn could not know what Waters did.

He could not know that Cole, while weak where his vices were concerned, had always been a rock about the big things. Friendship. Loyalty. Fatherhood. At his core, Cole—like Waters—had struggled to live up to the John Wayne/Henry Fonda images that their fathers had revered and tried hard to inculcate in their sons. Yes, Cole might sell a pumping unit for quick cash when he was in a bind. But what he had said at the country club still resonated. *I'd go down with my legs broken and a bullet in my head before I'd do something to hurt you or your family.* It might be naive, but Waters believed in the ultimate goodness of his best friend. If that was stupidity, he was willing to pay the price for it.

And Penn knew nothing of Lily beyond her public

face. He could not know that before she had her miscarriages, Lily had been an attentive wife and lover,
but not a gifted or accomplished one. Even if she *were*
trying to convince Waters that she was Mallory reincarnated, Lily could never separate love and lust
enough to handle him in the brutally physical manner
that she had last night. It simply was not in her.

Across the cemetery, the dark knot of mourners
began to break up and return to their cars. Gravedig-
gers would soon lower Eve Sumner's body into the
ground. But whatever she really was—whatever
made her *Eve*—had vacated her body three nights ago
in the Eola Hotel, if not long before. Who was the
woman he had made love to for two weeks? If he was
right about Cole and Lily, the answer to that question
was something no one would ever believe. Not Penn
Cage. Not Tom Jackson. Not anyone who hadn't lived
through what Waters himself had. Not without proof.

"I have to know," he said aloud. "Once and for all."

The mourners' cars pulled out of the cemetery like
a slow train with a big black Cadillac hearse for a ca-
boose. As he watched them go, Waters knew there
was only one place he could go to get the answer he
needed. Home.

Walking back toward his Land Cruiser, he glanced
at his watch. It was 2:24 P.M. His heart stuttered. The
sight of Eve's burial had made him lose track of time.
Annelise would be dismissed from school in six minutes. Lily could be waiting in line right now to pick
her up.

"Jesus," he whispered, and he broke into a run.

chapter 15

Waters ran a red light and accelerated to sixty-five as fear poured like corrosive acid through his veins. He'd missed Annelise at school. One cell phone call to the elementary school office had determined that Rose had picked her up, and Rose's cell phone wasn't switched on. Which meant Annelise might already be home with Lily. The implications of this were almost more than he could stand. At the cemetery he'd decided he trusted his wife and his best friend. That meant there was no conspiracy to drive him crazy or frame him for murder. Which meant everything "Eve Sumner" had told him was true. He had never even met the real Eve, except perhaps in the panicked seconds before he lost consciousness in the hotel. Yet while he "slept," his hands had strangled the life out of her, guided by the twisted soul of Mallory Candler. And now Mallory was alone with Annelise, hidden in Lily's unsuspecting mind.

Waters turned onto State Street, stomped on the gas

pedal, and rawhided the Land Cruiser through two lines of double-parked cars. His fear was not for Annelise alone. Right now, the real danger was to Lily. Penn's comment about Lily's resurgent sex drive echoed in his mind: *Don't look a gift horse in the mouth.* Some men might think having Lily Waters and Mallory Candler in the same body was a gift from the gods, especially if you got Lily for the day shift and Mallory at night. It was the madonna-whore fantasy brought to life. Only Waters knew that this state of affairs would not last. Now that Mallory was this close to him, she would not be satisfied to coexist peacefully with Lily. Mallory Candler did not *share*. She would use all her power to control Lily, to dominate her, and finally to exterminate all trace of her from the body Mallory sought to inhabit.

Then the danger would shift to Annelise. For no matter what fantasies Mallory might have of domestic bliss, she would ultimately view Ana as a threat. A living reminder of Lily. And sooner or later, she would act to remove that threat. Just as she had removed Eve Sumner.

"Mallory killed Eve," Waters said aloud.

He hit the brakes and swerved into his driveway, then tore up toward the house. Rose's Saturn was still parked out front, and this brought him palpable relief. With Rose still here, he wouldn't have to wait until Annelise went to bed to see Lily alone. He skidded to a stop by the front porch, shut off the engine, and ran inside.

"Daddy!" Annelise cried from the end of the hall. She was crossing between rooms with Pebbles in her arms.

"Hey, punkin!" he called, running to her and sweeping her up in his arms. "Where's Rose?"

"Who's running in my house?" bellowed Rose, coming into the hall. "I should have known. I'm glad you're here, Mr. John. I need to go early today."

"Where's Lily?"

"She sleeping. She been tired most all day."

Thank God. "Rose, is there any way you can stay an extra hour?"

The maid looked doubtful. "My sister needs me to stop off at the drugstore for her potassium."

"Is it critical? I really need you, Rose."

The black woman studied Waters's face, then said, "I guess I could get my no-count nephew to get them pills. If his car's running."

"Thank you, Rose. Can you take Annelise outside and play for a few minutes? I'll come join you before long."

Rose nodded, her face creased with suspicion. "Come on, girl," she said to Annelise. "Put that mangy old cat down and bring my cell phone out to the swing set."

"Pebbles isn't *mangy*," Ana retorted, knowing Rose's gibes were all in fun.

"Hmm," Rose growled.

Ana darted into the kitchen for the cell phone, then ran for the back door. Rose followed slowly, her big hips swinging with patient determination.

As soon as she cleared the door, Waters walked back to the master bedroom and opened the door. Lily lay on her side beneath the covers, breathing deeply.

He walked over and started to touch her shoulder, then drew back his hand. What could he say? How could he know if Mallory or Lily was in control at any given moment? He couldn't simply ask Lily if she was Mallory. If Lily awakened as herself, his words would confuse and even frighten her. And if she awakened as Mallory, she might simply lie. He closed the bedroom door, but before he could think of a sensible way to learn the truth, Lily rolled over and opened her eyes.

"John?" she said in a sleepy voice. "What are you doing home? What time is it?"

"I'm back from work, babe. It's suppertime."

She rubbed her eyes. "God . . . I must have slept all afternoon."

He sat beside her on the bed. "Do you feel sick?"

"No, just . . . out of it. It's weird, like jet lag or something. Where's Ana?"

"Outside with Rose. I asked Rose to stay late."

"Why? I'll get up."

"Not yet." He leaned over her. "Do you remember what you did today?"

Lily nodded. "Yes, I . . ." She blinked several times, then looked blankly around the room. "I guess I *don't* remember."

Waters looked into his wife's bewildered eyes. All his instincts told him Lily was herself now. But even if she were, what could he say to her? *I think you're possessed by the soul of my old lover?* No, what he needed to do was bring Mallory to the surface. But how to make her reveal herself? *Actions speak louder than words*, said a voice in his head.

Lily threw aside the bedcovers and started to get up. Waters took hold of her shoulders and gently pushed her back down. "You don't have to rush," he said. "Annelise is fine with Rose."

"I'm okay," Lily assured him. "Really. I can get up."

Waters laid the flat of his hand between her breasts

and rubbed softly. "What if I don't want you to get up?"

Her eyes widened in surprise.

"I've been thinking about last night," he said. "All day."

After staring at him for a moment, Lily reached out and touched his thigh. "That feels good," she said.

His fingers went to the buttons of her silk night-shirt and opened the top three. As he leaned down to her breasts, he felt her hands entwine in the hair behind his head. He kissed gently at first, but as the pink flesh swelled in his mouth, he withdrew his tongue and bit the nipple.

"*Hey*," Lily protested. "Easy, okay?"

Waters murmured his assent, but he knew he would have to go further to awaken Mallory. For a while he caressed Lily's breasts in the way she had always liked. Then he kissed his way up to her left ear. "I want you now," he whispered. "Are you ready?"

Lily shifted her thighs, then made a sound low in her throat. "I think so."

He unbuckled his belt and slipped off his pants. Lily took hold of his shirt and pulled him across her, then kissed his mouth. As she parted her legs, he touched her cheek and said, "I want to be behind you."

Lily looked uncertain. "I want to see your face."

"I know." He shut his heart and focused on what he had to do. "But you know what I like."

Confusion clouded Lily's eyes, but after a few moments of reflection, she kissed him, then rolled over and got onto all fours. "Go slow," she said. "I'm not that ready."

Waters knelt behind her, rubbing and kissing her

lower back. Lily remained still. Mallory would have arched her back, catlike, against his hand. He wasn't sure exactly what to do next, but he knew in his soul that he was right. Given the right stimulus, Mallory would betray herself. She would be unable to resist. He slapped Lily on the rump, hard enough to sting.

"*Ow*," she cried. "What was that for?"

"You know what I like." He spanked her again. "What do *you* like?"

"I don't like that."

He slapped her once more, and harder. Lily tried to jerk away, but he grabbed her hips, thrust forward, and went between her thighs. She froze. Poised in this odd position, this confusion of desire and resistance, Waters felt something change. The flesh under his hands seemed to shiver, and then, as he watched in fascination, Lily looked back over her shoulder, her eyes glinting with excitement and anticipation.

"Oh, I know what you like," she said, pressing her hips back against him. "And you know what I like. So *do* it."

Waters was paralyzed. The consciousness glittering in those eyes belonged to a woman he had first made love to more than twenty years ago, before he even met his wife.

"Mallory?" he whispered.

She laughed then, a low, throaty sound, and her eyes filled with dark amusement. "When did you know?"

Waters could not find his voice. To look at his wife's face and see no trace of her in it was more than he could endure. As he knelt with his mouth open, Lily reached between her legs and took hold of him.

Her touch jolted him like a defibrillator jolting a

dead heart. He had accomplished part of his goal, but what he needed to do next, he could not do now. He threw himself off the bed, grabbed his pants, and ran for the hallway.

"Johnny!" yelled the voice behind him.

He pulled on his pants by the back door and buttoned his shirt as he ran outside. He saw Annelise and Rose at the swing set, Rose pushing Annelise with the steady rocking motion of an oil-well pump. The moment Rose saw his face, she grabbed the chains of the swing and stopped it.

"What's the matter, Mr. John? Where's your shoes?"

"Nothing's wrong. Lily's too tired for supper. I'm going to take Ana to her grandmother's for a while."

Concern filled the maid's eyes. "Are you sure everything's all right? Lily don't usually sleep like that. Maybe you should give Dr. Cage a call."

"No, it's—"

"Mama!" cried Annelise. "Daddy said you were sleeping."

Waters whirled and saw Lily walking down the back porch steps. He ran toward her with his arms out.

"You need to rest, honey! You said you were dizzy."

Lily squinted at him and shook her head. "I'm not dizzy. I want to see Annelise."

"No," Waters said firmly. "You need to lie down."

"Don't be ridiculous. It's still daylight."

"Go back inside!"

"Daddy?" called Annelise. "Why are you yelling at Mom?"

Waters turned and saw his daughter walking up

behind him. "Mama's sick, baby. You stay right there."

"Sick?" Ana's voice cracked. "Sick how?"

Waters turned and saw Rose staring at him as if he had lost his mind. *Have I?* he thought. Then he remembered the eyes glinting in the bedroom. "Lily, *please* go back inside."

Annelise began to cry.

Lily looked back at him with such a hurt expression that he felt like a Nazi storm trooper. But was she really upset? Or was Mallory reveling in a role she'd been waiting ten years to play?

"Mr. John," Rose said in an indignant voice, "I think you the one needs to go back inside. Get yourself a drink and sit down for a while."

Lily's eyes remained on Waters, pleading for some explanation.

"Go back inside," he begged. *"Please."*

Lily burst into tears, then turned and ran back up the steps. Behind him, Annelise began to wail. Waters turned and saw Rose kneeling with the child in her arms, comforting her with soft words. But over Annelise's shoulder, the maid glared at him with eyes that could melt steel.

"Keep Ana out here," he told her. "I'll be right back."

He ran up the back steps and started down the hall toward the master bedroom. As he walked, he cut his eyes left and right, half expecting some kind of attack from his blind side. Mallory had done such things before, and he sensed danger now.

Finding the bedroom door closed against him, he began to doubt himself. What if Lily *had* snapped back to herself after he fled the bedroom? He put his ear to the cypress face of the door but heard nothing. Testing the knob, he found it locked.

"Lily?" he called.

No reply.

"Lily!"

Still nothing.

"Lily, open the door," he called in a reasonable voice. "I need to talk to you."

The silence mocked him. He looked down at the brass knob. There was a tiny hole at its center. Annelise had picked the lock many times with a paper clip. He was about to go in search of one when he heard a soft click from the knob. When nothing else happened, he grabbed the knob and threw open the door.

Lily sat cross-legged at the center of the bed, her palms upturned in the manner of a Hindu in meditation, her wide-open eyes burning with a light that rooted Waters to the floor.

She smiled serenely. "Close the door."

"You can't do this," Waters told her.

"It's already done. Come in and close the door, Johnny. I'll do the talking."

Waters did as she said.

"I want to tell you how my father died," Lily said. "Do you remember what I told you about him?"

Waters said nothing. He felt as though someone had injected him with the most powerful hallucinogen on the planet. To hear the voice of his wife speak Mallory's inmost thoughts—and in Mallory's diction—pushed him into a realm beyond fear. It inverted his sense of reality, so that the familiar engendered horror rather than affection, and dread replaced love.

"You know what I'm talking about."

For some reason an image of Penn Cage behind his desk filled Waters's mind. "That he abused you?"

"Mmm-hmm. You never believed me about that, did you?"

He tried to guess where she was going. "Why do you think that?"

Lily shook her head in reproof. "Because I was *inside* you, Johnny. I know your thoughts now. Your memories."

"Did it really happen?"

"Maybe not like you imagine. But it happened. From the time I was about ten, I started to feel uncomfortable around my father. He said things to me he shouldn't have said. He noticed things about me. It started as compliments, but the older I got . . . he talked about my beauty, all the time, of course. But then it was my body. And my 'way,' he called it. My 'beguiling' way. He'd walk into the bathroom when I was using it. Or trick me into coming into the bathroom when he was in there without clothes on."

"Did he touch you?"

"He wanted to. My friends knew it too. Some of them. He did the same kinds of things to them. Too much time with us instead of with the grown-ups. Touches that lingered too long. It was only lack of nerve that stopped him from doing something physical."

"If he never touched you, how do you know that's true?"

"I'll tell you. About fourteen months ago, when I first got back to Natchez, I wanted desperately to get into my old house. I wanted to remember what it was like, and to get some of my old things, if they were still there. I didn't want to risk it when I was in Danny. But once I got into Eve, I felt confident enough. I took the key from under the rock in the flower bed where they'd always hidden it, and slipped inside."

Lily's eyes glazed with the power of memory. "I had no idea what it would be like. I found my room exactly as I'd left it. It was like a shrine. My old clothes, my posters, my photos. My cheerleading uniform. Everything. It was like going to Graceland and seeing Elvis's old costumes on mannequins. They actually had my Miss Mississippi gown on a mannequin in the corner." She shuddered. "I had never felt as dead as I did in that room. Anyway, I took a few small things. Some snapshots. A cross my grandmother had given me. A scarf I'd had when you and I were together. In moments like that, you know which things are important. The things you can't live without."

"Your diaries?"

She nodded. "That's what I really wanted. I expected them to be in my drawer, but they weren't. I searched the whole house, but I couldn't find them. Then I went into the attic. We had a walk-in attic on the second floor. Remember? I found the diaries in a glass-topped box by the back wall. There was light up there, so I started reading them."

Waters thought he saw tears welling in her eyes.

"Reading what I'd written so long ago . . . it was the opposite of how I'd felt in my room. I felt more alive then—more myself—than I had since the night I was raped in New Orleans. There was my true soul, right there on the page. As I sat reading, I noticed something odd about the wall. The edge of a board was sticking out. But it wasn't like a warp. The board was propped there. I pulled it away and found a space. There was a book inside it. A big one. It was a photo album."

"What was in it?"

"When I opened it . . . I saw pictures of a naked girl. I thought it was just regular pornography at first. Then I saw that the girl was me." Disgust rippled through Lily's body. "*Me*, Johnny. I was about twelve, and I was in the bathroom. My own bathroom. I flipped the pages and saw more pictures of myself, from age eleven to about twenty. I was always naked or partly naked, and always in the bathroom. They were all shot from the same angle. Later, I found the hole in the wall that he'd shot them through. There were pictures of my friends too. Anyone who had come over to spend the night with me. When I saw those pictures . . . I knew that everything I'd felt when I was a child was true. Things I'd punished myself for thinking about my father . . . do you understand? I felt raped. By my own father. And I knew what he did with that book. He sneaked up there all those years and . . . you know what he did. It makes me want to throw up."

Waters remembered Benjamin Candler's odd combination of arrogance and smarmy glad-handing.

"Don't you remember how he took pictures of everything?" Lily asked. "Every football game, every pep rally, every school play. But those weren't the pictures he really wanted."

"What did you do with the book?"

"I put it back where I found it."

"Why?"

"I went back to Eve's house and thought about it.

Let it sink in. And then, three days later, I went back. But that time I took a gun."

Waters's stomach tightened. "Why?"

"I knew he'd deny it. I went on my mother's bridge day. That was his afternoon off. I waited for him in the kitchen. When he walked in, he saw Eve Sumner, realtor, standing there with a gun."

"What did he do?"

" 'What's the matter, Ms. Sumner?' " Lily cried in a hysterical voice. " 'Are you in trouble? Is someone chasing you?' I laughed and said, 'No, I just want to talk to you.' He asked what about. 'Your daughter,' I told him. 'My daughter's dead,' he said. 'Are you sure about that?' I asked. He said that wasn't appropriate conversation. He asked me to leave his house. I refused. I said, 'I want to talk to you about why you molested your daughter.' "

"Jesus."

"He looked stunned, but he didn't kick me out. He asked what the hell I was talking about. I told him I knew about the pictures he'd been taking all those years. His face went white, Johnny. I was like the ghost of Christmas past. He told me to get the hell out, but you should have seen him staring at me. I knew what he was thinking. He was wondering if I was one of those other girls who'd come to spend the night. He said he'd call the police if I didn't get out. I dared him to do it. He told me I couldn't prove anything about him. Then I opened the drawer next to me and took out the photo album. I'd gotten it from the attic before he came home. That was all it took. He turned gray, like there was no blood going to his face. Then he started to cry. He asked me who I was."

"What did you tell him?"

"The truth. 'I'm Mallory,' I said. He didn't believe me until I started to talk. I told him things only I could know, like I did with you. I reminded him of things he'd said to me, things no one else could possibly have heard. I'd been talking for about two minutes when he grabbed his left arm. I ripped the phone out of the wall and walked out with the photo album. That night, I heard that he'd died of a heart attack."

Savage satisfaction entered Lily's face.

"Why did you tell me this?"

She cocked her head and smiled. "An object lesson. You betrayed me too, Johnny. Not like he did. You looked me in the face when you did it. You tried to ease the pain as much as you could, but in the end you only made it worse."

"Mallory—"

"Don't worry. I forgive you. I'm trying to, anyway. I know why you did what you did now. I felt your guilt when I was inside you. You were so young. You couldn't even imagine being married. It takes men longer to see what the important things are in life. I know that now. We had some bad luck . . . but now we have a second chance."

"Mallory, listen—"

"We don't have time to talk about this now," Lily said, uncrossing her legs and sliding to the edge of the bed. "We have to take care of Annelise. She's scared, and she doesn't understand what she just saw."

He remembered his daughter's tear-stained face. "Mallory, you can't . . . This is all wrong. You can't do this to my wife."

She shook her head as though he were speaking nonsense. "I *am* your wife now, Johnny."

"Mama? Where are you?" Annelise's frightened voice echoed up the hall.

As he turned toward the door, Waters heard Rose call, "Mr. John, this baby's upset! She got to see her mama!"

"In here, Rose," Lily called.

Annelise shot through the door like a missile, then froze and looked from father to mother. Lily held out both arms.

"Come here, baby! Mama's right here!"

Annelise leaped onto the bed and hugged Lily tightly.

"What ya'll want me to do?" Rose asked from the doorway, her voice strangely suspicious.

Waters sighed in surrender. "Go home, Rose."

"There's nothing but cornbread made. The pork chops and macaroni still got to be done."

"I'll do that," Lily said from the bed. "Go on home and rest old Arthur."

Old Arthur . . . Rose's nickname for arthritis. Mallory could access Lily's memories at will. No one would ever be able to discover the truth by probing her with questions. Only Waters, who saw the differences revealed behind the bedroom door, would know Mallory lay hidden behind Lily's eyes. Perhaps with time Rose would sense something amiss, but by then it would probably be too late.

"All right, then," Rose said reluctantly. "I'm going on." She gave Waters a last look of disapproval and walked down the hall.

"Are you really, okay, Mom?" asked Annelise.

Lily gave her a storybook smile. "Sure I am. You go with Daddy and start the water for the macaroni. I'll put on some real clothes and then make the pork chops and the salad."

Ana hugged her again, then climbed down from the bed and came to Waters. "Do I get to cook the macaroni by myself?"

"Do you think you can?"

"Mama said!"

"Okay, then. Come on."

With a last hard look at Lily, Waters picked Ana up and ran for the kitchen. She giggled all the way there, but Waters's heart felt like a stone. He wanted to run right out the front door to the Land Cruiser and put as much distance as he could between Annelise and the lost soul dressing in the bedroom.

But running was not an option. Mallory wouldn't even have to chase him. She could simply call the police and accuse him of kidnapping. He'd be lucky to get a hundred miles from town before he was arrested. And no judge in the state would believe one word of his story.

Twenty minutes later, the pork chops were simmering in a skillet full of gravy, and the macaroni was boiling on the range top set in the marble island. Lily had tried to make preparing the dinner a family affair, but it took all Waters's will to simply play the role of a sane father.

Lily and Annelise were working on the salad now, and whenever Ana's attention was diverted, Lily would wink or smile at him. As the charade played on, one question filled his mind: *Where is Lily right now?* While inside Eve, Mallory had described her host as "sleeping." What did that mean? The only encouraging thing Waters could recall—as horrible as the memory was—was that Eve seemed to have snapped back to herself before she was murdered. Which meant that her true self had survived, even after a year of possession. Mallory had been inside Lily for only forty-eight hours.

Lily lifted a butcher knife from the block and began to slice tomatoes. Watching her deftly handle the blade, Waters recalled Mallory sitting in a fetal position in an empty bathtub, methodically cutting parallel lines into her wrists. He felt a scream building behind his lips. The only thing that kept it there was his desire to spare Ana the trauma of seeing her father lose control. Yet how long could he spare her? He was trapped in a situation no one would believe: while a murder investigation moved ever closer to him, his daughter lived under threat from the real killer—a woman everyone would perceive as her mother. And if no one believed him, no one would help him. He would have to solve his own problem. There was only one solution that he could see. Mallory had to leave Lily's body.

"Hey, punkin?" he prompted Annelise. "Time to get the Velveeta ready."

While Ana worked to tear open the foil packet, he strained the macaroni in the sink, then transferred the noodles to a ceramic dish. "You want to stir the cheese in this time?"

She clapped and grabbed a big spoon from the drawer.

"You know how to do it," he told her. "I'm going to show Mom something in the dining room. We'll be back in a second."

"Okay." Ana climbed up on a chair and began squeezing Velveeta into the noodle dish.

Waters took hold of Lily's wrist, pulled her into the dining room, and shut the door behind them.

Lily seemed amused by his action until he grabbed her throat and pushed her up against the wall.

"Listen to me, Mallory," he hissed. "You can*not* do this. You have to get out of my wife."

She gave a constricted laugh.

Waters squeezed harder, cutting off her air. "You know as well as I do that I can't kill you. Because I can't kill you without killing Lily. You're like AIDS, or cancer. But there are things I can do."

"*Such as?*" she croaked, her eyes still bright with laughter.

"You think you felt dead when you saw that room at your parents' house? If you don't get out of Lily, this is how it will be. When Annelise is around, I'll treat you just as I would Lily. But the minute she's gone, you won't exist. I won't look at you. I won't speak to you. I won't acknowledge a word you say. I won't sleep with you. Ever again."

Lily's eyes seemed to dilate with fear, but the moment he loosened his hand, she laughed. "You're so naive, Johnny. I'm going to let this little outburst go, because I know you're in shock. But you don't tell me what I'm going to do. You strangled Eve." She batted his hands away from her neck. "All I have to do is give them your name, and they can match the DNA to the semen you left in her body. Okay?"

Waters's mouth fell open. "My God. That's why you killed her."

Lily's mouth flattened to a thin line, and her eyes went arctic cold. "You have no *idea* what you put me through. You gave me two babies, and you made me kill them. Then you *walked away*. Well, for once you can't walk away from me." She reached up and touched his cheek. "Do you know what it's like to hate someone enough to kill them, but love them too much to do it? I thought of killing you a thousand times. And *her*. But I'm glad I didn't. Because now I have you." She pinched some skin on her arm and pulled it up. "And her too. And that's all I want, Johnny."

Fear ate through his bowels like a ravenous worm.

"I know exactly how things are going to work out," Lily said, "so you may as well accept it all now. Six months from now, you won't even remember Lily—"

Waters seized her throat again and squeezed with enough force to crush her windpipe. His arms quivered from the strain, and Lily's face went red, then blue.

"Mama?" Annelise called.

Waters let go the moment the dining room door opened.

"The macaroni's— *Mom?* Your face is all red! What's the matter?"

Lily knelt and hugged Ana. "Nothing, baby. I bent over to look under the table, and the blood just went to my head. It's nothing. Let's go eat!"

She smiled at Waters and led Ana back into the kitchen. He waited a moment, then followed, his hands shaking at his sides.

Lily was brushing mushrooms into an empty bowl, which she then handed to Annelise. "Do you remember how to take the stems out, baby?"

"Of course I do. That's easy."

"Will you do it for me?"

Annelise nodded and sat on the floor, the bowl between her knees. Lily turned to the cutting board and resumed slicing the tomatoes.

"I hope Pebbles doesn't come in here and try to eat from this bowl," Annelise said. "She won't like mushrooms." She looked up at Waters. "Will she, Dad?"

Tears stung Waters's eyes as he looked down at his daughter. "Probably not, punkin."

A bright reflection suddenly flashed past his eyes. He looked up at Lily, and his heart stopped. She was dangling the butcher knife over Annelise's head like a miniature sword of Damocles. Its point swung back and forth as Ana patiently picked stems from the mushrooms.

"Your daddy's in a funny mood today," Lily said, her eyes mocking Waters. "I think he ought to realize how much he has to be thankful for. Don't you think so, Ana?"

Annelise pursed her lips as she worked at a thick brown stem. "Daddy knows what to be thankful for."

"I wonder sometimes." Lily lowered the knife to within a half-inch of the crown of Annelise's head. "Do you, John? Do you know what to be thankful for?"

"Yes," he said in a shaky voice. "I do."

Lily smiled, then lifted the blade about twelve inches. Waters felt slight relief until she dropped the knife and caught the flashing blade just above Annelise's head.

"Oh!" Lily cried in an exaggerated voice. "I almost had an accident!"

"Be careful," said Annelise. "More kids get killed from accidents than from getting sick or anything else. I learned that in school yesterday."

Lily winked at Waters, then went back to slicing the

tomatoes. He fell to his knees and hugged Annelise until she told him to stop.

Ninety minutes later, Waters was tucking Annelise into bed upstairs.

"Why isn't Mama tucking me in too?" she asked.

"Mama still feels tired."

"She said she was all better."

Waters nodded. "Mothers fib a little sometimes, so daddies and little girls don't worry so much. But she'll be fine. You sleep tight. Hang on to Albert tonight."

Ana clutched her stuffed rabbit to her chest.

He kissed her forehead, then walked to the stairs.

"*'Night! Love ya! See ya in the morning!*" Annelise called, and she laughed when he repeated it back to her.

As he descended the stairs, he realized why Mallory had let him put Ana to bed alone. She wanted to emphasize just what was at stake if he didn't get with her program. For Waters, the stakes did not need emphasis. But as his foot hit the bottom step, he realized that Mallory's latest object lesson cut two ways. Everyone feared losing someone, and Mallory was no different.

He found Lily in the bedroom, lying across the down comforter in a nearly transparent camisole that she had received as a gag gift at a friend's bridal shower. She had never worn that piece of lingerie before tonight. He walked to the foot of the bed and spoke in a voice devoid of emotion.

"I want you to listen carefully. You think you hold

all the cards, but you don't. The final card, I hold. And if you don't do what I tell you to do, I'll play it."

She must have heard something new in his voice, for her smile vanished, replaced by a crafty attentiveness. "What card are you talking about?"

"The death card. The ace of spades."

Lily twined a lock of her short blond hair around her finger and began to twist it. "What do you mean?"

"Before I let you destroy my wife and child, I will blow my fucking head off. And you will never have me."

She seemed not to have heard his threat. Or perhaps not to have fully understood it.

"You know me, Mallory. If you leave me no choice, I'll kill myself."

Lily shook her head. "You won't. You wouldn't leave Lily and Annelise without you."

"You're right. I'd take Lily with me. A bullet in the head for her. Then me."

She went still, her eyes wide with fear. At last he had rattled her. "You wouldn't do it," she said, sounding not at all sure. "You wouldn't abandon Annelise."

"Here's why you're wrong," Waters said. "When I shoot Lily, you die with her. I couldn't live with myself after killing my wife, so I'd finish the job on me. But Annelise would survive and be safe. She'd go to live with her grandmother. That's already arranged in our wills."

Lily's head moved slowly back and forth. "That will never happen."

"You don't think so? Do you know why I survived the hell that was the end of our relationship? Because I'm stronger than you are. How many times did you try to kill yourself? Four? Five? But you couldn't do it.

It was all theater. But I don't act, Mallory. You know that. The day I decide to do it, consider it done."

Lily got up and began to pace the bedroom, her mouth working in frustration. She gave off the desperate fury of a wild animal pacing a cage. Suddenly she stopped and met Waters's eye.

"You said you'd do that if I don't do what you wanted me to do. Well? What do you want me to do?"

"Leave Lily alone. Get out of her head."

"If I do that, what will you do for me?"

"Why should I do anything for you?"

Her hand went to her neck and twined another lock of hair around her finger. "Because you love me. But if you can't face that yet, you should do it because I'm the only thing keeping you out of jail."

Waters fought back his anger. "I do love you."

Lily's eyes softened.

"I just can't let you destroy my wife. That's why I want you to go into another woman."

She watched him in silence, trying to work out his thoughts. "Who?"

"I don't know yet."

"But you pick this woman, you mean?"

"Yes."

"Someone you like."

"Whose face and body I like," he said.

She stared at him for nearly a minute, her eyes growing dark with suspicion. "If I go into this other woman, you'll kill her. That's what you're thinking."

"You know me better than that. I couldn't kill an innocent person."

"If you thought you were saving your family, you might."

"I'd kill myself, Lily, and Annelise, before I'd kill an innocent person."

Morbid curiosity flickered in her eyes. "Why?"

"Because I'm responsible for this. For you being like you are. Lily and Annelise are part of me. They're involved, even though they didn't ask to be. The sins of the fathers and all that. But I can't visit this karma on anyone else. If someone has to pay, it should be me and mine."

She tilted her head, studying his eyes. "You know what, Johnny?"

"What?"

"Lily is too old, anyway. We're going to have our own babies, and thirty-nine is too old for that." She lifted the camisole, grabbed a dimple of cellulite from her upper thigh, and pulled. "*Yuck.* Pick someone under thirty, okay?"

Waters struggled to suppress his rage. "I don't have any problem with that."

She walked forward and took hold of his hand. "Just one more thing, Johnny. Pick her soon, okay?"

Lily smiled as though things had arrived at the exact point she'd chosen from the beginning. "Now, get those clothes off and get into bed. I want you to finish what you started this afternoon."

He pulled his hand free. "That's not part of the deal. First you move into someone else. Then I come to you."

She laughed. "Who do you think makes the rules here? I agreed to your idea because of the childbearing issue. But don't forget that you could be spending the night in jail. I know all this has you freaked out, but I want you, Johnny. Now. And I'm going to have you."

Waters made no move toward the bed.

"Re-*mem*-ber," she said in a singsong voice. "If Mama ain't happy, *no*-body's happy." Lily walked to the dresser, opened a drawer, and brought out a shining pair of handcuffs.

"Those look like Eve's," he observed.

"Of course they are. Your wife doesn't have anything like this hidden in her underwear drawer. Not even a vibrator."

Lily pranced toward the bed, dangling the handcuffs as though to provoke him. "These *were* Eve's, I should have said. Possession is nine-tenths of the law, right?" She laughed. "Isn't that what they say, Johnny?"

Waters stared at the handcuffs, a shining little metaphor for his situation. He recalled Eve cuffing him to the bed at the Eola. Thinking of that made him think of Mallory, not as she was now, but when they were together. In those days, Mallory had bound him with scarves, not handcuffs. He saw himself tied to the headboard of her parents' bed, wondering if Ben Candler and his wife would come home unexpectedly and discover their princess *in flagrante delicto*. When he thought of Ben Candler, he felt something shift deep in his mind, and he saw what Mallory had described earlier: the local politician who liked to take secret snapshots of little girls. In the dark glow of that image was born his next move in the emotional chess match he would have to play for possession of his life and family.

"Take that slutty rag off and get under the covers," he said in a harsh voice.

Lily looked curiously at him, trying to read his intent. "You first," she replied.

"I'll join you in a second. I have to do something first."

"Like what?"

"Just get in the bed. And turn off the lights."

A wary look in her eyes now. "I want the lights on."

"I can't do it with the lights on. I can't look into Lily's face and make love to her when she's not there."

"I thought you'd like the idea."

"I don't. You can use your handcuffs or whatever kinky stuff you want. Just turn off the lights."

"All right. But where are you going?"

"What are you worried about? I can't hurt you without hurting Lily."

Pouting with her lips but not her eyes, she went to the bed and slipped off the camisole, then climbed under the covers and switched off the lamp.

Waters walked to the door.

"Tell me where you're going!"

"For God's sake, just lie back and enjoy it."

"I intend to."

He walked quickly to the den. Inside the cabinet under the TV was the camcorder he had scolded Annelise for using without permission. It was a Sony PC-110, a handheld digital camera with more special-effects functions than he would ever use. But the PC-110 also had one capability that he had found both fun and useful. Called Super Night Shot, it allowed you to shoot video in total darkness, by projecting an infrared beam onto a subject. He and Annelise had used it to film Pebbles hunting in the backyard at night. Tonight he would use it to try to save his life.

He inserted a fresh tape into the slot, then removed

the lens cap and switched on the camera. The Super Night Shot switch was on the side. He activated it, then turned off the lights in the den and looked through the viewfinder. A ghostly green image of the room filled the screen, the camera autofocusing wherever he turned it.

"Okay," he said softly. "Let's make a movie."

He took off his shirt and wrapped it partly around the camera, but took care to leave the lens and the infrared beam generator exposed. On his way back to the bedroom, he stopped in the hall bathroom, dug under the sink for a minute, then continued on, the camera and shirt held carefully in his left hand. At the bedroom door, he walked quickly through the darkness to Lily's low dresser and set his shirt on it, the camera lens facing the bed. Then he walked around to his side of the bed and began removing his pants.

The lamp on Lily's side flashed on, temporarily blinding him.

"What did you do?" she asked.

"Nothing."

She looked at his pants on the floor, then up at him. Then she leaned off the bed and lifted the pants to look under them.

"Looking for a gun?" he asked.

A white plastic bottle of K-Y Silk-E lubricant lay beneath the khakis.

"My mistake," she said. She lay back on the bed and stared at his nude body. "You still look good, Johnny."

"Get on all fours and handcuff yourself to the bedpost."

"What are you going to do?" she asked, a mocking smile on her face.

"Teach you a lesson." He reached over and switched off the lamp.

Her voice came out of the dark. "How are you going to do that?"

Waters climbed onto the bed, looked in the direction of the camera, and silently mouthed three words. *I'm sorry, Lily.* Then he faced forward, took hold of the familiar hips in front of him, and slapped one cheek. "You know what I like, Mallory," he said.

He heard a metallic snick as the handcuffs snapped shut.

"Yes, I do," came Mallory's low voice. "And you know what I need."

Waters set to work with a will.

chapter 16

When Waters walked into his office at nine the next morning, he found Penn Cage waiting behind his desk.

"You wouldn't be here unless there was bad news."

"It's not catastrophic," Penn said, "but it's serious."

"Tell me."

"The police say they have a videotape of your Land Cruiser in front of the Eola Hotel one hour before Eve's estimated time of death."

The floor seemed to shudder beneath his feet. "That's impossible."

"Maybe not. They say there was a traffic accident at the intersection of Pearl and Franklin streets that night. A car hit an MP&L cherry-picker truck. Do you remember that?"

Waters tried to keep his facial muscles still. "Yes."

"There were lots of squad cars there. Ambulances, a fire truck, and a sheriff's department cruiser. For some reason, the sheriff's car had his videocam running—the one they switch on during traffic stops. He was pointed the wrong way up Pearl Street, and the police say his camera recorded your Land Cruiser turning from Main onto Pearl, stopping, then backing onto Main again and disappearing. The tape is date- and time-stamped."

"*Shit.* Do they have my license plate on tape?"

"I don't know yet. But a Land Cruiser is a rare vehicle in this town, and they've asked that you give a DNA sample for testing."

"Oh God."

"Obviously they'll want to compare this to the semen taken from Eve Sumner's corpse."

"And it will match." Images of Parchman Prison filled Waters's mind: endless rows of soybean fields and angry inmates, himself locked in a barred box. "The police called you?" he asked. "How did they know you were my lawyer?"

"Lily told them," Penn replied. "Tom Jackson called her just as you left the house. She told him I was your lawyer, and that he should call me. I came straight here."

"Lily didn't know you were my lawyer." Fresh fear poured into him.

"Obviously she did," Penn said.

"She must have been following me."

"Your wife?"

Not my wife, Waters thought, touching his back pocket, where the Mini-DV videotape he had shot last night rested. He had felt so confident about his plan, but now . . .

"Am I going to be arrested?"

"I don't think so. Tom wanted to bring you downtown for questioning today, though."

"Jesus." Waters felt inevitability closing around him like a noose.

"I requested that he interview you at the law office of a friend of mine. Since you've cooperated so far, Tom agreed. That may not seem like much of a gift, but it's a lot better than going through this in some interrogation room at the police station. It's set for three this afternoon."

"What about the DNA test? What should I do?"

"Comply immediately. That's what an innocent man would do."

"But I know my DNA will match."

"That's not the point right now. DNA testing takes a long time to complete. Months, sometimes. I've seen tests come back in three weeks with the FBI pushing, but this is a local case. By agreeing to the test, you buy yourself three to twelve weeks. Closer to twelve is my bet."

Waters felt his breath returning. "I can't be arrested, Penn. I have to stay free."

"You will."

"If I'm arrested, will I get bail?"

"Almost certainly. You're a pillar of the community with no criminal record."

"But it's murder."

"Take it easy, John."

"What if they trip me up during questioning? What if they arrest me then?"

"I think that's unlikely. Tom might ask you to take a lie-detector test, though."

"I can't do that!"

Penn held up both palms to reassure him. "You won't have to. I'll advise you against submitting to a polygraph, and I'll do that in Tom's presence. The refusal will look more like my decision than yours. The police here still see me as a big-city prosecutor, and that's to your advantage right now."

"He'll ask me if I had an affair with Eve. What if I deny it, and they have a witness or something?"

Penn answered carefully. "I will never advise you to lie, John. I can't do that. But I will say this: If, after today's questioning, the police still believe that you weren't having an affair with Ms. Sumner, I'd wait until the day before the DNA test was due back, and then I'd tell them the semen found in Eve was probably yours. You were having an extramarital affair with a woman of dubious sexual character, and she happened to get murdered. You knew that getting mixed up in that could destroy your marriage. As an innocent man, you hoped—and even assumed—that the guilty party would be caught before the DNA test came back, which might obviate the need for any ruckus to be made about whose semen it was. The odds of that would be low, considering the nature of this case, but a scared husband will tell himself many things. The police understand reasoning like that. Being guilty of an affair does not make you guilty of murder."

Waters found it hard to concentrate on his lawyer's words. He looked around his office as though for an avenue of escape.

"John? Do you understand what I'm telling you?"

"When do they want the DNA sample?"

"Adams County Path Lab is ready for us as soon as we can get there. I suggest we go immediately. There will be police representatives there. Probably Tom Jackson."

A bubble of panic ballooned in Waters's chest, cutting off his air. If he were arrested today, Mallory might abandon her intention to move out of Lily and into another woman, as she had agreed to do last night. He had to let her know what was happening.

"You look like you might faint, John. Sit down."

"I need to use the bathroom."

Waters hurried from his office, went to Sybil's desk, and grabbed her cordless phone from its cradle. She looked up in surprise, and he put his forefinger over his lips. Then he slipped into the conference room and called Linton Hill.

"Waters residence," Rose said.

"It's John, Rose. I need to talk to Lily."

"Lily gone swimming, Mr. John."

"Okay, thanks." He clicked off and dialed Lily's cell phone. It rang five times, and then a recorded message told him "the subscriber" was either unavailable or out of the service area. Desperate now, he hung up and walked down the hall toward Cole's office. Cole had said to come to him if he needed help, and Waters definitely needed it now. Cole might not believe his story about Mallory being in Lily, but at bottom, that didn't really matter. Because Cole would do what Waters asked, even if he thought he was crazy. But when he opened the door, he found Cole's office empty.

"He hasn't come in today," Sybil said from behind Waters. "I don't know where he is."

"Shit."

Sybil looked genuinely worried, and not about Cole. "Is there something I can do to help you, John?"

"I wish you could, but no." He squeezed her arm, then walked back to his office.

Penn was standing at the center of the room, examining a dragonfly trapped in amber and mounted on a black pedestal.

"Feeling better?" he asked.

"A little. Penn, we have to talk, and I mean for real."

The lawyer looked up, concern in his face. "What is it? Have you been holding something back?"

"In a way. Last night, Lily told me she was Mallory. She *told* me that."

"What did she tell you? Exactly?"

"That the theory I put to you yesterday is true. That she moved from Eve, through me, into Lily."

Penn rolled his eyes. "John, we've been over this."

"*Please* try to listen with an open mind. Last night I secretly videotaped Lily and me in bed. She's doing things on that tape she's never done in her life."

"And you want to show this tape to me?"

"No, because you don't have any frame of reference to judge it by. You don't know what she was like before. I'm talking about kinky stuff, though. Bondage, handcuffs."

Penn cleared his throat. "Handcuffs aren't that kinky, John."

"In Lily's mind, handcuffs belong on felons, nowhere else."

"As far as you know. Tell me what else happened."

"Lily threatened Annelise's life."

Penn drew back, incredulous. "How?"

"She held a fucking butcher knife over her head!"

"Well . . . did Annelise see this?"

"No."

"What else did Lily say to you?"

"Too much to remember. Penn, I know you think

I'm psychotic, but it's *her*. It's Mallory! She told me she killed her father!"

"That's crap. Ben Candler died of a heart attack."

"Yes, but do you know what caused it? Remember you told me some people had told you Ben was a little strange? What word did you use? Pervy?"

"Pervy. Perverted."

Waters quickly related Mallory's tale of the secret photos and the gunpoint confrontation with her father. As Penn listened, his expression changed from skepticism to fascination.

"Jesus," he said when Waters finished. "It's hard to imagine Cole Smith making up that story. Maybe Danny Buckles, the child molester, did something like that, and Eve or Lily modified the story to use on you. We know Eve knew Buckles, because she warned you about his abuse at the school."

"Are you *kidding* me?" Waters asked. "You're grasping at straws!"

Penn walked over to Waters's desk and sat behind it. "I don't think so. And Ben's heart attack . . . maybe Cole and Eve were trying to shake him down the same way they did you. They tried to convince him Mallory was alive, and it killed him."

"You still see a conspiracy behind all this? Do you really think Lily would threaten her own daughter with a butcher knife?"

"I'm afraid so. By doing something a loving mother would never do, Lily convinces you beyond all doubt of the fantasy they want to sell you. She's not Lily anymore. It's like Eve cutting herself. That's the only rational explanation for the events you've described."

"There's one other possibility."

"What?"

"Eve was telling the truth from the start!"

The lawyer slammed his hand down on Waters's desk. "For God's sake, wake up! You're about to be at the center of the biggest murder case this town has seen since I reopened the Del Payton case. You could go to prison for life. You could get the death penalty! And you're so far down in denial, you can't see anything. Do you understand what I'm telling you?"

"Yes."

"I don't think you do!"

Waters threw up his hands to show he understood the obvious. "I don't want to go to prison. But compared to a threat to my wife and daughter, prison is nothing. I can't ignore what all my instincts tell me is true." Waters put his hands on the front of his desk and leaned toward Penn. "You were a prosecutor, right? What happens when human beings have sex? Biologically. The seventh-grade sex-ed version."

The lawyer shook his head in exasperation. "The male deposits sperm in the vagina of the female."

"Exactly. An exchange of bodily fluids."

"From male to female," Penn clarified.

"You don't think anything goes the other way? Forget intercourse. Just think about kissing. That old expression, swapping spit? That's exactly what you're doing. And scientists can do DNA tests on cells in saliva."

"What are you getting at, John?"

"What do we really know about human consciousness? The top neuroscientists in the world can't tell you what it is. Where in the brain is consciousness located? What if there's consciousness in every strand of DNA in your body? Or what if your consciousness is at least *linked* to every strand of DNA in your body?

We know our individual consciousness grows out of our DNA maps. It has to. That's where our brains come from. Do you dispute any of that?"

Penn waved his hand impatiently. "If we were sitting in a bar or a college seminar, I'd love to bat this around with you. But you're in real trouble, and you're proposing as an explanation something that defies all physical laws."

"*Known* physical laws. Every Sunday, people go to church and pray for their immortal souls. Is there an immortal soul, Penn? If you believe so, you're saying it survives past death. If that's the case, who's to say that in certain situations—extreme situations of violence or desire for survival—that the soul can't move into another person the way Mallory said hers did?"

Penn sighed but did not argue.

"Mallory said the transfer can happen only during sex. And not just any sex, but during orgasm, when the individual self is blanked out. That creates a window of opportunity for the incoming soul—or consciousness—to gain a foothold. Do you deny that your conscious self, your identity even, basically blanks out during orgasm? Isn't that how it feels to you?"

"In a way, yes. But this idea of soul transfer . . . it's like some crazy blend of New Age science and Eastern mysticism."

"That's what quantum physics sounds like too, if you read much of it. Penn, have you ever slept with two women at the same time?"

"*What?* No."

"I don't mean in the same bed. I mean, have you slept with two women concurrently? Both for a long period of time?"

The lawyer shifted in his chair, obviously uncomfortable with some memory. "I was in that situation
once. For a couple of months."

"Two months isn't really long enough. I was in that
situation for five months one time. And something
happened that I remember to this day. When I started
sleeping with the second woman, her periods were
three weeks off from those of the first woman. But by
the third month, their periods had synchronized. And
they *stayed* synchronized."

Penn nodded thoughtfully. "I think it's well known
that women who live together—roommates, or girls
living in the same dorm hall—sometimes get synchronized periods."

"Yes, but something mental could be operating
there. What I'm describing is different. Neither
woman I was sleeping with was conscious of the
other. Certainly not of when the other woman's period was. And all I can think is that somehow, something was passing between those two women. And it
could only have been passed through *me*. You see?
Hormones, cells of some kind . . . I don't know. Cole's
had the same thing happen to him. This is weird stuff,
but all I'm trying to show you is that even in this day
and age, we understand very little about some
things."

"I'll concede that much. But what do you want me
to do about it?"

"I want you to keep your mind open enough to
help me in the way I really need help. That's all. I'm a
hell of a lot more afraid of Mallory Candler hurting
my wife and child than I am of going to prison for
murder. So . . . what do you think?"

Penn took a deep breath, sighed, and looked up at

Waters with deep compassion. "I think I'm your lawyer, John. And I think no jury in this state is going to buy what you just told me as a defense for murder. Not unless we're going for a verdict of not guilty by reason of insanity. That's all I know for sure. And today, that's what we have to work with."

Waters wasn't sure what he had hoped for, but Penn's refusal to even consider what he believed to be the truth drained something out of him. A debilitating fatigue settled into his limbs.

"I'd be irresponsible if I told you anything else," Penn added.

"Of course. I understand. So. What do we do now?"

"We go to the path lab and give blood for the DNA sample."

"Right." Waters took the Mini-DV tape from his back pocket and slid it across the desk.

"What's this?"

"The tape of Lily and me in bed. If I'm arrested at the lab, I don't want the cops to find that on me."

As Penn put the tape into his shirt pocket, Waters suddenly thought of Annelise sitting in class at school, oblivious to the storm gathering around her. "I need to call St. Stephens before we go."

"All right. Anything wrong?"

"I just want to make sure my daughter's in class. Where she's supposed to be."

Penn looked long and hard at his client. "I understand. No problem, John."

The pathology lab was housed in an unobtrusive medical plaza near St. Catherine's Hospital. Penn drove them over in his Audi. The nurse took them straight back to the lab when they arrived, but instead of finding Tom Jackson waiting for them, they found a technician from the police crime lab. Penn seemed pleased, and Waters soon saw why: the forensic technician said little and asked no direct questions.

Waters sat in the phlebotomist's chair while a med-tech inserted a needle in the antecubital vein in the crook of his elbow. As his blood ran into the tube—evidence that could one day end his life—he watched Penn standing nearby, likely pondering the intricacies of murder defense. Waters thought only of Annelise, whom his phone call had verified as being safe in class at St. Stephens. He would check on her constantly today, for until Mallory moved out of Lily and into someone else, Ana was in critical danger.

The med-tech ripped off the Velcro tourniquet. "Press down hard," she said, pointing at the cotton swab she'd placed over his vein. She took a scraping from the inside of Waters's cheek, then dismissed him.

Penn looked at the police technician. "Satisfied?"

After the cop nodded, Penn took Waters's arm, led him outside, and helped him into the passenger seat of the Audi. Then he got behind the wheel and started the engine.

"I know that was hard to take. Makes you feel like a felon, doesn't it?"

"I'm fine. I'm glad Tom Jackson wasn't there."

"Yes. Informal questioning is hard to control. When your mind is on something else, you tend to say things you might not have meant to say." Penn pulled the Roadster out of the lot and onto the highway. "But I have a feeling Tom is going to hit you hard this afternoon."

Waters nodded, but his mind was already far away.

The little convertible quickly ate up the distance to downtown, and as Penn turned into the back lot of Waters's office, Waters glanced down Main Street and saw Cole's silver Lincoln protruding from the line of cars parked on the left.

"What are you going to do between now and three?" Penn asked.

"Probably stay right here."

"Do you mind me asking why?"

"I'm going to try to do some work. Some mapping. It's all I can think to do." He lied because Penn could not help him in the way he needed help. "Something normal, you know?"

"I understand. But Cole may show up today. Be careful about confrontations at this point. Today is a critical day, and we don't know what he knows about you and Eve."

"I doubt he's even coming in today."

Penn squeezed Waters's arm and gave him a warning look. "Don't trust him, John. Never again. Cole Smith does not have your best interests at heart."

"I hear you. Do you have my tape?"

Penn reached into his pocket and brought out the small plastic case, then passed it to his client.

"Thanks." Waters shook his hand, got out, and closed the door.

"I'll pick you up here at a quarter of three," Penn said.

Waters nodded, then turned and trotted up the back stairs.

Cole sat at his desk, staring at the signed Number 18 Ole Miss jersey framed on the wall, but the glassy sheen in his eyes made it clear that his mind was elsewhere. Waters walked softly into the room and stopped a few feet from the desk.

"Hey!"

Cole whipped around as though he'd heard a gunshot. "Shit, Rock! Don't sneak up on me like that."

"Are you expecting company you don't want to see?"

Cole splayed his hands on the desktop as if to steady himself. "I'm always expecting that." He slid open his top drawer and took out what appeared to be a short-barreled Magnum .357.

"What the hell is that for?"

Cole laughed. "Don't worry, it's loaded. Where you been?"

"Giving a blood sample to the police for a DNA test."

"Shit." Cole's smile vanished. "Did Penn Cage tell you to do that?"

Waters was taken aback. "How do you know Penn is my lawyer?"

"Lily told me. She called up here a little while ago, worried sick." Cole slid the .357 back into the drawer.

What the hell is Mallory up to? he wondered. *She could have called my cell phone. Why would she call Cole?*

"I didn't think Penn Cage took clients. I thought he just wrote books."

"He's doing it as a favor to me."

"Celebrity lawyer, huh? I hope he knows what he's doing."

"He knows what he's doing in court." Waters let his eyes drill into his partner's. "But that's not the kind of help I need right now."

Cole's big head turned slowly, like that of a battle-scarred old bull. "Talk to me, John Boy."

"I need to stay out of jail. I don't give a damn what happens later, but I need to stay free right now, for as long as possible. And to do that, I need an alibi."

Cole looked at him with sympathy. "I'd like to help you. But it's too late. Cowboy Tom Jackson called me an hour ago and asked where I was the night of the murder. I had to tell him I was home watching HBO all by my lonesome. I couldn't say you were there, because for all I knew, you'd already told him you were somewhere else."

"*Shit.*" Waters cursed his paranoia. Because he hadn't trusted his friend, he'd screwed himself on the alibi.

"I warned you about this."

"I know."

Cole stood and squeezed his powerful hands together. "Sit down, Rock. You look like you're about to pop a blood vessel."

"I don't want to sit."

"Sit your ass down. I can't think with you standing up."

Waters took the leather chair opposite Cole's desk, and the big man began to pace the room.

"How much time does Penn think you have before the cops bring you in?"

"Probably not much. They're questioning me this afternoon."

"Well, let's just cut to the chase. Did you kill that crazy bitch or not?"

Waters looked at the floor. "My hands strangled her. But I didn't kill her. I know that now. Not that it's much comfort, given my situation."

"But that's your joy juice on the slides down at the crime lab?"

"Yes."

Cole gave a theatrical groan. "What about Lily for your alibi? I'm sure she'll swear you were home when the murder happened."

Waters looked up at his partner. "Lily's not Lily anymore. I can't trust her to act in my best interest. That's why I'm here."

Cole stopped in midstep and stared as though Waters had just sworn the world was flat. "I thought the possibility of being cornholed for forty years in Parchman Farm had finally cured you of this *Wuthering Heights,* Mallory's-back-from-the-dead bullshit. But it hasn't, has it?"

"No. And I'm here because you're the only guy I know who might be crazy enough to believe me."

Cole scratched the back of his neck, amusement in his eyes.

"But even if you don't believe me," Waters continued, "I know you'll do anything you can to help me."

"*Now* you're talking," Cole said. "Okay, lay the weirdness on me."

"Mallory's inside Lily now."

"Tell me I didn't just hear that."

"I'm serious. Mallory passed into me on the night Eve died. She killed Eve to shut her up, and to hold the murder over my head. Then she passed from me into Lily."

Cole began to pace again, moving in a wide circle around Waters. "Why would she do that?"

"Because she thought I'd never leave Lily for Eve."

"Huh. Would you have?"

Waters thought about it. "I'd like to say no, but I can't honestly tell you. Did I risk losing Lily and Annelise just to sleep with Eve for two weeks?"

"I guess now we'll never know."

"Don't be so sure. Last night, I convinced Mallory to leave Lily alone. To move into some other woman, on the condition that I would leave Lily for whoever it was. Now I'm afraid I might be arrested today. Penn says it won't happen, but I have a feeling it's going to. And if it does, Mallory might decide to stay right where she is. Inside Lily. She'll be alone in the house with Annelise, and I'll be stuck in jail."

"That scares you?"

"What do you think?"

Cole stopped behind Waters and laid a hand on his shoulder. "What exactly do you want me to do?"

"If I'm arrested, I want you to bail me out. I'm going to give you access to an account with enough money to do it."

"You don't need me for that. Lily will bail you out of jail in a heartbeat."

"I told you—"

"Lily isn't Lily anymore . . . right."

"That's right. And I have no way of knowing what she'll do until she does it."

Cole took his hand from Waters's shoulder, walked to his desk, and sat on its forward edge. "Okay, I'll bail you out of jail. What else?"

"The charge will be murder one. The judge could deny bail. If that happens, I'll need you to be my go-between with Mallory while I'm in jail. Obviously, she could visit me in jail as Lily, but only for a short time. I wouldn't be able to monitor her movements or state of mind, or keep her calm if she starts to flip out. You have to do all that, and keep her moving forward with my plan. She has to move into another woman."

"How do I do that?"

"Tell her I'll get out of jail one way or another. And when I do, I'll come to her. I'll run away with her. You have to keep her convinced of that."

Cole's eyes narrowed as he studied Waters. "Is that really your plan? Or are you just trying to get Mallory out of the way so you can run with Lily and Annelise?"

"Christ, man. First things first. I'm not even in jail yet."

"Seriously, John. I mean, Ward Cleaver gets the chance to run off to paradise . . . Does he take the wife and kid? Or his beautiful love goddess?"

Waters gripped the arms of the chair in frustration. "This isn't some hypothetical game! The police want my ass. And I'll be face-to-face with them at three o'clock!"

Cole held up his hands. "Easy, John Boy. I get the picture." He got off the desk and walked to within a few feet of Waters. "So, what are you going to tell the cops? I mean, if your lawyer thinks you're crazy with this Mallory stuff, how are you going to play it?"

"Penn may think I'm nuts, but he also thinks I'm innocent."

"He does? Who does he think killed Eve?"

Waters gave a hollow laugh. "Are you ready for this? You."

Cole blinked in surprise. "What?"

"Penn thinks you slipped in and strangled her while I was passed out."

"No shit." Cole folded his arms across his chest and looked at the floor. "Penn always was too smart for his own good."

Waters started to laugh again, but something in Cole's voice stopped him. "What do you mean?"

Cole stepped forward and crouched before the chair, his eyes inches from Waters's own. Up close, the blood vessels in his nose were a ravaged red network of lines, like worms flattened by a car tire.

"I mean I killed her."

The glint in Cole's eyes left no doubt as to the truth of his words. The hair on Waters's forearms stood erect, and a shiver went through his heart. He drew back in the chair, but Cole clutched its arms with both hands, penning him in.

"Penn was right?" Waters whispered. "It was you all along? You fed Eve all that stuff about Mallory and me?"

"You're so lost," Cole said, as though the subject were not worthy of discussion. "You don't know which end is up, do you?"

Fragments of Penn's merciless logic poured into Waters's mind with the crushing weight of hindsight. *Who's in a position to know all about you and Mallory? Who would benefit if you were to go to prison for murder? I think we both know who we're talking about. . . . I've seen things done between lifelong friends that you wouldn't believe. There's literally no depth to which human beings cannot sink. . . .*

Waters smashed his fists into Cole's forearms, knocking them from the chair arms, and jumped to his feet. "Goddamn it, *why?*"

"John—"

"Just tell me one thing, you son of a bitch! Is Lily involved in this?"

Cole stood up, his face bright red. "Not anymore. But why do you even care about that?"

"Why do I *care?* Lily is *all* I care about. Lily and Annelise."

Cole looked suddenly bereft. "Don't say that."

"Compared to Lily, you think I give a shit about you and your problems? You made a good living from this company, and you pissed it away on gambling and God knows what else. Now you want to take me down for murder so you can steal the company and get your ass out of a hole you dug yourself? And you use my wife to do it?"

Cole's lower lip quivered, and the hurt in his eyes dwarfed the pain Waters had seen at the country club the previous day.

"You don't understand!" he cried, taking Waters by the arms. "You've got to listen to me."

Waters tried to pull free, but alcohol and dissipation had not completely sapped the strength of the old athlete in Cole.

"Let go, goddamn it!"

He was about to slam his knee into his partner's groin when Cole sobbed and drove him back against the office wall like an offensive lineman. Waters's head hit the painted bricks hard enough to blind him. The first thing he saw when the stars cleared was Cole staring at him like a madman begging for understanding.

"You don't know anything about Lily!" Cole shouted. "You think you know her, Johnny, but you don't!"

Johnny? Waters tried to think through the blur in his brain, but Cole kept talking, his face wet with tears and mucus, his right arm across Waters's chest, pinning him to the wall. *"Listen* to me, Johnny. I'm trying to do what you told me to. But you don't even care!"

Waters remained frozen.

"You lied!" Cole screamed. "You said you'd give

up Lily and come to me if I went into another woman. But you were lying!"

Waters's heart stuttered, then kicked off again with an arrhythmic beat that he feared would not sustain consciousness. He shut his eyes against confusion so profound that it felt like psychological whiplash.

"Say something!" Cole demanded. "Look at me!"

Waters opened his eyes. His partner's face, livid a moment ago, was now pale, and his mouth worked in a silent struggle between rage and despair. Even as Waters's emotions tried to convince him that Cole was only playing another scene in a drama written to deprive him of his sanity, cold reason forced him toward the awful truth. Cole was not that good an actor. He could dissemble in front of husbands whom he had cuckolded, but the pain and confusion in his face now were utterly foreign to the man Waters had known all his life. Cole Smith simply did not panic, and to mimic it like this was beyond him.

"Oh God," Waters breathed. "No . . ."

A strange light suddenly shone out of Cole's eyes, and his lips curled into something like a smile. Horror unlike anything Waters had known in his life turned his bowels to water. This morning, while he was talking to Penn or giving blood to the police, Mallory had followed his order of last night in a way that must have given her savage pleasure. As Lily, she had seduced Cole, and by this single act had both violated the wife Waters loved and robbed his best friend of his mind. The image of Cole thrusting inside his wife drove Waters to a point of fury that bordered on madness. He rammed his knee into Cole's testicles, then slammed an uppercut into the soft area under his jaw. The big man fell back, gasping for air, and Waters retreated behind the desk. Two blows wouldn't stop a man of Cole's size for long, so he reached into Cole's drawer and brought out the Magnum .357.

"Tell me what you did!" he shouted, aiming the gun at Cole. "You made Lily sleep with Cole, didn't you?"

Cole tried to straighten up but could not. The blow to his groin had effectively crippled him. But he did raise his face, and when he did, Waters saw the light of triumph in his eyes.

"It wasn't"—Cole gasped—"wasn't like it was the first time they'd done it. It didn't take much convincing to get your partner over to your house, Johnny. It took even less to get him to provide service in the bedroom. Lily bought a fifth of Johnnie Walker to warm him up. Then she fluttered her eyelashes and shed a few tears, and he was on her like a hound dog."

"Lily never cheated on me with Cole!"

"Not after you were married. But Cole has *very* fond memories of Lily as a college freshman. Mostly because she's your wife, I think. Lily wasn't anything special in the sack, but she was young and firm. A nice diversion on a Friday night."

Waters hoped this was one of Mallory's lies, but the sick feeling in his stomach told him it probably wasn't. He choked back a response and cocked the pistol's plowshare hammer.

"And neither one of them ever told you about it," Cole said. "The whole time you were falling in love with her, showing her off, telling Cole how great she was, he was thinking about the times he did her. That's friendship, isn't it?"

A strange sense of relief rolled through Waters. By trying so hard to damn Lily and Cole, Mallory had made him realize that both were innocent of anything beyond a college fling. There was no scam, no conspiracy. Both were pawns in Mallory's twisted plan. Lily probably wouldn't even remember having sex with Cole. Unless . . . like Eve, she had "awakened" to find herself naked and under Cole—

"Where's Lily?" he asked. "Right now? Did you hurt her?"

"Why would I hurt her?" Cole asked. "What happens to Lily later doesn't interest me, but I don't want you to feel any guiltier than you have to when you come to me."

"You swear she's all right?"

"I don't want to talk about her!" Cole snapped. "You told me you'd leave her, but she's all you care about! You *lied*."

"I wasn't lying," Waters replied calmly, trying to get his thoughts back on track. He let down the hammer and set the pistol on the desk. "What did you expect me to do? You'd blotted out my wife's mind. You threatened my daughter's life—"

"You threatened me first! You said you'd act like I was dead!"

You should be dead, Waters thought. "This is just like twenty years ago, Mallory. You don't trust me to love you. You think you have to *make* me love you. But you can't make anyone feel love. Love doesn't work that way."

"I know how love works!" Cole screamed. "I know how you felt with me when I was in Eve. You were lost inside me! You loved me then. And you will again."

Waters wasn't about to argue. If Mallory decided to hurt Lily and Annelise, he had no way to stop her.

Certainly the police could do nothing to prevent it. He
slid the .357 back in the drawer, closed his mind to the
male face across the desk, and spoke as tenderly as he
could.

"I always loved you, Mallory. And you always sab-
otaged us with your paranoia. But now . . . now I see
that you're doing what you promised. You left Lily
alone, and you're going to go into someone else. And
I intend to keep my part of the bargain."

Cole wiped his eyes and walked toward the desk.
"But how long is it going to take? Who am I going to
go into?"

"I don't know yet. I have to find a woman I think I
can live with."

"What about Sybil?" Cole said, his eyes suddenly
bright. "Cole already sleeps with her. Or he did until
a month ago, anyway. She's pretty, she's only twenty-
eight, she's got a wonderful body . . . and no husband
or kids to worry about. Nobody to ask questions.
She's perfect. I even know she's fertile."

"How do you know that?"

Cole's face articulated pure sadness in a way that
Waters had not seen since Cole was a child. "She got
pregnant when she was in high school," he said. "Her
parents made her get rid of the baby."

Waters didn't want Mallory thinking about abortion. "Sybil could be the one," he said. "But I don't
know yet."

"I don't want you to take too long. You know me,
Johnny. I need intimacy." Cole was coming around the
desk now, and nothing about his bodily movement
was familiar. He was like 250 pounds of graceful
woman stuffed into khakis and a button-down shirt.
"You know," he said, "having experienced sex as both

male and female, I have to say I like being the man better. I was always more of an aggressor in sex. But . . . I couldn't ask that of you."

Ask what? Waters wondered, realizing the answer even as he asked the question.

"Unless," Cole said softly, "you don't mind the idea."

Cole took hold of his hand, and before Waters could overcome his shock, Cole kissed his wrist, then slid his tongue along Waters's inner forearm.

Waters jerked his arm free with a cry.

Cole laughed. "I knew you'd be like that. Oh, well. Men can't bear children, anyway."

Waters's stomach churned with fear and revulsion. "Tell me one thing before I go. When you told me how you moved from person to person, you said it took you a while to control people's minds. How are you doing it now? To people you just entered?"

Cole smiled cagily. "I learned a lot in ten years, Johnny. And some people just aren't very challenging. Lily is depressed. She still blames herself for her miscarriages. Basically, she's just *weak*. Cole is a burnout case. Eaten up with guilt about his debts, insecure about sex with his young conquests. His mind is a nest of snakes drowning in scotch. He takes Viagra to cheat on his wife, for God's sake. There's not enough of the original Cole left to resist me."

Waters shook his head. The parallels to virus transmission kept hitting him; when a person's resistance was down, the virus gained a foothold and grew exponentially.

"The people in your life are empty," Cole said. "They could never make you truly happy. But I can. You know I can."

Cole pressed a button on his desk phone. After a moment, Sybil said, "Yes?"

"Could you come in for a minute, Sybil?"

"I'm pretty busy." Her voice was clipped and cold.

Cole chuckled and whispered, "She's pouting." He raised his voice. "Come on, Syb. It'll only take a sec."

He turned off the intercom. "Take a good look, Johnny. I like her."

Waters stood mute as Sybil walked in wearing a classy skirt suit. Her hair was pinned up, showing her long neck to advantage, and her smoldering Cajun eyes settled on Cole with open resentment.

"What is it?" she asked. "Hey, John."

Waters only nodded, knowing he could never make his voice sound normal under such stress.

"Damn, I forgot what I called you in for," Cole told her. "My mistake. I'll remember what it was in a minute."

Sybil expelled air from her lips with obvious anger, then turned and marched out. Cole's eyes followed her tiny waist and shapely hips as she went through the door.

"What do you think about her?" he asked. "Cole may be a mess, but he does have an eye for beauty."

"She's beautiful," Waters replied. "But I'm going now. Tell me, will Lily remember having sex with Cole?"

"Probably not. Of course, she'll always remember the first times they did it. Nothing I can do about that, I'm afraid."

Waters bit off his reply and turned to go.

"What about Sybil?" Cole called after him.

Waters paused in the door but did not turn.

"Maybe. I have to think about it. Right now I have a date with the police."

"A lot of clocks are ticking, Johnny. Don't take too long."

chapter 17

The police grilled Waters for sixty-four minutes. They would have gone on longer, but as the questions became aggressively repetitive, Penn protested that the interrogation was bordering on harassment of a model citizen who had cooperated from the beginning. If there were new questions, Penn told them, he would get the answers from Waters and relay them to police headquarters.

Tom Jackson handled the interrogation, flanked by a silent partner with a pockmarked face who glared at Waters as though he held some personal grudge against him. Waters decided it was class resentment. Both detectives seemed uncomfortable in the upscale law office of Penn Cage's friend. Most of the questions were about Eve Sumner, the rest intended to uncover the current state of Waters's marriage. Where Eve was concerned, Waters mostly lied. He denied ever having had sex with her. As for the videotape of his Land Cruiser by the Eola Hotel just prior to the murder, he explained that the EPA investigation of his company had been giving him sleep problems, and that he had recently done a lot of late-night driving. Tom Jackson was forced to admit that he'd stopped Waters late one night in the act of doing just that. On the night of the murder, Waters told them, he'd driven downtown with the idea of having a gin and tonic at one of the bars near the Eola, but the rainstorm made him reluctant to get out. He'd turned onto Pearl Street with the intent of going home via Franklin Street. At that point he saw the crowded accident scene, and decided to back up and take a different route home. He couldn't tell what Jackson thought of his explanation, but it was clear that Jackson's partner thought he was lying. Still, no one placed him under arrest.

After the police left the law office, Waters gave Penn an inquiring glance. Penn shook his head, as if to say, "Not until we're outside."

Once they were in the Audi, Penn started the engine and turned to Waters with curiosity on his face.

"You're a hell of a liar, John. I think you could have passed a polygraph if you'd been hooked to one during those questions."

"My family's at stake," Waters said quietly. "It's really that simple. I'll do whatever I have to do to save them. You'd do the same."

Penn looked as though he was recalling something troubling, and Waters suddenly remembered that the lawyer in Cage's novel had lied to the police about several important events.

"You *have* done the same."

"Lying to police is tricky business," Penn said.

"They tend to get pissed off when they find out you did it."

"But you said—"

"Nothing," Penn finished. "Nothing at all."

He pulled into the street and headed toward Waters's office. "When the DNA match comes in and you recant your statements, I presume your position will be that you concealed adultery to save your marriage?"

"Does it matter? At this point, I don't really care."

"That worries me, John."

"Don't give it another thought."

Penn stared but said nothing else as he drove down Main Street. In the parking lot of Waters's building, Waters shook his lawyer's hand, then got into his Land Cruiser and headed for home, his mind on the videotape that now rested in the glove box. The next few hours would be the most difficult of his life.

Waters found Lily asleep in the master bedroom and Rose sitting on the back steps, watching Annelise ride her motorized scooter on the patio. He sat beside Rose and watched his daughter make circle after circle on the stones, waving and smiling each time she passed them.

"Something ain't right with Lily," Rose said. "She usually goin' like a top from the time she wake up till she lay down at night. You know that."

Waters nodded soberly. "I think she's been a little depressed lately."

"Depressed? That girl been depressed since she lost them babies. You knows that too. What's really going on, Mr. John? You playing around on that poor girl?"

"No."

"You'd best not be. You need to get Lily to Dr. Cage. He'll fix her up quick, or else get her to a specialist who can."

"I may do that, Rose."

"You promise?"

Rose's words reminded him of the promise he had made Mallory so long ago. "I think I know what's wrong, Rose. And I don't think a doctor can fix it. I have to fix it."

The black woman turned and looked deep into his eyes. "You sure you ain't been goin' in the street with somebody?"

"I'm sure."

She shook her head in surrender, as if to say, "White people's problems," then grunted and stood and waved at Annelise. "I'm going on, girl. Your daddy got you now."

"Bye, Rose!" Ana yelled. "See you tomorrow!"

"Mmm-hmm." Rose waddled up the steps and into the house.

Waters let Annelise make a few more circuits of the patio, then took her inside and fed her the supper Rose had left in the oven. Fried chicken, mashed potatoes, gravy, broccoli, and salad. Ana skipped the salad, but she put away two chicken legs and three helpings of potatoes and gravy. Waters wondered where the food went; his daughter still weighed only fifty pounds.

When he finished rinsing the dishes, Lily had still not appeared, so he took Ana into the den and listened to her read aloud from J.R.R. Tolkien's *The Two Towers*. She had quickly graduated from the Harry Potter series, and now loved nothing more than hobbits and elves. As the struggle of good versus evil played out in his ears, Waters realized he had rarely looked at his own life in those terms.

Despite all Mallory had done in his distant past, he had never attributed the word "evil" to her. But now . . . an image of Lily dangling the butcher knife over Annelise's head flashed into his mind, and he knew in his bones that Mallory would not stop until Lily and Annelise had been wiped from the earth. He could see only one solution: Mallory had to be destroyed. And yet . . . she could not be killed without killing the innocent person who contained her—

"John?"

Waters got to his feet as Lily walked into the den in an old blue housecoat. Her eyes were puffy from sleep, and her newly cut blond hair was pressed flat against the left side of her face. Annelise looked up from her book, and her eyes went wide.

"Mom?"

"Sit down, babe," Waters said, leading Lily to the sofa. "Do you feel all right?"

"Not really. I'm exhausted. I have been all afternoon." She looked at Annelise, whose eyes were filled with confusion. "Hey, baby."

"What's the matter, Mom?"

"What did you do this morning?" Waters asked. "Did you run again?"

Lily squinted at her watch. "I'm not sure. What day is it?"

Annelise laughed, but the sound rode an undercurrent of fear.

"Wednesday."

Lily shook her head, then covered her eyes. Waters feared she would begin crying in front of Annelise.

"Mom, what's *wrong?*" Ana asked.

"I've got a headache, honey. You keep reading."

"I'm tired of reading."

"Well . . . turn on the TV, then."

"I don't want to watch TV."

Waters got up, switched on the television, and set it on the Disney Channel. Annelise sighed in frustration, but she began watching all the same. Waters did not sit again, but walked behind the sofa and massaged Lily's shoulders. As he worked his way up to her neck and scalp, she moaned and leaned forward. He gave her about fifteen minutes of that treatment, and then Ana's program ended.

"Time for bed," he said.

"Why?" Ana asked, looking ready to throw a fit. "It's not time yet."

"Mom doesn't feel good, and I have some work to do."

"I can just stay in here and watch TV. I'll be quiet."

Waters shook his head and held out his hand. Ana hesitated, then got up and closed her hand around two of his fingers.

Lily said, "Is it all right if I don't go up to tuck you in, baby?"

Annelise gave her a hug. "It's okay. You better take a pill or something."

Waters went upstairs and helped his daughter into her pajamas. He kissed her and stroked her hair for a minute, but he left without reading a story. He was anxious to get back downstairs before Lily nodded off again. With Mallory so unstable, he could not afford to wait another night. There was also the chance that Tom Jackson would turn up more evidence linking him to Eve, and that might be all it took for Jackson to arrest him.

Lily was back in the bedroom, sitting in her chaise with her feet propped on the ottoman. She still wore the old housecoat, and in the brighter light of the bedroom, he saw black rings beneath her eyes.

"Is Ana all right?" she asked.

"She's fine."

Lily squinted up at him. "You look worried."

He walked over and sat on the ottoman, then laid his hand on her knee. "I want to talk to you about something."

"That sounds ominous."

"I don't mean for it to. But this is serious. You've been having trouble with your memory for the past couple of days, haven't you?"

Lily looked strangely at him. "How did you know?"

"Have you noticed anything else out of the ordinary?"

She looked away, deep in thought. "I don't really feel like myself," she said in a careful voice. "I've noticed some . . . physical things."

"Like what?"

She looked embarrassed. "I'm bruised, John."

"Where?"

She opened her housecoat at the waist, revealing her left hip, which was mottled with dark blue spots. "Both hips are like this. Bruises like hand marks."

He swallowed. "I did that."

"When?"

"Last night."

Confusion clouded her eyes. "I don't remember. But at least it explains some things."

"Like what?"

"This morning when I woke up and went to the bathroom, I felt like . . . no, I *knew* that I'd had sex. And it frightened me."

"And you don't remember it at all?"

"No. And the same thing happened this afternoon. Did we make love this morning?"

Waters closed his eyes in anguish. "No."

"But . . . did you do this?" She pulled open her housecoat at the chest, and Waters saw two purple suck marks above her breasts. "No," he whispered. "I didn't."

She stiffened. "Then how did they get there?"

He took her hand and squeezed it. "That's what I want to talk to you about. This is going to be the hardest conversation of our lives."

"You're scaring me, John."

"I know. We're in trouble, Lily. And we won't get out of it unless we do it together."

"Tell me. Don't make me wait like this!"

He was still unsure how to start. "What I'm going to say will sound crazy to you. But I want you to promise to keep an open mind and hear me out until the end. All right?"

"Yes."

"Do you remember that day at the soccer field when I asked you about Eve Sumner? I didn't know who she was."

"Of course. And then we saw her at the Mardi Gras party. She asked about selling our house." Lily's long-term memory was clearly still up to the mark. "What is it? Do you know something about Eve's death?"

"Yes."

Just as with Penn, he started his story at the soccer

field, but this time he did not end at the Eola Hotel. He told it all the way up to the agreement he'd made with Mallory about finding a new host. He did not break his narrative with apologies or pleas for forgiveness; it would not alter what he had done or Lily's perception of it. He thought she would interrupt long before he got to the end, but she didn't. She sat like a woman forced to watch the execution of her family, pale and blank-faced, until he described Lily dangling the butcher knife over Annelise's head. Tears poured from her eyes, and she began to shake so badly that Waters finally stopped speaking.

"Tell me the first thing that comes into your head," he said. "Anything. I don't care what. Tell me you think I'm insane."

Lily closed her eyes and wiped away her tears. "Were you in love with Eve?"

"No. I thought she was Mallory."

A hysterical laugh burst from her lips. "I guess I asked the wrong question, didn't I? Were you still in love with Mallory?"

"I don't think so. I think I was just lonely in a way that hadn't been dealt with in a very long time."

"And you thought that *Mallory* could relate to that part of you?"

He felt like he might throw up, and they hadn't even begun to deal with the true horror of the situation.

"I suppose so."

She shut her eyes again, and more tears flowed.

"I know you think I'm crazy with this talk of possession. I only risked telling you because I know enough has happened to you in the past couple of days that you might believe it."

"There's more you haven't told me, isn't there?"

"Lily . . . last night we put Annelise to bed, and then we had sex."

She flinched as though he had slapped her. "So you and Mallory 'make love,' but we 'have sex'?"

"What we did last night wasn't making love. Lily, there's no way you'll believe what I'm about to tell you unless I show you something. Can you stand to watch something painful?"

"How could it get any worse?"

"If you watch, you'll know."

"Is it a tape of you and Eve?"

"No. You and me."

She wrapped her arms tightly around herself. "Show me."

He went to his dresser drawer and removed the Sony video camera and remote. One cord was all it took to connect the small camera to the bedroom television. Then he removed the Mini-DV tape from his back pocket, loaded it into the camera, and went to sit beside Lily.

A ghostly green bedroom scene lit the television screen, much like news footage shot at night during Desert Storm and the Afghanistan war. The infrared beam from the Sony was not very powerful, but sufficient to illuminate the two naked bodies kneeling on the bed.

"I can't see her face," Lily said. "Is that me?"

Waters took her hand. It was as limp as a coma patient's. "You tell me."

Onscreen, Waters turned to face the camera and mouthed, *Lily, I'm sorry.*

"What did you just say?"

" 'Lily, I'm sorry.' "

She stared as though hypnotized at the haunting green image. When her husband took hold of the hips of the woman kneeling in front of him and went into her, the woman turned toward the camera in a caricature of startled pleasure. Waters felt Lily's body jerk when she recognized herself. In tomblike silence they watched Lily perform acts she had never spoken of in her life, and probably had not even known were possible. First in handcuffs, then freed from them, she copulated with a manic energy and abandon that the man onscreen looked hard put to match. As the tape spooled across the heads, Lily's hand remained motionless in his. Waters had known this experience would traumatize his wife, but he saw no other way to shock her into belief.

"Is there sound?" Lily whispered.

"I didn't want to put you through that. I thought the picture would be enough."

"Turn it up."

"Lily—"

"Turn it up!"

He picked up the remote and raised the sound to an audible level. Guttural grunts that had never before issued from Lily's throat filled the bedroom, but the most shocking was Waters's voice crying *Mallory!* as he urged his partner to greater depravity. When Lily pulled her hand out of his and began rocking slowly back and forth, Waters switched off the camera.

Lily looked dazed, like the victim of a violent crime. Which was exactly what she was. Only no law had ever been written to cover the crime she had suffered, except perhaps in some medieval manuscript.

"Those things on the tape," she murmured. "Have

you been wanting me to do those things all these years?"

"No." Waters realized he wasn't telling the complete truth, and he didn't want to lie to Lily ever again. "Sometimes," he admitted. "It's not that I want you to do *those* things . . . but to try new things. I want you to want to please me the way I want to please you. But it's been so long since we've had even a basic—"

"I know that. I was trying to change when . . ."

"When this happened. I know."

At last she looked him in the face, and the abject fear in her eyes shook him in a way that nothing in his life ever had. "I don't remember doing that," she said in a monotone. "Any of it."

"I know."

"Did you give me drugs or something?"

"No."

"Then why . . ." The whites of her eyes grew as the implications of Waters's story of possession broke through her last defense mechanisms.

"Oh God," she whispered.

Waters reached out to her, but she jerked away from his hand.

"Don't touch me!"

"I won't."

Lily jumped to her feet and looked around as if to find somewhere to run, but there was nowhere. In her own home there was no sanctuary.

"Why did you tell me this?" she screamed. "You're trying to drive *me* crazy! That's what this is!"

He tried to keep his voice calm. "Why would I do that, Lily?"

"I don't know. You want to leave me."

"No. If I wanted that, I'd just leave."

"Maybe you want to keep all your money! How do I know? Maybe you have another girlfriend somewhere!"

He held up his hands in supplication. "I made this tape to show you—Lily Waters—what had happened to you. To us. That's not you on the tape, Lily. You know that."

She splayed her shaking hands in front of her and stared at them like a mental patient on the verge of collapse.

Waters ran to the kitchen and poured a shot of vodka from a bottle in the freezer. When he got back, Lily lay panting on the floor, close to hyperventilating.

"Drink this," he pleaded, kneeling over her.

She obeyed like a sick child, then squeezed her eyes shut against the burn of the alcohol.

"That's it."

"Oh no—" She scrabbled to her feet and ran into the bathroom, where she dropped over the commode and began to retch. Waters knelt beside her and held her convulsing body.

"Take it easy. Get your breath back."

She planted both elbows on the toilet seat and raised her head. Her face was wet and blotchy red. When Waters took her arms to lift her, she didn't resist, and when she got her feet beneath her, she went to the bed and sat on her side of it.

"What can I do?" he asked.

She looked up, her eyes hollow and exhausted. "Am I myself now?"

"Yes."

"But if what you told me is true—if Mallory is inside me—where is she now?"

Relief cascaded through him with the force of a religious epiphany. After days of isolation and ridicule, someone else believed. "She's inside Cole now."

"Cole Smith?"

"Yes."

"And she was in me before that?"

He nodded.

"But that means . . ." Lily closed her eyes, then went deathly white.

"Don't think about it, Lily."

"Cole and me."

"I'm sorry."

She raised a quivering hand to her face. "I can't take this, John. I can't listen to this."

"I won't say any more."

"Did I really threaten Annelise with a butcher knife?"

"That wasn't you. It was Mallory."

"This is madness!"

"I know it seems that way." Desperate to pull her back to the present, he followed a perverse instinct. He got to his knees before her and spoke softly. "Lily, tell me something. I promise I won't get upset by your answer. Did you sleep with Cole during college?"

Her eyes instantly locked onto his, and he saw a different kind of fear in them.

"It's all right if you did," he assured her. "I just . . . Mallory told me that you did, and I wanted to know if she was making it up."

Lily's chin started to quiver. She bit her lip and

looked away from him. "I did. I slept with Cole at Ole Miss."

The stark admission from her own lips hurt him more than he had expected, but it had the intended effect. By putting Lily in a position where she felt momentary guilt, he knew her desire to console *him* would overpower the shock of the situation.

"I know you must have imagined all kinds of terrible things about why I didn't tell you," she said. "The truth is, I hardly remember being with him. I certainly don't remember what it felt like."

He shook his head. "It's all right. You don't have to make excuses."

"But I want you to know why I kept it from you. When I came back to Natchez after SMU, and you and I went out on our first date, I really fell for you. I mean, I knew then—right then—that you were the man I'd been searching for all my life. On that same night, I found out Cole was your partner. I couldn't believe it. I wasn't about to bring up something like that on our first date, and by the time we were close enough to talk about it, I felt too awkward to do it. I was afraid you'd be so disappointed that you'd leave me. I was petrified Cole would say something to you. You know how guys are. But one day I came by your office when you weren't there, and he brought it up. He was a real gentleman about it. He said, 'Look, John's my buddy, he's a great guy, and he really cares about you. As far as I'm concerned, what happened between us never happened.' I almost cried, I was so relieved. Neither of us ever wanted you to think it had been more than it was, which was nothing."

"I understand," he said. "Really."

Lily slid down off the bed and hugged him, and he felt tears soaking his shirt.

"Listen," he said, holding her to him. "Do you really believe the things I told you? Do you believe Mallory is alive?"

Her reply was a warm vibration against his chest. "If you hadn't shown me that tape, I wouldn't have. But yes, I believe it." She looked up at him, her eyes alive with terror. "She wants you, John. And I don't see a way to stop her."

"I do. I've thought about nothing else from the moment she went into you."

"How? It seems impossible."

He took Lily by the shoulders and held her away from him. "We have to kill her."

Lily blinked. "But . . . you said she can't be killed without killing whoever she's inside. Didn't you?"

"That's right."

He could see the thoughts spinning behind her bloodshot eyes. "You mean commit murder," she said. "Cold-blooded murder. Kill someone like . . ."

"Cole," Waters finished.

Her lips parted slightly. "Do you mean that?"

"Yes."

She looked into his eyes for a long time, then walked back to the bed. "There have to be other options."

"I don't think you'll like them."

"What are they?"

"We could run. Mallory actually suggested that, but for a different reason. To escape the murder charge."

"Run where?"

"Central America, maybe. Costa Rica. Find a place

without U.S. extradition. We'd have to leave everything behind. Change our names. I'd be a fugitive because of Eve's murder. Running would make me look
guilty, and the DNA match would prove it."

Lily's mouth opened, but no sound emerged for
several moments. "So . . . even if we manage to get rid
of Mallory, that DNA test could put you in prison for
life."

"Don't think about that right now. We have to focus
on one problem at a time. Do you want to take Annelise and leave the country forever? She might never
see your mother again. You'd never be Lily Waters
again."

Lily looked around the room as though seeing it for
the first time. "Before today, I'd have told you those
weren't the important things. Things like names and
where we live. What job you have. What school Annelise goes to. But they *are* important. Those details
are what make up our lives. I think if we throw all that
away to run like criminals, then we'll lose part of ourselves."

"I think so too."

"What other option is there?"

"I could plead guilty to Eve's murder. You and Annelise would be safe then. And maybe Mallory would
get tired of waiting for me."

"That's not an option," Lily said forcefully. "You
are *not* going to prison."

Waters sighed. "I don't think it would stop Mallory
anyway. She's already been in prison once. She'd find
some way to get in and get close to me." He sat beside
Lily on the bed. "I honestly don't think there's any option but to destroy her. And to do that, we have to kill
an innocent person."

"Can you kill Cole in cold blood? You've been friends since you were little boys."

Waters thought of Cole knowingly yielding to "Lily's" seduction only hours ago. That was affecting his judgment, but he saw nothing to be gained by reminding Lily of the event. "I said someone *like* Cole. It doesn't have to be him."

"Who, then?"

"Remember my deal with Mallory? I promised her that if she went into another woman—a woman chosen by me—I would leave you and Annelise to be with her."

Lily closed her eyes and wavered on the bed. He reached out and steadied her.

"I'm all right," she said. She stood up and looked him full in the face. "Who would it be? The woman? Who would you pick?"

"Mallory suggested Sybil."

"Your receptionist?"

"Cole's already sleeping with her. Or was, until recently."

Disgust wrinkled Lily's face. "How in God's name does Jenny stay with him?"

"How are you going to stay with me?"

"That's different. You did what you did because . . . I've been less than a wife to you for far too long."

"That's no excuse."

She folded her arms across her chest and looked at the floor. "I never thought I'd say this, but it's a mitigating circumstance."

Her forgiving attitude stunned him, but before he could fully absorb it, she grabbed his arm and said, "Wait! What if we found someone who *wasn't* innocent?"

"Like who?"

"I don't know. Like that Danny Buckles character who molested the little girls at school."

Waters thought about it. "He's in jail. And he's a man."

"Okay. But you know what I mean."

"I don't know any female criminals. Even if I did . . . who are we to decide that someone deserves to die? Even Danny Buckles?"

Lily flipped away his comment with an angry hand gesture. "I'm not saying anyone *deserves* to die. But if I had to throw someone out of a sinking lifeboat to keep it afloat, and my choice was between Sybil Sonnier and Danny Buckles, I'd throw out Danny."

The steel in her voice sent a shudder along his spine. Lily was not really talking in hypothetical terms. She had accepted the necessity. If murder was required to save her family, she would do it.

"We're going to do it," Waters said. "Aren't we? We're going to take an innocent life."

Lily nodded soberly. "The only question is who."

He closed his eyes as the reality sank into the marrow of his bones.

"You should pick someone we don't know," Lily said. "That way the guilt wouldn't feel so personal. It would just be this anonymous person."

"An anonymous person that I killed."

"*We* killed."

"Okay, we. But after you read the newspapers for a week, you'd feel like you knew her. And how do you think we're going to kill her? From a mile away? There's no way to soft-pedal this. If we decide to do it, it's going to be bad. We'll never get over it. The only real choice is whether it's Cole, Sybil, or some other woman."

"You *can't* kill Cole. You couldn't live with that."

Waters had given this question a lot of thought. "Let me tell you something about Cole. His life is already in danger. He's borrowed heavily from loan sharks to pay his gambling debts, far more than he can ever pay back. He keeps a pistol at the office now. They may literally send someone to kill him."

Lily shook her head. "You'd never let that happen. You'd pay his debts yourself. Don't kid yourself that you wouldn't."

"Normally, I'd agree. But it's a lot of money, Lily. Over six hundred thousand dollars. And if the EPA rules against us, I won't *have* the money to pay that debt."

Her mouth fell open.

"So. Even if we pick Sybil or someone else, Cole could still be murdered. If he doesn't come up with that money, I mean. And where's he going to come up with it, except from us?"

"And we may not have it," Lily said. She knit her brow and walked slowly around the room. "I don't care. If you killed Cole, you'd be like that pathetic Poe character who heard the heart beating under the floorboards. You'd go crazy."

"And I won't be like that with Sybil?"

"Not as bad. You don't really know her." Lily stopped in midstep. "*Do* you?"

Despite her professed forgiveness, his affair with Eve had irreparably damaged her trust in him. "No," he said. "She's nice, but all I really know is that she's a South Louisiana divorcée who needed a job. One of thousands."

"Does she have children?"

"No."

This seemed to settle the matter for Lily. "Cole has three children, and we know them all. Do you want to see those kids' faces when they hear their father has been murdered? Knowing it was you who did it?"

Despite all his ruthless theorizing, Waters could not imagine that reality.

"When are you supposed to tell Mallory who to go into?"

"She was pressuring me when I saw Cole this afternoon."

Lily's cold eyes and set jaw showed the depth of her resolve. "Tell her tomorrow," she said. "Tell her your answer is Sybil. And tell her not to waste time. You've been thinking about Sybil all night, and you want her."

"Why the hurry?"

"The murder investigation. From what you told me, you could be arrested before supper tomorrow."

"What if Cole sleeps with Sybil tomorrow? Will we be ready to deal with it?"

Lily sat on the bed in a posture of absolute concentration. He imagined this was how she looked when she knocked the top out of the CPA exam. "We'll be ready," she said. "It's just a job. Like doing an audit. Drilling a well. We'll plan every step. Then we'll execute those steps in the safest, most efficient way possible. We'll overlook nothing."

Waters thought of Sybil Sonnier's sincere eyes and her desire to please. Then he remembered a Nietzsche quote from college: *In revenge and in love, woman is more barbarous than man.* Looking at his wife's face, a study of moral detachment chiseled in ice, he believed it. And for the first time, he sensed that he had come face-to-face with Mallory Candler's match.

chapter 18

The morning sun was already high when Waters started up the back stairs to his office, his eyes burning from fatigue. After their discussion the night before, he and Lily had decided to put Annelise in their bed, and her constant shifting made sleep almost impossible. Likewise, Lily had decided to keep Ana home from school for the day. She didn't want her vulnerable to Mallory in any way while Waters tried to manipulate Mallory into Sybil.

Waters paused at his office door, started to go down the hall to Cole's, then went into his own. If he went into Cole's office and found only his friend and partner, he did not know if he could keep his emotions in check. To see Cole unaware of the dark presence submerged beneath his conscious mind would be like talking to a friend who did not know he was dying of inoperable cancer.

Waters walked to his desk but did not sit down. Turning to the picture window, he opened the door that led to the balcony and went outside. The river flowed gunmetal gray today. Usually a rusty brown, it now looked dead and deep, like it could swallow anything dropped into it without a trace. The twin bridges moved with desultory traffic, log trucks and big diesels mostly. Some steel was being replaced on the eastbound span. Antlike workers crawled over the girders with surprising speed, and for fifty yards there was nothing but a makeshift guardrail to keep you from dropping eighty feet to the river below if you drifted over the line.

That's what I've done, Waters thought. *Drifted over the line. And now I'm a few short steps from prison.* That he had been pulled over the line would be a fact only in his own mind, not those of the jurors who would convict him. All that his recitation of the "facts" as he saw them might accomplish would be to get him sentenced to the state mental hospital at Whitfield rather than to Parchman Prison in the Delta.

"Johnny?"

He whirled and found Cole standing three feet behind him, clean-shaven and dressed in wool trousers, a custom-tailored shirt, and a silk tie. This and his use of "Johnny" made Waters think he was facing Mallory, but he wasn't sure enough to open a dialogue based on that assumption.

"Hey, Cole," he said in a casual voice.

Cole's smile disappeared. "Why do you do that?"

"What?"

"You know it's me."

Waters looked into the smoldering eyes. "I didn't know for sure."

"Now you do."

He turned back to the rail and gazed over the river

to Louisiana, flat farmland stretching to the horizon. He felt a hand on his shoulder.

"I want you to decide today," Cole said. The hand squeezed his shoulder with a near-painful grip. "By the end of the day, Johnny."

Waters turned to face his partner. "I've already decided."

Cole's finger went to his neck as though to twist his hair, but there was not enough hair to twist. "Who?"

"Sybil."

The big man's shoulders sagged with relief. "I'm so glad. I thought you might be thinking of someone else."

"Sybil makes the most sense. She has no family to ask questions. No one that I know of, anyway."

"She has an aunt in Houma. And a half-sister in Boutte. But she's not close to either of them."

Waters nodded. "I guess that's it, then."

An unfamiliar vulnerability entered Cole's face. "Is that all you have to say? 'I guess that's it'?"

"You're right. There's a lot more. There's Eve's murder. Lily and Annelise. The EPA investigation."

Cole huffed with exasperation. "Are you going to be in the office all day?"

"Except for lunch, I guess."

"Good." He leaned toward Waters's face, then stopped himself. "I want to kiss you, Johnny. But I know it would make you uncomfortable."

"Sybil won't make me uncomfortable."

Cole laughed softly. "I had a feeling she wouldn't."

Waters passed the remainder of the morning by pretending to work, mostly to keep up appearances for Sybil and any visitors who might stop by. Things needed to appear normal to the very end. Tragedy should appear to strike in the midst of humdrum existence. Oddly, he saw no further sign of Cole. Around noon, he heard his door open and looked up to find Sybil standing in it. She was smiling, and her eyes sparkled.

"What is it?" he asked, trying not to look her in the eye.

"I just wondered if you wanted me to keep holding all your calls."

Waters nodded, doubting what she said was true. Sybil was practically glowing—she wanted to tell him something. But he could hardly look at her. Twenty-eight years old. Beautiful. Her whole life ahead of her. Why did she deserve to die more than Cole, who had squandered almost every blessing he'd ever been given? Because Waters hadn't taken the time to get to know her well?

"Why do you look so happy?" he asked at last.

Sybil bounced on her toes like a giddy cheerleader. "Oh . . . I don't know. It's just a good day."

A hollow feeling spread through his chest. "Anything to do with Cole?"

She looked at the ceiling, but her smile only broadened. "I don't know what I should say."

"It's all right. Nobody's getting fired, Sybil."

She looked him in the eye, unable to contain her news any longer. "I'm seeing him tonight."

Waters tried to keep his face impassive.

"John, he's leaving his wife. He's finally doing it!"

In that moment, Waters almost cracked. He had a sense that Mallory had told Sybil this out of cruelty, but then he reconsidered. Soldiers sometimes offered a doomed prisoner a cigarette or told him a joke be-

fore shooting him in the back of the head. A small
kindness before the end.

"I'm glad for you, Sybil. I hope it's the right thing
for you."

She nodded with the excitement of a young bride. "It
is. I *know* it is."

Waters could think of nothing to say.

"It is for him too," Sybil added with sudden severity. "He's been unhappy for so long."

"Yes. He has."

"Well . . . I guess I should get back to work."

She smiled and went out, closing the door softly
behind her.

Waters put his head down on his desk, already
grieving for Sybil and for himself. *Tonight.* He had not
expected Mallory to move so fast. If he went through
with what he and Lily had planned, tonight he would
lose a part of himself forever. Just as he had when he
committed adultery with Eve. Only this time would
be different. Not long ago, he had questioned his belief in an immortal soul. Today, he felt for the first time
that his was in mortal peril.

He could remain in the office no longer. He stood,
took his keys from the drawer, and walked down the
hall to Cole's office.

"I'm going home for lunch," he said as he walked
in.

Cole did not respond. He sat with his head on his
desk, snoring loudly. Waters sensed that if he woke
Cole now, he would find his old friend looking out of
the familiar eyes. But he could not be sure. And if all
went well, Cole would be himself again by tonight.
That thought pushed Waters across the room to Cole's
side of the desk. He felt strangely compelled to lay his

hand on his old friend's shoulder, to give some parting gesture while Cole was actually Cole. He extended his right hand, then froze.

The desk drawer stood open about six inches, and Cole's right hand lay in it. The fingers of that hand gripped the finely checkered butt of the .357 Magnum Waters had seen yesterday.

The thought that Cole might be this close to suicide stunned him. If he and Lily carried through with their plans for Sybil, and then Cole took his own life . . . the irony would be unendurable. But *was* it suicide Cole was planning? Perhaps he was holding the gun for protection. Maybe he was too afraid of Vegas enforcers to sleep without a gun in his hand. But somehow, Waters didn't think that was it. Instinct told him that his friend, already stressed to the breaking point by his debts, now had blackouts, memory loss, and exhaustion to contend with, just as Lily had. Beyond this, Cole had knowingly slept with his best friend's wife. If he had not been too drunk to remember this, even Cole would suffer intense guilt over such a transgression. Taken as a whole, all this might be enough to drive him to suicide.

Waters was thinking of trying to remove the gun from Cole's hand when he saw an ugly scab on the inside of Cole's left wrist. Bending at the waist, he saw that the scab was one of several wounds there, some so fresh the blood was still drying. At the center of the web of cuts were three deep, parallel gouges, much like those he had found beneath Eve's watch. Only these were far worse.

The sight of those wounds caused a profound change within Waters. Though inflicted by Mallory, they seemed emblematic of the pain Cole had been car-

rying with him for the past several years. By choosing
Sybil as their surrogate for Mallory's murder, Waters
and Lily had spared Cole. He would live on, making
the same mistakes he had always made, searching for
happiness and never finding it, and probably die
young of a heart attack, or from the complications of
the diabetes he so religiously ignored. It suddenly
struck Waters how simple it would be to lift Cole's
gun hand, put the barrel of the Magnum to his temple,
and pull the trigger. By the time Sybil came running
in, Waters could be on the other side of the desk, gap-
ing in shock and weeping genuine tears of grief. Mallory would be dead, and Cole's death would be ruled
a suicide. Hell, with Cole's money troubles well
known in town, no one would even question it. Cole
kept a couple of Polo shirts in the closet across the
room. Just to be safe, Waters would wrap his hand in
one before he fired, to keep any powder residue off
his hands.

He looked from the scars to the gun, then at the
back of Cole's big head. The growing bald spot there
looked almost pathetically human. *Cole's got life insurance through the company*, he thought. He had verified
this himself, along with all other policies, after Cole
had let the liability premium lapse. If the $500,000
death benefit were used to pay off Cole's Vegas debts,
that would leave a $150,000 balance, which Waters
would have to pick up. He would also have to pay
substantial sums on a regular basis to keep Cole's wife
and children living in even a shadow of the style to
which they were accustomed. *If I pull that trigger*, he
thought, *that's the least I can do.*

Somehow, this thought did not revolt him as he
knew it should. The simple fact was, if he killed Mal-

lory now, the danger to Lily and Annelise would end immediately. Cole would probably lose several years of life, but there was a strong chance that he might not live more than a few days anyway.

Waters prodded Cole's shoulder.

His partner groaned but did not move.

With a strange sense of detachment, Waters went to the closet, took a red Polo shirt from it, wrapped it around his hand, and went back to the desk. Cole was still snoring.

Bending his knees, Waters laid his cotton-swathed hand over Cole's and lifted the .357 into the air. There was a hitch in Cole's breathing, but the snoring resumed. Very slowly, he moved the barrel against Cole's temple and slipped his own finger inside the trigger guard. This close to his partner, he could smell Cole's distinctive odor, a mix of sweat and aftershave and cigar smoke that Waters would know anywhere with his eyes closed.

God forgive me, he thought, and began to squeeze the trigger.

Before he applied sufficient pressure to break the trigger, Waters saw a vision of a room filled with people. Older people mostly, row upon row of them, and a man in black was speaking about God. As he droned on, Waters turned in his pew and saw a lone boy like himself sitting between two adults. The boy was Cole Smith, a freckled thirteen years old, but his face held enough empathy for a man twice his size. The empathy was for John Waters, who had just lost his father.

Waters froze with the trigger near to breaking, and in that horrifying lacuna of time, he heard Sybil coming up the hall.

"Cole?" she called. "Hey, sleepyhead!"

He dropped Cole's gun hand back into the drawer and tossed the Polo shirt under the desk.

"What are you doing?" Sybil asked from the doorway.

Waters nearly jumped out of his shoes. "Trying to be quiet. Cole's still sleeping."

"He's been asleep half the morning."

Waters quickly crossed to the door. "Maybe he drank too much last night."

Sybil frowned like a future wife. "He's not drinking tonight. He says things he doesn't mean when he's drunk. And I've had it with that. Tonight I'm getting the truth."

Waters wanted to pat her arm, but he could not bring himself to touch her. He slipped past her and went into the hall. "I'm going home for lunch. I may not be back."

Sybil nodded and peeked into Cole's office. "Maybe I should wake him up."

Waters looked over her shoulder and tried to calculate the probabilities of what would happen if she did. Who would awake? Cole? Or Mallory?

"I'd let him sleep," he said, catching the scent of perfume from Sybil's neck. "You want him rested and clearheaded tonight."

She gave him a preoccupied nod. "You're right. Hey, what were you looking for?"

"Oh . . . I lent him my dictation recorder yesterday. No big deal."

She nodded again. "No scotch for that boy tonight."

Leaving Sybil standing in Cole's door, Waters walked to the back stairs, his mind focused on Lily and Annelise. That was the only way he would survive the night's work.

Waters drove slowly through the darkness of North Union Street, Lily rigid in the seat beside him. Annelise lay asleep on the seat behind them, a gun under the seat beneath him. Large Victorian houses lined both sides of the road, their gingerbread trim strangely threatening in the night. He wasn't driving his Land Cruiser or Lily's Acura. An hour ago, Lily had dropped him a quarter mile from an oil field equipment lot on Liberty Road, where an old four-door pickup always sat with a key under the mat. It belonged to a well-checker Waters knew, a man he hadn't spoken to for more than two years. That was one virtue of small towns. Things changed little, and when they did, they changed slowly.

He braked on the 1200 block, scanning the house fronts for numbers. Sybil Sonnier lived in a detached apartment behind one of the larger Victorians on North Union. Many single people preferred to live in these cozy quarters rather than take apartments in the homogeneous complexes around town.

"There it is," Lily said in a taut voice. "Twelve-sixty-six."

Most of the houses here stood fairly close together, but 1266 was surrounded by more than an acre of land, and a second driveway led beneath twisted old oaks to a faint streetlight behind the main house. That light marked Sybil's apartment. Waters had scouted all this during the afternoon. No one could ask for more isolation in the middle of town, except perhaps at Bienville.

There was only one light on in the main house. The third floor. A bathroom, Waters guessed.

"Park a couple of blocks down," Lily said. "Like we planned."

Waters swerved right, turned into the driveway, and headed straight toward the streetlight behind the main house.

"What are you doing?" Lily whispered.

"This is better. If you sat on the street, a random cop could come by and talk to you. Even if you ducked down, he might check the truck because it's unfamiliar or because the plate's out of date."

Lily looked at him a moment longer, then nodded.

Thirty yards from the small two-story structure, Waters pulled behind a pile of old tires, then shut off the engine. He had no idea what the tires were doing there, other than collecting nesting water for mosquitoes, but they provided excellent cover. They sat in the punctuated silence of the ticking motor, watching a dim yellow glow in the second-floor window of the apartment. The pickup smelled of stale crude oil, cigarettes, and diesel fuel.

"Look," said Lily, pointing toward the first floor. "There's Cole's Lincoln."

Waters recognized the tail end of the silver land yacht sticking out past the far corner of the apartment.

"And there's Cole," she said.

Light speared into the night as a door opened on the second floor. Then Cole's bulk blotted out most of it. He seemed to stagger on the landing of the outdoor stairwell, but then he caught himself and turned back to the door. A much smaller form stepped into the light. Sybil, wearing a transparent gown with nothing underneath. As she reached up to Cole's neck with both arms, Waters cranked down his window and heard the tinkle of laughter. Cole bent and kissed her for a while, then slapped her on the rump and started down the steps. Sybil stood in the light, watching him go.

"How can we be sure Mallory went into her?" Lily asked. "If the woman has to climax for the transfer to be made . . ."

Waters had asked the same question that afternoon. Mallory had called and told him to come to Sybil's house after midnight, where they would have their first celebration. When Waters asked how she could be sure the transference would happen the first time, Mallory had replied, *If I were Cole, I might be worried. But I'm not, am I? Tonight will be the best sex Sybil ever had, and she'll have no idea that it's because I'm a woman.*

"You'll have to say something to her," Lily said. "See how she reacts. If she's Mallory, you'll know after the first few words. The second you do—shoot her."

The stately rumble of Cole's Lincoln filled the night, and then the bluish glow of headlights arced into the dark from behind the apartment. Sybil remained on the landing, watching to be sure her lover made it to the street without difficulty. Cole must have been drinking after all. After a few moments, the Lincoln backed up, stopped, then shot forward on the little drive and rolled past the pile of tires, headed for North Union Street. Sybil waited until Cole made the turn, then closed her door.

"Now we wait," Lily said, glancing at her watch. "One hour."

Waters sighed and looked into the backseat at Annelise. An hour seemed an eternity when you were sitting on someone else's property with a pistol under your seat. What if the owner had seen him pull in? What if the police had already been called to check out the suspicious vehicle?

"Take it easy," Lily said, laying her hand on his thigh. "We're fine."

"I know." But he didn't feel fine. He had wanted to leave Lily at home with Annelise. Then his wife could swear that he had been home with her while the murder took place. But Lily had insisted on coming. Without her there, she feared, his nerve might fail. A moral man was bound to question himself during such a terrible act, perhaps even hesitate at the moment of truth. She wanted him to know she was absolutely committed to perpetrating this crime in order to save her family.

Lily's presence made their alibi more difficult to carry off, but Annelise would save them. Lily had put her to bed at home at her regular bedtime, but not before slipping a good dose of Benadryl into her Sprite. All Ana would remember in the morning was going to bed at the usual time in the usual way—nothing of a midnight truck ride and certainly nothing of a murder. Before leaving the house, Waters had also ordered a Pay-Per-View film on a satellite channel. The film lasted two and a half hours, and he and Lily had both seen it during its theatrical release. By the time it ended, they would be back home again, their work done.

The wild card was Cole. Waters believed that once Cole was himself again, Lily's story would make him see the necessity of what they had done, and that he would support whatever story they told him was required. But even if he didn't believe them, what choice did he have? With Sybil dead, he would be in more desperate need of an alibi than anyone, and should he balk, they could easily frame him for her murder. All it would take was an anonymous call to the police. They would check Sybil's apartment for hair, fiber, and fingerprint evidence, and Sybil's body for Cole's semen. Cole rarely practiced safe sex with regular lovers. An anonymous tip would doom him as surely as Waters was doomed for Eve's murder. Much easier for Cole to swear he had been watching a Pay-Per-View movie at Linton Hill with his friends while their daughter slept upstairs.

Their only real problem was time. If Cole went to a bar now instead of going home to his empty house (Jenny had taken the kids to her mother's in New Orleans), it would greatly complicate Cole's alibi. But Waters had a plan for that too. A deep gully ran very close behind Sybil's apartment. From his childhood, Waters remembered steep, heavily wooded banks along the edge of the ravine, and he had verified the accuracy of his memory during this afternoon's ride, by traveling along a parallel street. If he dumped Sybil's body down that kudzu-choked bank, it might be several days before she was found. Forty-eight hours, at the very least, unless animals dragged her body into the open. Fixing an exact time of death would be problematic at that point, even with the highly efficient methods of an FBI forensic unit.

Lily touched his shoulder and pointed into the backseat at Annelise's prone form. "She's why we're doing this," she said softly.

"I know that."

"I know it's hard to wait. Think about something else."

"Like?"

"The future. Life is going to be different after this."

He swallowed. "No doubt about that."

She leaned close so that he could see her eyes in the dark. "Not like that. Not bad. I'm going to start taking care of you again. No more distance. No more coldness. Life is too precious for that."

"You're right. And we're about to take it from someone."

Anger tightened Lily's face. "Do you know what will happen if we don't? Mallory will kill her anyway. If you spare Sybil now, with Mallory inside her, you're not sparing her anything. It's the same as letting a truck run over her. Mallory wouldn't leave anything of her. She'd gradually devour her mind, like a swarm of locusts nibbling away."

"You're right. I know you're right."

He expected Sybil's upstairs light to wink out, but it didn't. He took this as a sign that Mallory had succeeded. If Sybil were still Sybil, and had just made love after a romantic dinner, he would expect her to be asleep by now. At least watching TV in her bed. But he didn't see the flicker of a television through any of the windows. He had a feeling that Mallory was sitting in the silent house, waiting for him.

"I'm going," he said, reaching under the seat for the gun.

"It hasn't been an hour," Lily protested.

"I don't care. I'm doing it now."

The gun felt cold in his hand. It was an old Smith & Wesson .38 Special that an uncle had given him when he was a teenager. His uncle bought it at a lodge auction, with no records of any kind made.

Lily watched him check the cylinder. He had

driven here with an empty chamber under the hammer, but now he took a shell from his pocket and filled it.

"Here," she said, dropping a pair of latex gloves in his lap. "Put these on."

"Where did you get those?"

"My makeup box. They came with some hair coloring, but they'll do the job."

The gloves were too small, but he pulled them on anyway.

"Keep them on until you get back here. Someone might be able to take fingerprints from the inside of the latex."

Her attention to detail amazed him. He nodded, then reached for the door handle, but Lily grabbed his shoulder and peered urgently into his eyes.

"Don't think of her as Sybil. You have to see her as Mallory."

"I know." He pulled the handle and kicked the stubborn old door loose from its frame. "When you hear the shot, start the motor."

"I love you, John. This is the only way."

He pulled himself free, opened the door, and climbed down from the truck. Despite his efforts to be quiet, the door screeched when he closed it. He winced but did not hesitate, running low and quick across the open ground to the first floor of the apartment.

Through the nearest window, he saw a combination den/living room with a kitchenette against the far wall. A staircase went up one wall on the inside. Good. He reached down and tried the window. Locked. There were three more on the ground floor. He moved to the next one and pulled. The window shifted in its frame. Setting the pistol on the ground, he put both hands on the sash and pulled up with a steady pressure. The window gave and slid upward.

In seconds he stood inside the dark room. He smelled vinegar. Probably some sort of salad dressing. Meat too. Glancing toward the kitchenette, he saw dirty plates with the remnants of rib-eye steaks on them. Sybil didn't seem the type to leave dirty dishes out, and he took this as another sign that Mallory had succeeded.

Drawing a deep breath, he moved to the staircase. The steps were carpeted, but he still put a foot on the second step and tested his weight. It didn't creak. If Mallory was upstairs, there was no reason to be quiet, but he couldn't shake the fear wrapped like tentacles around his heart. Gripping the gun with his finger on the trigger, he started up.

Lily sat in the pickup, listening to Annelise breathing. Once, the respirations got so faint that she reached over the seat and put her hand on Ana's chest to feel the reassuring rise and fall. For a few panicked seconds, she wondered if she had used too much Benadryl—then the inhalation came, weak but there.

Where was John now? On the porch? In the apartment? She prayed that he had the nerve to go through with it. Her husband had great compassion; that was one reason she had married him. Now compassion was his enemy.

"*Hurry,*" she murmured. "*Don't think. Just do it.*"

She had been sitting in the truck, and her eyes adjusted to the darkness. The cloak of night parted to reveal a yard with a swing set, seesaws, and a rose garden by Sybil's apartment. Lily could imagine Sybil out there on Sunday mornings, alone, doing her best to make her apartment seem like a home. That simple thought pierced her heart, but she shut her mind to empathy. It wasn't too difficult. All she had to do was focus on an image of herself dangling a butcher knife over her own daughter's head. Superimposed on this horrifying scene was another: naked figures thrashing in ghostly green light, her own face clenched in ecstasy as she demeaned herself in ways that nauseated her now. Mallory Candler had done all that.

Lily actually remembered Mallory from St. Stephens. Like Cole, Mallory had been a senior when Lily was in the ninth grade. Her clearest memory of Mallory was a tall, proud, and stunningly beautiful girl moving through the halls of the school, leaving a wake of staring boys behind her. Lily had been a gangly freshman then, obsessed with long-distance running, though in her secret heart she knew she used running as an excuse not to deal with her insecurity about boys. Someone like Mallory Candler was beyond her understanding, a girl so radiantly desirable that grown men fawned over her whenever she was around. Lily had once seen her own father become tongue-tied in Mallory's presence. Having experienced that reality, it was hard to imagine Mallory as the obsessively jealous psychotic her husband described. Yet she knew it could be true. What would it feel like to be such a creature and be denied something after so many years of having everything?

Lily went rigid, gooseflesh covering her skin, her eyes and ears alert. Something had snapped outside the truck. She didn't think an animal had made the sound. A large deer perhaps, but she was downtown, and her senses told her it had taken more weight than that to produce the sound she'd heard. She peered toward the main house, then the apartment, but she saw nothing. What would she say if the owner of the house suddenly appeared at her window with a gun?

Hi, I'm Lily Waters. My husband had to stop off and tell his receptionist something. I hope we didn't scare you in this awful truck. John had to go out and check a leak at one of his wells on the river . . .

"That's exactly what I'll say," she whispered.

And if a shot rang out while the owner stood there? What then? Would John have to kill him too?

Yes, said a voice inside her. *That's what happens when you start this kind of madness. . . .*

Annelise stirred in the backseat. Lily reached back and rubbed her shoulder, praying she would not wake.

Halfway up Sybil's stairs, Waters stood motionless against the wall. He had heard something. A groan or a snore, perhaps. But only one. He had to keep moving, yet something held him where he was.

Go, he told himself. *Don't stop.*

But his feet remained still. The gun had felt so natural in the truck. Now he wanted to throw it on the floor. He knew what horror awaited him upstairs. That was how he thought of Mallory now—not as a person, but as a thing. There was no human pity in her, no real love. He had no choice but to go on. Yet the image of Sybil smiling in his office today would not leave him. So young, so trusting. She had trusted Cole Smith with her heart, which was the height of lunacy. But she was not the first young woman to do it.

Waters shut his eyes and tried to visualize himself shooting her. *If you can't see it in your mind, you'll never do it in life.* A popular New Age platitude. And why should it be difficult? After all, he'd already killed one woman. At least his *hands* had killed her. But killing was not a thing of hands. It was a thing of the mind. Killing in cold blood demanded a cold mind. A gun made it easier, a matter of a momentary trigger pull rather than the eternity of crushing hands and bulging eyes it had taken to end Eve Sumner's life. But for a man with a conscience, a single finger's pull could be more difficult than lifting a mountain. Would shooting Sybil from behind make it easier? It seemed the act of a coward, but wouldn't it be better for *her* if she never saw it coming?

That's how I'd want it, he thought. *None of that life-passing-before-your-eyes bullshit.* If you saw it coming, those last seconds could dilate into a lifetime of regret and self-recrimination. But with a bullet through the base of your brain, there would be none of that—no white light or angel choirs either—only instant and utter darkness.

He gritted his teeth and forced himself up to the next step. Then the next. There was a small landing at the top. Two doors led off it. The one on the right led to a bathroom. He saw light reflecting off a stainless-steel leg bracing the sink. The other door, only slightly open, would be her bedroom. Yellow light trickled onto the landing as though in invitation.

Why is she up here? he wondered. *Why isn't she waiting downstairs with a bottle of champagne?* Maybe she was sitting naked on the bed in her favorite position, legs crossed yoga-style, silently awaiting the lover she had fought for a decade to reach. But then he remembered Cole, fast asleep at his desk that afternoon. Maybe Mallory was at this moment struggling to take control of Sybil's sleeping mind. If so, it was the perfect opportunity to destroy her. Before she had a chance to plead for mercy or fight back. Only if she was asleep . . . how could he be certain Mallory was inside her? He concealed the .38 behind his back and slipped into the bedroom.

Sybil lay on the bed, the covers pulled loosely over her chest, her lower body exposed in the sheer nightgown. But for her curves and pubic hair, she looked like a sleeping child. She still wore her makeup. Maybe she'd passed out from too much alcohol. He knew he should wake her. If she panicked, she was Sybil. If she smiled and pulled him into the bed, she was Mallory. Simple. But he could not find it in himself to touch her.

Do it! Lily shouted in his mind. *Hurry!*

Waters picked up a throw pillow and held it over the muzzle of the gun, then held the pillow above Sybil's face. His right hand began to shake. In his mind, he saw her eyes snap open, as ravenously alive as a vampire's, filled with hatred and fury at his betrayal.

"Come on," he whispered. *"For Annelise . . ."*

He tried to pull the trigger, but his finger would not obey.

Lily lay shivering in the backseat of the truck, trying to cover Annelise's body with her own. There was someone outside. Close. Moving carefully. She could hear them through the window John had left open. It had taken all her self-restraint not to start the engine and race away, but she couldn't abandon her husband. She wished she had brought a gun of her own, but there had seemed no reason. Shielding Annelise with her body seemed an ineffectual act, but she might keep Ana alive long enough for John to save her if an attacker came out of the night. If that happened, she would scream through the window and pray that John heard her. She was holding back a scream when a large black figure loomed in the driver's window.

"What the hell are you doing, Lily?" Cole asked.

Lily's throat locked shut.

"Do you think you're invisible back there?"

As she stared up in shock, Cole began to laugh, a dark, deranged sound that stopped the blood in her veins.

Oh God, she screamed silently, thinking of John and his mission in Sybil's little house. *Oh, no . . .*

Cole's laughter went on and on.

Waters pushed the shaking gun into the pillow resting against Sybil's head. She opened her mouth, and he knew from the smell that she had not brushed her teeth. As his finger tightened, she suddenly rolled away from him, groaned, and started to get out of bed. Waters stood silent as a tree as she walked to the door, crossed the landing, and went into the bathroom. The sound of urination reached him, and in his mind he saw his own wife as he had a hundred times, sitting sleepily on the commode, oblivious to the world, utterly and pathetically human.

I can't do this, he thought. *Walk in there and fire a bullet into her face?*

As the sound slowed to a trickle, he darted onto the landing and rushed down the stairs.

"Hello?" Sybil called drowsily. "Cole?"

Waters froze on the ground floor. *Why did she call*

out for Cole? Mallory would have said, "Johnny?" Maybe Sybil was stronger than Lily or Cole. Maybe Mallory couldn't control her as easily—

"Is someone there?"

As footsteps descended the stairs, he folded his body and clambered through the window, then sprinted for the truck, pulling off the gloves as he ran.

He saw the shadow of Lily waiting in the backseat and wondered if Annelise had awakened. Lily would be angry, but she'd have to understand. They'd have to find another way, that was all. He opened the door and jumped into the driver's seat.

"I knew you couldn't do it," Cole said, popping up from the floor of the passenger seat.

Waters tried to bring up his gun, but Cole's big hand was already pointing a pistol over the seat at Lily and Annelise.

"You could make me kill two babies," Cole said, "but you can't kill a secretary that's too stupid to live. Give me that fucking gun."

Waters handed it over.

The fury and hurt in Cole's eyes made him sick with fear.

"You felt pity for Sybil?" Cole said in a cracked voice. "I know it wasn't for me. If you'd thought it was just me in there, you'd have pulled the trigger without a thought."

"Mallory—"

Holding Waters at bay with his own pistol, Cole aimed his .357 at Annelise's head. "I should kill her. It's only fair, after what you made me do. Besides, you two need to learn a lesson."

Lily began to cry. Waters wished he had shot Cole that afternoon.

"Shut up! You simpering little *nothing*. What good are you? You hardly gave him one child. You can't even make love with him like a woman."

Lily covered Annelise like a blanket, her face empty of anything but terror.

"Don't do it!" Waters begged.

"Tell me why I shouldn't."

"The Mallory Candler I loved would never do that."

Cole shuddered. "What?"

"The Mallory I knew would never be that cruel. I hurt her terribly, yes. She was heartbroken. But she never really hurt someone physically. You say you're Mallory Candler. You may have started as Mallory . . . but in the ten years you've been like this, you've changed. Something's twisted you. Mallory *loved* me. You don't love me."

Fury contorted Cole's face into something horrible. "I love you more than anyone possibly could!"

"No. You want to *own* me. That's not love. You don't want to make me happy. You want me to make *you* happy. But I can't. Because you'll never feel loved enough."

Cole's lips quivered.

"Yes, I was going to kill you," Waters said. "I honestly thought you would be better off dead. At peace. God forgive me, but you were meant to die ten years ago. Something allowed you to survive . . . like this. But it's not natural. It's not fair for you to steal someone else's body, someone else's life, to live out what you think is the life you deserved."

A tear streaked Cole's face. "It wasn't fair for that man to rape me!" As he wiped away the tear, a savage light came into Cole's eyes. "Who are you to tell me what I deserve? You gave me children and then took them away. You left me an empty shell."

The gun shook against Annelise's head.

"For God's sake, no!" Lily pleaded. "She's just a child!"

Waters closed his eyes. "I loved you once," he said quietly. "Show me you're worth loving again."

Cole gasped, and his eyes locked on to Waters's face. "You think I *want* to hurt her? You're making me do this! You were going to kill me."

"What choice did you give me!"

Cole's left hand rose to his neck as if to twist a lock of hair around his finger, but there was no hair there. He seemed suddenly purposeless, disoriented. Waters was about to speak when Cole jerked the gun away from Annelise's head and leaped out of the truck.

Lily began to sob in the backseat. Waters cranked the engine and threw the truck into gear, roaring out of the little driveway like a man fleeing the scene of a murder.

When they pulled up to Linton Hill, Lily was still crying. Waters had not dumped the pickup as planned; he didn't think Lily could handle the logistics in her state. He parked the old Ford behind the house and lifted Annelise into his arms.

"Open the back door," he told Lily. "Go up and get her bed ready."

Lily ran to the door and opened it with her key, then disappeared into the house. Carrying Annelise up the stairs winded him, more from his nerves than her weight. As he pulled the covers up over her chest, Lily pulled him toward the door.

"What are we going to do? What *can* we do?"

Before he could answer, the downstairs phone rang. He bounded down the steps and checked the caller ID on the den telephone: UNKNOWN NUMBER. At 1:20 A.M.

He picked up the receiver but said nothing.

"John?" said a familiar voice. "John? It's Penn Cage."

"Penn! What's going on?"

"I'm sorry to call so late. I've been calling for the past hour. I was about to get in my car and drive over there."

Waters didn't think it was possible to be more stressed than he was already, but the edge in his lawyer's voice did the trick.

"What's happened?"

"Are you on a land line?"

"Yes."

"The police have a search warrant for your house. I'd expect them there by six a.m."

Waters felt dizzy. "Why a search all of a sudden?"

"They may have new evidence. There's just no way to know."

"Okay," Waters said, not at all sure what he should do.

"I'm telling you this," Penn said carefully, "because people often have things inside their homes they'd rather not see made public. Pornography. Recreational drugs. Sexual paraphernalia. Diaries or journals . . ."

Evidence of murder, Waters thought. "I hear you. I appreciate the heads-up."

"It won't do any real good for me to be there during the search, but call me as soon as it's over. You're liable to be taken in for questioning again. Things could go south very quickly from here, but stay calm."

"Yeah. Thanks." Waters hung up.

"That was Penn?" Lily asked from behind him. "What did he say?"

She had wiped away her tears, but she looked as though she might collapse at any moment. He wished he could spare her the truth, but she had to know.

"The police are going to search this house in four hours."

Lily's head began shaking like she had Parkinson's disease. "What are we going to do?"

"They won't find anything. I'll—"

"What are we going to do about *Mallory?*"

He started to go to her, but then he realized that the fear in her eyes had been replaced by fury.

"How could you do this to us?" she whispered. "How did we *get* here?"

"Lily—"

"You still love her, don't you?"

"*What?*"

Lily was nodding, her eyes flicking back and forth, focusing on nothing. "You still love Mallory. You always have."

"You know that's not true."

Her face was so white that he feared she might faint. "How could Mallory have done any of this if you didn't still love her? That's what's kept her alive all these years!"

Waters stepped forward, his hands held out to calm her, but Lily backed away as though afraid he would strike her.

"What kind of husband are you?" she cried. "What kind of *father* are you?"

"Lily, please. Listen to me."

"She told me about you getting her pregnant! While you were in Sybil's apartment. She told me about the abortions. She thinks my miscarriages happened because of what you made her do."

"That's impossible."

Lily's eyes were wild. "When I lost those babies, I knew there was a reason. I searched for some mistake I'd made . . . some sin I had to pay for. But it wasn't my sin, was it? It was *yours*."

Before he could reply, she turned and fled the den.

He stood alone in the roaring silence, his options exhausted, his hope all but gone. The second hand on his watch seemed to be flying.

chapter 19

Lily stood on the porch of Linton Hill and watched the police pull out of her driveway. Two squad cars, then a van from the crime lab. Each of her hands held a fragment of a Wedgwood coffeepot shattered by a careless policewoman. A family heirloom, Princeton pattern. Her husband's hushed voice sounded from the foyer behind her. He was talking to his attorney. The police had demanded John's presence at the station for questioning. In fourteen years of marriage, she had never heard her husband sound afraid, except during the worst of her depression, when for a week she had actually considered suicide.

He sounded afraid now.

As the police vehicles rolled up State Street, Lily felt the tears she had suppressed throughout the search. In addition to manhandling her family's most precious belongings, the searchers had also taken away several boxes of photographs, all three home computers—Annelise's Apple notebook included—

and an assortment of clothes from John's closet. The clothes had been unceremoniously dumped into plastic bags and thrown in the back of the van. The only mercy of the morning was Penn Cage's warning. An hour before the search, John had driven Annelise to Lily's mother's house, so that she would not have to witness the event.

"Lily?"

She turned. Even in his black cashmere sweater, John already looked like a man on the run. His face was drawn, almost haggard, and his bloodshot eyes had dark bags beneath them. He had spent the remainder of last night dumping the stolen truck and walking home while Lily slept with Annelise.

"I've got to go to police headquarters," he told her.

"They broke my grandmother's coffeepot."

He took the fragments from her hand. "I'll have it repaired. I'll send it back to England and have the factory do it."

"It won't ever be the same."

"No." He touched her arm. "But it will be all right."

"I'll go with you."

He set the fragments inside the foyer, then came out and hugged her. "Penn's going to meet me there. I don't want you exposed to any of that. You should go check on Ana."

"When do you have to leave?"

"Now."

A surge of panic went through her, but she steadied herself so that he wouldn't worry more than he already was.

"I'll call you and let you know what's going on," he promised. "Keep your cell phone on."

"I will."

John's face became as serious as she had ever seen it. "Depending on how the questioning goes, Penn thinks I could be arrested this morning."

She closed her eyes and reached for his hand.

"If that happens, Penn will contact you about bail. You should follow his instructions to the letter."

She wanted to speak, but all she could manage was a nod.

John hugged her once more, then went down the steps to his Land Cruiser. As he drove down the lane leading to State Street, Lily felt something deep within her give way. Last night's hysterical anger had withered into ashes during the search, leaving only terror at the impending destruction of her family. Her terror made her ashamed. Fear could not help her. Nor could it help John or Annelise. She had to overpower her fear and use the only weapon she had ever really had: her mind. The shattered china coffeepot in the foyer could never be made right again, but her family could. People were different from objects. After bones healed, they were stronger in the broken places. A family could be like that.

She could do nothing about the murder case. That was Penn Cage's job. But the other threat was something else. She allowed an image of Cole holding his pistol to Annelise's sleeping head to fill her mind, but instead of fear, she felt cold, implacable rage, all of it focused on the woman who had wrecked her life. Her hands shook with the power of her hatred for Mallory. As she stood on the porch of her violated home, she heard a voice that seemed the voice of a stranger, but it came from her own lips.

"You can't do this," it said. "Not to my family. I will *not* let you do this."

She turned and hurried into the house. In the kitchen, she drew an eight-inch carving knife from the butcher's block and ran her finger along its serrated blade. Then she grabbed her cell phone and her keys and ran for her car.

Waters sat in a plastic chair on one side of an aluminum table bolted to the floor, Penn Cage to his left. Detective Tom Jackson sat across from them, and Jackson's partner, the short, pockmarked officer named Barlow, paced the tile floor in the space behind Jackson.

An audiotape recorder sat on the table, the tape spooling slowly through the machine, but this was only for backup. A large video camera stood in the corner of the room, recording Waters's every nervous tic as he faced the detectives.

Tom Jackson treated the questioning as he had the whole business, with the regretful firmness of a friend forced by circumstance to carry out an unpleasant task. He acted as though Eve's brutal murder were a crime any man might have committed in the heat of passion.

"We're not arresting you yet," he said. "But things don't look good, John. We have a lot more evidence than you and your attorney are aware of, and I want to be straight with you about that."

Penn's skeptical look told Waters that his lawyer doubted the police would be straight about anything.

"You know that we have a videotape of your vehicle near the hotel within one hour of the murder," Jackson said. "You know you were twice seen going into Bienville with the murder victim. You *don't* know that for the last two nights, FBI forensic technicians have been going through that mansion with special lights and chemicals, and they've found biological evidence of considerable sexual activity."

At the mention of FBI involvement, Penn shifted in his chair.

"That evidence is now being sent to the FBI lab in Washington. It will be compared with the semen sample taken from Eve Sumner's body, and also with the blood you gave yesterday."

Jackson looked as though he expected a response to these revelations, but neither Waters nor Penn said a word.

"We also have your cell phone records. Those records show that for a period of two weeks prior to the murder, you received daily calls from three different pay phones. The bulk of those calls originated from one less than a quarter mile from Eve Sumner's real estate office."

Waters struggled to keep his face expressionless. So far, all they were talking about was evidence of an extramarital affair.

Jackson looked down at a file before him. "The DNA testing will take weeks, but we already know your blood type matches that of the perpetrator. AB negative. That's fairly rare. You're also what's known as a secretor. So is the perpetrator."

"You seem to be assuming," Penn interrupted, "that whoever last had sex with the victim also murdered her."

Jackson seemed surprised by this objection. "I *am* assuming that. I realize it's not necessarily true, but I'll be surprised if it's not."

"I urge you to keep an open mind," Penn said. "Assumptions of any kind are always dangerous in murder cases."

For the first time, Jackson showed signs of irritation. "Let's get down to it," he said, looking at Waters. "You were having an affair with this woman. All the signs point to it. And if the DNA is going to come back and prove it, what's the point in lying to us about it?"

Waters looked at Penn, but his lawyer's face revealed nothing. He had a distinct feeling that if he did not give Tom Jackson something today, he was not going to be allowed to leave this building. And with Mallory on the loose, that was simply not acceptable. He'd given some thought to a plausible story before the morning's search, and he was about to try it out when a uniformed cop came in and whispered something in Detective Jackson's ear.

Jackson got up and left the interrogation room without a word.

Penn reached out and squeezed Waters's shoulder.

"Ain't that cute?" said Jackson's partner. "You two ought to share a cell."

Lily Waters sat in her mother's formal living room, a pristine space that was hardly ever used. Like most Southern women of her generation, Evelyn Anderson viewed her living room as a showplace, a silent testament to her taste and decorum. Evelyn herself perched on the edge of a wing chair with her hands folded in her lap, her silver hair perfectly coiffed, her face lined with worry.

"Lily Ann," she said in a genteel voice. "What in heaven's name is going on at your house? A friend of mine called and told me she'd seen police cars there."

Lily got up and went to the door to make sure Annelise was still watching television in the den.

"Mom, I need to ask you something."

"All right."

"You know our wills state that you would get custody of Annelise if anything happened to John and me."

Her mother's eyes narrowed. "I know that. But what—"

"I don't think anything is going to happen to us. But if something did . . . do you think you would have any problem fulfilling that obligation?"

Evelyn's hand rose slowly to her mouth as the gravity of her daughter's question hit home. "Honey, I've never seen you like this. Has John done something illegal with his company? Has the EPA investigation gone against him? Oh God, are you losing your house? Is that why the police were there?"

"It's nothing like that."

"Lily, please. Maybe I can help."

"You can't help, except by answering my question."

Her mother sighed and shook her head. "Honey, if something happened to you and John, I'd make it my life's work to raise that little girl just the way I think you would have."

Lily's hands began to shake.

"Baby, please—" Evelyn was rising from the chair, but Lily held up a hand.

"Is there anything you haven't told me about your health? I know you keep things to yourself, like Dad did. You're not ill or anything, are you?"

Evelyn shook her head. "I had a physical just last

month. Dr. Cage says I'll outlive him and all his nurses."

In spite of her desperation, Lily laughed.

"Honey, has John treated you badly?"

"No. Don't ever think that, Mom. Whatever happens. John is a good man. And I haven't always been the best wife to him in some ways."

"Don't say that."

Lily sat on the sofa, propped her elbows on her knees, and began to rub her throbbing temples. "Losing those babies took something out of me. It was something I couldn't control, and it was very hard on John."

Evelyn gave a prim nod. "I know that, dear. I see more than you think. But you're still with us, and that's all I care about. That and Annelise."

Lily knew that if she stayed in this room much longer, she would never summon the nerve to do what she had to do. She stood and folded her arms across her chest.

"I'm going, Mom."

"Lily! You *must* tell me what's happening."

"I can't. Not yet. Just please keep Annelise here. I'll call you with any news."

Evelyn shook her head in frustration, but she stood and followed her daughter to the front door. "Aren't you going to say good-bye to Annelise?"

Lily fought back tears. "I can't. I don't want her to see me this way."

Evelyn reached out and squeezed her daughter's arm. "You go do whatever you have to. I know you'll do the right thing. And remember . . . your father's looking down on you. He'll help you if he can."

Lily sobbed openly then. Before it could get worse, she slipped through the door and ran out to her car.

Tom Jackson walked back into the interrogation room and sat down opposite Waters.

"Our crime lab tech has just completed a preliminary examination of several hairs taken from your hairbrush at home. He matched those to hairs found inside suite three twenty-four at the Eola Hotel the morning after the murder."

Waters said nothing.

"We've also learned that Eve Sumner had a safe deposit box we knew nothing about. That box is being opened now." Jackson laid his big hands on the metal table, reminding Waters of Cole. "Now, I don't know what we might find in that box. But I have a feeling it's the kind of stuff Eve didn't want anyone knowing anything about. The way she didn't want anyone knowing about you."

Waters looked at the table and wondered where Lily and Annelise were. And Cole? What was Mallory driving him to do now?

"Are you listening, John?" Jackson asked. "This is murder we're talking about. If you don't give me something, you're going to find yourself in a cell with Danny Buckles, and the reputation you've spent twenty years building will be ruined in a day."

"Stop right there," Penn interjected. "Detective, all you have done this morning is tell us that you have evidence of an extramarital affair. You've shown us nothing. But let's say that evidence exists. Do you arrest people for having affairs?"

"When one of the parties is murdered," Jackson said, "we often do."

"Damn straight we do," Barlow growled from behind his partner. "I say lock him up right now. He'll get tired of jail real quick. The rich ones always do."

The look in Tom Jackson's eye told Waters the detective remembered his old schoolmate better than that. "Okay," Jackson said. "If it was just an affair, why lie about it? Tell us the truth and help us get to the bottom of this."

You don't want to know the bottom of this, Waters thought. "All right, Tom," he said in a tone of surrender. "I had an affair with her."

Detective Barlow slapped his leg as though this admission sewed up the case.

Penn stiffened but said nothing, recognizing that Waters was following a strategy Penn himself had laid out days ago. Only Waters intended to go a little further.

"How many times did you see her?" Jackson asked.

"The whole two weeks before the murder. Every day but the day she died. Or the night, actually."

"What do you mean? You were with her the day she died?"

"Yes." Waters looked Jackson in the eye. "But I never went up to the suite that night. And I didn't kill her."

Barlow barked a derisive laugh.

"Why didn't you tell us this before?"

"Because I knew it would break up my marriage. I don't want to lose my wife, Tom. I knew I hadn't killed Eve, and I figured you'd catch whoever did it long before the DNA came back."

"Bullshit," said Barlow. "You did her, man. The only question is why."

Jackson looked thoughtful. "Who do *you* think killed her, John?"

Waters sensed Penn's anxiety without even looking at him.

"I honestly have no idea. I know she saw other men besides me. She didn't try to hide that. But I don't know who they were."

Barlow guffawed at this.

Penn leaned toward Jackson and said, "Eve Sumner was known to sleep with a lot of men. She previously had relations with Mr. Waters's partner, for example. And I'm sure you've turned up many other paramours over the past few years."

"That's true," Jackson admitted. "The lady got around. But not so much in the past year, it turns out. For the first few years she was back here, you couldn't hardly keep score of all her guys. But for the last year, she didn't do much in that line. Stayed at home a lot, mostly kept to herself."

Waters knew why, but Tom Jackson would never believe it.

"Tell me about seeing her the day of the murder," Jackson said.

Here was the tricky part. The best lies were always interwoven with bits of truth, and Waters's memory had not been reliable lately. "Two nights before she died was the last time I saw her in the Eola. That night, I tried to break it off with her."

"Why?"

"She was becoming obsessive. She thought she was in love with me."

"You just told us she was seeing other men while she saw you."

"She told me she was. I don't know. But I do know

she wanted love more than sex. And . . ." Waters trailed off, so that Jackson would have to pull part of the story out of him. The detective would value the lie more if he had to work for it.

"What?" Jackson prompted. "Go on."

"I hate to say it, Tom, but I think she was looking to marry up. She told me she was tired of selling houses. She didn't want to work at all."

The detective nodded thoughtfully. "Go on."

"The next day, when she called my cell phone, she asked me to come to the hotel that night. I told her that my wife was going out of town, and I had to baby-sit my daughter. She got very angry. It was a lie, of course, but she didn't know that. That night I slept on my porch in case she flipped out and came around the house to try to talk to me or to Lily."

"Did she?"

"A car parked out by the road for a while, but never approached the house. The next morning, I put on my cell phone and saw that I had about fifteen missed calls, all from pay phones."

"Fourteen," Jackson corrected. "Fourteen missed calls."

"Right. Well, she got me on the way to work. It only took a few seconds, but she got me."

"What do you mean?"

"I felt guilty, and I wanted to sleep with her. That was the first time in two weeks that I'd gone without her for twenty-four hours. I drove back to my house, and she met me out back, in my home office. It's in the slave quarters of our house."

"You had sex with her?"

"Twice."

"Did you use a condom?"

"No. I never did with her."

Jackson sighed and looked at the table. "What time did she leave?"

"I don't really know."

"But she was there for a while. If you had sex with her twice."

"Not that long, really." Waters let himself show a little male camaraderie. "Eve was talented."

"That's what I hear," said Jackson. "What about after that? Why did you go to the hotel that night?"

"I promised her I would. But when I got down there . . . shit, there were police cars everywhere, it was pouring rain, and I just didn't want to deal with it. I was trying to end it, you know? When I first heard she was found dead, I was scared to death that she'd committed suicide."

Tom Jackson exhaled like a man completing the first round of some difficult game. Then he leaned back in his chair and sighed. "You want something to drink?"

"No, thanks," Waters replied, trying to gauge the effectiveness of his story.

"Penn? Coffee? Coke? Water?"

Penn shook his head.

"Because we're going to be here for a while."

After leaving her mother's house, Lily headed for Linton Hill, her mind ratcheting down from the emotional turmoil she had felt leaving Annelise to cold reason. Using her cell phone, she called Sybil and asked if Cole was in his office. When he came on the line, he brusquely asked what Lily wanted.

"I want to talk to you," she said. "In private."

"What about?"

"I have a solution to our problem."

Silence. "You're leaving John?"

"No."

"Then I'm not interested in talking to you."

"I think you will be, when you hear what I have to say."

The hiss of the open line continued for some time. "Let's hear it."

"Not now. In person."

"After what you tried last night? You're crazy."

"I'm not going to do anything like that," Lily promised.

"That's right. You're not."

"If you don't see me, you won't have a chance of getting John for yourself."

"I've always had John," Cole said. "And you know it. That's why he came to me in Eve."

This dig had no effect on Lily's emotions, which were now locked deep inside her. "If you really believe that—if you think you can compete with me and win—then you shouldn't be afraid to talk to me."

"Compete with you?" Cole snorted. "Come to the office. I'll be ready for you. Don't do anything stupid."

"I'll be there in fifteen minutes."

Lily pulled up the drive to Linton Hill, parked, and ran inside. Rose stood in the main hall, nearly apoplectic at the mess the police had made of the house. Lily mumbled something about a legal mixup and hurried back to her bedroom closet. There she slipped off her flats and pulled on a pair of red cowboy boots. Then she took the butcher knife out of her purse, slid it down into her right boot, and pulled her jeans leg down over the boot.

Satisfied that her jeans looked natural, she went out the back door and made her way down to a ditch near the back of their lot. While preparing for the search this morning, John had taken the handcuffs Lily had brought into the house under Mallory's influence and dumped them there. After a couple of minutes, Lily found the cuffs and dropped them into her purse. As she hurried around the house to her Acura, she saw Rose staring at her through a side window, but she did not stop to explain anything. What could she say?

She made the drive to John's office building in four minutes. She parked in the back lot, removed the handcuffs from her purse, and slipped them under the front seat. Then, before fear could stop her, she got out and marched up the back stairs to the second floor.

Sybil didn't see her enter, and she was glad. After last night's near-tragedy, Lily didn't think she could look the receptionist in the eye without coming apart. She passed John's empty office and kept walking, but paused just short of Cole's door, which was half open.

"Come in," Cole called. "Keep your hands in plain sight."

Lily stepped into the doorway and froze.

Cole sat with his elbows propped on his desk, both hands gripping a large handgun that was aimed at Lily's chest. He smiled, and Lily knew from the strange glint in his eye that she was facing Mallory Candler.

"Hello, Lily," Cole said. "Throw me your purse."

Lily tossed the purse across the office. It landed in front of the desk. Cole got up and retrieved it, then dumped its contents onto the gleaming wooden desktop.

"Good girl," he said, finding nothing dangerous. "So why am I talking to you?"

"You think I'm weak, don't you?"

"I know you are. I've been inside you."

"Are you sure enough to try to prove it?"

Cole's smile disappeared, replaced by a look of interest. "What do you mean?"

"You want my husband? Give me a fair fight."

"How do you propose I do that?"

"Come back into me."

This was clearly the last thing Mallory had expected to hear. "Are you serious?"

"Absolutely."

"You would let me come back into you."

"Yes."

Cole laughed. "I'd destroy you."

"Maybe."

"I controlled you from the first day I was inside you."

"But I had no idea what was going on. I didn't know my family was at risk."

"You think that would change anything?"

"Yes."

Cole's eyes narrowed. "You're lying. What have you hatched in that little accountant's brain of yours? You're trying to find a way to kill me. Close enough to fuck is close enough to kill."

Lily had rehearsed her speech during the drive from Linton Hill. "You don't believe me because you don't trust anyone. I never really knew you at St. Stephens. You were so beautiful and proud, I couldn't imagine someone like you being insecure and jealous. But I guess none of us are immune to that."

Lily took three steps closer to the desk. "I'm insecure about a lot of things. But one thing I'm sure of—my husband's love. I *know* John loves me, that he wants to share his whole life with me. He was haunted by your memory for a long time, but that was only guilt, really. Guilt and lust. Those things were enough to make him fall for you in Eve. But they're gone now. After last night, you know that."

Cole's face twisted as if he were trying to say something but not sure what.

"I'm not afraid of you anymore," Lily went on. "That's why I'll take the chance of having you inside my head again. Without John's love, you'll eventually wither away and die. Like you should have done ten years ago."

Cole got to his feet and aimed the shaking gun at Lily's head. "You don't know *anything*."

Lily stood her ground as he came around the desk, his face reddening.

"He's always loved me," Cole insisted. *"I've been in his mind. I know what he feels."*

"If you really believe that," Lily said calmly, "come back into me and take your chances."

Cole raised the barrel of the .357 and held it against Lily's forehead, his finger taut on the trigger. "I think I'd rather kill you." He dragged the gun barrel down the bridge of her nose and pressed it into her left eye socket. "I can go into Sybil anytime I want. Or anyone else I choose. There are *millions* of women I can go into. Young, fertile women with their whole lives ahead of them."

Lily's bladder was close to letting go. "If you shoot me, Sybil will run in here and see. I doubt she'll be too wild about having sex with you after that. And by the time you find someone else suitable, John could be in prison. He's at police headquarters right now. They tore our house apart this morning."

Cole pressed her head backward with the gun barrel. "*You* don't tell me what to do."

"If you come into me," Lily gasped, "everything looks normal. No questions about another killing. And when John gets out on bail, you can fly to South America with him."

"That's right, I could," Cole said. He smiled with secret amusement. "You think you can overpower *me*, lily-white Lily?"

She swallowed. "I'm willing to try."

The light in Cole's eyes danced like little demons. "All right, then. Lock the door."

Lily hadn't expected this. "Not here."

"Why not?"

"I can't possibly relax enough here to . . . you know. Peak. It's going to be hard enough anyway."

Suspicion suddenly darkened Cole's eyes. "Where, then?"

"A motel. I'd rather it not be here in town. Everyone knows me. I thought we'd go to Vidalia."

"Across the river?"

"It's only a mile from here. Maybe two."

"No. You've set up something. Hired someone to kill me."

Wound tight as a piano wire inside, Lily found it took all of her effort to laugh. "I would have no idea how to do that. Look, you pick the place. The motel and the room. Just make it across the river, where nobody knows me. Call me on my cell phone, and I'll come to you."

Cole kept the gun against her cheek as he mulled the idea over. "I was going to say I'll regret not being able to kill you. But what I'm going to do to you once I'm inside you is worse. *Infinitely* worse."

Lily walked away from the gun, collected her purse and personal things off the desk, and marched to the door.

"I'll leave my cell on," she said.

chapter 20

"I think they're going to arrest you no matter what," Penn said. "I'm going to tell them to fish or cut bait."

He and Waters sat alone in the interrogation room, but Waters had no illusions that their conversation was private. He leaned in close to Penn and whispered, "I have to stay free. Unless you can guarantee that I'll get bail, I don't want to be arrested."

"You'll get bail," Penn said at normal volume. "You're a highly respected member of the community. You have no criminal record. They have no eyewitnesses, and no direct evidence that you murdered anybody. You slept with someone who got killed, you've cooperated, and you present zero flight risk."

Good performance, Waters thought. Or maybe Penn really believed he would not run. Surely he sensed that his client's qualms about pulling up stakes and fleeing the country were rapidly evaporating in the face of mounting evidence.

The door banged open, and Tom Jackson walked in

with a manila folder in his hand. His face was tight but unreadable. He sat opposite Waters and removed Mallory Candler's high school graduation photo from the folder.

"We found about fifty photos of this girl in a folder in your office."

Waters shrugged. "So?"

"That's Mallory Candler, right? Miss Mississippi? Graduated from St. Stephens with Penn?"

Penn looked distinctly uncomfortable.

"A year earlier," Waters said.

Jackson slid another photo of Mallory from the folder. Waters mentally dated it to about the tenth grade.

"We found this in Eve Sumner's safe deposit box. Along with some jewelry that was stolen from the Candler home about a year ago."

Waters swallowed but said nothing.

Jackson stared at him with a curious expression. "John, I'm starting to think I'm only seeing the tip of the iceberg here. You want to explain what you and Eve Sumner were doing with photos of Mallory Candler?"

Waters shrugged again. "I can't. I have no idea why Eve would have those."

Penn sighed with relief.

"You dated Mallory for a while, didn't you? In college?"

"Yes. That's why I have those pictures."

"And she died ten years ago?"

Waters nodded.

"Murdered in New Orleans, right? Was Eve Sumner a friend of hers?"

"Not that I know of. Eve was ten years younger than Mallory."

Jackson reached into the folder. "Maybe you can explain these?"

He removed four photographs and spread them out on the table. They showed a naked girl of about twelve standing in a bathroom. In one she was reaching for a towel, in the others drying off. Waters looked away.

"You've seen these before, haven't you?" said Jackson.

"No."

"You're damn right he has," snapped Barlow. "He's one sick son of a bitch."

Jackson frowned at his partner, then said, "This little girl is Mallory too, isn't she? Her face was almost fully formed, even then."

"It looks like her," Waters admitted.

"Show him the newspaper stuff," growled Barlow.

Jackson reached into the folder and brought out several newspaper clippings. Each was a story on the arrest and impending trial of Danny Buckles. Many had been written by Caitlin Masters, Penn Cage's girlfriend.

"We found these in Eve Sumner's house during the original search. Didn't think much about them at the time. A lot of people followed that story. But now, finding these kiddy porn pictures . . . it makes me wonder."

Waters tried to blank his mind so that his face would remain expressionless.

"It got me thinking," Jackson went on, "how it was you who exposed Danny Buckles in the beginning. You never quite explained how you did that, John.

Not to my satisfaction, anyway." He tugged at one side of his mustache. "Was it Eve who told you about him?"

"My little girl told me what was going on at the school."

"I remember. But I'm wondering how you knew what to ask. Because, see, we found these pictures in the safe deposit box too."

Jackson took a short stack of photos from the folder, these held together with a rubber band. He removed the band and laid out the photos. There were six men and five women, all candid shots. Waters recognized only one. Danny Buckles. As he stared at the odd collection of faces, a wave of nausea hit him. This collection was a catalog of the people Mallory had occupied on her journey to reach him. She had saved a photograph of each. Even Danny Buckles. But why? Did she feel some emotional attachment to her hosts? The way people felt attached to their old houses? Or was it merely morbid curiosity that would not let her forget them completely?

"You look pale, John," Jackson observed. "Do you know these people?"

"Just Buckles."

Jackson sighed wearily. "Okay. Here's what I want you to do. I'm going to turn off the camera and the tape recorder, and then go outside and get a cup of coffee. You and your celebrity lawyer here put your heads together and decide what you want to tell me about all this. Because I'm thinking this mess is a lot dirtier than a simple crime of passion. I don't know if Eve Sumner was blackmailing you or threatening you or what-all. And I *damn* sure don't know what a Miss Mississippi who's been dead for ten years could have to do with any of this." He sniffed and looked deep into Waters's eyes. "I've always liked you, John. I think you're a stand-up guy. So help me out here, okay? And yourself too. If you do, maybe you'll stay free to raise that little girl of yours."

Jackson got up and left the room. His partner switched off the camera, picked up the tape recorder, and followed him.

Before Waters could speak, Penn took a pen and notepad from his pocket and wrote: *Don't trust a word he says.*

Lily was driving on the westbound bridge over the Mississippi River when her cell phone rang. She had been riding circuits of the mile-long spans for the past hour, waiting for the call. The ID on the phone read SMITH-WATERS PETROLEUM. She took a deep breath and clicked SEND.

"This is Lily," she said.

"Well, this is *Mallory*," Cole replied. "Are you ready for me?"

"Tell me where."

"Straight to business? All right, the Stardust Motel. Room eleven. I'm already here."

Lily's stomach cramped suddenly. "I'm on my way."

"I'm looking forward to it, Lily. You don't remember the last time we did this. But this time you will. You'll never forget it."

Lily pressed down on the accelerator and covered the last quarter mile of the bridge at sixty miles an hour. The Acura shot down into Vidalia, Louisiana, a small town without a central business district. Its main commercial strip was lined with gas stations, fast-food joints, honky-tonks, and assorted farming and small-engine shops.

The Stardust Motel was a faded old motor court, one creaky rung above hourly rates. Under any other circumstances, Lily wouldn't be caught dead in it. Today, she cared nothing about the place. She turned off the highway and into the parking lot of a package liquor store, from which she could scan the motel lot. The low cinder-block building had peeling white paint and orange numbered doors. Cole's silver Lincoln sat in front of room eleven. The only other car in the lot was a four-door pickup with a battered horse trailer behind it.

Lily pulled slowly across the parking lot and parked beside the Lincoln. Before she could turn off the motor, the door to number eleven opened and Cole rushed across the space to her window, a pistol in his hand. He held the gun at waist level, aimed at Lily's neck, and motioned for her to roll down her window. Lily hit the button and the glass disappeared into the doorframe.

"Get out," Cole said, pressing the gun barrel against her neck. "Leave your purse in there."

As she climbed out, he spun her against the Acura and gave her a quick pat-down. Apparently satisfied, he took her arm and shoved her through the orange door into the room.

Slamming the door behind them, he threw her against it and searched her more thoroughly. She thought he was going to stop at the boots, but he slid his hands down into them, first the left, then the right. Her heart clenched when his hand closed around the haft of the knife and yanked it out.

"Was this for me?" Cole whispered in her ear.

"No. Just for protection."

"I see." The point of the blade pressed into her back, above her left kidney. "Do you feel safe now?" The knife point punctured her blouse, then her skin.

"*Don't*," she pleaded. "Remember why we're here."

Cole grabbed her shoulders and threw her onto the bed. Towering above her, he brandished the knife in his fist.

"Now that I know what you really came for, let me tell you what's going to happen. You and I are going to have sex. And if I can't get inside your head . . . I'm going to take this kitchen knife you brought and slit your throat. And you'll never see your little girl again."

Lily tried to shut out the horror of Cole standing above her, his fleshy face red with anger. Actually, *Cole* standing over her would not have been nearly so bad. Even if the real Cole meant to rape her, it would be infinitely preferable to this. The light in the eyes glaring at her now was malevolent and merciless, intending only her destruction.

"Take off your clothes," Cole said. "Now!"

Lily rolled away from him and obeyed. When she was down to her underwear, she slid under the covers and waited.

Cole was still staring at her, but his face was no longer as red as before. Setting the knife on a high closet shelf, he began to undress. When his shirt came off, revealing a mass of pasty fat over decayed muscles, Lily felt a rush of nausea. Twenty years ago, she had voluntarily slept with this man. She was a lonely freshman, he a senior from her hometown. The familiarity of his face had so relieved her loneliness that when he pleaded for sex late in the night, she had given in. Cole had been a strapping young college boy then. The man before her now weighed seventy pounds more than the boy he had been, and his health was wrecked. Lily suddenly doubted whether the scenario she had envisioned was even possible. How could she climax with a man for whom she felt only revulsion? Even to save her family. Some reactions simply could not be forced.

When Cole was naked, he slid under the covers beside her. Lily lay as rigid as a board, afraid he would try to mount her like an animal. But Cole did nothing like that. He turned onto one elbow, raised a hand, and began to stroke her hair above the ear, the way her mother had when she was ill as a child.

"I know it's not your fault," Cole said softly. "You didn't know about me when you married John. What we really had."

He continued to stroke her hair, and Lily tried to relax. After a time, Cole's hand moved lower, but he did not go straight to her genitals, as she had expected. He took his time, his touch feather-light, then firm, as he caressed first her arms, then her thighs, her abdomen, and finally her breasts. The real Cole Smith would never touch her this way, she knew. The tenderness in his fingers now was essentially and empirically feminine. The knowledge and instinct in them belonged to Mallory Candler. Lily tried to blank her mind and let physical sensation override her conflicted emotions.

"That's it," Cole whispered, as her nipples began to respond. "I know it's not easy, Lily."

She closed her eyes and tried to convince herself

that the fingers touching her now belonged to her husband.

"I'll tell you how to make it work," Cole murmured in her ear. "Think about John while we do this." He kissed her neck, then her earlobe. "That's what I'm going to do."

Tom Jackson walked back into the interrogation room with the air of a man expecting to hear a confession. Barlow followed like a smug acolyte.

"Well?" Jackson said.

"Either arrest him or let him go," Penn replied. "He's told you what he knows."

Jackson blew air from his cheeks and settled into his chair. "Penn, this is the wrong way to play this. It's obvious that John knows a lot more than he's saying. And if he wants to stay out of jail, he'll tell us."

"What do you want to know?" Waters asked before Penn could reply.

"You dated Mallory Candler ten years ago. Why do you have all those pictures of her in your office now?"

"I was cleaning out our storeroom and I found them. It was just a walk down memory lane."

Barlow snorted.

"Did you and Eve ever have a third party in the bed with you?" Jackson asked.

"What?"

The detective's eyes didn't waver. "You know what I'm talking about. Another woman, maybe? A man?"

"Hell no!"

"What about a kid?" asked Barlow.

Waters came to his feet, his face hot. "What about kissing my ass?"

Barlow balled his fists and started forward, but Jackson stopped him with an outstretched arm.

"I don't have to listen to this crap," Waters said.

"Yes, you do," said Jackson. "You're not giving us any choice, John. We don't know what the hell's going on. I've got guys going through your computer drives now. Is there anything you want to warn me about them finding?"

"Like what?"

"We get a lot of kiddy porn over the Internet, even here in Natchez. I'm wondering if Eve and Danny Buckles were into something like that. Running a BBS or something. They've got these naked pictures of Mallory Candler, and you're the only person involved with them who might have access to something like that, though I don't see exactly how."

Waters found himself speechless.

Penn said, "Those photographs were taken by Benjamin Candler. Mallory's father. Mallory discovered them in the attic during her reign as Miss Mississippi, and she suffered a breakdown because of it. She gave the photos to my client for safekeeping."

"Ben Candler?" Jackson asked. "The state representative?"

Penn nodded. "Tom, I believe Eve Sumner got sexually involved with John in order to blackmail him. I think she stole those photographs from his home during an attempt to find embarrassing materials to use in her scheme. And I wouldn't be at all surprised to find Danny Buckles was involved in all of that."

Jackson seemed unable to process what Penn had told him. Even Barlow had nothing to say.

"Ben Candler took those pictures of his own daughter?" Jackson asked finally.

"Benjamin Candler was a sexual deviant," Penn said. "I think minimal investigation into that will bear out all I've told you. The point is, your suspicion that my client is somehow involved in the distribution of pornography is ridiculous."

Jackson turned to Waters, who was staring in shock at his attorney. "Did Eve try to blackmail you with these pictures?"

"No."

"Did Mallory's father really take them?"

"Yes. I didn't even know Mallory when she was that age."

Jackson rubbed his eyes in frustration. "Tell me this. Did your wife know you were having an affair with Eve?"

"No. She does now."

"When did she find out? Before Eve's death?"

An alarm bell sounded in Waters's head. "What are you suggesting?"

Jackson looked apologetic. "It happens, John. A wife gets suspicious, starts following her husband. What if Lily saw you having sex with Eve in your slave quarters that day? What if she knew about the suite at the Eola? She might have followed Eve back to it and—"

"That's crazy. That would never happen."

"Jealousy's a powerful motive, John. Where's Lily now?"

"I don't know."

Jackson turned to Barlow. "Let's find out."

Lily came awake in room eleven at the Stardust Motel and sat up in bed. Cole lay naked on his back beside her, his mouth open, his eyes shut, and breathing so deeply that he might have been drugged. Shivering in her nakedness, she got out of bed, went to the bathroom mirror, and stared at her reflection.

"I'm *me*," she said to the face in the mirror. "But I know you're there. I'm the first person who's ever *known* you were there."

She rubbed her eyes and looked over at Cole again, then grabbed her clothes and dressed as quickly as she could. She found her keys on the dirty carpet by the door, picked them up, and started to leave. With her hand on the knob, she stopped and turned back to Cole.

She had to be sure.

Walking over to him, she reached down for his shoulder. The sight of his pale flesh filled her with revulsion, but she had to wake him. What did one touch matter after having sex with him? She grabbed the big shoulder and shook it. Cole groaned and pulled the covers up to his neck.

She shook him again. "Wake up!"

"*Unnhh.*"

"It's Lily. *Wake up.*"

Cole opened one eye, then squinted until it was nearly shut. "What the hell? Did I sleep over at your house?"

She looked into the bleary eyes, searching for deception.

"Where's John?" Cole mumbled. "Jesus. Is it morning?"

"What's the last thing you remember?"

Cole blinked, still more asleep than awake. "I don't know . . . the office? Sybil said something about meeting me. Shit—I don't know." He drew his knees up into a fetal position and pulled the covers over his head.

Hurry, Lily told herself. *You may not have any time at all. . . .*

She turned away from the bed and went toward the door. Her sense of balance left her, and she nearly stumbled. As she reached for the doorknob to steady herself, the room went dim. Pure terror flushed through her. That dimness wasn't in the room—it was in her mind. That dimness was Mallory.

"No," she whispered.

She slapped the door hard and focused on the pain in her palm. "I know you're there. You're inside me, but it doesn't matter. I'm Lily Ann Waters, born June twelfth, nineteen sixty-three." She opened the door and struggled toward her car. "My daughter is . . . Annelise. Born June fourteenth, nineteen ninety-five."

The dimness vanished and returned, flickering like electric lights during a brownout. "I feel you," Lily said, clicking the unlock button on her key ring. "Damn you, you can't . . ." She tried to cling to her identity by thinking about John and the threat of the murder case, but it wasn't working. The simplest facts became her mantra, her only shield against the force she felt growing inside her. *"Lily Ann Waters,"* she gasped. *"June twelfth, nineteen . . . Lilyannwaters . . . daughterborn . . . daughter June . . . fourteenth . . . Annelise born . . . lilyann . . . waters—"*

She opened her car door and dropped into the driver's seat. She tried to fit the ignition key into the slot on the steering wheel, but this simple task was beyond her, like trying to thread a needle in the dark. The fourth time she missed the slot, she began to weep, and darkness began closing around her.

She suddenly remembered her father, dying of cancer. At the end he had been afraid to go to sleep. If he did, he believed, he would never wake up. Superstition, she'd thought at the time. Now she knew his fear as a palpable reality. If she succumbed to the darkness now, darkness was all she would ever know.

"*No!*" she screamed, hammering the steering wheel with both hands. "Mallory is dead! You're *dead!* Your body's rotting in the *dirt!*"

A sudden flash of light drove back the shadows. She slid the key into the slot and cranked the Acura's engine.

"John hates you!" she screamed. "He *hates* you! He never wanted your children. . . . That's why he made you kill them. And he wanted to kill you last night!"

Agony knifed through her chest. She gasped but managed to get the car into gear and back away from the motel door.

"You're dead," she repeated. "You're rotting in the ground on Cemetery Road. You're a lost soul . . . fading into nothing. You're *nothing.*"

Light bathed Lily's mind like cool water.

She put the Acura into drive and pulled onto the highway. The bridge loomed in the distance. She wanted to blow past every car and truck between her and the bridge, but the police were aggressive about ticketing on this side of the river. Though she held the car to forty, the superstructure of the bridge neared rapidly. Soon she would ramp up onto it.

Thirty yards ahead, a pickup truck moved into the left lane, making room for her to pass on the right. A girl about Annelise's age sat in a wicker chair in the back of the truck, facing Lily. Her face was dirty and her arms bare in the cold, but her eyes shone as she waved at Lily. Pure sadness filled Lily's chest. At seven years old, Annelise was already remarkably independent, with a distinct personality that would only become stronger with the passing years. But she still needed help. She was so fragile in some ways—

The front of the Acura lifted onto the bridge and started up the grade toward the center of the span. Lily gripped the wheel, her mind filled with love for her daughter. That love warmed her whole body, so it was all the more terrifying when the rear of the pickup truck ahead wavered in the air like a mirage, and the sunlight went dim. With the dimness came a rush of malice from deep within her, like a tumor metastasizing at a fantastic rate, amorphous but swift, swallowing her spirit.

"No!" she shouted, battering the wheel with her hands. *"Stop it!"* The pain in her hands momentarily anchored her, yet still the darkness grew. *"You can't do this! You can't—"*

She could barely hold herself in the proper lane. At the limit of desperation, her mind searched back to childhood for some weapon to protect her. She had stopped going to church after losing her baby, but now words poured from her mouth in a flood, as though of their own accord:

"The Lord is my Shepherd, I shall not want; He maketh me to lie down in green pastures. He leadeth me beside the still waters. He restoreth my soul . . . He . . . yea . . . yea, though I walk through the valley of the shadow of death . . . I will fear no evil . . . no evil . . . He restoreth my soul . . . He restoreth my soul!"

As tears flowed freely from her eyes, blue sky burst into her vision, and the road and bridge appeared before her. Every physical detail burned itself into her brain: the cement surface of the road, the dirty face of the girl in the back of the pickup, the rivet heads holding the silver superstructure of the bridge together, a workman hanging suspended from the girders on the right side. He wore a red bandanna beneath his hard hat, and he looked directly into Lily's eyes, his expression timeless and kind. As Lily looked back, time seemed to slow, then stop, and in that timeless space began the only epiphany of her life.

She understood now, why she had done all she had since calling Mallory that morning. So simple and profound. She looked from the workman to the road, and as she did, the little girl sitting in the back of the pickup raised her hand and waved.

Lily raised her hand and waved back. *Farewell, little one.*

She reached beneath the seat, grabbed the handcuffs, and quickly cuffed her left wrist to the steering wheel. Then she yanked the wheel to the right and pressed the accelerator to the floor.

At sixty miles per hour, the Acura smashed through the makeshift guardrail and hurtled into space. The air bag deployed on impact, blowing into Lily's face and blinding her for the duration of the fall. Her stomach flew into her throat, her inner ear lost all orientation, and she floated through space like an astronaut in a ship without windows, her mind filled with bliss, a sweet peace that asked nothing of the world but to bid it good-bye.

The world snatched her back with an explosive impact, driving her head like a cannonball into the headrest behind her. She could neither breathe nor see, but only feel the strange weightlessness of the car bobbing in water. Then she heard a sloshing sound.

My feet are wet. . . .

The Acura had righted itself. High above her hung the underside of the bridge, getting slowly smaller as the powerful current carried her southward, spinning the car as it slowly filled with water. She looked down at her handcuffed wrist with detachment. It seemed to be the wrist of someone else. As she stared, she heard a scream of rage and terror, and she looked outside the car for its source. When it came again, she realized it had burst from her own mouth.

Her arms suddenly began to flail, and the cuffed wrist jerked the steel chain taut, trying to break free. Lily felt as though someone had wired her to a computer and begun operating her limbs with a joystick. The scream came again, and then the malignant force she'd felt on the bridge returned. She tried to resist, but resistance was futile. This time the light did not merely dim but disappeared altogether. She felt like a woman in a coma who hears people speaking around her but cannot speak herself. And the person she heard now was shrieking like someone being stabbed to death.

The interior of the car flashed white, then vanished again, as though illuminated by lightning during a storm. Only the storm was in her mind. She saw a black flashlight in her free hand, the heavy Maglite John had put in her glove compartment. It rose to the roof, then hammered down against the handcuffs. The Maglite rose again, but this time when it hit the steel cuff, the head of the light flew off. Lily heard a scream of fury, and on the next upstroke, batteries sprayed into the air.

The nose of the Acura tilted forward, and brown water rose to her waist. Her body heat leached out at a terrifying rate, causing her to shiver violently. _Let it be over_, she thought. _Dear God, let it be done._ But it wasn't. Blood poured from her wrist as the water rose over it, yet still her arm thrashed against the metal, utterly beyond her control. Another scream exploded from her throat.

"_You gutless bitch! You can't take him from me like this!_"

The Acura wallowed onto its left side. The water rushed over Lily's left shoulder and into her ear, then her mouth.

"Please God . . . forgive me," she gasped. "I did this for my family."

And then the water covered her.

chapter 21

John Waters stood bolt upright and gripped his left arm like a man having a heart attack. He was leaning over the sink in the bathroom of the police station when the pain hit. Now he staggered against the wall, unable to breathe.

Lily, he thought, and inexplicable terror filled his mind.

With soapy hands he pulled his cell phone from his pocket and dialed his wife's cell number. After five rings, an automated message saying the subscriber was out of the service area began to play. He hung up and dialed Linton Hill, but all he got was the machine.

"Damn it," he muttered.

He dialed Lily's mother's house, but no one answered there either, and Evelyn did not carry a cell phone.

Someone knocked on the door of the rest room.

"John? You okay?"

Tom Jackson wasn't going to let him out of his sight for more than a minute.

"I'm fine," he mumbled. "Stomach trouble."

"You need some Pepto-Bismol?"

Waters put his cell phone back in his pocket, rinsed the soap off his hands, then opened the door.

"Shit, John, you look bad."

"I'm worried about my wife and daughter. I know this thing with Eve is going to be public now, and . . . Jesus, if I hurt those two, I don't know if I can stand it."

Jackson could have said, "You should have thought about that before you screwed Eve Sumner," but he didn't. He took Waters's arm and gently walked him back toward the interrogation room, where Barlow and Penn waited. As they reached the door, Waters glanced down the hall at a fire exit. With Lily and Annelise unaccounted for, he felt an almost irresistible urge to flee.

"Don't think about it," Jackson said kindly. "That's no answer."

Waters nodded dully and took his seat.

Lily Waters sat in church between her mother and her grandmother, running her hand over her mother's treasured mink coat. Lily was six years old, and she never listened to the preacher. She watched the people and caressed the coat, the softest thing she had ever felt against her skin. She only stopped when it was time to sing. Her father sang out of tune, and he sang louder than anyone else. Sometimes people stared, but Lily was proud of him, because he loved to sing so much.

The church faded like a dream, and she found herself on horseback, her arms around her father's waist as the saddle bounced up and down beneath her. She smelled the sweat of the horse and the sweat of her father, mixed with the acrid odor of cigarettes and old leather. The leather smell faded into the scent of newly mown grass, and then she was running, her chest burning, a stitch in her side that screamed *Stop!* But she didn't stop. She kept putting one foot in front of the other, more distance between herself and the girl in second place. Only a tenth-grader, she was leading the two-mile run at the State Championship in Jackson. She heard the wind whipping the paper number against her chest and a distant roar, the roar of people shouting her name: *Lil-lee, Lil-lee . . .* She ran still harder, and then the athletic field morphed into another church, and she was running through its doors in a white gown as rice flew around her head. John helped her up into a horse-drawn carriage that waited to take them to Stanton Hall for their reception. Her mother and father waved, and John gripped her hand as though he would never let go. Strangely, the street led into a bedroom, where with shining eyes John watched her lay the gown across a chair and climb into their wedding bed. She lay back on the down mattress, as fulfilled as she had ever felt, and terrible pain ripped through her. Annelise was coming, and the nurse was screaming at her not to push, and then to *Push! Push!* She heard a slap and then a cry, the sound of life from her own body. Ineffable joy filled her heart, and then the nurse took Annelise away, and the doctor looked at her, his face changing from happiness to concern, his voice grave: *The fetus is already in hydrops, Lily. He can't live inside you, but he can't live outside either. . . .* And then the terrible sound of the heartbeat decelerating, like a little boy trying his hardest to beat a drum but wearing out in spite of his desire to play on, while Lily screamed and her mother talked to her as though she were a baby herself and still the drumbeat slowed, faded, down into silence so black and deep that nothing ever returned from it. That was where she was going now, into that silence. Without color, without echoes, without warmth, without love—

From the inmost chamber of her heart, a force beyond anything Lily had ever known burst forth, suffusing her mind and body with a will to live. She screamed, an explosion of bubbles that burst into blue light with a white sun shining in the midst of it.

The Acura had bobbed from its side onto its tail, and the waters had receded. She sucked in a lungful of air and looked down at her handcuffed wrist. Soon she would sink beneath the surface, lost to the world.

Mallory had tried to free herself, tried and failed. An image of a butcher knife came to Lily, but the knife was back in the motel room with Cole. *I couldn't cut off my hand anyway,* she thought. *I'd pass out.* She tugged again on the handcuff. *The real problem is my thumb,* she realized. She yanked open the glove compartment, spilling papers everywhere. There was a plastic ice scraper, but no knife. Panic ballooned in her chest, cutting off her air. As she stared at the thumb, swollen from Mallory's efforts to free herself, she saw the broken Maglite in her lap.

She grabbed the black tube with her free hand. There was only one battery inside. She wedged the tube between her legs and groped blindly on the floor of the car. Her hand closed around a battery. She picked it up and shoved it down the tube, then grasped the open end and slammed the makeshift club with all her strength against the base of her thumb.

Pain exploded through her body, searing and infinite. Tears poured from her eyes as she gasped for breath. She could not bear to do that again. But not to meant death. The car listed to the left, and water sloshed around her waist. Again she drove the Maglite downward, and her left arm went numb to the elbow. She yanked against the handcuffs, but still her hand would not come free. With a scream of animal rage, she drove the club down yet again, and this time bone snapped.

Her stomach heaved as the car settled deeper in the water. *"No!"* she screamed. *"Not yet!"*

As the car slid beneath the surface, she yanked her shattered hand through the steel cuff and hammered the Maglite against her window. The glass cracked, then gave way, and a flood of brown water poured over her face. She coiled her legs beneath her and sprang through the opening, driving herself upward and away from the metal coffin, following the bubbles that rose to the surface.

When she burst into the light, she felt the vast river pulling her downstream like the hand of God. You couldn't swim against that current, she knew. You had to go with the flow and work your way slowly toward the bank, far downstream. As the pain in her left hand curled her body into a ball, she pulled off her boots with her right, then forced herself to tread water and looked toward the nearest bank. It seemed impossibly distant, but she had conquered distance before. She imagined that she saw Annelise standing among the trees on the bank, waving her in.

She began to swim.

Waters had just returned to his seat in the interrogation room when a patrolman threw open the door.

"Dispatch just took a call from some construction guys working on the bridge. A car went over the side. All the way to the water."

Jackson looked irritated at the interruption. "What bridge are you talking about?"

"The Mississippi River Bridge!"

All four men looked at one another with disbelief.

"We're calling the sheriff's office," the patrolman said. "They've got the only rescue boat."

"Not much point," Barlow said. "That's a hundred-foot drop."

"Depends on the fall," said Jackson. "If it was a new car, it has air bags."

"Didn't mean to interrupt," said the patrolman. "Just thought you'd like to know."

He closed the door.

Penn said, "I don't think that's ever happened before."

As they stared at one another, Waters's cell phone rang. He looked at Jackson. "That's probably my wife. I told her I'd call her."

"Go ahead and take it."

Waters removed the phone from his pocket. The ID read COLE SMITH. He started not to answer, but when it rang again, something made him click SEND.

"Hello?"

"John! It's Cole!"

Mallory, he thought.

"Rock? Are you there?"

Waters knew he should not trust his ears, but something told him the panicked voice in the receiver truly belonged to his old friend. "I'm listening."

"Get hold of yourself. I was driving across the Mississippi River Bridge, and all of a sudden the guys working on the bridge stopped traffic. Somebody went through the rail."

"I just heard that."

"John . . . it was Lily's Acura."

Waters felt himself going into free fall.

"I'm stuck on the bridge now. The car floated for a while, but then it went under and . . . Jesus, she got out, John. *I saw her.* She made it to the bank south of the mat field. They just loaded her into an ambulance!"

"My God. Where would they be taking her?"

"Has to be St. Catherine's in Natchez."

Waters hung up and got to his feet.

"What's wrong?" Jackson asked. "John?"

"That car that went off the bridge was my wife's."

Penn jumped up and gripped his arm. "Are you sure? Who told you that?"

"Cole. He saw her make it to the bank. He saw the car sink. I've got to get to the hospital!"

Penn looked at Jackson. "Tom, I realize you may intend to arrest John today, but this is an emergency. You need to let him go deal with it."

The unexpected turn of events left Jackson unsure what to do. Waters started to leave without permission, but Barlow laid a hand on the gun at his belt.

"I'll stay with him," Penn promised.

"Now look, Penn," Jackson said. "I don't know what—"

"For God's sake!" Penn cried. "The man's wife could be dying. Come with us if you have to!"

Jackson hesitated another moment, then threw up his hands. "Shit, we'll meet you there."

The emergency room of St. Catherine's Hospital was abuzz with conversation about the freak accident. Over the years, several cars had gone into the river, but all from the banks, and most from boat ramps. Only the extensive repairs in progress had made the bridge accident even possible, and some nurses wondered aloud about the odds that someone would go off the road in the exact area that the steel was missing. More than once, Waters heard the words "suicide attempt" from behind a curtain down the hall.

He and Penn had beaten the ambulance to the hospital, but so had Tom Jackson. The big detective stood at Waters's side during Lily's transit to the ER, but it didn't matter, because she was unconscious. As the ER staff worked to stabilize her, Jackson escorted Waters and Penn to the waiting room.

Penn's father was Lily's doctor, and his office was only a hundred yards from the hospital. While Lily was in X-ray, Tom Cage came out to the waiting room and told them he didn't think Lily had suffered internal injuries—thanks to the air bag—but that she was still unconscious. Until they completed a CAT scan, they wouldn't know about the condition of her brain. She also had a shattered wrist and thumb and some broken ribs.

Seeing Dr. Cage in the St. Catherine's ER took Waters back to his father's death. The doctor's hair and beard had been black then. Now both were silver, but his strong hand on Waters's arm combined with his deep, reassuring voice kept Waters from giving in to the fear and guilt that were eating their way through him.

They waited one hour, then two. Dr. Cage came out twice: once to tell them that an orthopedic surgeon was repairing Lily's wrist, then again to say that he'd sent Lily's brain scans via computer to the office of a neurologist in Jackson. Two local radiologists felt there had been only a slight concussion, but Tom Cage wanted to be sure. Lily had regained consciousness, but she seemed disoriented and confused about her identity.

This revelation chilled Waters's soul. He wanted to ask more, but Tom Jackson was standing beside him, so he took Penn's arm and pulled him over to a corner.

"Did you hear that? About Lily's identity?"

"Don't talk about what you're thinking," Penn advised. "Lily's had a terrible accident. Anything could cause that confusion. All that matters right now is that she's alive."

"You're wrong, Penn. You don't know how wrong you are."

Penn sat him down in one of the plastic chairs bolted to the wall. "I just found out Cole is outside. He's been out there for an hour, but the police won't let him in."

Waters wasn't sure if he was angry or glad. "Why not?"

"Tom Jackson knows Cole slept with Eve. He'll want to question him separately about the safe deposit box evidence and so on. I just wanted you to know Cole's here. Let's get Lily out of the woods. Then we'll go back to your legal problems."

"John? Penn?"

Dr. Cage walked into the waiting room. "I just talked to the neurologist in Jackson. He says Lily's brain looks good. No intracranial bleeds. No severe injury."

Waters sagged with relief. Penn braced him.

"She's much more alert now," Dr. Cage said. "I'm going to admit her for observation. You can see her briefly."

Waters nodded, but suddenly Tom Jackson stepped forward. "Could you give us a minute, Doc?"

Penn nodded, and his father went back to the treatment area.

"Listen, guys," Jackson said. "I'm ecstatic that Lily is okay. It's a goddamn miracle. But I can't let John go back there and talk to her."

Penn drew himself erect. "You can't stop him unless you arrest him."

Jackson sighed. "I'll arrest him if I have to."

"Damn it, Tom, would you *think* for one minute?"

Looking at Penn's face, Waters realized that surface identities like "lawyer" and "detective" had just gone out the window. They were three guys who had grown up together, and they could have been standing on a playground or a football field.

"What can it hurt for him to see his wife?" Penn asked. "She's probably still in shock anyway."

"I don't know what's going on with this Eve Sumner mess," Jackson admitted. "But I know it's no simple murder. I need to question Lily *before* she talks to John."

"Then go do it. I'll tell my father you're going back."

Jackson looked almost apologetic. "Do you have any problem with me doing it now, John?"

"Not if it gets me in to see her. We have nothing to hide."

"Okay, then. I'll go talk to her."

Twenty minutes later, Tom Jackson came back to the waiting room and told them Lily was being moved upstairs.

"Did you learn anything that makes you think you should keep John from his wife?" Penn asked.

Jackson shook his head and looked at Waters. "You're a lucky man. The Lord was watching out for that lady today. Go on up. She's on the fourth floor."

Penn and Waters went to the elevators. While they waited, Waters took out his cell phone and called Cole's cell number. His partner answered immediately.

"John, what's going on in there?"

"Lily's going to make it."

"Thank God!"

"Cole . . . what were you doing in Vidalia?"

"Rock, I wish to hell I could tell you. I honestly have no idea. I woke up naked in a room at the Stardust Motel. If I was a woman, I'd say somebody slipped something into my drink and raped me. I even wondered if some woman did that and robbed me, but my wallet's full."

"Did you see Lily anywhere near that motel?"

"The motel? Hell no. I saw her in the water, man. And I'll never forget it."

Waters closed his eyes and asked the question he most feared. "Which span was Lily on, Cole? Which direction was she going?"

"West to East. Louisiana to Mississippi."

"And you woke up in a motel on the Louisiana side?"

"Right."

The elevator doors opened. Waters and Penn got inside with a black nurse.

"John?" Cole asked. "What's going on?"

"I have to go."

"Wait—"

Waters hung up and put the phone in his pocket. Blood pounded in his ears. What had Lily done? Whatever it was, she would have been trying to save her family . . . but how? Had she tried to kill Cole?

As the elevator rose, the nurse said, "You Mr. Waters?"

"Yes."

She smiled broadly. "Your wife's in four twenty-seven. People are already calling her the miracle patient."

Waters forced himself to smile.

When the doors opened, he and Penn walked quickly past the nurse's station. No one bothered to hide their stares. At the door to 427, Penn stopped.

"This may be the last time you talk to her for a day or two," he said. "Make it count."

"What do you mean?"

"Unless my instincts are wrong, Tom Jackson's going to arrest you after this visit."

"But—"

"He doesn't have a choice, John. Don't worry. If it happens, I'll get bail set as fast as is humanly possible. Now get in there."

Waters shook his lawyer's hand, opened the door, then froze.

Annelise was sitting on the edge of Lily's bed, playing with the IV tube running into her arm. Looking around for an explanation, he saw Lily's mother sitting on the foldout chair against the wall. Evelyn did not look glad to see him.

"Hello?" said Waters.

Lily turned her head toward him, then smiled faintly. Both orbits of her eyes were badly bruised, and her face was abraded near the chin. A splint with pins immobilized her left wrist, which had pins in the bones.

"*Daddy!*" Ana cried. "Mama's car fell off the bridge!"

"I know! Your mama's tough, isn't she?"

Ana laughed and looked at her mother with pride. With his heart still pounding, he walked to the bed and hugged his daughter, then looked deep into his wife's eyes.

"They want to put Mom on TV!" Annelise said.

Lily groaned. "I don't want to be on TV looking like this."

Waters lifted Ana off the bed, set her on the floor, then knelt before her. "Honey, I need to talk to Mama alone for a minute."

Ana's face seemed to go flat. "How come?"

"We have to have a grown-up talk. It'll just be a minute."

"But how *come*? No fair!" Ana was on the verge of tears.

He looked over at his mother-in-law. "Would you take her out for a minute, please?"

Evelyn looked to Lily, who nodded. Glaring at him, Evelyn got up and led Annelise out.

Waters hesitated before rising. He was almost

afraid to look Lily in the face with no one else nearby. But when he stood and looked down at her, he saw the same exhausted face he had seen moments ago, the face of the woman he'd married. He felt relief until he remembered Mallory's tearful performance outside Linton Hill on the day she had possessed Lily. Mallory could easily fool him. She could fool anyone.

He thought of asking Lily how she felt, but the question seemed silly. Instead, he dropped all pretense and asked the question foremost in his mind.

"Who are you?"

Lily looked up at him without blinking. "I'm me."

"Are you?"

She nodded, then touched his hand. "I went to see Cole, John."

"In the Stardust Motel?"

"Yes."

"Why?"

She looked toward the window and the indifferent sky. "I thought about killing her. You know who I mean."

"Mallory . . . But you didn't. Cole's downstairs."

Lily didn't say anything.

Waters's throat knotted. "What happened then?"

"We had sex."

Fear coiled in his belly. "Did he rape you?"

She looked back at him, her eyes free of deceit. "No. I gave myself to him. And Mallory came into me."

Waters shut his mind against the reality of what had been required for this transition to occur. "Is she inside you now?"

"Yes."

"How do you know?"

"I know."

"Who am I talking to now?"

She squeezed his hand. "I told you. Me. Lily."

"Where's Mallory?"

"Submerged. That's how I think of it. Somewhere under the water of my consciousness."

He shook his head, trying to follow her meaning. "What happened at the bridge?"

"I did that on purpose, John." Her eyes fixed his with a startling intensity. "I drove the car off the bridge."

He could not believe this. "You tried to commit suicide?"

"Yes."

"*Why?*"

"I thought it was the only way I could stop her. The only way I could save you and Annelise."

"Lily—"

"When it happened I thought it was spontaneous, but I realize now that I'd meant to do it all along. Kill myself, and Mallory with me."

"You mean you knew you were going to kill yourself before you ever went to see Cole?"

"Yes and no. I knew, but I didn't let myself know."

"I don't understand."

"It's like . . . sex when I was in college. I never went out on a date with the intention of having sex. But sometimes I had sex. And later—sometimes—I'd realize that I'd meant to do it all along. But I had to hide the intention from myself. You know? Because deep down, I thought premarital sex was wrong. I'd been conditioned that way."

She looked at the ceiling as though watching a film being projected there. "The bridge was like that. If I had admitted to myself beforehand what I was going to do, Mallory would have known. She would never have let me drive up on that bridge."

"How do you know that?"

"Because when I handcuffed myself to the wheel, she—"

Waters went pale. "You handcuffed yourself to the wheel?"

"Yes. With Eve's handcuffs. When I went through the guardrail and off the bridge, and I knew there was nothing she could do to save herself, I was glad."

"What happened when you hit the water?"

"I blacked out. When I came to, the car was floating but filling up with water. And then . . . Mallory tried to save herself. I only remember bits of it. For me it was like being trapped in a room with a strobe light. I could see for a second, then total blackness. I guess when I couldn't see, she could. For some reason, the separation between us wasn't as total as it had been before. Anyway, the car was sinking toward the front. Mallory was enraged. She hated me for outthinking her, and her hatred clouded her mind. She practically tore off my hand trying to get out of those cuffs, but she couldn't do it. If she'd been an animal, she would have gnawed my hand right off. Then the water went over my head."

Lily told the story as though she had observed the event rather than lived it, but her voice belied the shock in her eyes.

"I saw things, John. Not white light or anything like that. Just things from my life. Images."

"What images?"

She looked up at him with sudden urgency, her

eyes wet. "My father. Our wedding. Annelise . . . the baby we lost."

He tried to lean over and hug her, but she shook her head.

"And I knew then," she said, "that I couldn't give up my life. *My* life. Not for you or even for Annelise. I knew people had struggled to bring me to this earth and give me the gifts I have. And I knew I had an obligation to them, and to myself, and to you and Ana, to live as long as I possibly could." She wiped her eyes and laughed strangely. "So I took that heavy flashlight you put in the glove compartment and broke my thumb with it and got the hell out of there."

Waters could scarcely imagine his wife doing this, but his awe was displaced by fear that had still not been put to rest.

"What happened to Mallory?"

Lily reached for the remote control that operated the bed, and raised her upper body until her head was only a little below his. Her blue eyes had a provocative glint.

"She's right here."

Waters took a step back.

"I told you. She's still inside me."

He didn't know what to say.

Lily's eyes held something like pity. "I know you're wondering what to do. That's what men wonder: what do I *do*? But there isn't anything to do. Mallory is between us, John. You put her there. As long as you've felt love for her, or obsession, or whatever it is, she's been between us. But when you slept with Eve, you gave her power over us. It's like any married couple, when one partner cheats. The third person is always there between them. The memory of that betrayal. And they either live with it and try to move on . . . or they give up."

Waters started to speak, but Lily cut him off.

"But I'm not giving up. Okay? You and I share the blame for you going to Eve. We have a wonderful child. We love and respect each other. And that's worth fighting to save."

He stepped close to the bed and stroked the hair over her ear. "You know I believe that. But what about Mallory? What if I wake up one night and find her looking at me through your eyes?"

"It could happen, John. Tonight. Or five minutes from now." She took a slow, deep breath like someone testing their lungs, and he suddenly remembered that some of her ribs were broken. "But I don't think it will," she said. "When Mallory first came into me, I had no idea she was there. I had no idea my family was at risk. Or my life. Now I do. And after the bridge . . . and the river . . . she knows how strong I am. I don't think she'll ever control me again. She'll be like a tumor I carry with me, an inoperable tumor that reminds me just how precious life is."

Waters leaned down to hug her, but the door opened behind him, and Penn Cage came in.

"I'm afraid your time's up, John."

"Can I have just one minute?"

Penn sighed and shook his head. "They're going to arrest you. I wasn't going to say anything in front of Lily, but I'll need her signature on some papers to arrange bail, so . . ."

Waters closed his eyes and tried to marshal whatever emotional resources he had left. As he looked down at Lily, she smiled with a serenity he had not seen on her face since Mallory was last inside her.

"Go on," she said, taking his hand. "It's going to be all right. I know it is."

Waters hugged her, then followed Penn into the hall. Tom Jackson waited there, his face heavy with the burden of duty.

"John Waters," he said, "I'm placing you under arrest for the murder of Evie Ray Sumner. You have the right to remain silent. Anything you say can and will be held against you in a court of law. You have a right to an attorney . . ."

Waters felt Penn's hand squeeze his shoulder, but the rest of Jackson's words blurred into nothingness as Barlow walked up and snapped handcuffs around his wrists.

chapter 22

SIX WEEKS LATER

John Waters slowed his Land Cruiser, then turned off the gravel onto a dirt road that had not existed a week ago. Lily sat in the passenger seat, wearing blue jeans and a straw hat. Annelise was strapped into the back-seat. The river was still half a mile away, but he could smell it already.

"Where's the oil derrick, Daddy?" Annelise asked, scanning the nearly bare trees and brown fields.

"There's no derrick yet. Just a stake in the ground. This is a location, baby. A prospective well."

"That's no fun."

"I think it's pretty fun."

Lily laughed and rolled down her window, letting in a blast of cold air. "That feels better. The heater was giving me claustrophobia."

He was glad she could laugh. Waters had not

laughed much in the past six weeks. During that time, he had been free on bail, but "free" was a misleading term. The daily routine of life was illusory, a mock reality that could be snatched away by the jury that would be selected in less than a week. Still, he had worked hard to keep his family's spirits up and his oil company alive.

Two weeks after Lily's accident, the EPA had determined that the salt water that destroyed the Louisiana rice farm had leaked from another company's well. The relief this judgment brought was undercut by the effects of Waters's arrest for murder and the scandal caused by the revelation of his affair with Eve Sumner. The faces he met on the street were cold, and loyal investors stopped taking his calls. Even Cole's less reputable moneymen seemed to want to steer clear of the company. Waters spent two weeks doing nothing but damage control, but with his shattered reputation, there was little he could do.

He had paid off Cole's gambling debts to the tune of $658,000. In exchange, Cole signed an agreement by which Waters would recoup his money out of newly discovered oil production. The question was, would there ever be any new Smith-Waters wells? The first issue was personal. Cole had not once mentioned having sex with Lily while Lily was under Mallory's influence. But he had done it, and done it knowingly. Yet Mallory herself had admitted that she plied Cole with a fifth of Johnnie Walker during the seduction, and it was possible that he had no memory of the event. Beyond this, Waters had some doubt as to whether Cole would have yielded to Lily, had she been herself. God only knew what Mallory had done to draw Cole into having sex with her. Waters had thought long and hard about the situation, and in the end he'd decided that forgiveness was his only option. Cut off from his friendship and aid, Cole would become a shell of himself, and spiral down into depression, possibly even suicide. With the support Waters had shown him, Cole had joined AA and was now thirty-one days sober. Waters had no illusions about his friend's strength of character, but he did have faith.

The second issue was lack of investor support for the company. After two weeks of total rejection of their latest prospective well, Waters told Cole he was going to drill a well "straight up"—which meant he would fund the cost entirely out of his own pocket. And he was not going to drill the prospect they had been marketing. He was going back to Jackson Point, to the dry hole they had drilled just before he started seeing Eve. If he moved the site six hundred feet to the south, he believed, he would hit the reservoir he had missed on that unlucky night.

"Slow down!" Lily said, as the Land Cruiser bounced over a giant pothole.

"Sorry. My mind's somewhere else."

"I know. Remember, one day at a time."

He blew air from his cheeks and tried not to show his irritation. There were guys in Parchman Prison repeating the same mantra, and they would die behind those walls.

Waters jumped when his cell phone rang. In the current social climate, it didn't ring often, and the chirp still reminded him of Eve. He took the phone out of a plastic tray under the dash and looked at the ID. PENN CAGE. He pressed SEND and heard a burst of static.

"Hello?" he said. "Hello!"

More static. "John? Can you hear me?"

"Barely! You're in and out, Penn. What's going on?"

"I just got a call from the D.A. They got the DNA analysis back."

Waters wished he hadn't answered the call. The DNA match of his blood and the semen taken from Eve Sumner would be the final nail that crucified him in court.

"Are you there, John?"

"I wish I wasn't!"

"The test was negative."

"Well, we knew that."

"No! The samples *didn't match.* Did you hear me?"

The static was bad, but Waters had heard. "How can that be?"

Lily was looking at him strangely, as though she expected tragic news.

"I don't know," Penn yelled through the static. "Maybe Eve slept with someone else that day. But the lab says it wasn't"—static drowned the lawyer's words—"didn't show genetic evidence of two different men. And neither sample was corrupted either. Not your blood or the semen . . . DNA simply didn't match."

"You're breaking up!"

". . . exact words? They said, 'Close but no cigar.' You believe that?"

Penn's last words had come through clearly, so Waters stopped the Land Cruiser in the middle of the dirt road. "What does this mean for the trial?"

"Are you kidding? To convict you, the D.A. has to prove guilt beyond a reasonable doubt. His own DNA test proves that an unknown man had sex with Eve on the night she died! That's reasonable doubt right there. I'll be surprised if the D.A. even goes to trial now. I really will."

Lily took hold of his hand, and Waters realized he was shaking. "But . . ." He wanted to continue but could not.

"Who *cares* how it happened?" Penn exulted. "Don't look a gift horse in the mouth. This is the second miracle you've got in a very short time. Take it and run, buddy. Hug your wife and daughter. Live your life."

Waters put a quivering hand to his face and tried to hold the tears of relief in his eyes. He couldn't do it. "I have to go, Penn. I'll talk to you soon."

He clicked off.

"Daddy, what's wrong?" Ana asked.

"Nothing, punkin. I just got some good news."

"What is it?" Lily whispered.

"The DNA didn't match. Penn says there's no way I'll be convicted without it. There may not even be a trial."

Lily closed her good hand into a fist and brought it to her mouth, then shut her eyes in what appeared to be a prayer of thanks. "I knew it," she said. "I knew it would work out."

"I didn't. Not like this. This is impossible."

Lily shook her head. "After what we went through, how can you say anything is impossible? Let's go to the well, John. Drive on and don't look back."

He glanced back at Annelise, who looked more than a little afraid. "It's all right, baby," he assured her, putting the Land Cruiser back in gear. "Everything's okay."

As the Land Cruiser trundled over the last few hundred yards to the location, Waters pondered Penn's news. He was a scientist, and he was not prepared to accept what he had heard on faith. The DNA match should have been automatic. A formality. The semen taken from Eve had come from him—of that he had no doubt. How would it not match the blood he'd given at the pathology lab? Barring gross error on the part of the lab, there was only one conclusion he could see. Something had genetically altered either his blood or his semen in the time that separated the taking of those two samples.

That "something" could only be Mallory Candler.

Mallory had passed from Eve's body into him during the moment of his climax with Eve. His semen had obviously been produced prior to Mallory entering him. The vast majority of blood cells taken from his arm four days later would also have been produced before Mallory entered him, but with one difference. They had remained in his body during the roughly twenty-four hours that Mallory had possessed him.

That's got to be it, Waters thought. *I'm genetically different now, and I have been ever since Mallory entered me. The semen I left in Eve had my old DNA signature. The blood they took from my arm had the new one. The same alteration must have happened to Lily—and to Cole and Eve and Danny Buckles and all the rest.*

"John? Is that Cole?"

As they approached the well location, Waters saw Cole's silver Lincoln Continental parked low in the shadow of a stand of pine trees. Dressed in jeans, a Polo shirt, and Red Wing boots, Cole strode away from the car with a long wooden stake in his hand. A red cloth fluttered from the stake like a knight's battle standard.

When Waters parked, Annelise leaped out yelling Cole's name, but Waters took a moment to hug his wife. Things had been difficult for the three of them during the past weeks, though Lily was slowly thawing toward Cole, who remembered nothing of the time he spent under Mallory's influence, and seemed to have no memory of yielding to "Lily's" seduction. In public they were treated like disgraced citizens. The first couple of times Waters and Lily tried to dine out, the restaurants had fallen silent when they entered. When Cole heard this, he insisted on taking them to the Castle, the first-class restaurant behind Dunleith, and when the dining room fell silent and everyone stared, Cole hugged his wife to his side and bellowed, "What's the matter? You people never seen *class* before?" Then he led them to the best table in the house.

"I'm okay," Lily promised. "Go talk to him."

Waters got out and went to greet Cole, who was already dancing a jitterbug with Annelise.

"All right, Rock!" he cried. "You ready to stake this baby?"

"More than ready. Where do you want to put it?"

"You're paying for the well. You decide where the stake goes."

Waters accepted the stake and surveyed the ground. Mostly sand and dirt, it stretched flat and unbroken to the broad brown expanse of river. At this point, it didn't much matter where the stake went, give or take fifty feet.

"Ana?"

His daughter looked up from a puddle she had been studying twenty yards away.

"You want to stake the well?"

Her face lit up, and she ran to him and took the pointed stake from his hands. "Anywhere I want?"

"Within reason. Anywhere in a fifty-foot circle of where we are now."

She scrunched up her face, then began marching away from the river like a conquistador with an imperial flag.

Waters turned toward the Land Cruiser to check on Lily. She was standing by the hood, staring fixedly at the river. He was about to call to her when she lifted her right hand to the short locks of hair at her neck and twisted a strand tightly around her finger. His blood pressure dropped like a stone.

"Hey, Lily!" Cole yelled. "What do you think about this well?"

She looked vaguely toward them, but her eyes seemed blank, and the finger stayed in her hair.

"She's still not over the accident," Cole said under his breath. "What do *you* think about this puppy, Rock? We gonna go big-time again?"

His eyes locked on Lily's twisting finger, Waters tried not to show his anxiety. "It's a good play. But that oil is either there or it's not. And it's—"

"It's been there or not for two million years," Cole finished. "Shit. Hey, *Lily*! This guy won't give me a straight answer! Is this well going to hit or not?"

At last his voice seemed to register. Lily dropped her hand and smiled brightly. "It's going to be *huge*," she called. "The river's lucky for us!"

As she walked toward them, Waters said a silent prayer and turned to see Annelise triumphantly drive the stake into the soft earth twenty paces away. *She's going to be all right,* he told himself. *Dear God, let her be all right.* He raised his hands and applauded Annelise.

His daughter's face glowed with pride.

acknowledgments

Aaron Priest, gentleman and agent of the old school.

Phyllis Grann and David Highfill.

All the sales reps at Penguin Putnam, and particularly the old hands from Penguin USA, who did yeoman's labor beginning in 1993 with *Spandau Phoenix*.

Geoff Iles, for taking over all the work but the writing.

Courtney Aldridge, for his expertise in geology and character motivation.

Michael Henry, for his pragmatic advice and inspiration.

Ed Stackler, for his editorial advice.

Luis Mandoki, for teaching me about emotion and character.

Dianne Brown, for an early read and her expertise in real estate.

Jerry Iles, M.D., for consulting on every book at a moment's notice.

Betty Iles, for untold contributions over all the novels.

Carrie, Madeline, and Mark, for doing without me all those hours and days.

Miscellaneous contributions: Mike Worley, Armando T. Ricci, Ken Perry, M.D., John Holyoak, Johnny Waycaster, Simmons Iles, Lucy Childs, Lisa Erbach-Vance, and Elizabeth Shah-Hosseini.

As always, all mistakes are mine.

Greg Iles is the *New York Times* bestselling author of *The Footprints of God, Sleep No More, Dead Sleep, 24 Hours* (released as the major motion picture *Trapped*), *The Quiet Game, Mortal Fear, Black Cross,* and *Spandau Phoenix*. A graduate of the University of Mississippi, he performed in the musical group Frankly Scarlet for several years before writing his first novel. He lives in Natchez, Mississippi, with his wife and their two children. To learn more about Greg Iles's novels and films, visit www.gregiles.com.